Legacy

EDWARD W. RAMSELL

authorHOUSE®

AuthorHouse™
1663 Liberty Drive
Bloomington, IN 47403
www.authorhouse.com
Phone: 1 (800) 839-8640

Published by AuthorHouse 03/23/2016

ISBN: 978-1-5049-8473-7 (sc)
ISBN: 978-1-5049-8472-0 (e)

Library of Congress Control Number: 2016904131

Contents

CHAPTER 1

CONTACT

KLAXON! KLAXON! KLAXON! KLAXON!

"Hell'sKLAXONHonker!"

KLAXON!

The alarm klaxon slapped Dac in his concentration and he banged his kneecap on the console escutcheon. His kneecap flared electrically and Dac reacted physically, mindlessly. He rubbed his joint violently, then collected and focused his wits on the horn. The horn was not impressed, remaining largely impassive.

"Dammit!" muttered the Job's VP and CEO between klaxes. "That thing never went off before!" he thought viciously. "Must be broke. Like half the equipment on this scrap heap."

"Pappa," he barked at the console. "Take a look at that alarm system and get engineering down here to fix it." Actually, the console was not guilty, nor did it care about Dac's command. Pappa monitored everything everywhere and received input omnidirectionally somehow. Dac didn't know how that worked and didn't care as long as Pappa responded. That feature was definitely a plus jobwise and conveniencewise. In more intimate situations, however, it was a little distracting knowing that Pappa knew everything. To date, in spite of numerous attempts, Dac had been unable to turn Pappa off when the occasion called, another thing Pappa probably knew.

"The alarm is functioning to specifications, Mr. Olson," said Pappa, professionally understated. Pappa's mechanical but mellow voice did not

1

help Dac's knee at all. "In fact, I triggered the alarm myself. Please see your display on your right."

"You ...?" KLAXON!

He snapped Medical's report back onto Incoming, something about biological contaminants from Eco and the allergy upsurge. He made a mental note to get maintenance hot on the atmosphere filtration system and looked up at his board to see what the matter was. He stared.

"A Planet!?" muttered Dac Olson in annoyance. "What's a planet doing out here? We're a zillion KLAXON clicks from nowhere!"

"I'm sure I don't know about its existential reality, Mr. Olson," replied Pappa smartassily. "I am rarely consulted on such philosophical matters. However, you are quite right about its isolation from most everything," concluded Pappa, correctly interpreting Dac's zillion.

Dac settled back into his chair while he decided what to do. He knew what he was *supposed* to do; he was supposed to stop and investigate that rock that wasn't supposed to be there. He just had to KLAXON decide whether he was going to do it or not. Not much choice, he resigned to himself after a quick mental review of corporate regs. Pappa has already logged it and triggered Analyticals. It was more trouble than it was worth to explain to HO why he hadn't investigated. Dammit all to the Corporate Cops!

"OK, Pappa." But why the KLAXON alarm, he thought.

"But why the alarm? It's just another cold ball. Did you find gold this time or diamonds?" I wish! We're lucky to find coal.

"Neither, Mr. Olson. The object exhibits some unusual characteristics that fall outside of acceptable risk parameters and therefore I have no appropriate assessment algorithm solutions." Pappa managed to convey a little uneasy mortification at this lapse. "In addition, I did not notice it until we were quite close. I am concerned about that."

"What kind of danger, Pappa?" KLAXON! Dac forgot about his kneecap.

"I did not say danger, Mr. Olson. I said the characteristics are outside acceptable risk parameters. I have no basis on which to make a proper assessment of the risk because the analyticals do not seem to register reliably for me. Danger is in no way assessable at this time. I thought you would want to know."

"I guess I do now. Initial Contact protocol, Pappa," Dac ordered.

"The crew has already been fully alerted." Pappa chirped acquiescence.

"I'll bet!" Dac glanced sideways at the klaxon horn which returned his glance impassively. One of these times KLAXON! he would beat Pappa to the draw and tell him something he didn't know. Well, he retrenched, he did know some things that Poppa could not know. And never would. I think. I hope.

Veep Dac Olson slipped comfortably into the IC routine as easily as putting on his pants, flipping switches on his KLAXON! console with a practiced hand. He watched indicators trip to 'Go' as the IC sequence marched to its own tune: General alert, everyone to work stations. Evasion control on. Radar augmented, all frequencies. Lasers charging. Atomics armed. Fire control up. Antennas retracted. Planetary Analyticals up. Observation orbit computed. Intercept trajectory computed. Deceleration sequence queued. Product delivery ETA adjustment and cost overrun analyses initiated and transmitted. KLAXON!

"On my mark." Dac marked the occasion with an unnecessarily robust punch to the 'Doit' button and watched the status panel register acknowledgement as each staff chief logged in for command instructions. They know what to do, he thought with satisfaction as the last indicator winked on.

Olson reached up to the overhead control bank to punch up Objectives and gracefully flipped off the General Alarm on the way back to his keyboard. The klaxon would not stop until all emergency systems were up. The irritating dissonant warbling tinny electronic KLA! stopped instantly but left a ring in the air. He'd heard better blackboards. The whole ship sighed in relief.

"OK, Pappa. What's up?"

"What's that?" responded the engineer absently from the adjacent cubicle.

Engineer Marcy Phillips was busy neering some engine or other behind Olson, banging things around more enthusiastically than seemed prudent considering the delicacy, and cost, of most flight deck components. Absorbed in her own problems, she hadn't really heard Dac Olson's remark. An assortment of tools and parts and panels littered the deck around her, handicapping the already cramped way.

"Let's see what we have," mumbled Olson, ignoring the engineer who seemed satisfied with that arrangement.

"Showtime!" said Dac, aiming a pro forma "Dammit" at the recalcitrant console. A sharp thump with his fist got its attention. Then to Pappa, "Quantify."

Pappa hesitated only a moment, then snapped up Planetaries on the object he had detected: previously unknown planetoid, just over forty-seven million kilometers ahead, below and to the right, 2°03'103'' off their course. No proximate star or moons. No immediate collision hazard. Class III inquiry initiated. Pappa went back to work on the problem.

"What's that doing out here, Pappa?" he repeated, here being the Bubble. Pappa offered no clue to what it was doing out here. There isn't a charted star in sixty light-years in any direction and only a handful in a thousand. There is nothing out here. Nothing.

Correction, thought Dac. *Was* nothing.

That's why he took the Bubble in the first place, he thought; go from here to there through nowhere. Maximum speed, minimum erosion, no hazards. It was longer in inches but faster in seconds; he could safely work the ship to an almost significant relativistic fraction. Now we find rocks out here. Big rocks.

Dammit, Dac mumbled again to himself. He would have to decelerate, investigate the fool thing, plot its location, marker the hazard, make reports, all that corporate baloney. Then do a months-long Comprehensive for potential economic exploitation. By the time he got back on course he would lose the advantage of taking the Bubble, not to mention his on-time incentive. "Why didn't the sweepers take care of this!?"

"Pappa," said Dac in resignation to nowhere in particular. "What else have you got?"

Three more boards activated on Dac's console: diameter about 1,000 kilometers but that was ambiguous. Some evidence of refraction. Probably an atmosphere.

"Atmosphere?" Dac tapped the board. "Come on, Pappa. No rock that size has an atmosphere." Pappa persisted mutely.

Unless it's a very heavy rock, he thought to himself. Like solid iron. Or a very heavy atmosphere, like mud. Or both.

"Pappa, give me a reading on that atmosphere."

Dac checked other data quickly as it popped up on the board. He OK'd several screens and slid several more across his shell for immediate reference. He glanced back at Pappa's fresh atmospherics analysis. Pappa picked up his eye movement and slid that screen front and center.

"Hydrogen!?" He thought for a moment, smiled and reached for the console. "Okay Pappa, time for a bath."

Dac punched up Systems Diagnosis on Pappa and switched to Mamma, the back-up computer. Mamma was considerably slower and less human friendly than Pappa but every bit as powerful and accurate. And for safety's sake, as non-redundant and independent as possible. Mamma performed almost all of Pappa's responsibilities in real time in the background, ready to jump in and take over essential functions instantly. In that event, Mamma and Pappa reversed roles.

He requested Planetaries again. Mamma cranked through the analysis and finally ran out her results on the board, displayed as an incidence distribution by atomic weights and another broken down by chemical analysis. Mamma lacked Pappa's ability to compose a prose executive summary and displayed the raw data only. Dac stared as he assimilated the data, and then stared more intensely in disbelief.

"Hydrogen." Flat unbelieving statement.

99.9% plus hydrogen, in fact, with a trace of assorted common space gases. He turned back over his shoulder to the engineer.

"Phillips, come here for a second," he ordered.

Electronics engineer Marcy Phillips grunted as she rolled out from under the support systems console on the left flight deck. This had better be good, she thought. She clattered a few tools ostentatiously and kicked the sheet metal noisily as she struggled out of the cabinet. Dac didn't notice. Or rather, his display of not noticing was as ostentatious as her display of pique at being interrupted.

"Yo!"

Dac winced. It wasn't a gung-ho yes-sir-what-can-I-do-for-you-sir yo. It was more like a whaddyawant yo.

He couldn't stand yo. He was home office at heart, not field, and had probably gone overboard in cleansing the project of cute little paramilitary affectations, like yo. But left was left, not port. Or starboard or whatever the Hell, and yes was yes, not yo.

5

Besides, Marcy's yo didn't convey much respect, like she didn't really buy into the corporate pseudo-military command BS. Like he didn't buy into it either, which he didn't. Like because they were having sex she really didn't have to play soldier on the job like everyone else.

Well, he admitted, that did put an awkward spin on their working relationship. And there was no one else around right now. And she did look fetching on the floor like that, and he did feel an unofficial stirring, and what the Hell.

Marcy finally climbed to her feet, goose-stepped around the bench and stopped facing Dac, saluting, smiling. Marcy was one of those few women who looked good in a mechanic's utility jump suit. Full figure. Narrow hips. No tummy. High buttocks. Long legs. Long dark brown hair, full and wavy. And a smile that turned his brains into overcooked penne. She had the opposite effect on other of his parts, but right now his brain was noodled.

"Uh, Marcy, can you take a look at this for me?" Dac sounded different even to himself, and shook his head to clear out the mush. "Pappa's numbers don't make sense and Mamma agrees with Pappa. Something's out of whack, sensors or something. Can you take a look at it?" Pause "Uh, now if you've got a minute." Smile. "Uh, please?"

"You got it." Marcy smiled a 'that's better' smile, moved to her work station and went to work. Dac watched her move and watched her work for a bit too long really, shook his head again and went back to his own boards.

The geological analyses of the planet and atmosphere hadn't changed materially, only refined themselves somewhat. Gravity barely registered strongly enough for a valid reading, but that should be up momentarily. Astronomics showed no orbital vector but he didn't expect one; no sun, no orbit. Proper motion roughly towards Corporate north. Survey showed it was perfectly round.

That's a little odd, thought Dac, considering that it wasn't quite big enough to pull rock into a perfect ball. Water ice, maybe, but not rock. Most accretions this far out in the boonies were a little lopsided. Usually a lot lopsided. But if it was as dense as it had to be to have a hydrogen atmosphere, it was possible that it was dense enough to crush itself round. What else.

Atmospheric temperature minus 143 degrees Celsius. That figured. No surface ice of any flavor. That didn't figure; extremely cold atmosphere with no precipitation?

Rotational period just under one hour. One hour? Dac checked Planetaries again; still reading a perfect sphere with no discernable flattening of the poles or equatorial bulge. Hard little beebee, thought Dac. But that jives with the iron ball theory. Let's see if Pappa knows what this thing is made of yet.

"Rock!?" he exclaimed in disbelief. Marcy looked up from her desk, saw that Dac hadn't spoken to her and went back to work.

Rock! This time to himself. The planet was rock! At least the surface was rock to a depth of thirty kilometers. Thirty kilometers was on the edge of implausibility too. Geologics could rarely penetrate more than a kilometer, and then only in loose accretions like comets. Thirty kilometers, if that depth reading was for real, meant the planet was made of cotton candy. Given a one hour day, and given it was made of something radar could penetrate thirty kilometers, it would have to show some pronounced polar flattening. Pronounced!? he thought with amusement; it should look like a Frisbee. Especially with a one hour day. There was no sun so there wasn't really a day, Dac reminded himself. Rotational period then. He checked Planetaries again. Spherical.

"Marcy." His voice wasn't so commandeering this time but it wasn't mellow either. More like troubled, and Marcy caught it immediately. "Have you found the problem yet? I can't make sense out of this at all. Something broke?"

"Nothing's broken," said Marcy, a little troubled herself. "But I see your problem. I've got a few strange readings on that planet, too, but I don't find a thing wrong with systems. The planet is just strange. I launched a probe to get a free-standing analysis so we can verify Planetaries." She turned to the football player opposite her work station. "Mike? What have you got?"

"I've got a cotton candy planet that spins like a top," began Mike Hand, "but doesn't show any equatorial bulge or polar flattening. Density seems to be lower than cometary material yet it's retaining an almost pure hydrogen atmosphere.

"The atmosphere has small traces of space junk," he continued, reading from the console, "less than 0.001% total of water, methane, ammonia, carbon dioxide and trash in normal ratios. It's cold, cold enough to precipitate everything but the hydrogen but there is no surface ice of any kind. No subterranean ice that registers either." Mike looked up to the others, a bit hesitant.

"Okay, here's more now," he continued. "The surface is light rock, a smooth surface like a billiard ball, with no volcanism, cratering or fracturing. It's obviously an accretion of light space debris, but it looks as though someone dragged it every weekend for a baseball game. Surface temperature about zero, atmosphere 143 below."

"Wow."

Marcy stared at Dac in mild amusement, both realizing how that data sounded out loud. And how it would sound to HO.

"I don't think you'll like this either," began Marcy. "I found the same surface smoothness so I ran an analysis on the echo to see if there was some sort of anomalous propagation from the atmosphere that may be fooling the radar and giving us the smooth surface reading. The signal is real, the planet is smooth as your ball diamond. Smoother."

"And nothing's broke." A statement belying a question. Dac tapped his desk in agitation and impatience, uncomfortable with ambiguity. He liked things that fit together all neat and smooth, like greased machine parts. This was anything but neat.

"Not that I can find," she replied, resisting again the urge to correct his grammar. "Pappa's still working on redundancies, but there's nothing to indicate an analytics or systems problem that would produce those readings. It's for real."

"Okay" said Dac after a moment. "We'll proceed on the basis that what we see is what we get. It's strange, but so far it doesn't seem to be hazardous. Keep working on systems as you can, Marcy. Let me know if you find anything. Pappa, alert Unit One. Take her in to standard observation orbit."

Pappa chirped happily.

"Let's go down and take a look."

CHAPTER 2
APPROACH

"Holy South Hampton Institute of Technology!" oozed Dac slowly and with feeling, followed by a low inhaled whistle. "I see it but I don't believe it."

Dac, everyone, looked intensely at their screens as they approached the target planetoid. The image grew and slowly resolved into a clearly, indisputably nothing-like-a-planet shape. Their approach brought them up on the blank smooth side of the object but as they moved into a standard parking orbit the object appeared to rotate up over the horizon towards them. It was hypnotic and transfixed everyone's attention. No one moved or even breathed.

"Squared," agreed Marcy, hushed and awestruck. "Pun intended."

"I'll believe it when I walk up and kick it," said Jason Fielding, Unit One team leader, always the consummate pragmatist. He rapped the board with the back of a fingernail as though he could knock some sense into it. "Until then it's just a bug splat on the windshield. Where did you come up with this one, Dac?"

"We tripped over it. Hazard control went off and there it was. Don't worry about it, Jason, it's real," replied Dac, still stunned. After a moment his stun turned into a kid-at-a-birthday-party grin. "Well, we finally did it, gang. We'll go into the books for this. You're looking at the first by God bona fide alien artifact ever found!" Dac checked himself and then side-eyed the crew at the possible blasphemy. Ahh, who cares! "And Hell's Nina, Pinta and Goddam Santa Maria! The first sign of extra-terrestrial intelligent life anywhere in the known universe! And we found it! Nobody but us!!"

"Bzzzping," chimed in Pappa testily. "You will note for the record that I sounded the alarm, Mr. Olson, and I provided the initial interpretation. In fact, you tried very hard to discredit my completely accurate analysis of the planet." Take that Mr. CEO!, thought Pappa, probably. AI and machine intelligence and true thought were still unsettled concepts, both socially and legally.

Pappa had a little difficulty conveying a dented ego by inflection and tone but had no trouble at all with sarcasm. His human emulators had been designed to elicit more humane treatment from his operators, and therefore more reliable functioning in return from Pappa, but Dac felt Pappa was the more frequent abuser.

"It was also I," continued Pappa, loathe to forgo twisting it, "who first confirmed basic Analyticals. You'll find that all of my systems are properly maintained and functioning perfectly, Mr. Olson."

"Yes, that's true Pappa. Sorry about that." Mock finger in throat. Dac sincerely hoped Pappa hadn't seen that gesture or understood it if he had. "But you'll surely agree that while you first identified the planet, we first identified the alien artifact," said Dac with a conspiratorial smile to the others. "And I did say 'we' found it. That includes you, Pappa."

"Pt. Pt. Pt." Pappa retired from the contest only slightly mollified.

In fact, Pappa had missed the artifact entirely and still couldn't see it in spite of direct control from the flight deck. It simply didn't register on Pappa's instruments, although some secondary manifestations did. Pappa was trying to sort that out now.

The rest of Unit One began to trickle into the flight deck to see what the commotion was.

Pete 'Swingline' Bravo, Survey. Mercedes Mead, Geology. Gerry Ast, Communications. Edward 'Fats' Bic, Meteorology. Ross Label, Biology. Mike Hand, Engineering. Plus a few general purpose grunts. They hovered to the display boards like moths, mumbling to each other in subdued awe.

It was a crack crew, thought Dac, and I'll need a crack crew on this one. Unit One was one of six crew command units on the SBU Jobs, a Buffet class profit center out of the Bush system. The six crews competed for their rating partly to keep them in top trim and partly to pass the time, and Unit One hadn't lost in three projects. Unit One consisted of Dac's hand-picked professionals, as did Unit Two. Units Three and Four were younger workie-ups assigned more or less arbitrarily to the Jobs, good but unseasoned. Units Five and Six were entry level but talented green-weenies fresh out of corporate Career School. Dac never saw Units Five and Six, by design and by choice.

"I get to touch it first!" said Bravo, his sudden booming voice startling most. "Be sure to get my picture, just like Neil Armstrong." The others reacted jovially in mock disdain, each claiming hisser own piece of the action.

"We'll worry about dibs later," said Dac in his best let's-be-professional voice. Silence. "For now we'll learn everything we can from up here. We may never make planetfall, much less kick that box. You know the regs."

Yeah, they knew the regs; total quarantine on any planet with life sign until cleared by Biochemical Engineering. And the nearest BE installation was 'leventy-seven WaytheHells from here.

"You all know the routine. Take a few minutes to enjoy the view but I want your preliminary reports in two hours. Communications!"

"Yes, sir."

Gerry Ast, Senior Associate, Communications. Pushing middle age but very well preserved by space's light physical demands. Gerry was not really pretty, and didn't care. She was, however, attractive to everyone who knew her and worked with her. Strong and confident, knowledgeable and competent, totally without ego but packed to the gunnels with energy and spunk. She took complements gracefully and deserved them. She gave praise generously and appropriately, with no sign of patronization or politics. She had only one flaw, one that had persistently kept her from advancement in the corporation; she was absolutely honest.

"Ah, Gerry." Dac jumped in mock surprise and turned to Gerry who stood immediately behind him looking over his shoulder. "Open a secure line to HO. Tell them we've got something big here, Priority One Alpha. We'll need advice on how to proceed and probably a variance. Get Marketing, Legal, Claims, Engineering, Finance, anybody you can think of on conference." Dac thought for a minute, pondering the conflict between trying to limit publicity and trying to maximize HO support.

"Get people, anyone who can make decisions; we may only get one chance on this. And make that line super secure, double blind! Don't tell them what we've got because I don't know what we've got. Keep a lid on it. Questions?"

"Yeah. Are we in a hurry? Nothing will happen here for a year, if then. We won't even get a reply in a ..." Gerry finally tuned in to Dac's impatience and turned quickly to go. "Yessir! Now. You got it!"

"Communications!" Gerry stopped in the middle of starting.

"Yes, sir."

"See if you can talk to that thing," said Dac mildly, with a smile Gerry could see. "I want to know immediately if you get anything. But *after* you contact HO."

Gerry Ast did not need to be told to try to contact the aliens; that was standing order No. 1 in this situation. She did, however, need a little direction in the face of this monumental distraction. She smiled back a much more reasonable "Yes, Mr. Olson," turned and went to work.

Standing order No. 1, never invoked until now. He pondered that blankly, not having any previous experience on which to draw. No. 1: Upon identifying sign of intelligent alien life, secure the area, contact the HO, the aliens with HO guidance, and the Feds after assessing the economic situation, and don't touch! Or convoluted legalese to that effect.

Dac smiled after Gerry and returned to his display panels to finish dealing with the cook's complaint about running out of butter. I did that, he thought, ordered peanut butter instead of butter butter but the cook would never know. Go with the cheap spread and conserve the real stuff for special occasions, he ordered summarily; do the best you can. No cows out here.

Pappa was refreshing his board, now displaying the artifact at higher and higher resolution. The crew bustled silently, examining every bit and byte of data excitedly. All ship's sensors probed the planet, feeding the frenzy with every detail their electronic hearts could find. Dac checked all his monitors once over and punched up Diagnosis to be certain nothing dangerous was overlooked in the excitement. His responsibility was to bring everything home in one piece, alien artifact or no, and he couldn't afford the luxury of distraction.

"Pappa?" Dac had to rely on Pappa for tracking every one of the hundreds of approval codes needed to proceed. "You on this?"

"Level One sequences complete, Mr. Olson," responded Pappa immediately. "We should be able to complete Level Two through Level Five in approximately one hour, give or take."

"Give or take what!?"

"Discovery of the artifact has caused quite a commotion on board, in fact throughout the Jobs, Mr. Olson." Pappa actually chuckled! Or some random electronic facsimile of it. "It may take a while to get everyone back into their duty stations to attend to business."

"Understood." Dac had a little problem with the distraction himself. "Do what you can to facilitate things and keep me posted. I'll hold you to that hour!"

Satisfied, he leaned closer to his board and finally took the time to study the artifact in detail, comparing Pappa's construct to his optical image. The two screens automatically shifted back and forth, keying on his eye-attention until he locked them with a snap. He stopped to uncross his eyes and swear at the fools who came up with that idea! The reader-sized images did no justice to reality.

"Lock and expand," he commanded, also automatically. His other tasks minimized to make room. That's more like it.

The artifact was a perfect cube, no doubt about that. A gigantic perfect cube, sitting there all by itself in the dirt. One humongous cube dead center on the rotational axis pole that convention designated as South. There was no other structure of any kind anywhere else on the featureless planet. Checking the tentative dimensions on the display for reassurance, Dac tried to imagine its size.

Gigantic? Colossal. Stupendous. Big! The mother of all cubes, more than 40 kilometers on a side. That qualifies as big by any standard. A perfect cube with no features other than its cubeness and Pappa didn't see it! A block of something taller than the biggest volcano in the Solar system, bigger than many moons, and Pappa was blind. No wonder he had an attitude.

Pappa's scan showed the planet clearly, smooth as a billiard ball, the cube rotating visibly but slowly. In the South pole, canted to the left and towards the ship in the radar view, was a gigantic perfectly square hole in the planet. A hole that matched the cube that was all too obvious in Dac's opticals.

The opticals amplify photons in the visible spectrum, thought Dac, focused on it by lenses. Pappa's pixels are reconstructed by computer using data from the synthetic aperture radar. The radar uses electromagnetic radiation focused by magnetic lenses. So the radar uses photons too but from far outside the visible spectrum. That might be it.

"Pappa!"

"Chirp."

"Scan the planet at all available frequencies. Can you tune your radar to visible light frequencies?"

"Yes, but resolution suffers somewhat."

"Try that and any other frequency that occurs to you. Bracket the Hell out of it. I want a complete radiation profile on that thing. X-rays, neutrinos, the works."

"Chirp. On it."

Everyone was hard at their assignments, the excitement tingling the flight deck. Dac did as well, leaning close to the display to examine the cube, now several notches larger as they approached. Forty kilometers on a side, 64,000 cubic kilometers, give or take. Who... What... The obvious questions came to mind but were totally inadequate in face of the fact.

Dac had imagined that when, or if, this day ever came he would be ready, like Flash Gordon or Arnold. He would be supremely confident, commanding his crew like Patton, mastering the alien environment like a Heisenberg, confronting the aliens like Kirk. The day had come and he felt woefully inadequate.

His homocentric outlook on the universe, in spite of all evidence to the contrary, presumed a human scale to things, that aliens would be human sized, subject to human rules of peopleness. He did not have to abandon that idea, it was forcibly stripped away by this artifact that surpassed thingness, as a mountain range is not understood as a thing.

The image of a childhood toy flashed. The planet reminded Dac of those toy tops that flip over when spun. They were shaped like a ball with a round peg handle sticking out. This thing wasn't quite the same proportion, and this handle was a cube instead of a spinable cylinder, but the impression was there. What do they call those things?

"Pappa. What do they call those things?"

"I beg your pardon, Mr. Olson. What do who call what?"

"Never mind." Whatever.

Geometrics constantly revised its measurement of the planet, now close to 1,000 Kilometers in diameter and steady. Very low albedo indicating what? Normal for space rocks, probably, but it was hard to tell with no local sun. Precipitation? From what? Volcanism? Still no sign of any surface irregularity.

Pressure 2.2 Earth bars, with no gradient from planet surface to maximum measurable altitude. Atmospheric analysis unchanged since initial observation, almost pure hydrogen. No measurable atmospheric differential Doppler effects which implied no wind. Correction; the very cold atmosphere was stationary in relation to the planet surface, assuming the planet rotated with the cube at the South pole That was a suspect assumption as gas planets characteristically displayed banded layers of atmosphere rotating at different latitudes which might or might not rotate with the planet core itself. Time out.

Dac double checked his board, specifically the rotational rate. There were no surface features to key in on, except for the cube. It showed a rotation of about one revolution per hour. That's about like the minute hand on the old analog clocks. The cube must be sitting on something solid. That's a pretty good indication that the whole planet revolves at that same rate. Very solid to support a 42 kilometer cube.

Wait a minute! No wind? Hell's Tornado! With that atmosphere and that rate of rotation, the Corialis effects would be fierce. Corialis effects mean wind, and in this case there should be cyclones. This atmosphere rotates like it was solid!

"Mercedes! Help!" A good natured plea to Mercedes Mead, Geology. Dac knew he was at the limit of his tech background here. "Can you make sense of these atmospheric readings?"

"No, Mr. Olson. I can't." Flat out unapologetic statement of fact.

"Okaaay. Then can you fill me in on what you do know so far? I'm stuck."

"I have a few more details, Mr. Olson," replied Mercedes. "Atmospheric depth approximately 50 kilometers, subject to verification because of data ambiguity. Mild planetary surface temperature at slightly below zero degrees."

"Fifty kilometers? A planet this size shouldn't even *have* an atmosphere, much less 50 kilometers of atmosphere." Dac paused to internalize the new information and was no better off for it. "At this size any atmosphere would ordinarily be extremely thin, not two bars! And measured in meters, not kilometers. Fifty kilometers? Hydrogen?"

"No way," concurred Mercedes. "The physics just doesn't work that way. There's more. Sunlight blows hydrogen away even on Earth. There's no local sun but it takes a planet at least the size of Pluto to hold hydrogen, and then only because it's so cold and far away from the solar wind. This thing isn't big enough to hold more than a wisp of heavy gases like carbon dioxide, much less hydrogen."

"Check that temperature again, Mercedes."

"The hydrogen atmosphere is close to -143 Celsius top to bottom, as far as I can trust these instruments, and stationary with no stratification and no pressure gradient!" Mercedes was obviously perplexed at the readings, not the least because they might reflect on her professionally. "Yet the surface temperature is just below zero. A temperature differential that great would set up atmospheric instability and turbulence. Certainly strata. But there is no stratification, which is to say no pressure gradient."

"Now how do you account for the lack of pressure gradient," asked Dac, reasonably enough.

"Again, I can't. Any gas has weight and is springy, has pressure," said Mercedes, opting for the more technical term. "The lack of stratification implies there is no weight and therefore no gravity. But that's clearly not the case here; we can detect a light but clear gravitational field."

"Curiouser and curiouser," mused Dac mostly to himself. Then aloud, "Where's the Mad Hatter?"

"Who?" said Mercedes.

"What?" said Pappa.

"Never mind," muttered Dac, bemoaning public school education nowadays. "How about that cube, Pappa? Anything new?"

"Successive readings on the size of the cube are asymptoting to about 42 kilometers horizontally on each side, Mr. Olson. The top is a perfect square to the limits of my instruments. The cube is about 44 kilometers high so it isn't quite a perfect cube after all." Pappa stopped patiently to let Dac formulate a more specific question.

"Strange," said Dac. "Someone sure went to a lot of trouble to put this thing here and make it a regular polyhedron. Why is one dimension off by just a tad?"

"I'm sure I don't know, Mr. Olson." Dac pensed at Pappa in the person of the speaker on his console. The speaker awaited a more complete analysis but Pappa declined to elaborate.

The image was now too big for his board. Dac adjusted it to center the cube in the display and watched it slowly rotate as the ship maneuvered into a polar orbit. There was no sun in the vicinity so it was a little hard to see. Radar seemed to fail at all frequencies and the visible lighting from the ship was woefully inadequate for an object this size. To the naked eye it was almost invisible, delineated only by occluded stars. The optical intensifiers had only starlight to work with and damned little of that. He upped gain and contrast, losing a little definition.

"Hello!" he said aloud. No one noticed, each intent on hisser own Hellos. "Was that a flash of light from the cube?" A few did look up at that.

"There it is again! Is that a signal!? Pappa! Are you getting this?"

"Chirp. One moment, Mr. Olson." A moment.

"Nothing, sir. Can you be more specific?"

"I saw two distinct flashes of light near the base of the cube! Run the last twenty seconds again. Tell me if it was just my imagination." Pappa obliged.

"There. Did you see it?"

"Yes I did. Two distinct flashes, extremely short duration. No obvious meaning or intent. No further incidents. Returning to real time."

The image was now bigger by half again so Dac backed off the magnification to view the whole cube, looking for another anything.

"Chirp."

"Mr. Olson? Polar orbit established."

Dac checked the orbitals routinely and tripped over them. The period of the orbit was five hours! Five hours to orbit a 1,000 mile diameter planet at an altitude of 90 kilometers. Something's wrong. "Pappa!"

"Chirp."

"I've got your orbitals here, Pappa. Are they correct?" Dac tapped the readouts as if to say "You're wrong this time, Pappa. Gotcha!"

"Yes, sir. Sorry sir. I'm afraid they are correct." Pappa paused to refresh the display.

"The planet's average density is quite low, continued Pappa, "something on the order of 0.104 that of water. Surface gravity is 0.046 Earth Gs. Our orbital period is 4.897 hours at 91.34 kilometers, plus or minus .002 kilometers due to perturbations attributable to the alien structure. Adjustments to orbit should be made at approximately every 74 orbits. The orbit is slightly ellipsoid, probably due to asymmetrical density distribution within the planet."

"That's not possible, Pappa. That density can't be right. No planet that small with a density that low can pull itself into a ball, much less hold a hydrogen atmosphere. What's your problem, Pappa?"

Pappa was silent for an unusually long AI time, but actually for only a few seconds. Pappa could tell the difference between the figurative 'What's your problem' as in 'Your emotional involvement is affecting your judgment,' and the literal 'Find your mistake and fix it.' Pappa, correctly, was looking for the mistake.

"No problem, Mr. Olson. The orbit is as described and stable, standard observational orbit. You are correct," continued Pappa." The planet is unusually light and the other observations are puzzling at this point. Would you like to set a different orbit, higher perhaps?"

"No, Pappa," said Dac. He carefully considered that, crazy or not, the orbit posed no apparent hazard. "But watch things closely. I want all new developments immediately." One beat. "And Pappa?"

"Chirp."

"Take another hard look at the planet. Consult with Geology and run every probe you can think of. I need to know why things don't add up, Pappa. I need it now."

"Is now a good time, Mr. Olson?" The interrogative mode indicated that Pappa wanted to take the initiative.

"Yes," responded Dac, instantly hyper aware.

"May I propose a rough working hypothesis?"

"Yes, of course, Pappa."

"It is not a planet."

CHAPTER 3

CLOSEUP

"Not a planet …?"

Absolute silence on deck. Pappa, momentarily confused by the silence, paused to check that he was transmitting to the flight deck and that there were, in fact, people there.

"It looks like a small planet with an alien artifact on its South pole," continued Pappa, satisfied he was talking to somebody. "The alleged planet, however, is probably an artifact itself, with a little space litter sprinkled over it. A part of the internal structure can be seen protruding through the litter."

"You mean the cube?" asked Dac, reminded again of the child's toy. What did they call those fool things?

"Yes, sir. The cube which, of course, is a misnomer."

"Chirp."

"Chirp."

"I have confirmed Mead's calculations, sir," continued Pappa. "The alleged planet is probably hollow. A central void approximately 700 kilometers in diameter would account for the very low gravity well. That is consistent with my hypothesis that the whole structure is an artifact, Mr. Olson; hollow planets do not occur naturally. The cube appears to extend into the planet to the depths probed."

"And it's hollow." A statement.

"The cube? I have no idea at this time, sir."

"I mean the planet, Pappa." Confounded literal smart-ass computer. "The sorta-planet is hollow. You're certain about that?"

"No, Mr. Olson, not certain at all. However, Geology has just completed analyzing her soundings. Mercedes confirmed that the alleged planet is light rock to a depth of more than 55 kilometers but well within normal for a rock-type body. A solid body of this size and composition would have a gravity gradient between four and ten times the observed intensity. The planet's low gravity indicates extremely low density within, approaching a vacuum. Since this state is unlikely in a natural body, it is probably not natural, and is probably hollow."

"Chirp."

"Hollow!" Dac was having trouble believing he was hearing what he was hearing, but kept his poise as the crew listened intently waiting for what he might say next. Hell's Hearing Aid, he thought, *I'm* waiting to hear what I say next.

"Are you telling me that ... that thing is a space ship?"

"Not at all, Mr. Olson. Few hollow artifacts are space ships. This does not appear to be one of them. It is probably either a tool or a toy."

"A toy! Come on, Pappa, a thousand kilometer toy?"

"All non-tools are toys, Mr. Olson. Tools have a function. Non-tools, by definition, do not have a function other than to be the object of subjective aesthetic experiences."

"Then you think this planet is really a toy? Or a work of art?"

"I neither stated nor implied that, Mr. Olson. It is far more likely to be a tool."

"Then what's its function?"

"I haven't the slightest, Mr. Olson."

"Okay. Okay." Dac had to realign his thoughts. "Given your analysis of the planet's structure is correct, it only describes how the mass of this very light thing is distributed. It does not explain how this very light thing can hold a pure hydrogen atmosphere. Do you have a theory about that?"

"None whatsoever, Mr. Olson. However, you may be asking the wrong question." Pappa was being deliberately obtuse.

Pappa was basically a neural network computer, overlaid with human-like and non-human sensors, instrumentality and analyzers that allowed him to take initiative and function independently of human intervention. There were data input facilities, of course, needed in the same way humans need to read the newspaper from time to time. Pappa couldn't be everywhere and do everything so he had to be able to accept input. But while he would take instructions, he didn't need instructions. More or less, anyway.

In addition to his hardware and hard programming, Pappa had a battery of fuzzy logic human emulators designed to soften the social intercourse between computer and person. Beyond a certain level of intelligence, unfettered computers were a royal pain to work with, and humans even worse. The solution was a soft program that emulated human peculiarities and emotions that humans could relate to. More or less.

Pappa was a pretty good human but he was successful in dealing with humans largely because of Dac's highly professional human crew. They respected Pappa and Pappa respected them, forming the basis of all sound working relationships.

Sometimes, however, Pappa got a little bucky and this was one of those times. Another less sophisticated crew would not be so tolerant. His human emulators were on overdrive and he was enjoying playing tag with Dac in front of the crew.

Okay, play the game, Dac, you haven't got time for this.

"Your analysis is a stroke of genius, Pappa," cajoled Dac. "Sometimes I don't know how you do it. It makes so much sense now that you've laid it all out. I'll be certain the record reflects your role in the discovery."

"Good Lord," thought Dac, gagging slightly. "I don't get paid enough for this." Light chuckles and a finger-down-the-throat pantomime from a crewone subtended his pause to select his next words.

"By the way, Pappa." Said Dac, hoping Pappa hadn't appreciated the gesture. "There's still a point I don't quite understand." Pause to formulate a different approach. "Regardless of the internal structure, there still doesn't seem to be enough mass to retain the atmosphere. You said that was the wrong question."

"Quite. Since it is impossible for that mass to retain that atmosphere, it is obvious that it does not."

"Does not what?"

"The alleged planet does not retain the alleged atmosphere."

"Then what in Newton are we allegedly looking at?" Dac was quickly losing whatever good humor he may have held for Pappa. "That's 50 kilometers of pure hydrogen!"

"Yes, sir, it is that. But it is not an atmosphere."

"Okay, Pappa." Dac took a deep breath, glanced at the others on the flight deck who were about to split, and asked in carefully measured words, "If it isn't an atmosphere, what is it?"

"It is artifact. Or more precisely, everything you see out there, including the hydrogen, is artifact."

"Everything?" The crew was no longer laughing.

"Everything except the dirt."

"You're certain about this?"

"Oh, No, sir. As I said, this is a hypothesis, but it does accommodate the lack of stratification and turbulence in the hydrogen layer." Pappa slipped into his ingratiatingly pedantic mode again. "The hydrogen has been put there and is held there by some mechanism and for some purpose we have yet to discover, but I am certain the mechanism is not planetary gravitation. I am working on that now. I do have one other tentative finding."

"Let's hear it, Pappa. Maybe someone can key off it."

"The cube seems to be expanding," resumed Pappa.

"Expanding!" prompted Dac incredulously, with no question-ish inflection. "*Seems* to ...? There's a question?" Dac sure had a question if Pappa didn't.

"Okay. Yes. The cube is expanding," conceded Pappa. "Our initial measurements were imprecise because of the distance. The earliest measurements that can be relied upon were taken only 47 hours ago after settling into polar orbit. Based on those findings and measurements taken within the hour, the Cube has grown in all dimensions by a factor of 1.38095×10 to the minus 8 per hour. The rate of growth has been constant over that time period."

"How much is that in kilometers?" asked Dac, loathe to risk revealing his congenitally suspect math skills.

"Approximately one millionth of a kilometer, Mr. Olson. Perhaps it would be easier to think of it as approximately one millimeter."

"You mean the Cube is one millimeter bigger than it was when we arrived? Is that significant?" Dac had a problem visualizing a 42 kilometer thing adding a millimeter.

"I would not have mentioned it if the data were not significant, Mr. Olson. You understand that it is very difficult to obtain measurements this precise on an object that does not reflect radar signals."

"No, I mean is this important? Does it add to our knowledge in a way that must be considered significant, important?"

"There is no basis for a conjecture at this point, Mr. Olson."

"Track that growth and see if you can make some kind of a projection," said Dac without feeling. "A millimeter?"

"Chirp."

"Pappa!" shouted Dac with a jump out of his thoughts.

"Yes, sir." Very cold, even for electronic circuits. Pappa did not like to be shouted at and maybe needed his sensitivity tuned.

"Uh. Thanks, Pappa. That was a good job." Dac meant it. The crew saw that he meant it and Pappa understood that he meant it.

"You are welcome, Mr. Olson." Very warm, with a little triumph. "And by the way ..."

"Yes Pappa?"

"If my hypothesis stands, it means that I did in fact discover the alien artifact first. Is that not correct?"

"Yes, Pappa." choked Dac. "That is correct and noted."

"Chirp." Perhaps a little too chirpy.

"Well, what are you looking at?" They were looking at Dac. "Does Pappa have to do everything around here? You heard the story. I want you to confirm Pappa's theory or shoot it down. I don't care which!" Dac looked around the deck. "Now is good!"

They nowed in unison, not in fear but in excitement, each reassessing hisser data in light of Pappa's insight.

"Phillips?"

"Yes, sir?" Engineer Marcy Phillips responded dutifully, the flight deck being crowded at the moment. 'Thanks' said Dac to Marcy with his eyes. All I need is another ego game, he thought completely to himself.

"Phillips, what did you tell me about the planet? Something about it ringing like a bell."

"That's right. Hand and Bravo have both confirmed it. The planet resonates like a bell." Marcy referred to her board. "We've been monitoring it at, uh, 11,792.1749 Hz for an hour now. Not the slightest variation in frequency over the whole planet for that time."

"What about the atmosphere, or whatever it is. Does it vibrate too?"

"We went to work on that as soon as we heard Pappa's theory." replied the engineer. "We're not completely confident at this point but it seems not. The planet vibrates but the atmosphere doesn't. That's tentative but likely. There's something else."

"I'm sitting down."

"The atmosphere has a surface!" Marcy scowled at herself, struggling with the concept.

"How's that?" Dac recalled his basic physics classes wherein having a discreet surface was a property of solid and liquid matter but not of gas. "You mean you could water ski on it?"

"Uh, I guess if you really wanted to badly enough," rejoined Marcy. "The pressure in the hydrogen atmosphere is constant throughout. It doesn't drop off with altitude like you'd expect."

"We know about the pressure already. So what else is new?" Dac was losing interest a little.

"I'm talking about the surface, not the pressure. The pressure doesn't drop off at all until you get up to the very surface of the atmosphere. Then it drops to zero within less than one centimeter. It has a surface almost like a liquid but with no slosh."

"Slosh? Is that a technical term?" Dac was thoughtful and didn't really expect an answer. "One centimeter. You don't mean one kilometer?"

"No, sir. One centimeter, and maybe less than that. We're still refining the figures. The surface behaves like a very precise lens. Taking the size of the thing into account, the sphericity is more precise than any optical lens we could build."

"Anything else?" Pause. "Of course there's something else."

"Yes, there is. While the atmosphere has a surface, the surface doesn't." Even Marcy was a little bewildered at that.

"Right."

"I mean the surface of the planet, where all the dirt is. You would expect it to have a more or less hard surface, like any small moon. Lots of rock and dust from meteor impact. Space trash and the like." Marcy paused to check her notes. "It looks solid enough but radar shows a fuzzy surface, more like a very heavy sublimating gas, or a heavy suspension of particles. The depth of the fuzz is about sixty meters, then it seems to be somewhat more dense. Not solid at all, but denser than at the fuzzy surface. We think it may have something to do with the vibrations but we're not sure exactly how."

"And all the fuzzy dirt is vibrating but the atmosphere isn't?"

"Yes, sir. That's correct. All observed surfaces vibrate precisely in unison. That means each particle of dirt vibrates precisely with the whole, with no perceptible inertial lag. Perhaps the vibration accounts for the relatively warm surface. The hydrogen layer does not vibrate."

"You said the surface seemed to be a suspension. In what? What's the medium?" Dac was distracted and would not have been particularly interested were it not for Marcy's personal surface.

"There doesn't seem to be a medium, not even the hydrogen." Marcy hesitated, noticing Dac's noticing herself. "At least nothing's shown up yet. There appears to be nothing but space between the particles of dirt."

Marcy Phillips lowered her note pad and looked at Dac, as though waiting for further instructions but expecting none.

"Nothing but space," he repeated, his thought processes getting mushy again.

"Yes, space," she repeated. "I think you should take a look at my figures, if you have some time."

"Yes. It's best to look at the raw data before jumping to conclusions." Dac pretended to look at the clock. "Snoon. Sqweet."

CHAPTER 4

⁊◎ ◐⁊

GAP

"Translate those light signals yet, Gerry?" asked Dac as he entered the flight deck. He slid into his work station, flipped on Administrative Updates, checked the status of systems with a few more flippitys and satisfied himself everything was nominal. He turned to the display of the planet showing a perfect, featureless ball. "Let me guess; War and Peace?"

"Yeah, Right," said Gerry Ast with a lop-sided smile. "Those flashes must be a signal of some sort, but I have no idea what they mean. It's pretty hard to decode two light flashes. The only recording of the flashes is from your opticals. Those flashes are four or five times removed from the source, passed through a couple hundred miles of hydrogen at that low angle, and are artificially reconstructed at that. If there is any information compressed in those flashes, we probably lost it." Gerry Ast stopped, thinking about her next thoughts, her uncertainty holding Dac's attention. "In addition to the flashes, there seems to be a lot of clutter, a very dirty signal as signals go. Not what you'd expect from a culture that could build that thing. The light isn't coherent or monochromatic at all. It seems more like what you'd get from a firecracker. We're trying."

"I understand," replied Dac. He actually did understand. "What's the problem and what can I do to facilitate things?"

"Well, the problem is that when we observe light, we generally have very little need to know which photon came first, which second and so on. Recording light photons sequentially, however, is a real trick even under controlled laboratory conditions." Gerry eyechecked Dac. "A spectrometer analysis, for example, records an accumulation of photons over time but it

26

records the total array of photon energy levels, not the sequence in which they impacted the medium.

"Analyzing the extremely brief light flashes requires recording the stream of photons sequentially as they occur. Like a voice recording; the sequence itself is important. That's pretty loose but you get the idea. Standard electronic and chemical visual recorders merely sample the image, leaving out most of the signal and relying heavily on persistence of vision or audition to fill in the gaps." Gerry paused indicating a change of tack. "Actually, photon flow analysis is quite possible but we really weren't set up for it when the light flashes occurred unexpectedly; caught us completely by surprise, that. We're building a system to be ready for next time."

"Good, Gerry, good," observed Dac. I should have thought of that, he thought. "Have you found anything else that might be a communication?"

"No, sir. It's just a dirt ball, mostly," said Communications, slipping into her official report mode. "The most likely source of any signal is the cube, of course, but we've been on the North side of the ball for some time now, about three hours. We're just now coming up to a good position to view the cube. We'll pass directly over it, clearing it by about 50 kilometers. I turned on everything we've got. If there's anybody waving at us, we'll spot it. I'm broadcasting a basic hailing sequence on all available electromagnetic frequencies at assorted standard modulations. I also tossed in X-ray, McCraken and EPR transmitters for good measure. That should wake them up."

"Okay, Gerry. What do you need from me?" Dac knew this would be a whopper but he had to ask.

"Well, I need to dedicate a *big* chunk of free RAM. Like maybe most of it, for a while anyway. I've got the instruments to do sequential photon recording and recording one flash isn't a big deal; those we have only lasted a fraction of a second." Gerry paused to let Dac brace himself. "But we have no idea when the next one is coming. That means we have to be recording full time twenty-four seven. At least until we figure out what's going on down there, and maybe a lot longer after we do. That might hurt."

"You're right. That will hurt. Pappa? Did you hear that?"

"Chirp. Yes, Mr. Olson."

"And you concur?"

"Yes, Mr. Olson. In fact, I ..."

"Okay, Pappa. Do it. Whatever Gerry needs. Don't ask again unless it hurts. Keep me informed, Ast." Dac regretted that comment immediately; of course Gerry would keep him informed. "As per your usual fine job," he added quickly. Gerry wasn't fooled but she appreciated Dac's sensitivity.

Dac returned to his console and checked the updated displays. One complete orbit coming up. *How in the love of Kepler can it take five hours to orbit this thing?* he asked himself for the fiftieth time. *Even given that it's an alien artifact, it should still obey the laws of physics, shouldn't it? Gravity and celestial mechanics and physics and all that?* He shrugged mentally and focused again on the image of the cube coming up over the horizon.

Dac studied the facsimile of the Cube. It was beautiful in a dark foreboding sort of way, like a gothic castle at midnight, or a warship passing silently in the night. Without augmentation the Cube was very dark, visible mostly because it was silhouetted by eclipsed background stars, darker even than the ball. The Cube had taken on an upper case identity among the crew and, he pondered, himself; a proper name now however and whenever that came about. Marvelous, whatever it was. "Come on, Cube, talk to me."

"Chirp. You called, Mr. Olson?"

"What is it, Pappa?"

"You called … Five more flashes, Mr. Olson."

"What!" Dac lurched up from his slouch and grabbed for the display to see for himself. "Where are they?"

"There were only five, Mr. Olson, there have been no more. One extremely faint, two somewhat brighter, one relatively quite bright, one more like the second and third. On a scale of five the sequence is 1-3-3-5-3. Those are rather gross approximations; I will refine them in a moment. Some other indistinguishable clutter or static, mostly random photons and gamma rays."

"Gamma rays!?" *From a light bulb?* thought Dac.

"Yes, sir." Pappa paused, anticipating Dac's follow-up question. Getting none, he updated his personality profile on Dac and continued. "The flashes were almost simultaneous, all occurring within 0.073 seconds. I am analyzing the light for modulation now. The initial analyses are puzzling."

"In what way, Pappa?" *What isn't puzzling about this thing?*

"They are from point sources but the light is not coherent. In fact, it is a wide spectrum of frequencies from the far ultraviolet down through low radio. Heavy in the X-ray, infrared and visible light spectrums. A surprising number of neutrinos. Each flash is slightly different from the others. The apparent signal is not at all signal-like."

"How's that, Pappa? How would *we* know if it wasn't signal-like? Like we know what alien signals are *supposed* to look like. Or like they know what we'd be looking for. Or would care."

"That is all true and astute. However, a prime characteristic of any signal," responded Pappa, "is its artificiality. It can be identified by its exhibiting a stable frequency, for example, or coherency, directionality and modulation among other characteristics. These alleged signals have the characteristics of explosions, and dirty explosions at that. A common flashlight produces more structure."

"Run them back for me, Pappa." Maybe I'll see something Pappa missed. Yeah, right.

Pappa did, twelve times, until Dac was satisfied he'd seen it all. Something sure looked familiar but he couldn't put his finger on exactly what. Returning to real time Dac saw that they were now directly over the Cube.

"Thank you, Pappa. Communications!"

"Sir?" Communications associate Gerry Ast swiveled toward Dac, her head lagging behind while she finished a calculation.

"What do you make of this, Ast?"

"Nothing yet, sir. Taken with the first two flashes and without, there seems to be no meaning. No modulation of any sort we can identify. The timing of the flashes is completely random as yet. However, there is one avenue we haven't completely explored yet."

"And that is?"

"The Location of the point sources," replied Ast. "They were arranged in a perfectly straight horizontal line very close to the planet surface. That alone is significant."

"In what way?"

I'm speculating here, but the straight line arrangement implies the flashes are part and parcel to the structure of the Cube itself. But," cautioned Gerry, "I have no idea exactly how. Not even a guess."

"The arrangement and sequence in which they occurred may mean something, too," added Gerry. "The signal may be a combination of location, timing, intensity and perhaps something else we haven't noticed yet. Whatever they're saying, it's very subtle and very fast. In short, sir, we really don't have anything yet."

"Keep up the good work, Ast," said Dac absently in his shared frustration. "Something will pop up eventually."

Dac slumped back into his chair, slipping deeper into the cushions as he slipped deeper into the mystery. *Something's there blinking lights at us so they know we're here. They have to know we're here*, he thought with a little rise; *they winked at us when we came down to orbit and they winked again as we came up on the other side!*

"Pappa!"

"Chirp."

"Pappa, can you tell one side of the Cube from another?"

"No, sir. The four sides are identical. Why do you ask?"

"We detected flashes twice. Can you determine whether those flashes came from the same side of the Cube or from two different sides?"

"Yes, sir, a simple matter of counting the intervening revolutions. One moment."

"Chirp."

"The flashes came from different sides, Mr. Olson. Counting the side from which the first signals came as side 1, the second set of signals came from side 3. Is this important?"

"I'm not certain," he replied uncertainly. "But if the flashes came from different sides, they apparently knew where we'd be when we came up on the first orbit. Does that make sense?"

"Yes, sir, but it may be a simple matter of signals being sent in all directions, like a marker buoy. If you are thinking the flashes are signals meant for us, your hypothesis is not exactly conclusive of the evidence."

"Well Dammit, Pappa! You got any better ..."

"More signals, Mr. Olson." Pappa would not ordinarily have interrupted Mr. Olson but for his admonition to inform him immediately of any developments. "Three flashes, in line at the bottom of side 4."

"Why do I always miss it?" Dac whipped back to his console.

"I'm sure I don't know, Mr. Olson. Perhaps it would be profitable to pay closer attention to your board. Shall I replay them?"

"No!" Closer *attention*? Why bother. "Just figure out what they mean! Communications?"

"I'm on it, Mr. Olson."

"Meteorology?"

"Nothing about the signals, sir."

"Survey?"

"I don't know, sir. *Something* happened." Pete Bravo, Survey, hummed a little tune while several of the crew looked up. Something happened? "I'm checking with Geometrics right now."

Pete 'Swingline' Bravo, Senior Associate, Survey. Very young but very bright and savvy beyond his years. Pete managed an unprecedented move from Unit Five to Unit Two on his first project. That was based on his analysis of survey records compiled by previous profit centers operating in the GM region. He found fabulously rich mineral sources that previous teams had overlooked and his 0.001 cut made him fabulously rich. A prospector at heart, Pete stayed on just for the fun of it.

Pete got his nickname from an incident in school, a duel with staplers over a point of honor involving a cheerleader. The staple was never removed, ostensibly out of respect for her remarkable talents, and could still be seen under the skin on the back of his left hand.

"Got it!" rejoined Pete. "I don't know what this means but the last two events were perfectly time-symmetrical in relation to the polar axis."

"What in Hell's Axle does *that* mean, Survey!?"

"Well, sir," responded Pete, excited. "The time interval between the second signal and our passing over the South pole is exactly the same as the time between passing over the South Pole and the third signal."

"Great!" redunded Dac. "What in Hell's Poles does that *mean*?" but more gently this time.

"I don't know, sir. I checked out the first signal, too, but it was not symmetrical, probably because we were not yet in orbit. If that's the case, the timing of the flashes might be incidental to our orbital position rather than to deliberate alien control. However, there is one peculiarity." Pete paused.

"*One* peculiarity!?" One? Really?

"Yes, sir. In all three cases our positions were aligned with each other on a plane perpendicular to the vertical faces of the Cube."

"Survey, I know any three points in space will lie in the same plane. Tell me something I don't know."

"Not just in the same plane, sir," reiterated Pete Bravo. "In the same plane perpendicular to the rotational axis. There's a little fudge in there because we are moving and the signals have a non-zero duration, but it is too close to be coincidence."

"Anybody make anything of that?"

"Yes, sir." It was Bravo again. "Well not *that* exactly, but I found something else. As you know, the Cube does not reflect radar at any frequency we use. It just soaks it up. So I was surprised to get an image when I analyzed the flashes at extremely high gain.

"There is a faint, uh, leakage of light in a straight line around the base of the Cube. It's extremely faint but it seems to go completely around the Cube in a straight line parallel to the surface of the planet. We know it is not a reflection of our signal; it appears to be composed of point sources." Pete paused under the intense attention of the crew. "Uh … The intensity is constant and stable. The light leaking from the line displays typical hairline slit diffraction. The distance from the line to the top of the Cube is exactly the same as the width of the Cube. The line is slightly brighter than the Cube, but no more so than, say, ambient starlight."

"Pappa! Let me see that line!"

"I am sorry, but we are too far over the horizon. I will draw up an image from Bravo's data. One moment."

There it was! A line around the base of the Cube. On the display it looked like candlelight seeping under a door. Pappa colored it artificially warm for contrast to the cold blue of the Cube. It seemed the Cube was a cube after all, of a sort.

"Track that down everyone! Make sense of that." Dac was excited. Everyone was excited. "Thank you, Pete. Good job! Do it again!" Swingline Bravo beamed.

The next several hours out of sight of the Cube were uneventful. Dac threw himself into a persistent problem with payroll administration and tried to unscramble the mess. Nobody was getting what they thought they had signed on for and everybody was mad.

"Screw it!" Dac muttered. He looked sideways in his immediate locale to see who caught that. He promoted a clean and professional work environment but apparently nobody noticed his lapse. "Pappa! Just pay everyone whatever they thought they were due and kiss it all off."

"K …?"

"Pay them and make it go away!" Sheesh!

Everyone probed and analyzed the artifact in hisser own way, Dac noted, but added little more to the basic facts. No meaningful signal, no explanation for the physics of the thing, no whys. In fact, it …

"Chirp."

"Yes, Pappa."

"According to my preliminary calculations we will receive another series of flashes in 32 seconds. It will be four flashes, on a scale of five, 3-1-1-5. It will last exactly 0.1801 seconds. The flashes will be arranged along the line Mr. Bravo identified, in the sequence displayed now on your console. If my calculations are confirmed, these flashes, like all previous flashes, will have no meaning. If you move quickly, Mr. Olson," said Pappa mildly, "you may see it this time."

Dac jumped for the screen, stopped to question Pappa's outrageous prediction, then decided to see it first. If Pappa was right he'd sure have questions! There would be a few if he was wrong for that matter. Hell's Flashlight, he thought. I've got too many questions now!

Dac saw the light flashes this time. Everyone saw them this time, exactly as Pappa predicted. Except for one point.

"Pappa!"

"Chirp."

"Nice work, Pappa." Dac looked at the replaying loop of the fourth signal thoughtfully. "Everything you said checks out but one. You said the signal would have no meaning. If you understand the first three signals well enough to predict the fourth, then it must have a meaning. Right?"

"Wrong," stated Pappa incontrovertibly, brooking no response. "You are asking the wrong question again. The flashes of light are random but quite predictable. They have no direct meaning as such. Howeve …"

"You're going to have to explain *that*, Pappa." Dac mentally cocked his hammer and released the safety. This had better be good. The crew had stopped completely.

"What we are seeing as flashes of light," explained Pappa, "are actually eclipsed background stars momentarily exposed through an aperture. The apparent randomness derives from their random position in the background sky, but those random positions are known and fixed, and therefore predictable. The apparent signals occur when the ship passes in the plane of the aperture."

Dac was stunned. Bravo was grinning from ear to ear. Biology hadn't understood a thing. Marcy was stunned. Fats Bic was fascinated. The rest were in there somewhere.

"And?"

"And the line discovered by Mr. Bravo is actually random starlight from large numbers of relatively faint stars seeping through that same aperture. The apparent signals are merely the few brightest stars. It appears relatively bright because of the Cube's low albedo."

"And how did you come to this?"

"I noticed that the spectrum of the light flashes is typical of main sequence stars so I compared the location of the flashes to the background sky in the direction of our observations. They matched perfectly." Pause for questions that were not yet formulated. "Therefore the flashes were actually background stars. The only way we could see the stars through the Cube was if there was no Cube there or if it was transparent. It does not seem to be a transparent medium, so it must not be there, at least at the precise times and locations we observed the starlight passing through it."

"But, but," rebutted Dac, "if the Cube isn't there in the aperture and allows the light to pass at precise intervals, isn't that proof that ..."

Dac didn't even buy that and tried again.

"Look, Pappa. How could the Cube not be there, just at the right times so we can see it?"

"The Cube is there, and so is the aperture through which the starlight passes. If the Cube is there in the aperture, by definition it would not be an aperture." Again Pappa paused for assimilation. "The location of the aperture is Mr. Bravo's line. There is no Cube in the aperture so we can see through it and light can pass through it." Pappa seemed to be experiencing some frustration, evidenced by the redundancies.

"Okay, Pappa. Thanks. Anyone else?"

Nothing.

"Not all at once." Dac looked from face to face, no one any more willing to challenge Pappa than was he himself.

"Sir?" Mike Hand, Engineering. "I think Pappa's right. I don't know how, but maybe that really is a Cube, suspended over a base, separated by a physical gap of some sort. We looked through the gap each time we went around in orbit and passed through the plane of the gap. It's easy to visualize but I have no idea how it's built, much less why."

"Quite right, Mr. Hand," said Pappa with approval.

"Hand! Do you have a measurement on that gap? How big or thick it is?"

"Yes, sir. A rough guess anyway. I show the Cube separated from the base by approximately 40 meters, subject to confirmation."

"Of course subject to ... Does that make sense Pappa?"

"Very close to my estimate, based on the length of the flashes and our orbitals."

"Okay, what holds it up? Magnetism?"

"No," from Survey, Geology and Pappa simultaneously. "No evidence of a magnetic field which would be easy to detect at that rotational speed," continued Geology. "Probably pillars stand the cube off from the base for some reason. Maybe the cube is set on something transparent, like a big plate of glass. Maybe some sort of field holds the Cube up and the light passes under it like those stacks of ring magnets on a pencil we all played with as kids." Mercedes stopped rather than finished, feeling everyone's eyes on her. "Maybe they're just windows."

"Okay. And how does it spin exactly in line with the base? Why doesn't it wobble all over the place?"

"Once started, why wouldn't it stay in line?" responded Survey. "There's nothing to deflect it. Everything's moving in lock step."

"Biology! Outside of those alleged flash signals, do you have any sign of life down there?"

"No, sir, but that doesn't mean there isn't any," answered Ross Label, Biology. "I get a pretty good view from up here and I'd say there is probably no life. Better than 97% probably. I'd need to get on the ground to go to 100%. Compared to what you guys are doing, I've been pretty bored."

"Communications! Get on the horn to HO again. Tell them the artifact is dead, no sign of life, intelligent or otherwise."

"Anything else?"

Dac grinned just a little, then a lot.

"Yeah. Tell them we're going down!"

CHAPTER 5

PLANETFALL

"All riiiight!!"

Equivalent emphatic demonstrations from everyone.

"Going DOWN!"

Even Pappa and Mamma celebrated with a brilliant brassy fanfare. In fact, it was a stock hailing call that in other circumstances might precede a shot across the bow. No one cared.

"Okay. Okay," said Dac as the ruckus moderated, officially stern but grinning like a fool with the rest. "We'll take another couple of orbits to double check everything. Biology, anything moves down there and planetfall is off. You are charged to aggressively find something that moves Understand that?

"Communications? Same charge. Make sure nothing down there talks but us." Dac paused to eye check the deck. "You hear a sneeze and we're outta there soonest. I want a record of everything we do. Everything.

"Survey," Dac continued," build your flight plan and find the best spot to land, close to the Cube. Engineering and ... Hell's Hounds! You all know what to do. Report in two hours. Make me proud!"

Everyone scrambled. They knew the drill, only the target was new; implement the procedures they were trained to do and had already set up. Biology was the trigger on planetfall, of course, so everyone had monitored Ross Label's progress. Progress was zero, no life. So everyone had prepared for planetfall. Only the light signals from the Cube held up things and that issue had just evaporated.

"Going down!" turned into a celebratory chant of sorts. Not quite melodic, many of the crew having lead ears, but gleefully expository nonetheless.

Dac watched as the general commotion settled into purposeful activity. He hadn't seen this kind of genuine exuberance since we left port. We were certainly successful so far on this expedition, he mused, but the work was routine and uneventful, like casting a net in known waters; you'll always get *something* useful. But this? This is the kind of discovery that will make everyone unbelievably famous and rich beyond imagination. And we're doing something that has never been done before in all of human history, and probably the aliens' history too. They deserve the fun. Let it go.

"But I've got a job to do," thought Dac in counterpoint. "Time to relax later."

"Mamma?"

"Boit."

"Give me a status check. Everything nominal for planetfall?"

"Unit One is in readiness sequence. All EVA-specific indicators are nominal," returned Mamma. "Standard planetfall equipment being prepped and should be ready in six hours. I will need a breakdown of mission objectives and planetaries to put the rest of it together.

"Conditioning for this planet's atmosphere initiated," Mamma continued. "Gravity may be a problem if they stay down more than ten cycles, same parameters as empty space EVA. Shuttle being prepped and on schedule for five cycles plus standard safety contingencies, if that is all right. Crew sterilization sequence started an hour ago."

"An hour... Who ordered all of this an hour ago?" Dac looked up at the crew who just barely looked down in time to avoid eye contact.

"Boit."

"Mamma? Come on back." The hour head start wasn't really a problem, Dac knew, but there was a little problem with protocol that needed to be clarified.

"Mamma!"

"Yes, Mr. Olson?"

"Somebody thinks they're more qualified to make decisions than me, and seems to get information before I do. I want to know who and how." This was mostly for the benefit of the crew. Mamma didn't really care one way or the other about who gave the orders as long as it didn't interfere with Internals.

"How, sir?" Mamma responded. "Why everyone knew there was no sign of life. And Pappa's work is always available in real time, if you can read Lesmar. Pappa's hypothesis about the light signals has been in the system for two hours while he developed it."

Dac always felt learning AI speak was a waste of time when you could just ask. He may have to reevaluate his thinking on that. But he was the VP on this project; he wasn't supposed to be spending his time on that sort of street-level nuts and bolts, was he? Just the same, there was a principle afoot here. To wit, I am the boss. Mental pause. Did I just say To wit?

"All right. All right, that's how. Now who?"

"Boit."

Lots of silence, even from Mamma, which was unnerving in its passive rebelliousness.

"It was me, sir." Me was Mike Hand, Engineering Associate. "I, uh, figured it was a given, and the sooner we started the sooner we could get back on schedule and make up your lost time, and the incentive and all. Pappa's analysis made sense to everyone, and ..."

"Are you telling me, Mr. Hand, that everyone in this room conspired in your little usurpation of authority?"

"No, sir!" he exclaimed, glancing around the room in mild panic. "It was just me, sir!"

"I see." Dac really did see. All of them wanted to go down and he couldn't blame them. Hell's Starting Pistol, he was itching to get down there himself. The greatest event ever and he wanted to be in on it. He couldn't blame them, and admired their initiative. However ...

"Mr. Hand."

"Yes, sir!" Mike glanced sideways at the others who looked back helplessly wide-eyed.

"Mr. Hand, you seem to be the protagonist in all of this. I have a special task for you." Dac paused to secure everyone's full attention. "We can see everything on the Cube from up here. We don't know what it is or what it means, but we *can* see it all. Agreed?"

"Yes, sir!" agreed Mike, anxious to be agreeable in the extreme.

"No, sir, Mr. Hand. We *cannot* see all of it. We can't see *inside* it, can we Mr. Hand?"

"No, sir!" Another apprehensive glance at the others.

"Yes, sir, Mr. Hand. We *can* see inside it. Do you know how we're going to see inside it, Mr. Hand?"

"Yes ... No, sir." Mike shot a look of desperation at the crew and a look of defeat at Dac. "I ... I think you're going to explain how we are going to look inside it. Sir!"

"Not we, Mr. Hand. You." Not quite what Mike Hand expected but probably better than he expected.

"Me?"

"You, and whoever you need to get into that gap in the Cube and see what's in there. How soon can you report back on your plans to enter the Cube?"

"Preliminary report in one hour, sir." Mike tried heroically to suppress a grin but failed catastrophically. "Final project design in one cycle. Sir!!"

"That," allowed Dac, with mild amusement and a fixing eye contact to each crewone, "will do nicely. See me in one hour. Dismissed."

Dismissed? Did I just say that!? Dac had never before dismissed anyone. He surprised himself that he did it now, but it was needed now. He checked sideways at the crew and was certain he detected way too much merriment. Me too, he thought.

Mike and most of Unit One all but fell over themselves to get to work on planetfall. Hell's Checklist, thought Dac, they've probably got it all worked out already. But channels is channels and you can't be too careful if there is any risk involved. The Cube certainly qualified as any risk.

"Okay, Jason. What have you got?"

Dac settled at his circular conference table and cleared most of the debris from the immediate area, a pile of yet-to-be-reconciled invoices for cargo and supplies from the stop before last at Gates Port. He flipped the monitor to standby and looked up to Jason Fielding, Unit One Team Leader and Mike Hand, Mechanical Engineering. Mike settled into the chair across the conference table while Jason sat to Dac's left. Dac moved a note pad to within striking distance and looked up to Jason Fielding.

Team Leader Fielding was tall, lean, old as this business goes, leathered, wise and take-no-prisoners. He looked like a survivor of the OK Corral, mean enough and quick enough to catch bullets in his teeth. He was, however, the nicest guy on the ship, kindhearted to a fault. He was just thoroughly seasoned, weathered even, and anyone on the ship would follow him into Hell.

In fact, if Dac himself saw the need, Jason Fielding would march into Hell, but not into HO. Jason had never been there, didn't like corporate political crap and didn't like corporate crats and didn't like corporate procedures and didn't like corporate personalities when they functioned as such, Dac included. He did, however, respect Dac as competent at what he did, and liked Dac as a person when he dropped the crat crap. That, thought Dac, was good enough.

Mike Hand was responsible for the crew of six that kept the machinery going on this profit center. Mike was not an intellectual but he was very bright in a motor control context. Very skilled, very intuitive when quick action was required, and very good at getting things done in ambivalent situations. Mike didn't make mistakes, at least not when it counted, and Dac trusted his judgment implicitly.

Mike was the closest thing to military of any in his crew. He really liked the tight corporate organizational structure and thrived in narrowly focused objectives, which in Fielding's eyes kept Hand permanently suspect. Hand was also the most physical of his crew, a world-class soccer player in his youth and skilled at a variety of sports even now. This job might be physical and it was certainly unprecedented so Mike Hand was the natural choice to go in first.

They settled in and looked expectantly at Dac to get things rolling. Okay, he thought, how about this;

"Go."

It took a second for someone to shift into Go. When they did, it was Jason.

"Unnh. Well, for starters, we came up with a few definitions so we all know what we're talking about," began Fielding. "Most of these are current practice anyway but this will formalize it. Mike?"

"Good thinking, Jason. Let's hear it."

41

"First of all, that isn't really a planet out there," began Mike, "so we knocked it around and came up with calling it the Ball, capital letter Ball. By the same token, the hydrogen layer isn't really an atmosphere, so now it's the Wrapper. The hollow void in the center is the Pit, as in avocado." Mike paused for approval.

"I assume you're willing to put your name on the report to HO, Jason?"

"Uh. yes, it was a joint effort, Mr. Olson." Jason glanced at Mike who smirked back. "We all just sorta' fell into this."

"I can believe that. Go on."

"Well, the thing that looks like a cube will be called the Cube, capital C," continued Mike. "It sits on the Base, separated from it by the Gap. As Pappa suggested, the four vertical sides are numbered in the order they appear to a viewer as they rotate to the East, beginning with the side toward us when the first stars were spotted through the Gap. Pappa will keep track of that. The other two sides of the Cube are the Roof and the Ceiling. With me so far?"

"No."

"Well, imagine you're in the Gap, standing on the Base. From your perspective you will be standing on a Floor. Above you will be a Ceiling. Above that you would expect to find the Attic, whatever's inside the Cube, and above the Attic is the Roof. Got it?"

"Okay, I've got that. But why?"

"Well, we kept getting a little confusion as to whether we were talking about the top of the Cube or the top of the Base, so we went to the analogy of a house. Using that analogy, what would you call the interior of the Base?" asked Jason expectantly.

"The, uh, Basement?" Dac felt a little foolish in spite of the good sense it made.

"Right!" Mike exclaimed. "And the whole thing, Cube, Base, Ball and all, is the Thingy." Dac looked up to Jason at that, then to Mike but didn't ask.

"Okay," said Dac, not entirely certain that it was. "Now what's the plan?"

"Unit One," began Jason, "will take a shuttle down to the Ball for reconnaissance. We will launch one hour before we come over the horizon towards the Cube on the next orbit, about seven hours from now. That will allow maximum time to maneuver while Pappa is able to observe us directly. Then we'll ..."

"Excuse me, Jason," interrupted Dac. "How will Pappa be involved?"

"We may have a problem with navigation, Dac," replied Jason. "The surface of the Ball is still giving us ambiguous readings; we're not exactly sure where the surface actually is. It has to be somewhere, of course, but the shuttle's radar and laser ranging systems sometimes have trouble finding it. We think Pappa's shipboard systems are more accurate and he can relay harder data to the shuttle to navigate by. In addition ..."

"Excuse me? We don't know where the surface is!?" Dac feigned incredulity; he was aware of the fuzzy surface problem. "That is a go-no go criteria, you know."

"Yes, we understand that. We think the anomaly is in the radar readings of an unusual surface composition, not the fact of the surface itself. It's there somewhere. We just have to be careful on touchdown. Any problem and we abort soonest."

"Or sooner!" Dac was becoming more than a little apprehensive about planetfall without more solid information, specifically about solid ground. "Help me out here, Jason. What's your honest assessment of the risk. I know everyone wants to go down; me too. But I have to be sure we don't do anything dumb. Or dangerous."

"Understood," replied Jason. "Every planetfall I've done was hazardous in some way; some completely unexpected and really hairy. If something goes wrong or even a little dicey, Pappa will be overhead in position to help. We'll be close to the surface, about one kilometer from the Cube when Pappa comes over the horizon. That will give us just over one hour to maneuver for touchdown while still in view of the ship.

"Because of the heavy reliance on Pappa," continued Jason, "the shuttle will set down before Pappa passes out of view. We'll make a grand tour around three sides of the Cube and set down on the side facing the ship as it drops towards the horizon. You know me, Dac, I take risk but I don't take blunder."

"Good. We understand each other." It better be good, thought Dac; I don't have a better plan. "Go on."

"The surface seems to be perfectly smooth, so there shouldn't be a problem finding a place to land," Jason went on. "We'll monitor hazards as we approach and try to get as close as possible. With a little luck we'll be able to inspect three of the four sides on the way in. The only interesting feature we can see from here, of course, is the Gap so we'll check it out before landing. We'll take a good look into it, see if we can figure what it is and how it's made and what's holding it up. We'll focus communications on it too; if there's anybody to talk to down there, they'll be in the Gap." Jason paused to give Dac a chance to respond. Dac didn't.

"From what we can see from here, there's no reason we can't just land next to the Cube, like stopping at a drive-in for a burger and fries," Jason continued, picking up a little uncharacteristic enthusiasm. "That will leave us a kilometer below the Gap so we won't be able to examine it too closely. We should be able to get contact data on the Cube itself, however, and the Ball. Okay so far?"

"Yes, Jason," said Dac, not 100% sure about the Okay. "No problem as far as I can see. You've made planetfall often enough that I won't second guess you. I do have a concern, however. That surface."

"You mean the ambiguous readings?"

"Yes."

"I have a little problem with that too," agreed Mike Hand. "Our best guess based on the data, such as it is, the surface is something like an expanded matrix of space debris, light in structure, like popcorn. We get the same sort of readings from planet surfaces covered with extremely dense and deep vegetation, and from some comets that are unusually frothy. I guarantee there is no vegetation on the Ball.

"There is no sign of movement like a wet surface," continued Mike, "and certainly no volcanic or tectonic action. The uncertainty is within the range of previous experience. We'll deploy the floatation pads at very low pressure to dissipate the weight, which won't be much anyway at five hundredths G. We may have trouble walking on it, but I don't think we'll have any difficulty with touchdown."

"Okay," replied Dac. "What kind of difficulty with walking? Walking is pretty consequential to going out for samples and all those scientific things you guys do. Would snowshoes help?" Dac was serious.

"Well …" hedged Mike while he decided if Dac was serious. "Actually, the decision to go outside and walk on the Ball may have to wait until we get there on the surface. But if the surface will support the shuttle, it should support people too." Mike turned to Jason for confirmation; Jason was stone-faced as usual. "We'll take along snowshoes. They're standard equipment on planetfall."

"They are?" Dac hadn't known that.

"Yes, sir," answered Jason. "Standard issue in case of snow, deep fine sand, thick seaweed beds and the like." Didn't Dac know that?

"Okay. It may support people but what about that foaminess?" rebutted Dac. "What if it really is foam and you sink up to your knees?"

"Well ..." interjected Mike. "The landing probes will tell us how firm the surface is. The ground effect skirt will help, too. That's what they're designed for, you know."

"Okay, fair enough." Yeah, I know. "What else?"

"If there are no particular problems," said Jason, "we'll stay on the surface for one orbit. Collect samples, analyze the Cube any which way we can and deploy a few monitoring devices. We'll lift off before the ship comes over the horizon and rendezvous over the Cube. Standard reconnaissance procedure all the way."

"Redundancies?"

"Pappa is running simulations now to establish a nominal baseline," said Mike Hand. "Unit Two is prepping for backup and will monitor all systems in real time. Mamma will double up on Pappa's navigational data. The shuttle will be prepped for five orbits. In fact," added Mike in a conspiratorial tone, "everyone wants to get in on the act. This'll be the most over-backuped expedition I've ever done. The biggest problem is fending off all of the well-meaning help without offending anyone. I'd say we're all set."

"Do it!" said Dac with a smile. "But planning and preparation only. I pull the trigger, understand?" with a pointed look at Mike Hand. "Without my explicit consent, nothing leaves this ship!" Reluctantly he returned to his game of invoice solitaire. "And that goes for Pappa and Mamma, too."

"Chirp"

"Boit."

"Thar she blows!" said Jason with heartfelt bravado. However, there was more genuine awe in his voice than his many rugged years of space exploration might have otherwise allowed.

"Yeah," answered Mike Hand. "And it would really be something if you could see it."

The shuttle powered swiftly up over the horizon toward the South Pole, toward the rectangular blackout of the background sky that delineated the Cube. The blackout grew dramatically as they watched, rising from a line at the horizon to full black curtain spanning the breadth of their view through the port. The rising enveloping blackness reminded Gerry Ast of the black overcasting plague arising from Sauron's evil power in Mordor. Ross Label recalled raising the top of his convertible one romantic night under an unexpected shower. Mercedes Mead saw the menacing black bat wings of the demon on Bald Mountain. Mike Hand saw a playing field to be conquered, a goal to be scored. Jason Fielding saw a flat wall, big, black and imposing to be sure, but only a dead hunk of stuff to be dealt with.

"Atmospheric insertion in 30 seconds." intoned Shuttle. "Deceleration sequence beginning ... now."

Everyone lurched forward as thrusters brought the shuttle down from orbital speed to atmospheric insertion speed in a smooth but rapid transition. The surface of the hydrogen Wrapper was very discrete, transitioning from hydrogen at 2.2 bars to empty space in less than a centimeter. In effect, at orbital speed the surface of the Wrapper was hard as water; a standard tangential entry to dissipate energy would be like slamming into a solid wall. In order to minimize the impact, and maximize the time under Pappa's watch, the shuttle went to within fifty kilometers of the Cube in space and decelerated rapidly to below the speed of sound in the Wrapper. It then dropped at a steep angle into the Wrapper at a comparatively leisurely atmospheric maneuvering speed. Ross, ever the romantic, relived his favorite amusement park ride, a log sliding down a chute to splash into a water sluice. Splashdown!

"Bring her up alongside the Cube at Gap level, Mr. Hand," instructed Jason unnecessarily. "Let's give it a once over."

The shuttle was quiet as a tomb, everyone struck dumb at the sheer size of the thing and totally absorbed in trying to see the all but unseeable.

As the shuttle approached the face of the Cube, the sky disappeared completely to a line directly overhead. Jason was whole-heartedly thankful for Pappa's backup on navigation; there wasn't a damn thing his eyes could focus on.

"Damn!" Nobody disagreed.

The shuttle's instruments were equally uncertain, hunting constantly for stability even with Pappa's help. Pappa had been able to draw up a very accurate radar image of the whole Thingy from space by iteratively averaging massive amounts of vague data over relatively long periods of time. It was something else, even for Pappa, to determine the shuttle's position second by second to within a few safe meters when the shuttle moved randomly at the will of its operators in close proximity to an all but invisible wall that rotated at one revolution per hour.

"Damn!" An increasingly common epithet. "Damn!" See?

Pappa managed by calculating the shuttle's position in relation to the edges of the blacked out sky, as observed both from space and from the shuttle, refined by his radar positioning of the shuttle. This was cross-checked and adjusted a hundred thousand times per second against the shuttle's own navigation system and Pappa's projections of their position. Mamma watched and jumped in whenever she didn't agree.

"So far, so good," muttered Jason, not completely comfortable about that. "Mike, bring her in a little tighter and let's take a look in the Gap."

"Might as well," rejoined Mike under his breath. "There's nothing to look at down here. Good lord this place is barren!"

In fact, the place had the charm of a crease in a sheet of black paper; it didn't take long to satisfy your curiosity. They anticipated more details as they approached the Ball and the Cube but there were none to provide a feeling of scale. The face of the Cube had no texture, no shine, no reflection, no translucency or depth. It didn't seem to be black, like black paint, but rather black like the inside of a vast hall with the lights out. At this range, so close that peripheral vision did not include the edges, it was impossible to judge the distance to the face without the instruments. Jason was also apprehensive about the trustworthiness of his instruments.

"Close enough," said Jason. "Try the floods."

Nothing.

"Those floods on?" asked Jason. Mike checked the indicator lights. They were on.

"The floodlights don't light the surface any more than radar does," muttered Jason.

"Probably for the same reason," remuttered Mike, "whatever that reason is."

The shuttle rose to the lower edge of the Gap, the Floor, with motion identifiable only by instrument. Then starlight suddenly appeared before them, as though the Cube had instantly disappeared, or opened like a camera shutter.

"Whoa!" shouted Mike. "What ..."

He stopped when he looked up reflexively to see that the vast blacked out sky above was still blacked out. Directly in front, however, a horizontal line of stars crossed the view port, seeming to blaze in contrast to the complete blackness of the Cube. They were looking directly into the Gap, completely through the Cube.

"Hold her right there, Mike," ordered Jason. "Hold it!"

Mike jerked his attention back to the task at hand and stabilized the shuttle in place.

"Wow!" Largely the same reaction from everyone, in hisser own choice understatement.

The clarity of space renders the perpetual starlight in the night sky very bright and very close. There is no atmospheric haze to give the eye a feeling of depth. The line of star-filled sky visible through the Gap was just as bright and just as close. Perhaps it seemed more so by contrast with the blackness of the Cube itself, even though seen through a slit 42 kilometers away.

Mike noticed the total lack of reflection of the starlit gap on the underside of the Cube, the Ceiling. No reflections on the Floor either. That fact made the slit of starlight appear to be immediately in front of them, in spite of its distance.

"You can look completely through it!" amazed Mercedes Mead. "Everywhere!"

"What's holding it up?" breathed Ross Label. "Modesty?"

"Get instruments on that," commanded Jason. God that's dumb, he thought immediately, there's nothing there to get instruments on. "Scan the Gap and find out what's holding everything up. And don't tell me Charles Atlas."

"It's clear, Mr. Fielding," said Ed Bic. "There is nothing in the Gap, unless it's so thin it doesn't occlude stars." ... "Who's Charles Atlas?"

"Never mind!" spat Jason." How wide is that Gap? Fats?"

"Mike, run the shuttle up and down a few times, past both edges of the Gap so I can get a measurement," replied Fats Bic. "You know. The Floor and the Ceiling."

"While you're at it, Mike," said Pete Bravo, "rotate so we can take a look to the left and right. Maybe there's some support at the corners."

Done.

"Nothing, Mr. Fielding," said Pete. "No distortion or refraction or occlusion of the star field that would indicate support of any kind."

"Bic?"

"Right at forty meters, plus a tad," replied Fats Bic. "Confirming previous estimate."

"Anyone else?" called Jason back over his shoulder without taking his eyes from the port. "Radiation?"

Nothing

"Okay, Mike," said Jason deliberately. "Take her into the Gap. Very slowly. Bail out at the first sign of anything unusual."

"Unusual?" Mike Hand looked at Jason and Jason looked back with a straight face.

"Anything different from what we see right now. Okay?"

"You got it," said Mike with some enthusiasm. "Geronimo!"

"Wait!" barked Marcy Phillips. "It could be solid!"

"Solid? What do you mean?"

"This might be a big sandwich," she continued, "with a thick slice of something perfectly transparent in the Gap, with a refractive index of one. We might fly into a solid wall."

"Good thinking, Marcy," said Jason after a moment's consideration. "Mike, set landing probes forward and take it *very* easy."

Mike eased the shuttle forward toward the Gap. As he advanced, he raised and lowered the shuttle to confirm that he was centered on the Gap.

The thin line of stars ahead seemed to widen as he concentrated on them to keep his orientation. Just an illusion, he told himself, we're only a few meters closer. Closer. Looking good.

Suddenly the shuttle lurched to a wobbly stop, sending those who were standing into a stumble, like missing the landing at the bottom of an escalator. Exclamations everywhere. The shuttle's deck floated uncertainly, like an ice floe in choppy water.

"Abort, Mr. Hand!" shouted Jason. "Get out of here now!"

Mike was already backing the shuttle away as Jason gave the command, reacting instinctively to a subtle shift in the feel of the flight controls. They had not quite gotten into the Gap so they did not actually get out of it, but the shuttle stabilized almost immediately.

"Everything OK?" asked Jason as he scanned the crew. "Mike, what was that?"

"I don't know, Mr. Fielding," he replied. "We ran into something soft but apparently fairly firm. A magnetic field maybe. Bravo?"

"Nothing magnetic, Mike," responded Pete Bravo immediately. "No indication of radiation of any kind. Let me check ..."

"Mr. Fielding?" interrupted Fats Bic, Meteorology. "I have something here. It doesn't make sense, but when I scanned all radar modes I found a Doppler effect. In the Gap."

"Doppler effect? Translate that, Bic. A wind shear?"

"Something like that," said Fats cautiously as he studied his meteorological instruments. "There's a strong wind coming out of the Gap. It's moving straight out of the Gap at us. It stops in a pressure front directly in front of us. Wind speed approximately 90 kilometers per hour. Is that what we hit?"

"I don't show any wind, Fats," said Mike Hand, checking his navigational instruments. What's that pressure front?"

"There is no wind right here, Mike," said Fats. "Only in the Gap. It seems to stop at a front about two meters out of the Gap, ten meters in front of us now. From there on out the atmosphere is apparently motionless. That front must be what we ran into, like a big pillow."

"That's just what it felt like," agreed Mike, "a big pillow. Okay, what now?"

"We're sure as Hell not going into the Gap," said Jason with authority. "We're getting behind schedule, Mike. Take it on around to the far side as planned, Gap altitude. Fats, monitor that wind as we go around, see where it's coming from. Let's get settled some place cozy and let Pappa chew on this for a while."

Mike piloted the shuttle around the Cube, stopping periodically to confirm observations.

Confirmed; the wind blew out of the Gap in all directions at the same speed, with the same pressure front on all sides.

"You tell me," said Jason to no one specifically. "Is that wind holding up the Cube, like a ground effect machine or something?"

"That's a possible, Jason," responded Mike. "There's no way to tell what the cube weighs, but in this gravity that idea's within reason. But given that the Cube floats on the wind, I can't imagine what keeps it stable. Or for that matter what generates the wind."

"And where does the wind come from," added Fats. "There are no inlets, at least above the surface. Maybe it pumps gas from the interior and out through the Gap. That might relate to the hollow interior somehow."

"Okay," said Jason. "That's good for an opener. Then there should be an outlet in the Gap somewhere. And there should be some movement of the atmosphere, some flow. Anything like that on the charts?"

"Nothing yet," said Fats. "I'm on it."

"Mike, let's keep on schedule," said Jason. He flipped through a series of displays to verify time and location. "It's time to set her down. Find a place with a view."

Mike Hand prepared to set the shuttle down on the Ball as he cleared one face of the Cube. The point of touchdown was selected to keep line of sight contact with Pappa as long as possible as the Cube rotated, approximately one hundred meters off one corner. From that vantage point they could also see two faces of the Cube and six edges by which to navigate, four against the sky and two against the surface.

Mike leveled the shuttle and brought her down gently, flotation deployed in a limp skirt that hung below looking like wet laundry. On touchdown the weight of the shuttle would spread the skirt and gas would fill the bag just enough to lift the shuttle free of the surface. Unlike the

Cube, the Ball was visible by radar and by their floods, but absolutely featureless and a little fuzzy.

"This look like a good spot, boss?" asked Mike with a straight face.

"No, over there a little," replied Jason with a jerk of his head to his left. "It looks like ants here."

"Talk me down, Pappa," said Mike casually, with a sideways glance at Jason. "I read altitude at twenty-two meters, descent at point-five meters per second. Please confirm."

"Confirmed, Mr. Hand."

"Twenty meters."

"Confirmed."

"Fifteen meters."

"Confirmed, Mr. Hand."

Mike monitored the probes and the floatation sensors as he played the instrument panel by feel. It was an instrument, thought Mike, a musical instrument that worked with his body, responded to his body like a lover. He smiled as he pushed aside the persistent image of Marcy Phillips. Focus, Dammit!

"Ten meters. Attitude nominal. Slight drift to your right, Mr. Hand."

Mike tweaked the stick absently, intent on the displays. He could see the surface of the Ball through the open view port but the abject featurelessness of the Ball provided less control feedback than his instruments. In effect, he was flying blind but he was so completely absorbed in his mental construct that the shuttle felt more like a suit of clothes than the clumsy life support package it was.

"Five meters. Good correction, Mr. Hand."

The probes should touch any second, thought Mike. Nothing yet. Where's the surface? He glanced at the floatation sensors. Nothing. He glanced out the view port pointlessly; all he could see was the featureless fuzzy haze out to the limit of the floods. It looked the same from five meters as it did from fifty.

"Confirm altitude, Pappa. I read two meters but the probes don't register. I'm holding here."

"Confirmed, Mr. Hand," responded Pappa. "You are holding at two meters. No drift. I have no readings from the probes. Floatation deployment confirmed but no pressure yet. You may proceed."

Mike dropped the shuttle more slowly and noted with satisfaction that the flotation sensors finally responded. Their measurements were weak and erratic, however, indicating minor skirt movement and a slight increase of pressure. Very light pressure. Strange, thought Mike. The shuttle had an Earth weight of nearly five thousand kilos. Even here it should squash the floats and show a lively pressure reading by now. Mike checked floatation integrity for leaks. No indicators, but if there was no pressure there would be no leaks. A cold Dammit squirmed across the back of his neck. He looked apprehensively over to Jason who returned his professional concern but nodded reassurance.

"Go for it, Mike." Jason was stone.

"Talk to me, Pappa."

"Two meters, Mr. Hand" responded Pappa. "Negative."

"Negative!?"

Mike was experienced enough to take his hands from the controls, take a deep breath and size up the situation. Don't do anything dumb, fast, jerky or unexpected, he thought sternly. No danger, yet. Everything's nominal. Except the probes that still showed no contact. His navigation instruments confirmed Pappa. Two meters, negative. Three meters ... negative.

"Pappa?" he said deliberately.

"Submerging, Mr. Hand," said Mercedes Mead. Her voice was carefully cool but strained. "We may lose radio and radar contact."

"The port!" shouted someone.

The view port was blank white, covered by the Ball stuff, whatever it was, and illuminated by the floods. No visual capability.

Mike checked his instruments rapidly, adrenaline pumping but directed professionally. Contact probes? Nothing. Floatation? Nothing. Radar? Blank, uniform medium in all directions but up. Atmospheric pressure? A perfect vacuum! That can't be, thought Mike momentarily, that means we're back in space! Altitude? Altitude? The display was out of control, changing readings rapidly, apparently at random.

"Pappa?"

No response.

"Pappa?"

No response.

"Abort, Mr. Hand," said Jason, without emotion.

"Abort!" he repeated, firmly. "Let's take her back up to the ship."

"But ..." Mike stared in frustration.

"Now, Mr. Hand, while we can still catch her!"

Mike responded immediately, in spite of his confusion. He fired thrusters to lift the shuttle vertically at full throttle and punched emergency retrieval. Mike heaved back into his chair and looked at Jason.

"Emergency retrieval initiated," said Pappa without emotion. "ETA ninety-seven minutes."

Mike's controls died instantly as Pappa took over. Relax, thought Mike, we're all passengers now.

Pappa was orbiting away from the shuttle now, descending over the horizon. He would have to catch up with himself bringing the shuttle back up to orbit.

"That was just fine, son," said Jason. "Good work."

"But there was no immediate ..."

"We didn't have any choice, Mike," said Jason. "There was no solid place to set down. We lost radio and radar contact, most of our navigation capability, and Pappa was about to disappear over the horizon. I didn't want to have to fly around in circles without navigation until Pappa made a complete orbit. Too many blank spots."

Mike nodded. Jason was right, of course.

"I want to see what's down here too, Mike," said Jason with a smile, "We'll come back tomorrow."

CHAPTER 6

STRATEGY

"The Roof?"

Dac was genuinely puzzled. "Why the Roof? The Roof's 42 kilometers above the Gap. Why not just fly the shuttle into the Gap?"

"We considered that, of course," said Jason. "We decided against it for several reasons. First of all, we don't know what's in the Gap; look what we ran into on the Ball! In fact, that's precisely why we're not going in, we don't know. If there is some unanticipated hazard, radiation or something that could disable the shuttle or crew, we'd be stuck. It looks dead in there but we don't know."

"All right, fair enough," Said Dac tentatively. "What else?"

"The wind," said Mike Hand. "It blows out of the Gap in all directions. The Cube doesn't suck hydrogen in anywhere we could find; it just blows it out. The wind speed, or I suppose the Wrapper speed, is close to 90 kilometers per hour in the Gap."

"Chirp. The speed of the gas exiting the Gap is precisely …"

"90k, hunh," reflected Dac. "That's a hurricane!"

"Yes, sir." Mike tried to sound matter of fact. "Even allowing that it's hydrogen, it's still a heavy wind force because of the pressure, about two bars. The wind force is approximately the same as Earth atmosphere at sixty kph at sea level. Even if we flew in we couldn't do much that we couldn't do from here."

"Chirp. In fact, the wind force is precisely …"

"That wind," he continued, unabated, "would require power up virtually full time, making an EVA difficult to impossible, and limiting

55

the exploration to fuel supply. In addition, the shuttle isn't really built for that kind of abuse; not many hurricanes in space. Finally, the shuttle isn't streamlined at all and has minimal control surfaces for open atmospheric flight, just reaction motors. The unpredictable flight characteristics may overwhelm the reaction control system. In open air or space that's not a serious problem but I don't want to risk flying a shuttle with sluggish flight characteristics into a 40 meter hole. Particularly in the dark without reliable navigation capability."

"Chirp. The opening is not a hole as that term is generally ..."

"Okay. I'll buy all of that," agreed Dac. "Go on."

"There's another strange thing, Mr. Olson," said Mike. "The speed of the gas coming out of the Gap drops off to zero within one meter of leaving the gap."

"Let me get this straight. The hydrogen wind blasts out of the Gap at 90 kph and then just stops? You know what my next question is."

"Chirp. I'm sorry. sir, I do not ..."

"Yes and yes," replied Jason. "We wondered about that too. The only possibility is that the whole Wrapper expands to soak up the hydrogen, but in a controlled way right at the interface with the Gap. That's only a theory; we have no idea how it works. But you can see the insertion problem for a shuttle with no practical atmospheric control surfaces."

"Pappa has confirmed all of this?" asked Dac after a moment.

"Chirp. No!" Pappa has an exclamation point?

"Yes. So you can see why we don't want to fly into the Gap. Later maybe, but for now we plan to set down on the Roof."

"Chirp. This is new, Mr. Fielding. I'm sure I didn't ..."

"That puts you 42 kilometers from the Gap," deduced Dac. "Are you sure there's no way to put down on the surface?"

"The visual and radar surface seems to be a suspension of fine dust particles," responded Jason. "It appears to be mostly rock dust but the average density of shaving lather down to at least sixty meters, with practically no viscosity. We're not sure the Ball is solid even at that depth. We didn't touch bottom on our first try and we might just sink on in forever. The shuttle sure didn't float on it. We've scanned the Ball thoroughly and the only hard surface on the Thingy is the Roof."

"Chirp. Quite."

"Yeah," said Dac with a sly smile. "I followed your adventure with considerable interest. But how are you going to get into the Gap from the Roof?"

"This is really neat," responded Mike enthusiastically. "We'll run a cable down the side of the Cube, into the Gap and up the other side. We'll use it to pull me through the Gap against the wind. If there's an accident we can use the cable to pull me out. What do you think?"

"Chirp. I am thinking I missed part of this conversation. In fact …"

"You don't want to know what I think," replied Dac, certain he did not know what to think. "And where in Hell's Warehouse are you going to get, what, 150 kilometers of cable?" Dac knew the answer to that immediately.

"Chirp! I know! I know!"

"Uh, 350 kilometers, Mr. Olson," corrected Jason mildly.

"Oh, no! No you don't," said Dac in disbelief. "Not the antennas! No way!"

"Chirp," Pappa was loath to take sides in most differences, but really! "No way!"

The power antennas, six 500 kilometer long nanotube multi-filaments that the Jobs whipped like a vast Weed Eater through the ether, cutting through the almost non-existent magnetic fields of near-empty space to power the ship. It carried a complete set of replacements but the antennas were essential, like water. You don't play games with them.

"We'll only need one of the spares," responded Mike quickly and earnestly. "The risk should be minimal; no profit center has ever had to replace them all on a project. In fact, the worst disaster ever only required replacing three, and that was mostly because of pilot error." Pause. "And we'll bring them ... unh ... *it* back in one piece!"

"Chirpity chirp! ..." Pappa was at a complete boggle. "Chirp. My antennas!? Pardon my metaphor but that's like giving me a vasectomy!" That got their attention. "You want to snip my source of power, as it were?"

"You're talking about the Mandelbrot? Pilot error, maybe, in the face of a series of completely unpredictable catastrophes." Dac paused to think it through a little, torn between his duty to the safety of the ship and his desire to find out what the Thingy really was.

"We're in a completely unpredictable situation here, Mike, and I don't want to get caught with my cables down like that." Dac's change of tone said 'Give me a better reason,' and Mike picked up on it.

Pappa agreed earnestly but silently.

"Just think of it, Mr. Olson!" said Mike, encouraged. "First you rappel 42 kilometers straight down a sheer cliff. Then you hike right on through an alien building or whattheHell, through a virtual hurricane. Then you climb back up a sheer precipice, another 42 kilometers. Talk about your triathlon!"

Mike's rash enthusiasm was catching and Dac resented it at the same time that he succumbed to it.

"Do you really think you can do it?" asked Dac. "That sounds like a lot of work."

"The gravity is only an Earth fraction, negligible really. The climb down is easy as falling off a log. Coming back up will be easier if anything, I'll just take a nap while they pull me up. Both of those legs will be like riding an elevator, powered by winches on the shuttle." Mike stopped to consider the traverse of the Gap.

"Chirp. About that Gap, I think …"

"The Gap is something else," he continued realistically. "That kind of wind might be tough. We'll take it nice and easy. The winch will pull me through so it won't be that much work, but it will be dangerous. And we don't know what we'll find in there. That's the risk element, but that's why we're going. We're trained for exploration and if everyone does their job, it should be no more dangerous than any other initial planetary contact, with the usual assortment of hazards. These are just a little more unusual.

"I'd place the risk at about the same as typical undersea exploration," said Mike. "In fact, the Thingy seems very benign, so far." Everyone in their own way noted the 'so far' qualifier. "We've both seen far worse."

That was true enough. Planets were either dead rocks or they were Hell's Fire Sale. The planets worth anything to HO tended toward Firesales; corrosive or cyclonic atmospheres, volcanism, extreme high or low temperatures, ionizing radiation, whatever. This, this Thingy hadn't so much as sneezed. Well, thought Dac, that hurricane in the Gap sure qualified as a sneeze. But as Mike said, they'd all seen worse.

"Besides!" added Mike, almost shouting. "What are our choices? We can stay here and direct traffic until the guys from HO take all the glory or we can leave and let the guys from HO take all the glory."

That jerked Dac's bobber.

"Chirp. As always in these situations, there is probably a third alter ..."

"There's a big difference between just finding an alien artifact," Mike continued, setting the hook, "and getting down there to walk on it and kick it and stick your nose into it. And maybe talk to it. Nobody knows who discovered the moon but everybody remembers who walked on it first. We found it and we should get all the glory. There's enough for all of us!"

"Chirp. I presume I would be included in any ..." Had he had one and had he known what it was, Pappa's bobber would also have been jerked.

Dac considered Mike's words for a moment. As much as the idea appealed to him, the moon analogy would be found wanting under even the most casual scrutiny. At last he called for help.

"Pappa? Feasibility?"

"Mr. Hand is right." Pappa hesitated, expecting to be interrupted again, "We have seen worse."

"That's a little vague, Pappa," said Dac, surprised that Pappa seemed to take sides with Jason and Mike. In fact, Dac thought it was deliberately evasive. Pappa was supposed to be completely objective.

"Yes, Mr. Olson," replied Pappa happily. "The objectives of this excursion are vague so it is difficult to assess the feasibility of achieving them. Mission objectives appear to be closely related to uniquely human motivations that could be described as personal aggrandizement. The scientific objectives are as yet ill-defined."

You've got that right thought Dac, reassessing Pappa's astuteness upward a notch. "Jason?"

"We want ... need to find out what it is." responded Jason impatiently, "and how it works. We can see everything except the inside of the Gap and the inside of the Ball. We're going to look at the inside of the Cube for the same reason we're looking at the outside; we need to know if it's a hazard and what to do about it." As a final appeal to Pappa's math coprocessor he added, "And if there's a profit to be made, how to exploit it." In his exuberance, he continued quite unnecessarily and certainly imprudently, "Next we'll go inside the Ball."

Dac choked on that but managed a prompt, "Pappa?"

"The proposed activity will probably succeed in traversing the Gap as planned, Mr. Olson. The probability of gathering any useful and as yet unspecified data is completely undeterminable."

"Close enough. Mamma?"

"Just be careful what you bring back into the ship, Mr. Hand."

"That sounds like a go," said Dac. "I want a full engineering workup on the mechanicals, Mike. Proofed by Pappa and Phillips, confirmed by Mamma. Overspec everything by a factor of ten. No chances on this, Mike. I want to be 100% satisfied everything works right the first time or no go. Understood?"

"Yes, sir!!" Mike and Jason in unison, already moving toward the door.

"And Mike?" added Dac, retrieving an interrupted memo to HO about the abrasive toilet paper on this run. "Thanks for talking me into it."

CHAPTER 7

꩜ ◉◈

BALLFALL

"She's all yours, Shuttle," delegated Jason Fielding.

Jason had maneuvered the shuttle down to spitting distance of the Roof, mostly for the fun of it, and then let Shuttle take over. The landing, or rather the Roofing, would be a little tricky, a *lot* tricky. Particularly in the dark with almost useless instrumentation, so Jason switched to Shuttle for the detail work.

"Affirmative," replied Shuttle mechanically. Dac, monitoring the affair from above, winced mechanically at the sorta-military speak he worked so hard to outweed. Damned programmers!

Shuttle was not as sophisticated as Mamma or Pappa, particularly in its human interface, nor as broadly talented. It was, however, a superb navigator; that's what it did. Shuttle managed the shuttle, period, with the determined single-mindedness of a washing machine. Pappa and Mamma could override Shuttle at any time for any reason, but rarely did as Shuttle was hard-linked into the heavyweight computers for guidance in all things disputational.

Because of the Cube's low albedo in light and radar frequencies, Shuttle's navigational instruments were seriously handicapped. To manage Ballfall, Pappa set up an approach program based on his projections of the position of the Cube which were in turn based heavily on his previous observations of the Cube's occlusion of background stellar radiation. Pappa monitored the position of the shuttle and sent coordinates to Shuttle microsecond by microsecond. Shuttle navigated accordingly while Jason flew by wire, the process completely transparent. Now Jason was out of the loop and sat back to watch the show.

The Thingy spun at one revolution per hour, more or less. Since they needed to see the edges of the Cube for navigation, they would land on the Roof near one of the corners about a hundred meters from both edges. The Roof at that point was moving in a circular path at 88.83 kilometers per hour. It was like a night landing on an aircraft carrier making a sharp turn without benefit of lights or radar.

"50 meters, Mr. Fielding," paced Shuttle.

"Looking good, Shuttle," cheered Jason.

Looking. Yeah, right. Darker than Hell's Coffin and no radar. Shuttle was navigating by the location of the edges of the black interstellar sky against the Roof. There were no landmarks, lights, runways or pads, no nothing. Jason checked and rechecked all displays looking for anything outside flight parameters.

"Talk to me, people," encouraged Jason. "Everything okay?"

There was a flurry of affirmative responses; everything nominal.

"10 Meters. Approval for touchdown?"

"Go for it, Shuttle." Jason controlled his excitement nicely, reflecting Shuttle's own businesslike tone, and braced for contact with the Roof.

"Touchdown, Mr. Fielding." There had been no bump. Shuttle was pretty good at this, thought Jason. "You may disembark anytime."

"Nice work, Shuttle. All right, you heard the man. You know the drill." Jason upthumbed Mike Hand, switched navigation back to manual and rose to his duties.

"One moment, Mr. Fielding." Shuttle.

"What is it Shuttle?" There was no response for an uncomfortably long ten seconds.

"I have a problem. Something ... Abort, Mr. Fielding." As deadpan as a faceless machine can be deadpan.

Shuttle was not prone to abort missions, much less sentences, except in extreme circumstances. Jason froze, a wave of goose bumps tingling the back of his neck down to his shoes.

"What's going on Shuttle! What ..."

"Abort, Mr. Fielding," repeated Shuttle without emotion, then adding an electrifyingly shrill, "Now!" Nice programming touch, that.

That scared the equilibrium out of Jason and handily frosted the rest of the crew.

"What's happening, Shuttle! I'm blind here!" Jason leaped into his seat, flipping switches like playing a pipe organ. The tune was "Abort" in whole notes.

"I am blind also, Mr. Fielding. I don't know ..." Shuttle regained its composure. "We are going over the edge in three seconds, Mr. Fielding."

Jason hit propulsion the instant the shuttle flipped over the edge of the Roof nose first. It dropped lightly in the low G of the Ball, but it did drop. The flip over the side and the propulsion blast combined to precess the shuttle out of control. In the light gravity the shuttle floated down like a leaf, dropping inexorably towards the surface of the Ball. The crew, caught off guard, scrambled for their stations more or less successfully and struggled to make sense of the situation. Jason struggled to find which way was up.

"Dammit!" hissed Jason. "We're losing it!" A surge of unprofessional panic melted his bowels as he struggled with the blast of adrenaline.

Get a grip on yourself, thought Jason frantically, get your bearings, take a breath. What's the situation! What's the situation!

The surface is forty-four kilometers down. Okay. That should give me several minutes in this gravity. Yeah, but the Cube is right next door. We'll slam right into it. Where's the Cube! Got it, got it! Tweak impulse right ... now. Good, we moved away. I think. Where's the ground. Got to level out for a landing. Where's the Goddam ground! No! The surface is sixty meters of shaving lather. Don't land! Got to go back up!

"Shuttle! I need a little help! Now!" No programming necessary.

"One moment." Shuttle's voice was reassuringly professional. "I am anticipating that the shuttle will be upright in ... Fire left full, two second burst, on my mark, Mr. Fielding. Three, two, one, mark."

Jason hit left full, with all his heart, and the shuttle stabilized. Release.

"Full ahead ... Now."

Jason pounded the 'Stomp' button and got out of there like Hell's Bats. Sloppy but good enough, he thought as the shuttle cleared the Roof again. Jason took it up to orbit to catch up with Pappa.

"Shuttle? What happened!"

"Sorry Sir. I am not sure what the problem is. We made a successful touchdown, on spec. The first anomaly was increased sky glow in the direction of the corner of the Roof. The increased radiation resulted from a greater exposure of the sky to the sensors from below the Roof edge. Because of the high mounting of the sensor array, that could only mean we were moving towards the edge. I am sorry if you were discomforted, Mr. Fielding."

"Discomforted!?" Damn! "Okay! … Okay." Everything's under control, thought Jason. Nobody got hurt and emotions won't help. "What happened, Shuttle?"

"I just told …"

"I know what happened!" shouted Jason, reversing himself on the emotion bit. "I want to know what happened! Why did we start to move in the first place!? What went wrong?"

"I don't know, Mr. Fielding." Probably as contrite as Shuttle could get.

"Okay." Jason mumbled darkly for a moment. "Patch in Pappa!"

"Chirp."

"Did you see that, Pappa?"

"Yes I did. It was fascinating. Nice work, I think."

"Thanks," replied Jason ruefully. "What's your analysis of the incident? What pushed us off?"

"I have no conclusions at this time, Mr. Fielding, but if you think aliens are responsible, I am certain you were not pushed off the Roof."

"What do we do now?" Jason was steaming.

"Why, attempt the touchdown again, Mr. Fielding. Of course."

"Again!?" Jason exploded. "You saw what happened! We went right over the Goddam edge and almost ploughed into the shaving lather."

"Shaving lather?"

"Never mind!" OK, deep breath. "I'm not going down again until I know exactly what happened and what I'm getting into."

"I understand, Mr. Fielding," replied Pappa in a more understanding voice than Jason thought possible. "But I need a little more data to make a firm analysis of the hazard. I propose you set down farther from the edge, at least one or two kilometers in. That will give you more time to react. Based on the first incident, you should have at least a minute before sliding over the precipice. We also know what to expect so there will be minimum reaction time wasted."

"I want you to know that we appreciate your understanding, Pappa. Let me think about this."

"May I remind you that the ship will be out of range over the horizon in 47 minutes."

"Okay. Let's do it before I change my mind!"

They did it, and slid off the Roof again. Well they slid, same as the first time, but Jason easily lifted the shuttle from the Roof without further incident.

"Okay, Pappa, what in Hell's Skating Rink is going on?"

"It appears that the surface of the Roof has an extremely low coefficient of friction. It is extremely slippery. In fact," added Pappa, "your trajectory indicates virtually no surface drag. In addition, the Ball's gravity is quite low, the Ball is spinning at almost one revolution per hour and the surface is perfectly flat. The result is that inertial force threw the shuttle off the edge. Or to be more precise, your inertia held you in one place The Roof simply rotated out from under you."

"Solution?"

"Why, Mr. Fielding," responded Pappa with mild surprise, "set the shuttle down in the center of the Roof."

CHAPTER 8

ROOF

Jason Fielding poised to take the first step onto the first intelligent alien artifact ever discovered in the whole universe. Ever! In an ebullient splurge of playfulness no one had even thought possible, Jason struck his best hero pose for the record of this momentous event.

"Get a picture of this!" One small step... Jason practiced silently. One small step... Don't flub it like Neil.

The first man to take the first step on the first alien artifact fell majestically, even gracefully flat on his back and spun slowly away from the shuttle hatch. He flopped about like an overturned beetle. Jason finally regained his footing and dignity with the help of a thrown line garnished with probably way too much merriment.

"You want billfolds?" asked Gerry Ast, Communications. "Gotta special today only!"

"No thanks," replied Jason with a grimace and a "Smart-ass mumbledydump" mumbled prudently to himself.

"One more time. Gimme that line!"

Jason managed to keep his footing this time, barely. He skated a little as he located his center of gravity over his feet, like stepping into a pram. The low gravity made it even trickier, minimizing whatever friction he had to work with. The flood lights lit up Jason's caution orange pressure suit nicely but had no effect on the surface of the Roof; Jason appeared to be floating in space with nothing under his feet but starlessness. After fooling clumsily with his trappings, Jason got his sea legs and managed reasonably well in a squatty sort of flat-footed shuffle.

"Okay, come on in. The water's fine," grunted Jason. "Let's tie the shuttle down and get to work."

Gerry resumed recording the event, and even caught very impressive hero poses by each of the crew in turn as they went about lassoing an incredible alien Thingy. *Every* pose was heroic in its way. They would be a sensation back home. Ever the professional, Gerry deleted the first take.

"Ever see anything like this?" grumbled Mike Hand to no one in particular. Nobody in particular answered, each too busy trying to maintain hisser own footing. "Like walking on oiled buckshot!" General grunts of agreement.

"More like hot snot, not to put too fine a point on it," observed Gerry crudely, revealing a previously unsuspected grossy side. "And not that I have any significant experience with hot snot."

"Whoa!" Mike's feet went out from under him as he wrestled equipment off the shuttle, going down slow-motionly into a graceful but unconventionally awkward split. He was saved from slow-motion disaster by the constraints of his life suit and the light gravity. He wasn't hurt but it was a struggle to get back onto his feet encumbered as he was by his rigging. "I'm okay! I wanted to do that!" Nobody paid attention.

The rest of the crew moved busily but deliberately about the shuttle, intent on unloading paraphernalia, opening crates, checking lines, setting survey equipment, standing up.

Life suits allow little tactile feedback, and the light gravity provides little tact. Accordingly, everyone hit the deck several times before adapting, the occasional flash of a helmet work light signaling each pratfall. Once they abandoned the idea they were walking on a firm surface and let their EVA training take over, they found moving on the Roof was like floating in space. Hand-over-handing the accumulating lifeline mesh worked far better than walking.

A big hassle was untangling safety lines that tethered everything to everything, like a great backlash. The mess of lines reminded Jason of too many fishermen crowding a hot fishing hole struggling to keep their lines free. Inevitably a few unsecured tools and truck disappeared into the murk to add their mass to the meager gravity well hereabout.

"How big did you say that cable is?" asked Ross Label, Biology. "That's one big honkin' spool!"

"You mean how long?" answered Mike Hand absently. "Each reel holds a little less than 500 kilometers of antenna wire. We have six." Mike paused to admire the gigantic spools of antenna attached to outriggers on the back and top of the shuttle.

"Six!?" Ross was impressed. "Did you say six?"

"Well, actually, there are twelve total," refined Mike. "Six are deployed at all times for power. The other six are standby reserve, like this one. We rotate them to spread the wear, like rotating tires."

Lordy! Ross paused in contemplation. Six thousand kilometers of wire!

Dealing with safety lines was simple enough, standard EVA precautions, but the amount of new untested equipment involved was complicating things considerably. The huge reels of cable and the equipment to handle them were a little out of pattern. A lot out of pattern, in fact, as was trying to keep everything as nearly possible to the center of the rotating square Roof and in balance to the mass of the shuttle.

Keeping the shuttle and its trappings centered on the Roof was Mamma's job. She monitored a battery of accelerometers on the shuttle that detected any movement. Momma in turn notified Mike Hand of an imbalance and suggested remedial action. Mike then scurried with a dedicated team to move equipment appropriately. The closer they kept everything balanced directly over the center of the Roof, the axis of rotation, the easier to make relatively minor adjustments. They had all followed the shuttle's misadventure slipping over the edge and had a strong visceral impetus to keep the shuttle where it belonged.

Mike slipped again as he turned quickly, caught himself and shuffled nonchalantly back to the shuttle to get a grip on things. His feigned bravado probably didn't fool anyone, had heshe been paying attention. It was really tricky out here and demanded everyone's full attention to hisser's own task at hand.

Mike never panicked on a mission and he rarely even became nervous, but he was definitely apprehensive about this job. The gravity was just enough for his body to think it was walking and his eyes thought they saw a horizon, but the movements involved in navigating on the Roof were more like your basic EVA. Working in empty space was easier than this, thought Mike; at least you didn't have to fight your own engrained but conflicting eye/muscle coordination. His anxiety showed and it affected the crew. Keep busy, he told himself.

"You're go for analytics on the Cube, Pappa." Mike shook off his ill ease, set Pappa's remotes on the surface, latched onto a passing line and yanked it to check for security. Somebody whooped. A headlamp flashed as the line snagged a leg or something.

"Sorry." He adjusted his helmet work light and went back to setting up his rig for the traverse. "Let's see what this thing's made of."

They couldn't seriously consider nailing the shuttle to the Roof, at least until they knew far more about it. In order to have something to pull against to drag Mike through the Gap, the shuttle would be first secured to the Roof. Essentially they would tie it onto the Cube like the ribbon on a Christmas package.

Because of the extremely low drag on the cables, securing the shuttle was easier than anticipated but it was not easy. The plan; shoot a loop of cable out to the edge, taking advantage of the same slipperiness that had thrown them off the edge on the first attempt to land. To Roof.

Like space, a thrown object continued in a straight line until something happened. The low coefficient of friction on the surface would impart a rotational acceleration to a body moving radially, the resulting increased centripetal force offsetting the drag. The propulsion force came from small utility rockets. Once fired, the coil-sled should slide the full 20 kilometers to the edge unassisted. The cable would then secure temporarily with large block hooks over the edge, like bricklayer's hooks, Mike's idea. The hooks should work well enough because of the Cube's perfect right angles. After things were tied down to the four edges, they could make a more permanent lashing by looping the cable completely around the Cube.

The cable in this case was one of the spare antennas the factory ship whipped around for power. At full length in pairs, they made a 1000 kilometer array that tore through the tenuous magnetic fields in deep space. It was thin, light and springy, about the weight of light fishing line. Lighter, and barely visible in this setting.

"This is it?" Mike fingered the filament apprehensively up close for the first time. "When you guys said cable, I thought you meant CABLE! I could break this like a spider web!"

"Try it, but don't cut your gloves." Jason seemed amused but he wasn't playing. He knew Mike had to have complete confidence in his equipment.

"Okay, Jason." Mike wasn't quite mollified but did not take up the challenge. He had far more confidence in Jason than in the cable and knew he didn't joke about safety. "You're happy, I'm happy." A second sidewise glance at the huge cable reel sealed the deal.

In fact, the cable/antenna was deceptively strong, and accordingly frightfully expensive, essentially a coaxial bundle of hundreds of 500 kilometer long Buckytube molecules only a few atoms thick surrounding a central hair thin ultraglass conductor. The cable could support itself against the force that spread the antennae kilometers into space and could easily handle the stress of this unorthodox application in this light gravity.

Cables would be fired in opposite directions from the shuttle forming the loop around sides 1 and 3 of the Cube. Another loop would secure sides 2 and 4. Crewones would then slide along the cable, secure the edge blocks and return with little more than an occasional puff with a One-On-One. The centripetal force was not really strong, even at the edge, and the surface was extremely slick, so the 'uphill' climb back to the shuttle would be a piece of pie.

The cable was already wound from storage, on a free-wheeling spindle mounted on customized skids so the line reeled off one end without developing a twist or kink, like a spin casting fishing reel. The magnetic driver operated along the length of a long shaft through the spindle's axle. Once at the edge, some of the skid parts would make up the permanent hook over the edge.

"Let her rip," commanded Jason, satisfied everything was in order.

"I'm sorry, Mr. Fielding. Leterip?"

"Oh, for God's sake, Shuttle. Do it!" Manoman!

"Fore!" shouted Mike Hand in his enthusiasm. "Hang onto your butts!"

Shuttle energized the drivers on cue, sending the spindle on its 20k slide. It moved away slowly at first, accelerating visibly even as it dimmed out of range of the floods. The crew watched it dwindle and disappear.

They returned to work on the second spindle for launch in the opposite direction.

"Hold it!" shouted Bic, eyes locked on his Pappa-readouts. "Shuttle's moving. She's moving!" Bic immediately regretted his lack of professional demeanor in spite of the startling situation. "Unh … Significant movement towards the edge. Slow but accelerating. Orders, Mr. Fielding?"

Generalized ineffective scramble in place, the place being the Roof.

The shuttle was indeed moving, slowly but inexorably in opposition to the magnetic thrust delivered to the spindle that was on its way to the edge. The network of tangled cables and lines moved as a whole, sliding like a mesh of seaweed in the tide.

"Shuttle!" Jason took a moment to size up the situation and smiled at the commotion. "Shuttle, can you cancel that movement for me. Just put it back where it was."

"Yes, Mr. Fielding. A correction of 0.02g for two seconds should do it."

Shuttle blinked on the warning lights, pulsed the reaction motors briefly and stopped the slide of the shuttle.

Taking literally Jason Fielding's command to 'put it back where it was,' Shuttle fired a second blast to send the shuttle sliding back in the direction from whence it came. To the center of the Roof.

With a quick calculation Shuttle fired the opposing reaction motors a third time to bring the shuttle to a dead stop exactly back where it was.

And blasted a strong puff of exhaust at Ross Label who, against all EVA protocol, had disconnected his safety catch to move to an out-of-reach line.

"Whoa!" shouted Ross as he tumbled onto his stomach, spinning a little. "Hey! HEY!! I'm loose. Help! Help! I'm loose!" Ross' lack of professional demeanor was completely understandable and justifiable.

It took a second for the crew to locate Ross, the voice in their headsets not being at all directional, and another second to react. Several more to overcome their inertia and get moving. Several deadly more to coordinate a plan of action, find a free line, fasten it and set out after Ross. In those too many seconds Ross disappeared into the perpetual night.

Mike Hand quickly secured himself to the cable unspindling into the darkness and set out after Ross. He made frustratingly little headway on the slick Roof, certainly not enough to overcome Ross who had been launched by the shuttle's reactors pushing against its considerable mass.

"Come on! Gimme a shove!" he ordered as he grabbed a free hank of safety line. "Gimme a shove!"

Bravo, Mead and Fielding caught on immediately and moved to grab Mike as if he was a bobsled. They aimed Mike at the receding light on Ross's helmet and on 'three' threw him into the void. They pushed against their own combined mass and went sprawling into the piled crates and tangled equipment behind them. A sudden silence fell over the comm as they watched the line snake into the dark after Ross Label, after Mike Hand. One rapidly dimming intermittent light chasing another dimmer one, like fireflies thought Jason. Or tracer bullets.

"Pappa!" shouted Jason once he realized there was nothing more to be gained by watching. "Pappa! Get Shuttle Two down here! Get Unit Two down here as soon as possible. We've got a man loose! He's going over the edge!"

"The emergency alarm has been sounded, Mr. Fielding," responded Pappa. "It will take the Unit Two about one hour to assemble, prep the shuttle and launch. We are almost out of line of sight over your horizon now, Mr. Fielding."

Pappa hesitated, recognizing Dac's agitation and reluctant to aggravate his anxiety further. Pappa also understood that the final point was what Dac needed to know right now.

"By the time they can launch we will be almost a third of an orbit around the Ball and I will be unable to navigate." Pappa audibly winced to the limited extent of his speech generation subroutine.

"Dammit, Pappa!" cried Jason in frustration. "Do something! I'm going to lose a man down here and I need help!"

"I was able to take a sighting on their work lights, Mr. Fielding," Pappa offered. "They are moving away from your position at just over five kilometers per hour. That speed should remain more or less constant or accelerating slightly. The following light is gaining on the leading light and should overtake it in approximately four hours."

"Four hours!" gasped Jason. He paused to make a quick calculation, but mostly to regain his composure. "Four hours. Pappa, how soon will they reach the edge?"

"They will approach the edge of the Roof in approximately four hours, depending on the coefficient of friction that ..."

"Wrong answer, Pappa! We're not going to let that happen! Okay?" Of course four hours! Jason had to physically control his rampant exasperation and wrest his composure into obedience. Then more moderately after a second, "When can you get help down here! Launch Shuttle Two now before it's too late!"

"I understand your instructions and your frustration, but there is a single overriding consideration," replied Pappa.

"What overrides my guys going over the edge. Get that shuttle down here ASAP!"

"Yes, Mr. Fielding. I can launch the shuttle in the amount of prep time necessary, but not before. As you must know, procedural constraints prevent me from unsafe act ..."

"It's already unsafe, Pappa!" Jason was becoming unsafe himself. "What's unsafe about launching a shuttle?!"

"The primary problem is navigation." Pappa paused to allow for another outburst from Jason. Hearing none for a moment, Pappa proceeded. "I cannot navigate the shuttle precisely without visual contact. I must use the occultation of stars to accurately find the edges of the Cube. By itself the shuttle does not have the capability to navigate in that way and barely manages with my constant assistance. Sending the Shuttle Two down now to operate a cappella, as it were, might very well endanger not only Mr. Hand and Mr. Ross but also another shuttle and its crew. I cannot accept that risk now."

"Okay," said Jason, barely mollified. "I knew that. So when *can* you launch?"

"I will launch Shuttle Two just prior to coming up over the horizon to maximize the time available to navigate the ..."

"When!" Jason felt his self control struggling with his brain.

"The shuttle's descent should take approximately twenty-two minutes."

Jason choked in disbelief but managed to throttle back his rage and frustration. Pappa had picked up on Jason's emotionally stressed state and was reluctant to say anything that would exacerbate it. Jason had to force himself to allow Pappa to relax. One. Two. Three. Slowly.

"When will you be able to provide assistance, Pappa." Jason's voice was strained but calm. "Give me your earliest best estimate."

"Just over four hours, Mr. Fielding."

Jason couldn't respond. He turned around, figuratively turning his back on something, anything in denial, and saw Mercedes struggling into a One-On-One. She caught Jason's eye.

"If no one's going to do anything ..." she growled.

"No," said Jason simply. His voice was pure command and it stopped Mercedes instantly. "We've got two crew out there now. I can't risk three."

"But ..."

"But nothing," said Jason, catching the attention of several more crew. "That squirt gun won't do it. You'd have to accelerate hard to catch up with Ross, decelerate harder to stop both of you, and then accelerate both of you to get to Mike. Or get back here and leave Mike behind for some other way to get him back. Or if you had any fuel left you'd have to accelerate three of you back up the line, and decelerate all of you again. No way *that'll* happen."

Jason paused, looking at Mercedes then the others.

"I understand. You all need to do something. I know that," he said quietly. "But you all heard Pappa. It'll be close but we can get them back. We *will* get them back. Right now I need you to think smart, not rashly." Rashly? He thought to himself. Is that even a word? "Everything's a good idea until it isn't."

Mercedes dropped the O-Cubed thruster dejectedly, knowing it would have been futile. She straightened.

"Shuttle One!" she shouted. "We can get them with Shuttle One!"

Jason was caught off guard; he hadn't thought about using Shuttle One. He knew there was a reason it hadn't occurred to him but the reasoning was autonomic and visceral. He took a second to weigh the idea consciously.

"Pappa?" he said, looking at Mercedes as a placeholder. "Analysis?"

"It's certainly possible, Mr. Fielding," replied Pappa instantly. "Based on the seven hours spent unloading and rigging the equipment, you should be able to disconnect everything and abandon it in something over three hours.

"Abandon?"

"Reloading everything will take approximately ten hours, Mr. Fielding. Everything was packed when you unloaded; it will have to be reacquired and repacked before reloading. The only timely alternative is to abandon the equipment for the time being."

"Risk?"

"The relatively high mass of the shuttle secures the equipment now, and will secure it against the pull of the line and sled now extending to the edge. Without the shuttle's mass, the loose equipment will probably begin to slide. This will then require urgent recovery procedures to prevent its total loss, immediately upon the measures to rescue Mr. Hand and Mr. Label. The crew will have to embark to ensure their complete safety."

"And if Shuttle One detached and launched, Mike would lose his lifeline too."

"Yes, Mr. Fielding."

"What was that 'indeterminate' time element, Pappa? It shouldn't take much time to fly this crate twenty clicks."

"You would have to navigate without my assistance, Mr. Fielding. May I remind you that your pilot is out there on the Roof. Even if you were able to locate them before they reach the edge, you would have to return to the center of the Roof unassisted."

"Unassisted!?"

"I *am* about to move beyond your horizon, Mr. Fielding," reminded Pappa.

Jason weighed the crew and equipment against the two men skidding to the edge. Your guts were right the first time, he told himself. Dammit!

"We won't use Shuttle One, Pappa," he said deliberately. "But as God is my judge, that backup shuttle will be down here in time or I'll eat your chips for ..."

"Jason?" It was Dac, in the ship above.

"Yes. Yes, Dac," responded Jason with a jerk. "What *is* it!"

"I've been monitoring things, Jason. You made the right decision. I'm with you on this. We'll get down there as soon as we can. We'll do what we can and more, you know that." Dac paused, searching for something encouraging to say. "Jason, what's the worst thing that can happen?" Wrong choice of words, thought Dac, instantly angered with himself.

"I mean even if they do go over the edge, they will fall slowly, just like you did when you went over the edge. The Ball isn't solid and they won't hit it with much speed. The suits are rugged and with any luck they'll just bounce or something. They should keep until we get to them."

"For crissakes, Dac, that's a 44 kilometer drop! Just how fast do you think they'll be going when they hit the Ball!?"

"Ignoring Wrapper drag," interjected Pappa, happy to be useful, "Mr. Label will be moving at 54.64 meters per second at impact. The drag of the gas, however, will ..."

"Dammit Pappa!" raged Jason. "I don't care how fast he'll hit because he isn't *going* to hit! You're going to stop him! Let's make something happen, people! Somebody do something and do it now!"

"Take it easy, Jason. You know we're on it," soothed Dac. Then he added, "And Mike might just catch Ross in time anyway."

"Yeah, right!" Jason hesitated, got himself under better control. "I know the situation. Let's just get them back. Okay?"

"Come on, Ross!" shouted Mike Hand, as though the comm was inadequate for the task. "This way! Closer!" Mike followed Ross Label into the dark for hours, sliding motionlessly but slowly overtaking him.

"Pappa!" Mike hollered. He paused just an instant to flip his comm to Pappa only. "What's happening!? I'm not making any progress; Ross is just there. I'm not gaining!" Mike's redundancies betrayed both his frustration and his confusingly ambiguous environment. There are no road signs on the Cube, no clues to speed or direction or location any more than there are in open space, except for the light gravitation holding him against an invisible surface. "Where am I going, what do I do?"

"You are doing just fine, Mr. Hand." Pappa understood the situation well enough, particularly the emotional concomitants, that he needed to evoke confidence, rational thought and action, not panic.

"Your glide path does not directly follow Mr. Label," Amplified Pappa. "You are slowly overtaking him but to one side because your trajectories do not precisely coincide."

In fact, they were moving to the edge on radial paths which separated them. Ross' path was slightly away from the main spindle line; his speed moved him slowly away from the line. And away from Mike Hand.

"One moment." Actually more than a moment in the event. Pappa held everyone's attention by his uncharacteristic silence.

"Now what?" asked Dac omnidirectionally to the whole blessed system. "One moment what!?"

"I have been able to analyze the trajectories of Mike and Ross more precisely, Mr. Olson ..." Dac was sure he heard Pappa's gears grinding. "They are very difficult to locate precisely relative to ..."

"Spit it out, Pappa! What's the problem?" It had to be another problem, didn't it?

"Spit ...?"

"Dammit, Pappa! What *is* it!" Dac massaged the bridge of his nose fiercely. It probably sucked no more than anything else so far.

"Mr. Hand and Mr. Label are accelerating towards the edge of the Cube," responded Pappa, correctly interpreting Dac's overriding urgency. "And the rate of acceleration is accelerating."

"Hell's Demons, Pappa!" Why doesn't something go right for a change!? Just once? Dac paused mentally to ratchet down a bit, to reassure everyone, because everyone was listening, now. "How can that possibly be, Pappa?" Better. "If anything, they have to be slowing down. There isn't much drag on that skating rink down there but there is some. Right?"

"Correct, Mr. Olson. But while that slight friction coefficient does act to retard their forward movement slightly, the rotation of the Cube produces a vector at almost a right angle to that motion. At their location approaching the edge of the Cube, the surface is rotating at just less than 71 kilometers per hour."

"Okay. So?"

"So," responded Pappa reluctantly, "that vector imparts a slight centripetal force acting in the direction of their travel. It's a little like the childhood game of 'Crack the Whip'."

"How do you know about ..." Never mind. "Again, So?"

"As a result, that accelerating force exceeds the decelerating drag. Slightly, but the acceleration is significant, under the circumstances extant."

Pappa was really reluctant to continue with the next point, knowing it would not be welcome, and so didn't.

"What is it you're not telling me, Pappa?" There had to be something, thought Dac; we haven't used up all the somethings yet. "Let's hear it."

"Yes, Mr. Olson." Pappa could almost be heard taking a virtual deep breath. "Because the Cube is rotating, they will reach the edge sooner than anticipated. I originally projected they would reach the edge near a corner which is further away and therefore their arrival would have been later. Instead they are approaching midway between two corners which is significantly closer, and therefore sooner."

"How sooner?" That was a pretty good something conceded Dac. Sober as the situation demanded, he pursued, "What do they need to know?"

"They will reach the edge of the Cube nearly an hour earlier than originally projected. Subject to further refinements in my ..."

"You hear that, Unit Two?" Dac popped back into command mode of necessity. "Do what you have to do but I want you down there in time if you have to blast off pants down and doors open!"

"Easy does it. Easy." Mike encouraged both Ross Label and himself. He tried to guide his own trajectory across the Roof to Ross to no apparent effect.

He had tried various techniques to establish some control, like an ice skater or swimmer. The best tactic seemed to be simply walking toward Ross' helmet light. Actually, walking wasn't quite right; he shuffled as if on roller skates at the business edge of a pratfall.

Ross walked toward Mike but made very slow progress against the divergent paths drawing them apart. Eventually they narrowed the distance between them to an optimistic hundred meters.

"C'mon, Ross. Attaboy. Keep moving, Ross," coaxed Mike. "Take it easy now. Just move on over. That's it."

Mike had attached his safety line to the main line spinning from the huge 500 kilometer spindle, the launch of which caused this predicament. He fed out his line as he moved to meet Ross. He looked back only to see he was quickly running out of line.

"I can't go any farther, Ross. No more line."

"No more line!?" A little panic. Then a lot. "Jeez, Mike! I'm trying!" Grunt. "Where are we, Mike. It feels like we're standing still." Wheeze.

"I don't know, Ross," replied Mike truthfully. "We've been out here more than three hours; we must be approaching the edge. Jason, what's going on at your end?"

"The profit center is coming over the horizon in a few minutes, guys," cut in Jason Fielding, who had monitored every minute of the chase. "They should have launched Shuttle Two already. They'll be right down to get you soon."

"How soon, Jason," grunted Ross. "When!"

"Pappa thought it would take a half-hour for them to get down, locate you and make a pickup. If they started already, it should be about that. A half-hour."

"Where's the edge, Jason," asked Mike, the strain apparent in his voice. "How soon do we hit the edge?"

"We can only make a guess, Mike," replied Jason. "The Roof is rotating out from under you. When you get to the edge depends on exactly where you meet the edge; in the middle of a side or a corner or somewhere in between. We'll know exactly when Pappa comes over and can get a good fix on you. I can't tell much from here."

Jason was patient as he retold the same story he told them a dozen times in the last four hours. He couldn't help his own helplessness, or theirs, but he could be patient and understanding.

"Dammit Jason! When!?" Mike.

"Worst case, Mike," said Jason reluctantly, "ten or fifteen minutes."

"Then you better run your little heart out, Ross," shouted Mike with renewed energy, and in surprisingly good spirit. "We're almost home. Just keep on keep'n on." Upon reflection Mike added, "Maybe pick it up a little."

A few more minutes of grunts and wheezes punctuated the silence as Mike and Ross struggled in their dance to the edge. Jason watched the sky, checked his watch, scanned the horizon, shook his head and repeated the sequence ineffectually as the minutes slipped by. A burst of noise jerked him alert.

"Ross!" called Mike. "I think you're close enough now. I'm going to throw you a line. Heads up!"

Mike unhitched the hank of line and secured one end to his belt. He wrangled the rest of the line into a throwing coil and swung it around his head. And fell flat on his back. Two more tries resulted in two more pratfalls so he decided to compromise with reality and throw from his knees. He drew a bead on Ross Label's work light and released the coil into an overhead arc. Mike tried unsuccessfully to keep the coil in his light beam as it rose into the darkness.

"Ross! Did you get the line? Ross?"

"I didn't see a thing, Mike," responded Ross. "Try it again."

Mike did, six more times, without success, and stopped for a moment to reconsider his strategy. As he rewound the line he felt a light touch against his leg that shouldn't be there and jumped, startled. Mice?

He looked down to see his safety line accumulating slowly at his knees. A wave of apprehension swept him as he suddenly realized slinging the rope at Ross had propelled him slowly away from Ross. I can't do that too many times, he thought to himself, or I'll be right back where I started.

"Damn!"

"What?" replied Ross. "What Damn!?"

"Never mind," said Mike, angered at himself. "Here she comes again." This time Mike swung the line underhand and released it like a bowling ball to slide to Ross, hoping that it wouldn't tangle.

"I see it!" shouted Ross. "I can see it! Wait. Oh no! No."

"What is it, Ross?"

"It stopped!" cried Ross. "It stopped! I can see it. It's about ten meters away. All tangled. I think I can get to it."

"No, we may not have time. I'll throw it again."

"No!" shouted Ross. "I can get it. You may miss six more times. At least I can see it now. Don't move it!"

Mike was sure he could throw it again and get to Ross, but the panic in Ross' voice forced him to relent. It was Ross' call, a bird in the hand and all that.

Mike and Jason and the crew listened to Ross wheeze and gasp and grunt his progress as he shuffled frantically to get to the line lying now just out of his reach. Ross was not a physical person, in spite of HO's rigorous physical requirements, and did not respond well to physical demands. His muscles tightened and his nerves raveled, making his motions jerky and inefficient. His net movement to the line was painfully slow, putting more strain on his motor system. Two meters now. One meter.

"No!" cried Mike Hand. "Oh God, no!"

Ross froze. Jason froze.

"The line!" shouted Mike. "Get the line now! My safety's caught!"

Jason realized, too late, what happened. "Mike!" called Jason. "The sled stopped. It's programmed to stop!"

The sled carrying the spindled line was programmed to brake as it approached the edge. Since they didn't know exactly where the sled would reach the edge, it had been set to slow down at nineteen kilometers and stop within another half kilometer. It would be a hand job the rest of the way.

"Who the ..." Mike restarted and let his survival skills take over. "Okay, Okay. Got it. Ross? Did you hear that?"

"Yeah. I got that!" For the first time in all this Ross was really pissed. "So I guess I better get it." And went for it.

Whoever or whatever it was that thwarted them at every turn, Aliens or faulty design gremlins or misguided judgment calls or all of the above, they won.

Mike's safety line was hooked onto the main spindled line and the snatch hook slid along the line as Mike slid along the Roof. Until the sled stopped and the hook stopped and the line stopped and Mike Hand stopped. And the line Mike had thrown to Ross Label stopped.

Ross Label, however, did not stop.

The coil of line disappeared in an instant, from under Ross' reaching hand and disbelieving eyes. He stared in the direction the line had gone, an afterimage burned in his retinas. He could not move again, expecting somehow that the line would come back to him. It *couldn't* be gone!

Ross lay paralyzed by his loss. He slipped gracefully over the edge of the Roof, offering no further resistance. Mike saw the work light wink out and knew what had happened. The silence told Jason what had happened. Pappa told Dac what had happened.

"He's gone," said Mike simply. He could add no more.

"Pappa! Status?" barked Dac.

"Ross Label is now descending to the surface of the Ball, Mr. Olson," intoned Pappa. "He will impact the surface in approximately eight minutes, at approximately 37 meters per second."

"Where's that shuttle, Pappa?" Dac was controlled and professional.

"Two kilometers above the point of impact, Mr. Olson."

"Can they get there in time?"

"If you mean will they be able to attempt to rescue Mr. Label before he reaches the surface of the Ball, yes," replied Pappa. "However, they should not do so."

"Not ...!?" began Dac. "Why not!? Why are we going down there?"

"Mr. Label fell over the edge of the roof midway on one side of the Cube. His descent will take approximately eight minutes. The Cube is rotating at one revolution per hour. In eight minutes, the oncoming vertical edge will rotate perhaps 30 degrees towards Ross, effectively keeping him pinned against the wall. It will be extremely hazardous to attempt to rescue a falling body while maneuvering against the wall."

"Okay. Okay. Get me Unit Two, Pappa."

"Unit Two here. Alex." The voice was hurried, impatient with the interruption. Alex Castell, Unit Two team leader, first in line for promotion to Unit One if and when a vacancy occurred.

"Dac Olson, Alex," called Dac. "Fill me in on your plans, Alex. Can you get to Ross in time?"

"We'll be down to the surface in plenty of time, Dac. In fact we can see his light now. We're planning on standard sea rescue measures for openers. We're also trying to build a net out of the cargo slings to throw on the surface before he hits. That's kinda' Wild West but we're going to try everything and be ready for anything." Alex paused and then continued. "We really didn't have much time to think this through, Mr. Olson."

"I understand, Alex." Dac understood completely "What else?"

"We're in contact with Ross now and we can monitor his location pretty well. We'll be there waiting for him. Ross is also going to try a few things to help."

"Like what?"

"He's attempting to inflate the suit as much as possible. That should slow his descent some and make the impact more tolerable. That will give us a little more time as well as make him more buoyant. He's going to sky dive away from the wall too. We'll need all the room we can get."

"Right," paced Dac. "Pappa filled me in on the wall problem already. Good. What else."

"He's going to try to belly flop to spread the impact and minimize penetration."

"Penetration?" Dac considered that. "What happens if he misses the net?"

"That's our major concern, Dac," replied Alex. "We don't think the impact will be serious, about like those high divers at Acapulco. If he penetrates for some reason, we think he will just float to the surface. Pappa is making projections on that now."

"Pappa?"

"Mr. Label will not float, Mr. Olson," replied Pappa.

"He won't float!?" Dac was incredulous. "Ross will be a balloon in that pressurized suit; he'll bob like a cork."

"That's not correct, Mr. Olson," said Pappa with a hesitation indicating his reluctance to contradict his superior. "The Ball is not an atmosphere or an ocean. There is no hydrostatic pressure to create buoyancy."

"Hell's Bobbers, Pappa! Even good old mother earth's dirt has enough buoyancy to float solid rocks."

"Quite so," replied Pappa. "But buoyancy is the result of gravity forcing materials towards the center of gravity, the denser materials displacing the less dense materials. The resulting moment of force is perpendicular to the force of gravity and is commonly referred to as hydrostatic pressure."

"Okay, Pappa. We went to school." Pappa was about to inquire about the relevance of their formal education to Ross' predicament when Dac urged, "Go on, Pappa."

"The Ball, however, consists of fine particles apparently in some form of suspension. The particles are not suspended in a medium; there is nothing between the particles but empty space. They are not held in place by gravity; the Ball has been assembled and maintained in position artificially, an artifact. The particles do not move to a center of gravity; they exert no hydrostatic pressure and they cannot displace anything regardless of density. I believe that nothing will float on the surface of the Ball." As an afterthought, misinterpreting the stunned silence as expectation, Pappa added, "Nor, for that matter, will anything sink."

"Unless forced to sink by some outside force," continued Alex cynically, "like a 44 kilometer free fall."

"Precisely, Mr. Castell."

Okay, Pappa," said Alex. "We've got a serious problem here. If Ross misses the net, how far will he penetrate the surface?"

"I can only guess at the effective viscosity of the Ball, Mr. Castell, and ..."

"How deep!?"

"Terminal velocity will be affected by the aerodynamics of the suit and Ross' attitude on impact."

"How *deep*!"

"Ross' lateral movement due to his effort to sky dive away from the wall will ..."

Pappa was caught between his mandate to provide dependable information and his programmed inclination to avoid inflicting pain.

"Dammit, Pappa!!" That ought to spank his programming.

"Thirty meters, plus or minus ten meters."

"Do what you can, Alex," said Dac after a moment.

Ross Label missed the net. His position relative to the shuttle obscured his work light. The net was too small. The shuttle was on the surface barely in time to deploy the net. The net tangled. Ross kited in the last stage of his fall and overshot the net. Ross could not see the net anyway. It was not to be.

"Where are you?" sing-songed Nraa Post, Unit Two Electronics. "Come to mamma."

Her voice was steady and light but stressed as she scanned the depths of the Ball with barely effective sonic and ground penetrating radar probes. "This stuff is like a sandy fog." In frustration, Nraa switched frequencies to sweep different depths in the area of Ross' last known location. Nothing.

"Pappa? You sure I'm looking in the right place?"

"You are searching in the most likely location to find Mr. Label," responded Pappa. "While the Ball material is quite permeable and motile in character, it seems to stay in a fixed location unless disturbed. The point at which Mr. Label entered the Ball material should have remained in the same relative location to that side of the Cube."

Nraa switched to several other strategies with no luck. "What's happening here? I can't get these fool machines to show anything down there!"

"I would not bother with the sonic apparatus." Pappa stated the obvious. "Sonic penetration, and particularly the reflected sonic return, depends on the medium being more or less solid.

"What!!?"

"The particles have to touch in order for the sonic wave to propagate in the medium. The particles in the Ball are separated by empty space, a very good sound insulator." Pappa stopped awaiting confirmation.

"Oh, Okaaay. Unnh ..." Nraa thought for a moment. "Then how about the ground penetrating radar? Why can't I get an image with it either?"

"I believe," Pappa responded, "the problem lies with the fact that Mr. Label, body and space suit together, are very close to the overall density of the Ball itself. The Ball, while in a suspended state like a dense fog, is in fact, rock for the most part. It's like looking for the proverbial black cat on a moonless night."

"Then what can I do?" asked Nraa Post plaintively.

"Crank it up, Ms. Post. Sensors at maximum gain. Scan and clip the resulting images at a minimum narrow range. Convert to maximum contrast, essentially black and white. Analyze with the narrow scan throughout your sensors' range. Now blast all Holy Hell out of that Ball!"

Most of the crew on deck looked up at that. Pappa, in his subsequent smug silence, seemed pleased with his command of the vernacular.

"Bingo!" shouted Nraa after a few dubious but dutiful minutes. "I have him!" She looked up at the speaker on the wall with new respect.

"Ross?" Who else, Alex grumbled at himself. "How far?"

"Just shy of sixty meters deep, Mr. Castell," replied Nraa. "His position is stable. He's not moving."

"Sixty ... !?" exclaimed Alex, surprised at the implied challenge. "He may be just stunned. Let's get him out of there. Drop that grappling hook. Let's move it!"

Unit Two scrambled to the winch, replaced the cargo net with the grappler hook and winched it out. The hook and cable settled out onto the surface of the Ball, the cable meandering onto itself like a thread of thick syrup, but it did not sink.

"Dammit," mumbled Alex. "I knew that." He did. Pappa had told them things would not sink on the Ball for the same reason they would not float. In addition, the meager gravitational force of the Ball was not enough to overcome its own viscosity.

That was good news, thought Dac; situation stable; Ross would stay put. Basically Ross was loose in space but we're blind in both directions. Retrieval would be inconvenient as Hell's Smoke Bomb, but doable.

"You'll have to fire a line down to him," Jason chimed in. Alex Castell paused at that, a vision of seventeenth century gunners harpooning whales. "Uh ... How do we do that?"

"Well, first you need to ..."

"Ross is responding, Mr. Castell!" Nraa shouted, unprofessionally but understandably agitated.

"Ross! Can you hear me?" shouted Alex. "Are you all right?" Nraa winced and quickly backed off the comm link's gain.

"Yes. Okay. I'm okay," replied Ross, slurred. "Can't see a damned thing. I can't even tell which way is up." Alex opined that it would be imprudent to point out there was no up in space nor, for that matter, in the Ball, so prudently he didn't. "Just get me out of here!"

"Listen Ross," said Alex. "You're sixty meters ... uh ... down and ..."

"Sixty meters!?" cried Ross. "Oh God! Oh God!"

"I know, Ross," reassured Alex. "But we can see you. We know right where you are and we're going to fire a line down to you right now. You'll be back on board in a minute. Hang in there buddy."

The minute stretched to a half hour of cobbling and arguing. The issue focused on the feasibility of sending a crewone down into the Ball stuff using a 'One-On-One' rocket pack. The call on that was left to Pappa and ultimately to Dac Olson.

"Pappa? Analysis."

"The idea has merit, particularly in a clear medium such as an atmosphere, and even more so in empty space. However, neither is the case here. The rescuer is basically blind and the medium is significantly dense. The One-On-One is designed to produce short measured thrusts to impart momentum that sustains the pilot through a low resistance medium.

"However, to travel through sixty meters of Ball stuff," continued Pappa, "the One-On-One would have to thrust continuously. Even if the rescuer could locate Mr. Ross quickly, the return trip would require even more thrust time. The fuel may very well be inadequate for such a rescue attempt, threatening the loss of both Mr. Ross and the rescuer."

"How long can the thrusters run continuously?" asked Alex.

"The duty cycle is 200 one-second bursts, total a bit over three minutes." Pappa paused to anticipate Alex' next question but decided to answer it first. "However, modifying them for continuous thrusting may degrade performance considerably; they are not designed for that level of continuous output."

"Okay. Put someone on modifying the One-On-One for a backup," charged Alex. The rest of you figure out how to shoot a line down to Ross. Now!"

They didn't really need a Now!

Finally, they finished their tribute to Mr. Goldberg and looked to Alex expectantly. Alex winced. As for a device to shoot a line and hook a target, a more or less blind target, Shuttle Two was woefully ill-equipped. The solution; propulsion from one of the compressed air life-suit tanks dragging a line Ross-wards. The ad hoc grappling hook was the most irregular and expendable piece of equipment handy; a chair. Alex Castell's station chair.

Alex glanced apprehensively to the crew. "Ready?" They nodded, he nodded and they fired.

Actually, 'fired' was technically inaccurate; there was no fire involved. There are few devices on board a shuttle for shooting anything anywhere. Back home a classic shuttle craft on a body of water, for example, might be reasonably well-equipped to shoot a line; literally shoot. But a space shuttle in standard configuration would have nothing on hand remotely resembling a gun, in either form or function. Given foreknowledge of the challenge and enough time to prepare, yes. Right now, no.

It took three shots to get the range. Ross couldn't see the line and couldn't move to it anyway, so the crew would have to hit him dead center. The jerry-rigged chair-hook and compressed gas tank assembly was aerodynamically capricious and slithered through the Ball stuff like an eel. In addition, the shuttle was not fixed to a surface point, there being no surface points, and had to maneuver constantly to hold station. After several shots it occurred to someone to set out a marker buoy, a bright caution flag, which they assumed would stay put. It took seventeen more shots to finally get close enough to drag the line across him. Seventeen shots, a second line, two hours, several tanks and another chair.

"I think we got him!" shouted Nraa. "Yes! We snagged a keeper!"

"Ross! Are you there?" called Alex. "Do you have the grappling hook?"

"I have something that is kinda clunky and pointy, but I don't know what it is," responded Ross. "I can't see a thing!"

"You got it, Ross. Good job!" reassured Alex. "Just hang on to it for all you're worth and we'll pull you up."

"I hope you guys know what way is up. I don't have any bearing at all!"

"Up is that line and home," replied Alex. "See you soonest!"

The shuttle's floodlights focused on the taut line pulling Ross Label to the surface. The line whipped slowly, oscillating as Ross' body Lazy-Iked through the depth of Ball stuff. Progress was deliberately slow because of the drag and because they didn't know how Ross was secured. Pulling too hard might break him free or, worse yet, tear the suit and expose him to both the known hazard of empty space and the unknown hazard of the Ball dust.

"There he is!" said Alex in a controlled shout. "Get another line on him and get him the Hell in here! Move it!" Those instructions were completely unnecessary and in the fact, belated. The crew *moved* and got him the Hell in there.

Ross emerged feet first, with the line tangled about his legs and waist. He hugged the chair like it was a teddy bear as he spun slowly in the light, suspended a few meters above the surface.

"Lordy! Look at him," said Sci User, Mechanicals, as he helped lay Ross on the floor of the airlock. "That Ball dust is all over him."

"Dust? What the ..." replied Nraa as she wiped at Ross' visor. In fact there was no dust at all. "He's been sandblasted!"

Her fingers stroked his helmet, buckles, air tanks, fixtures, everything hard. The visor was frosted over completely, with ablated shallow pits like an ablated meteorite. All hard surfaces were frosted and pitted to various degrees. Resilient parts, like the rubber-ish soles of his boots were frayed, like suede leather. The heavy cloth suit itself was abraded as though it had been through five hundred spin dry cycles. There was, however, no dust on the suit.

"All over," continued Nraa. "Good Lord! He was getting ground up into Ball dust!"

"Look here! It's almost worn through in spots," said Sci, fingering the visor. "There's no ambient pressure down there so this could have really popped. Let's get him out of that thing."

Cheers and applause greeted Ross as his headpiece came away. He blinked at the light, at the grinning faces and at his hands. For the first time in more than three hours he could see clearly and focus on something beyond the tip of his nose.

"What can we get for you?" asked Alex.

"A change of clothes and a bath," replied Ross sheepishly. "I don't think anyone's going to use this suit again."

CHAPTER 9

GAPPING

"You're sure this is going to work?" asked Jason, not entirely in jest. "We could look pretty silly." There was no *could* about it. "Maybe stupid too but I'll be happy with just silly."

"Don't worry," said Mike, worriedly. "What can go wrong? It's just like lassoing a steer but bigger. Easier because the Cube isn't runing away. No wind, no friction, no snags, no problem."

"Right," interrupted Dac from the ship above, "and maybe no Mike."

Dac had called in Jason's landing, uh, Roofing team almost daily for technical updates. That alone was disquieting and helped spread among the crew a general feeling of foolhardiness at the enterprise.

"Whatever, we're ready any time you are, Mike. Good luck!"

"Thanks, Mr. Olson."

And so they began the task of looping a line completely around the Cube, cables that would be Mike's life line as he explored the Gap.

Conceptually the process was simple enough; make a 200 kilometer loop of cable, slide it out to two adjacent corners, throw it overboard, snag the lower corners of the Cube and reel it in.

Nothing is as simple as planned; this stunt being no different and certainly not simple. However, several factors favored our heroes. The cable had a nice springiness to it and was nearly unbreakable. While *nearly* held a certain cachet of disaster, the cables had been in common use since anyone's memory as a combination communication antenna and electrical generator. Essentially they comprised an array of six cables whipped around through space like gigantic 500-kilometer long fan blades to sweep through space's meager magnetic fields. The array also acted effectively as a 1000-kilometer diameter communications antenna, no small asset in deep space.

The cables would not break, designed as they were to withstand the centripetal force that held them taut. They were also springy as a watch spring or a band saw blade, although no one on board would know what either meant.

One point of anxiety, among many, was the risk of damaging or cutting the cable on the edges of the Cube. The cables were designed for deployment into space, abraded only slightly by the extremely slight litter of the void and protected only by a thin insulating coating. The perfect ninety-degree edges of the Cube were knife sharp and hard; the cables would be dragged over these edges as Mike traversed the Gap, a process guaranteed to scrape off the thin insulation.

The solution was a set of wheeled grab blocks, like bricklayer's line blocks but appropriately bigger, which would let the cables ride easily over the edges. Such machinery was not standard equipment on the Jobs, nobody having anticipated a sharp-edged alien encounter, so Engineering whipped up the contraptions to order.

"Hey!" shouted Mike when it worked. "It worked!"

Two lines set at right angles to each other provided directional control, like a big Etch-A-Sketch. Shuttle would manage the cables through servo controls at Mike's signal relayed along the cable itself, which was essentially a conductor at heart. In theory and in effect, Mike could drive himself anywhere in the Gap, literally flying by wire. In addition, he could pull himself along the cables with either powered winches or hand ratchets.

The process of setting the cables around the Cube confirmed one shipboard observation; nothing held the Cube up. Mike had hoped they would find some physical support under there but no luck; it was completely free-floating giving Mike prudent pause.

What if the Cube's night shift guy closed up shop, he thought with a shudder, and turned off whatever held it up! It was easy to imagine the Cube dropping on him like a hydraulic press. Talk about a bug under a heel! Mike shrugged off a wave of claustrophobia and went back to work.

"Pappa," said Mike, still trying to get a handle on the odds. "Any idea what the Cube is made of yet?"

"Yes, Mr. Hand. X-ray scattering indicates that it is probably solid metallic hydrogen." Pappa deliberately added no more.

"Hydrogen?" repeated Jason.

"Yes, Mr. Fielding."

"Metallic hydrogen!?" repeated Dac.

"Yes, Mr. Olson."

"What do you mean probably?" asked Mike, a bit more focused by his immediate needs. "That's a little vague, Pappa." He squinted suspiciously at his remote hand paddle as though Pappa resided there.

"The Cube is vibrating at an extremely high rate, close to molecular oscillation frequencies. That's a primary reason the surface is so slippery. These vibrations severely interfere with my analyses, but metallic hydrogen is the most likely material."

"Vibrating!? Like the Ball?" Mike flashed back to an early childhood day at an amusement park, trying to keep his footing on a very noisy vibrating floor in The World's Greatest Mad House. He had lost control and wet his pants, as he recalled. He sincerely wished he hadn't thought of that.

"No, not like the Ball," responded Pappa. "The Ball is vibrating radially, it expands and contracts. The Cube is vibrating longitudinally only, along the axis of rotation. In addition, the frequency of the Cube is far faster than the Ball by a factor of 10 to the 44th if my instruments can be relied upon."

"What about the temperature?" asked Mike, shaking himself from his reverie. "The atmos ... Wrapper is nowhere near cold enough to freeze hydrogen. Are we missing something I should know about?"

"I show no temperature reading for the Cube, Mr. Hand. However, it seems that the Cube is not frozen hydrogen, it is metallic hydrogen."

"There's a difference?" asked Dac.

"It did not freeze in the sense that it passed through a phase change," responded Pappa, "reduced in temperature from above its freezing point to below. It was probably assembled as metal. It is not crystalline, however; it is a glass. It is metallic probably for the same reason that the hydrogen Wrapper has no pressure gradient."

"And that reason is?" encouraged Dac.

"I don't know." Pappa punctuated that admission with a weak little fizzle. He didn't really have an ego to speak of so he had no problem revealing a void in his analysis, but he did detect an unresolved sense of urgency and apprehension in his questioners.

Everyone looked up at that admission. Pappa didn't know!? Their Pappa confidence index tilted toward unease.

"Give it a shot, Pappa," said Dac in a milder tone. Pappa was reluctant to speculate except under direct orders, in spite of his fuzzy logic.

"Shot?"

"Guess!" Grumble.

"Structure has been imposed on both the Wrapper and the Cube but in completely different functionalities," responded Pappa, "through the operation of some processes or devices I have yet to discover. Excepting possibly the aggregate dirt particles, none of the artifact is in a natural state."

"What else?"

"Very little else at this time, Mr. Olson. I am having a little difficulty with the confidence level of my probes. The Cube seems to absorb radiation completely at most frequencies and returns ambiguous signals at others. Metallic hydrogen should not behave that way, even allowing for the high oscillation rate.

"It does not evaporate or sublimate even in direct contact with relatively hot materials like the shuttle's landing gear," continued Pappa. "That would ordinarily make metallic hydrogen gasify uncontrollably. Those flood lights should have caused a small hurricane. There must be other factors I have not yet identified."

"Great," muttered Mike. "Let me get this straight, Pappa; we're standing on a hydrogen bomb? A 42 kilometer big hydrogen bomb!?"

"Not quite, Mr. Hand. It is probably hydrogen but it cannot explode. At least not in the manner of a nuclear fusion device."

"Then it *can* explode some other way?" asked Mike, persistently.

"That is not exactly conclusive of the observed facts and would be wildly speculative at this time."

"Then it *can* explode," even more persistently.

"Yes, there are circumstances in which the Cube might deconstruct catastrophically. However …"

"That's all I need, Pappa," said Mike with a grin. "Just needed a reality check." Then after a moment, returning to the task at hand, "I *love* this job!"

Mike paused to watch Unit One's progress. They were good, very efficient once they mastered the Roof Shuffle, and gung ho as Harpies. They made him proud.

What do I see here? What do I really know about this fool thing? Should I be taking this risk with something so strange that even Pappa was confused? Those are indeed good questions he thought to himself, and they sounded more confounding every time he recounted them. Mike Hand, Chief Engineer Unit One, mentally ticked off what he saw:

First of all. The Cube, and presumably the Base, was hard to the touch. Very hard and so smooth that it should have reflected like a mirror, but didn't. They tried vacuum pads and several types of stickum but nothing would stick to the surface. Mild probes would not penetrate the surface either Not knowing what they were doing they hadn't tried very hard anyway, he thought gratefully.

Secondly, nobody agreed on the Cube's color and it didn't really look colored. It didn't reflect a virtual image like polished metal or glass, and it didn't reflect selectively like colored stuff. It didn't reflect light even at very low incident angles and wouldn't mirage out to the limits of vision. Because of that, no radiation at any frequency they had tried would cast a shadow. It wasn't matte either, exactly, but looking at it strained the eyes as though looking through a light fog, with eyes hunting in and out for focus. It was close to being a perfect black body. Close.

Third. The five accessible sides of the Cube were absolutely plane, the twelve edges absolutely straight. The square surfaces were absolutely square to a degree exceeding the limits of their instruments. The sides were absolutely perpendicular to each other, forming precise knife edges. There was no refraction as those edges occluded stars. Cube was the only word for it, the essence of cubeness.

And last, it made no noise, vibrated a zillion times a second and was harder see than a cloudy sky at night. It wasn't hard to see, thought Mike, because it was transparent or dark or camouflaged or concealed. Quite the opposite. It was hard to see because it was so blooming *big*. You couldn't focus on it in the same way you can't focus on a clear sky.

Big, and dark. People could see it, barely, because of their cumulative night vision and persistence of vision, and imagination, but they were unable to work effectively without amplifiers. Floodlights lit the crew and the equipment but not the Cube, sometimes giving the illusion that they were in space itself, up against an infinite plate of glass. Mike was reminded of a travel poster for some tropical paradise, a photograph of a boat seemingly suspended above the sea floor in perfectly clear water.

Mike surveyed a field of trash with some amusement. Some genius discovered that a scattering of metal washers and confetti and toilet paper made the surface more apparent, more manageable.

"I hope the aliens don't think we're trashing their back yard," thought Mike.

There could be nothing more monolithic, dead and stubborn than the Cube. It was certainly lifeless according to corporate regs. It gave off no radiation, not even infrared. It didn't have a detectable temperature, at least not at any frequency examined. Aside from the imperceptible vibration, nothing moved.

"So what's the problem," he asked himself.

"No problem," he answered aloud, pumping himself mentally. "This Thingy is mine! We were here first, and I win!"

"I beg your pardon, Mr. Hand." Pappa did a pretty good imitation of clearing his throat. "It's time to start."

CHAPTER 10
DOWNSIDE

"One molecule." A statement not really believed but offered only as a polite 'This better be good' inquiry for more information.

"A five-hundred kilometer long molecule," confirmed Fats Bic, Meteorology.

Mike Hand fingered the slender line thoughtfully. It was about the thickness of a fine lead for one of those high-end push button automatic pencils, but with a fatish Wankel rotor triangular cross section. Thinner.

"Yes, Mr. Hand," confirmed Pappa. "In fact, technically, the molecule's length is the full 500 kilometers on this spool."

"I'll take your word on that. But you'll guarantee it can't break. Right?" Mike looked up at the gigantic spool, figuring somebody must have known what they were doing when they made that! And I can't believe they managed to wrestle it down from the ship lashed to the back of a shuttle. "Man! That's a honkin' big fishing reel!"

"I made no such observation, Mr. Hand," replied Pappa without even a hitch on 'honkin', "much less a guarantee. However, there has never been a structural failure with a cable in service."

"But you *can* break it?" 'In service' had a hedgy sound to it.

"Yes, although that has never been observed outside laboratory testing for manufacturing quality control."

"Thanks." Close enough, thought Mike Hand, Mechanical Engineering.

Curiously, the cable had begun to fluoresce a mild pink in such proximity to the Cube, which fact not only prompted wild speculation about its usefulness in uncovering new information about the Cube itself, but also made the line a Helluva lot easier to handle in the darkness.

The line was stiff and springy, like a dueling foil, which thought he immediately regretted. In space this stuff would snap straight out to its full length without much more than a good whippy shake and a Howdyoudo.

Mike flashed back to the time he had taken the spring out of an old watch his dad had given him.

"Part of your formal education," his dad had once said. "You can learn a lot by taking a watch apart and putting it back together. Builds character." Recalling the inevitable result, Mike wondered what kind of character all those leftover parts built. But dad had probably been right. Always was.

Considering he was about to jump over the side of a 42 kilometer cliff, with nothing between glory and that dust bowl down there but one disquietingly fine life line, Mike figured he was entitled to whatever information he needed for a proper assessment of his prospects.

"Well, just the central conductor," disclaimed Fats, giving the line an unnecessary whip. They both watched the pink wave undulate out of sight, seemingly kilometers out. And down. No seemingly about it; kilometers.

"The rest is the same stuff they use to hold up those centrifugal elevator satellites." Fats thought for a moment and corrected himself. "Unh, tie down."

"Down?" said Mike, momentarily confused, but only slightly distracted from checking out his rig.

"Yeah. The line that holds the satellite down so it doesn't fly out into space. Same stuff. Modern living through technology and tax dollars."

Mike registered that science fact clearly and found himself comforted. Being a space guy, he visualized the tethered binary earth-satellite system from the satellite's end, the earth being the whippee of a geosynchronous whipper satellite.

Mike looked around the Roof one last time, seeing crew and equipment and glare of lights. No faces were visible behind the metallic visors, normal but now a little unnerving. They looked like big insect eyes, or those overhead surveillance camera domes. Although he couldn't see eyes, he knew they all looked at him. Nobody moved.

"That guy's got brass garbanzos!" they might be thinking. Or maybe, "I'm glad *I'm* not jumping off that cliff!" Probably more like, "That's one crazy schmuck."

In the rush of the recent intense events he hadn't the time to get up close and personal with his crew, and he felt he was on his own, mostly. Everyone was in on the game but he was still basically on his own. Mostly. The point, Mike concluded to himself, was that he wasn't sure which he preferred; the gung-ho go for it rapport or the impersonal business as usual nonchalance. Both would be good.

"Ready, Mr. Hand," intoned Pappa flatly.

"Ready, Mike," said Dac, uncertainly, trying hard to sound certain.

"Ready," said Jason firmly. "Good luck, Mike." No doubts there.

"Ready," said Fats, sincerely, sounding it.

"Let's do it!" he shouted. Mike head-bumped Fats, nodded to the rest and jumped butt first over the edge into probably the highest longest rappel ever.

The gravity was so low on the Roof that Mike felt little effect of falling, instead experiencing the illusion that the crew were ascending on an elevator platform. Mike watched them until they disappeared upward as far as his helmet allowed and turned his attention downward.

The basic plan was to free fall for, say, thirty-five or so kilometers, then start braking, the descent taking something less than an hour total down to the Gap. Pappa would control the brakes remotely, with Shuttle on backup orbit behind him coming up over the horizon as he approached the end of the descent.

Poppa planned for a maximum allowable terminal velocity of 200 kilometers/hour to insure Mike could stop within the last 5 kilometers. With the low gravity and atmospheric, drag nobody thought Mike would reach anything near that speed. Even if he configured himself to minimize drag, he would probably make no more than 75kph, 100 max.

"You're sure about that, Jason?"

"Sure. Why not. Just go for it." That wouldn't sound too comforting from anyone but Jason. "We've got your 6."

In the fullness of time, however, Mike found himself seemingly standing still. Or rather falling still. The vast dim gray featureless horizon showed only a very gradual flattening over time. The nearly unseeable side of the Cube appeared virtually motionless.

"Woof!" He shouted in frustration. "Manoman! This is ..."

"I beg your pardon, Mr. Hand." It was Pappa, apparently unconcerned with Mike's frustration. "You are about to decelerate."

The only clue to motion was the faint whisper of the supporting line occasionally sluicing against its constraining guides and brakes as the centripetal effect of the Thingy's spin and the natural springiness of the line itself ballooned him, as planned, out from the wall by as much as two kilometers.

That clue and the regular "How ya doing, guy? Looking good," from the crew as they checked vitals. Pappa ticked off the distance to the Gap every five kilometers until 35, then every kilometer. Early on, Fats regaled him with a few more or less gross jokes until Dac shut him down. Then Dac turned on Wagner's Die Valkyrie until Mike shut him down in turn. Mostly it was quiet.

They allowed considerable slack in the line so that it, and Mike himself, would not be forced and dragged around the square but razor sharp edge of the Cube into the Gap. He was to make a round house sweep into the Gap, moving almost horizontally directly into it at that point. Until then, there was nothing to do but enjoy the alleged view that was disappointing in many ways.

Mike slipped into a fond childhood memory, of floating on an air mattress on an intensely bright day in Grampa's swimming pool. Grampa gently pushed the raft here and there, rocking it over the water wavelets and bouncing it off the side of the pool like a big puffy billiard ball. Double dribbling he called it. Mike the kid would just float away with the ease of it all, the gentle nudge and ...

A high, faint hiss jolted Mike's reverie, just before he felt his body settle gently into the lower inside surfaces of his life suit. Poppa had braked to initiate the mildly accelerating kilometers-long deceleration.

Presently Mike felt himself rotating slightly, then rather quickly as he moved onto the end curve of the line into the Gap, slinging him outboard of the line which pulled him back in towards the Gap. His rate of deceleration increased steadily for some time, mocking gravity, then all but stopped.

After a time, it did stop. If everything was nominal, he should be no more than 100 meters from the wall, hopefully much closer because each meter from here on in and through was his job.

His hitch mounted the line in front of him so that he would enter the Gap feet first and on his back. Once in the Gap he would rotate himself, hanging by several connections to the line. There he would assess his situation and reorient himself as necessary.

"Your turn," called Jason. "Time to get off your butt and get to work."

"You have control ... now," stated Pappa.

"Take care of my antenna," warned Dac.

"See you on the upside," encouraged Fats.

"Come back in one piece. Okay?" Marcy!?

The situation seemed stable as he first moved into the Gap but deteriorated quickly when he hit the outflowing gas. The Pillow of gas, now affectionately capitalized, was not unexpected, of course, but the difficulty in passing the transition was. Mike went into wild slow-motion gyrations each time he tried to enter. The line, attached as it was only at the Roof on this side and on the opposite side of the Cube, was a loose, free-swinging loop almost 130 kilometers long and he a pendulum with irregular flight characteristics. The sharp edges to the relatively narrow Gap made entry particularly dicey. After the third unsuccessful try, they all agreed to back off and sort things out.

"We could patent *that* ride," said Mike, heaving heavily. "Let's hear plan B. Jason?"

"Unnh ... Plan B?" Some sheepish voice somewhere 42k above him.

"Look, Mike. All we need to do is stabilize you somehow until you get in." Fats. "Take up all that slack and get you past the Pillow."

"Sounds good to me but I forgot to pack my gyroscope. I felt like I was a dart thrown backwards!"

"Well then, we'll just have to throw you in frontwards," replied Jason with a little audible amusement. "How does this sound? Part one: We winch in the line from the far side. Part two: Shuttle hooks onto your line up here and moves down there to pull against the winch, with a long snubber in between somewhere. That should stabilize you until you get inside."

General quiet while each crew assessed their responsibilities and liabilities in implementing the plan.

"I like it!" shouted Mike suddenly, sensing there were no serious objections overhead. "When do we start?"

Plan B went just fine through the Pillow and into the Gap, right up until it went wrong.

Insertion proceeded as planned. Mike secured the bumper sleeve at the edge and slipped through the Pillow with little more than a few minor wobbles. He dangled from the line still being held stable by Shuttle and managed to more or less right himself. He locked the cinches so he could put his weight down on the Floor and called for Shuttle to release the line.

Mike was breaking a good sweat by the time he finally got himself inside, upright and feet on the ground. Floor. The relaxed line allowed Mike to settle to the Floor just long enough to relax. He had no more touched foot down when he began to kite in long swooping arcs in the outflowing gas, the bob at the end of a 42 kilometer horizontal pendulum. Shuttle, having already released the line was helpless.

"Got a problem, guys," grunted Mike, struggling with his harness. "Still oscillating. Not as wild as before but I'm still out of control. I need a recommendation or I'm releasing the brake and getting out of here soonest. Nothing personal, Okay?"

"Okay, Mike. Just relax. We'll get you out in a minute and go back to the drawing board. Just relax." Jason was frustrated but calm and steady. There was no blood yet; no problem.

Mike took Jason literally and relaxed, dropping his arms to his side in exhaustion. In less than two complete oscillations Mike settled into a stable configuration.

"Hold it! Hold it," commanded Mike to the support crew. "Something happened! I'm stable now! What did you do!?"

"Nothing," was the hesitant reply after the crew looked at each other blank-faced. "You're still free floating in there. What did *you* do?"

"Nothing! Wait. That was the problem. When I move my arms or legs the oscillations start up again. But I can control it!" The crew heard a little whoop. "Hey! I can do this! I can fly! Just like a kite on the end of a string." Sput. "... water skiing on Boji!"

"Sput. You Okay, Mike?" It was Jason, confused at Mike's sudden reversal of fortune and attitude.

"Yeah! Great! I got this thing whipped and I'm going in. Just gimme a minute. See you on the upside!"

"Sput."

"Guys?"

CHAPTER 11

TRAVERSE

He squinted at his rigging, checked that everything was secure, and prepared to move on. The surface was so hard and smooth, and the wind so strong, that Mike could not walk on it. Had he tried, he would have been blown out of the Gap like a spit wad. His traverse was possible because of his rig, basically a sophisticated rescue sling with life support systems. The primary cable, anchored on the Roof, ran completely through the Gap. His rig was attached to it. Hooks, clinches, ratchets, snatches, winches and the like. Crude but workable.

He stopped for a moment to stretch his back and shoulders, resting against the inside of his suit which in turn rested against the sling which pulled against the wind.

Mike was tired. Not exhausted tired but achy tired, deep muscle lactose pain tired. All over.

He flipped casually into detention study hall, in some middle grade or other, in one of those musty old public buildings that smell unmistakably schooly; dust and wood, urine, disinfectant, wax, old scrub water. Gabe, the faculty hatchet man presided.

"Mike!" bellowed Gabe. "Mike! You know why you're here, don'tcha? Can't keep your mouth shut, that's why. Right?"

"Right, Gabe." That wasn't disrespectful in Gabe's world.

"You still can't keep it shut, can you? CAN you?"

"No, sir."

"What!?" Gabe strutted a bit across the front of the dais, visually checking the freshmen to his left, some of whom actually cowered. "WHAT?"

"No, sir, Gabe."

"Tell you what I'm gonna do, Mikey. You get your choice. You get 'The Treatment' or you get another week's detention. What'll it be?" Gabe smirked at the freshmen.

Mike thought only a moment. "The Treatment."

"You got it, Mikey." Gabe positively beamed. "Assume the position."

Mike slid out of the torture rack they called a desk and onto his knees, arms outstretched as in a swan dive. He looked back at Gabe and then to the freshmen. He smiled defiantly at Gabe but in the general direction of the freshmen, particularly one freshman. Or rather freshette. Gabe caught that.

"Mikey, you spend so much time on your knees you wore out my dictionary. Positively wore it out! I had to get me a new book, one that would hold your attention."

Gabe hoisted a two-volume set of the Encyclopedia of Astrophysics and Astronavigation. Third edition. Library bound. He swaggered over to Mike-on-his-knees and placed a volume on each of his up-turned palms, letting it drop a few centimeters to gain momentum.

Mike stiffened and swayed back to counter the weight, wincing inside but defiant outside.

"There," said Gabe with some relish. "That should make a good impression on your lady friend over there. Keep 'em up boy. Ten minutes till the bell." Snickers.

He kept 'em up, all right. He bent and sagged a little, but he kept 'em up. God did that hurt! He'd show Gabe just who ...

A sharp whistle near his right ear jerked him back to the task at hand. Gabe disappeared, along with the study hall and the freshette. The pain remained.

He hurt like that now, all over. Pulling and leaning against that constant wind frayed every fiber in his every muscle and he was just plain hurting tired of it. Thank everyone in the universe that this job is almost history. And history it would be. Mike would be the first person to traverse the 42 kilometer Gap and he did it on foot. Or rather he did it on hand. Mostly anyway, and even that had been mostly unintentional.

He would be a hero, and the most knowledgeable person in the universe about the Gap. Except, of course, for whoever built it. He would be on talk shows, magazine covers, videos and toys. They would hang on every word about his experience in the Gap. That is, until they figured out he had nothing to say. Well maybe not ...

"What was that!?" He said that aloud in spite of his complete isolation.

Mike jerked to his left and twisted to the limit of his suit. An unexpected surge of adrenaline tingled through his body, major motor muscles first then settling in his gut. He was being followed. Again!

He picked up the devil when he passed the halfway point, at the center of the Gap. He could never quite see It, like a floater in his eyeball, or an afterimage from a bright flash of light. It was persistent and devious. And fast! Every time he tried to spot It unawares, It was gone. That trick earned It the capital "I" in Mike's confined world, a sign of both apprehension and Its acquired reality.

Mike could not say what It looked like; he'd never seen It.

He almost saw It this time. Just there, behind him. Getting closer each time! He could feel It now!

Mike flashed a long forgotten panic he remembered from his childhood, from the basement of his home. If he had to go down there for a tool or a chore, he panicked on the way back up, when he had to turn his back on the devils down there. He would fly up the stairs two at a time, more. The relief at the top of the stairs was instant; he had escaped again!

He hadn't escaped this one yet.

"Come on, you bastard!" Mike muttered under his breath so It couldn't hear "Come on."

Mike's aggravation had accumulated since his transit from the center of the Gap, at the nexus of the wind. He could feel the flexible wiggly column at the vertical line where the wind radiated out in all directions. It felt alive and squirmy, like It tried to escape his grasp. He felt Its anger at being disturbed. Mike couldn't see It, couldn't really feel It aside from the quickly changing pressure pushing his hand one way or another. Like he felt as a kid trying to hold back water from the garden hose. But this was different. It felt alive and madder than Hell.

And It was following him. From the center of the Gap, every inch of the way to the edge of the Gap. Relentlessly, as if It were tethered to him. Even when he stopped to rest and looked back, It was there somewhere in the gloom.

"I'll catch you, smarty pants!" Mike once thought to himself, quietly so as to not give himself away. "You can't outfox this old hunter!"

Mike stopped on his traverse and waited quietly, not moving a muscle, until he was certain It had also stopped. Then he slowly rotated his body head to toe so that he faced whatever dogged him. He spent maybe an hour, he wasn't really sure how long, unfastening the harness one step at a time, refastening everything carefully as he slowly edged around to face his tormenter.

Mike was finally able to look back up the line, back towards the center of the Gap. Slowly he turned to the limit of his visor, then even more slowly turned his shoulders to the limit of the harness. He could just see the pink glow of the line oscillating gracefully into the distance, towards the center of the Gap. Towards It.

Nothing!

"Where are you, you … !"

Mike froze, his senses sparking. It was behind him again, still behind him! Watching him!

"What do you want!" he shouted into his face plate loud enough to feel the reverberation. "What do you want! Come out where I can see you! Fight me like a man. Whatever you are!"

Mike held still for minutes while his rancor settled.

"Wait a minute," he mused to himself. "What am I doing here anyway?" He was here along with the rest of the crew trying to find life, or the lack of it. Either way was a success and he was in the middle of the mix. I even "volunteered" for this job. "Let's find out which, real or not. Me or It."

"Okay, mister sneaky guy," he said aloud. "Do your worst, or best. Whatever."

Mike waited unmoving for maybe an hour. It's hard to tell how long in this supremely desolate environment. And how long is long enough to this alien spook? Mike considered an hour was long enough, although he was not certain that this standoff had been an hour; it could have been a week.

There came a time when he felt the lifting of the shadow. Rather, he didn't feel the lifting, but there came a point when he realized It was gone. Like you don't realize the moment that overstuffed Thanksgiving dinner passed into a kind of relative comfort. Just relief sometime during halftime when you reach for another slice of leftover pie, with a little leftover apprehension.

"I'm glad that's over," Mike mumbled. "Must have been that last piece of pie."

Mike reorganized himself and continued his quest, feeling better with the wind literally behind him. And one last look behind him.

Mike squinted into the Upside Gap. Or rather out of it.

The thin black-on-black horizontal line of stars extended in all directions and surrounded him completely. It was wider here in front of him because it was closer. Well, that wasn't quite right either, he thought, amused; he was in the Gap so he couldn't be any closer to the Gap. The star line was wider here because he was closer to getting out of it, closer to the edge.

"Come on," he growled at himself, pointlessly aloud. "Shake it off. Get alive!" Mike stretched himself as far as he could in the air suit, stretched his face, and clenched his fists until they hurt then splayed his fingers to the other extreme. He was getting a little sloggy lately, tired and sloggy, and had to force himself to think coherently. "Stop and get your bearings," he ordered himself out loud. "Focus! Hot tub! Focus! Cheeseburgers! Focus! Money! Focus! Beer! Focus! Marcy! Focus!"

This hedonistic litany, modified variously for the occasion and each then current passion, had served him well in times of need, appealing as it did to most of his basal needs. Like an old friend, it didn't fail him now.

Ah, Marcy. One of those what-might-have-been episodes in every lifetime but with an added slather of melancholy of seeing her every day, working closely with her every day.

Theirs had been a torrid affair by any measure; almost immediate violent attraction, intense physical exploration and childishly exhilarating companionship. An affair with the brilliance and life expectancy of a flashbulb. Whatever the Hell that was.

The gods had been kind, allowing the affair to end with finality and, incongruously enough, with love and respect. Mike remembered that day too well. It was the day Mike embarrassed himself at the dinner table trying unsuccessfully to keep up with the conversation about the origins of neo-neo-classical music in the twenty-first century. Mike knew now that he should have stuck to soccer scores and sports cars. Too late. He had lost Marcy's infatuation before desert.

"Thanks, Mike," were Marcy's exact words, "But no thanks." He put two and two together the next day when he saw Marcy at dinner with CEO Dac. Talking about horticulture. Whatever the Hell *that* was! Ah well.

Looking back in somewhat better focus, Mike could see a clear horizon in all directions, uninterrupted by even the slightest hint of support for the Ceiling. He always felt a claustrophobic shock wave of fear at the thought of the Cube overhead with no visible means of support, so he didn't think about it. Much.

Mike looked at the last few hundred meters before him as though it was a tree to be felled. It wasn't a matter of quitting; he had no choice and nowhere to go but out and up. Quitting would never occur to Mike Hand in any event; he came here to do a job and it would get done. He never failed what he started, which was probably why Dac had chosen him to explore the Gap. Well, he admitted to himself, he had failed once, but they had to carry his burned and broken body out of that one. Close enough.

In the longest dimension behind him, towards the corners almost 50 kilometers away, the horizon was no more than a hairline, but that hairline was perfectly clean; no reflection from the Floor or Ceiling, no refraction, no mirage. Just a clear, bright light line across the inside of his visor. The Gap is actually very dark, he thought, really dark. Only starlight leaks into the Gap. He could see nothing without the photomultiplier boost, not that there was anything to see.

The intensity of the amplified starlight had increased dramatically over the last kilometer to the edge, more quickly than his eyes were accommodating after five cycles in near total darkness, so he squinted against the light while he adjusted his visor. Better.

He keyed the intercom and checked for any trace of a carrier signal. Nothing yet. No problem, he thought; if going out worked the same as going in, he wouldn't get a signal until the last few meters out of this thing.

Whatever the reason, Mike had been out of communication with Unit One for virtually the entire traverse. Radio didn't work in here. Neither did transmission through the cable past the first 100 meters or so. Modulated electromagnetics were heavily suppressed in the Gap.

His recorder didn't work in here either so he made a note to himself to include that fact in his written report. On second thought he realized Unit One learned that radio didn't work in the Gap at the same time he did. Hell, include it anyway. He was too tired to argue with himself about it.

That's why he was so tired. His rig was supposed to be powered by winches on the Roof, with his movement controlled by radio. But he could send no radio signal so he got no power. He had tried to establish a code of some sort by tugging on the thin cable along which he dragged himself. That didn't work well because Unit One had no idea he was doing it. After a few minutes into the Gap he realized that it was impossible to jerk a long cable in a meaningful way. A 42-kilometer cable.

Unit One did the right thing when they lost contact, however; they did nothing. In the absence of Mike's signal they did nothing as long as they could see he was moving deliberately.

They could see him all right, and they could probably see his hand signals through their telescope. The problem was without a telescope he could not see their signals, if any. Not having anticipated the communications blackout, no contingency plans had been made in that direction.

Unit One could have powered the rig on through the gap without Mike's guidance but he would have been unable to move freely to take measurements at his leisure or opportunity. They correctly decided to leave him to the backup device and his own devices, but as a result he had to provide the power himself, one manpower. Ruefully, he struggled to fully appreciate their confidence in him. Ruefully because it was his own idea, in spite of his own reservations.

"Okay," Dac had interjected into the discussion of the mobility problem. "This scheme of your looks like it will probably work. Probably, mind you. But what if it doesn't?"

"Unnh… Like what probably?" Jason was still selling the proposition and wasn't attuned to the possibility of failure. "What did you have in mind?"

"Well, for instance, what happens if the cable breaks or the servo motors zonk out or you get a kink in the cable or you lose power down there and Mike has to walk home?"

"Good points, Mr. Olson. But have you ever heard of a cable breaking in service?"

"Well, no. But…"

"And did you ever try to put a kink in a cable? Or tie a knot in one?" Jason pressed the advantage. "That's why the cable reels are 10 meters in diameter; that's just a tad more radius than they can go. And the tensile strength is measured in tens of tons to withstand the centrifpetal force in deployment."

"That's true. I always wondered about that."

"And as for power loss or servo failure," responded Jason, "we will have four servos connected, two for each of the two cables operating at right angles. What do you suppose are the odds of all four servos and both cables going down at the same time?" Jason paused for effect, knowing that Dac was at his technological limit.

"Let me put it this way; something *will* go wrong, guaranteed." Dac eye-checked Jason and Mike Hand, who for his part was listening more than closely. "You tell me what that will be and tell me how we get Mike out of there in one piece regardless of the why and how of the problem."

Mike was really listening now.

"Uuuh …" Jason had to think about that for a moment giving Mike a chance to jump in.

"Look, Mr. Olson." Mike got his dander up a little, impatient with what he saw as unnecessarily cautious whatifishness. "I'm the bait here and here's how I see it. There will be four lines attached to me at all times. That gives me a lot of options. If everything breaks down simultaneously, I can walk out. Been there, done that, as the saying goes."

Dac and Jason both nodded, allowing as how Mike had indeed been there and done that, more than once.

"But," said Dac incontrovertibly, "you never did it into a ninety mile per hour gale. And you won't be able to walk at all; your only power would be your arms."

"True, but pulling with my arms is about the same at pulling a buddy up a mountain, or doing pull-ups. I can do that all day."

"Yeah, but," rebutted Dac, "for forty-two miles!?"

"Kilometers, Mr. Olson. Actually, at worst it would only be twenty-two kilometers. Half of way the wind would be at my back. I think. That's about the same distance as swimming the English Channel back home, with the tide." Mike paused for the kill. Dac paused reflecting that Mike swam the English Channel more than once. "And pulling on the cable is very much like swimming, muscle-wise."

Dac looked at Jason and Jason looked at Dac and they both looked at Mike. Mike looked confident and pleased with himself. That was it and all systems were go.

Mike shook his head to get back on the task at hand.

He turned to look back on his path and squinted into the wind. Although the wind could not touch his face through the faceplate, the wind was there. He felt it in the list it imposed on his body and he squinted reflexively. He had been getting squinty a lot lately.

The pain itself was only part of it; he had to listen to that confounding wind. He lived with the wind every second, like living in a vacuum sweeper hose, and he felt the pain every second. They reinforced each other, did the pain and the wind, like Curly and Mo. God could he hear it.

He had measured the wind at a constant 90 kph throughout the Gap. But they knew that before he went in. More precisely, wind speed was 87.574839 kph. Close enough.

Now that he thought about it, that *was* new. Not the wind velocity itself so much as the fact that the velocity was exactly the same throughout the Gap. As he moved from his entry at the edge of the Gap towards the center of the Cube he expected the wind to accelerate on the assumption that it came from some source and slowed as it expanded and spread out to the edges. It didn't, which was impossible, of course.

He had pulled himself against the unvarying wind until he hit the dead center of the Cube and then been flung forward in an instant as he passed the center. The wind that pulled him back against his cable for 20 kilometers suddenly reversed and threw him forward, taking up the slack that had accumulated behind him. That little free fall added interest to an otherwise dull hike, thought Mike.

He had worked his way back to the center to determine how the wind reversed and found that it hadn't. The wind blew out from a point at the center equally in all directions and he had simply crossed that point. He could feel the invisible point, actually a vertical line, with his hand, like gripping a very springy spongy tube. There were no visible pipes, outlets, grates or fixtures of any kind on either the Floor or the Ceiling; the wind just blew. Impossible, he thought as he returned to reality.

He suffered the shriek constantly, the only variation arising from the various surfaces of his suit. Whistles, shudders, whizzes and rattles. The noise wasn't so loud actually, the suit did a good job of dampening, but the wheezing and tearing was unrelenting.

One rest period he tried to play a tune on his suit, moving arms and legs to catch the wind on the tubes and plates just so. It didn't work well, sounding more like a pre-schooler on a harmonica than E. Power Biggs, but it passed the time and took the edge off the meanness he felt towards the relentless wind. In spite of his confidence that he could eventually master the trick, he would recommend a negative noise suppressor for the next guy. If anyone would bother with another pointless transit.

Wind speed in the Gap had no relation to location and did not vary over time. The air simply moved through the Gap at 90 kph. All the time. From the center out in all directions. The weird thing was the atmospheric pressure remained constant throughout his traverse, which, of course, was physically impossible. As far as Mike could tell, the wind moved without the slightest variation, at least not in the five cycles he spent in the Gap, and not with the instruments at hand.

In his tedium, he tried to calculate the amount of stuff blowing out of the Gap. Let's see, the Gap was about forty meters high and the Cube is 42 kilometers on a side. That's equivalent to an outlet duct of almost 7,000,000 square meters, 7 square kilometers cross section! Mike tried to imagine an outlet pipe 7 square kilometers. Can that be right!?

The square root of 7 is ... Wait a minute, about 2.645. So, a pipe twenty-six hundred meters on a side. A pipe over two and a half kilometers on a side!? That didn't help to conceptualize the situation. Too big. Check that math again; Haven't got anything better to do. Close enough for now; better stuff to worry about.

Like that gawdawful wind.

Wind speed, stuff speed is blowing out at almost 90 kph, which works out to 25 meters per second, give or take. 7,000,000 square meters of Gap at 25 meters per second translates into 170 or 180 million cubic meters of passed gas per second.

That's one Helluva fart, he thought, smiling to himself. And where does that put me?

"Where does it all come from?" thought Mike without emotion. The calculations had been done many times before he got here and his ciphers only confirmed the few basic facts he was given when he volunteered for this job. "From nowhere" was the only possible answer.

Atmospheric pressure in the Gap measured about 2.2 Earth bars throughout, center to edge. Check. The atmosphere was absolutely pure hydrogen. According to Pappa. At that pressure a cubic meter of hydrogen weighs about 3 grams. So the weight of hydrogen flowing from the Gap was 3 times 180,000,000 cubic meters. That works out to 540,000,000 grams per second. 540,000 kilograms per second. More than half a billion grams per second. Twenty tons per second!

And that all comes from nowhere! Thought Mike Hand, Engineering Specialist. At least nowhere I could find.

From the look of things Pappa thinks the Cube is very old, perhaps millions of years. Check that out. There are 60 times 60 times 24 times 365 seconds in a year. 31,536,000 seconds in a year. At 540,000 kilograms per second, this fool thing is spewing out 17,000,000,000,000 kilograms per year. Give or take. For maybe a million years. Give or take. GOT for short.

Mike quit at that point and got back to work.

The laminar flow on the top and bottom surfaces of the Gap moved at exactly the same constant speed as everywhere else, which is to say there was no laminar flow. Duh.

Both surfaces of the Gap, the Floor and the Ceiling, were perfectly slick and held no drag on the wind at the interface. They also held no friction for his feet, same as on the Roof. Wait a minute! he thought. We could walk on the Roof and it wasn't perfectly slick up there. There was some traction up there. Not much but a little.

He might as well be on roller skates down here. Thanks to the Gods and the engineers who protect fools, the rescue sling held him against the wind. Without it, he would squirt out of the Gap like wet soap between two palms.

But there's no friction at all here in the Gap. Is that significant? "Gaaah! That's dumb! Of course it's significant," Mike thought savagely to himself. "That's how they built it and that's why I'm here; to find out what the deal is. Come on! Get professional!"

"But why is that the case?" thought Mike. "There are six sides to the Cube but only one is frictionless. Correction: The Ceiling is the sixth side of the Cube. The Floor is a seventh face, also frictionless. That implies the Gap surfaces are different from the rest of the contraption somehow." Mental note on that.

Coming into the Gap against the wind, from the edge to the center, he was climbing the cable in a more or less standing position so he could see ahead through the limited aspect of his visor. He knew it was an illusion, but after eight or ten hours, the Floor seemed to lift into a steep, then vertical gradient.

It was the constant drag of the wind into his face that created the illusion of gravity, of course. That constant and unvarying pull backwards against his forward progress tricked his sensation-deprived brain into thinking it was walking straight up a wall.

From the center of the Gap out he felt like he was rappelling, face down. Again in a standing position. No toe holds, no spikes, no nothing. Just climb in/up to the center and declimb out/down. That was why he was so tired; he had been supporting his own dead-weight body for 5 cycles now. His own mass and the 400 kilos of equipment and ballast he carried that kept him from kiting. A good but necessary idea, that. I think.

Now that he could see more stars through the Gap his world was starting to return to normal. The Floor now felt more like a floor and less like a wall, horizontal instead of vertical. He was looking ahead, not down. It was just as much work to ease himself out of the Gap as it was to get into it, but at least things were right side up again.

Mike's expedition had been successful in one sense; everything worked as it should have. Even the radio worked properly; it sent out a consistently strong signal at all times. The problem was the Gap ate the signal. There were no incidents, no accidents. There was only one real problem. He hadn't learned a thing.

Nothing.

That was the gist of it. He spent five cycles in the Gap and learned virtually nothing. Well, not actually nothing; he had confirmed and refined the few firm measurements made by the remotes. His confirmations were somewhat more precise, but that was about it.

Looking back on his adventure, he felt like those guys who sit on a flagpole for a week. It was a grand gesture and showed determination, singleness of purpose, stamina and courage of a sort, but it didn't really prove a thing. Mike hadn't proved a thing either.

No one had a clue as to the why of all of this. For all his trouble, he had no clues either. Why the Cube and why the Base and why the Gap?

And why was he here? He had volunteered, of course, but he was expected to volunteer. Go where no one had ever gone before, know something no one ever knew before, or something like that. Well he hadn't found out anything new for all his trouble, but he had gone there.

Mike reflected on the chain of events leading up to now. The discovery of the planet where there should have been none, identifying the alien artifact, the Cube, the Gap. Incredible! In these last hours he couldn't help remembering that fantastic series of discoveries. But nothing new in the Gap.

In a way that was probably a good thing. Who knew what a discovery in the Gap might be. Maybe aliens who eat you like in the vids. Or a big grinder-upper. Maybe nothing is good.

He would worry about that later. Right now the problem was the edge. The edge of the Gap and the 42 kilometer vertical climb to the Roof, in the dark.

CHAPTER 12

DEGAPPING

"Time to start," said Mike aloud to himself, recalling Pappa's words when his traverse began. He shook himself to clear both his mind and his joints. "And now it's time to stop!"

The events leading up to his traverse of the Gap were past history. Great history. Fantastic history! And he was right in the middle of it! I'd better get something out of this, he thought. His idea of something ran in the direction of the world's greatest massage at the hands of Marcy Phillips, the world's greatest electronics engineer. Money. Marcy. His own profit center, fame and fortune. Marcy.

Come on Mikey! Focus!. You've got a job to do.

He snapped on the comm again, not really expecting to make contact; it was still a hundred meters to the edge.

"Mike Hand here," he said to the inside of his faceplate. "You guys still sitting on your thumbs up there?"

Nothing.

"Hey, how about a ride. Ready or not, here I come. Come on back."

Nothing.

The com hummed stupidly. The SWR meter indicated everything was functional. He tapped the transmitter sharply to no end. If the dampening effect in the Gap was symmetrical, he should have contact by now.

No problem, he thought, yet.

The cable was taut behind him, holding him snug against the blast of the gas blowing out of the Gap, but hung loose in front of him. He whipped the loose cable pointlessly and watched the wave flow up the line to the edge of the Ceiling. The line was clear, no snags.

He mentally rechecked the ascent procedure; Secure himself three times to the cable, secure the rig, release himself from the rig and ride the line up to the Roof like an elevator. Visualizing his ascent recalled a wonderfully sunny windy day of his youth spent flying kites in a field. He and a buddy sent 'messages' by tying strips of cloth loosely on the string to be blown up to the kite. He didn't get answers then either, he thought ruefully.

He carefully disengaged himself from the climbing apparatus, one snatch at a time, like playing that game with the different sized rings on three pegs; hitch this, check that, unhitch that, check this, release a clip, fasten a binder, do this, undo that. He would go up unencumbered; the rig would be pulled up later.

He finally felt ready to release his last connection to the rig. When he did, he would fly out of the Gap with the hurricane and find himself either dangling at the end of a 42 kilometer elevator or swimming in a sea of shaving cream a couple hundred kilometers deep.

The routine was familiar; he had done it exactly 41 times before, every half kilometer. When he found that the wind speed and pressure didn't vary in the least as he moved into the Gap, he decided to measure them both at the Ceiling as well as on the Floor. To do that, he released himself from the rig as he was doing now and skydived to the Ceiling. The wind speed and pressure measured exactly the same throughout the Gap, top to bottom, 41 times. The routine was familiar, he warned himself, and therefore dangerous; familiarity bred dumb.

He checked everything again, not so much out of fear; he was beyond that, but out of deeply ingrained professionalism born of near disaster. He had almost killed himself, and others, too many times to allow the least margin for error. When in doubt, check.

No doubts. But check again anyway, like proof-reading his undergraduate thesis. Check again. Again.

Mike gripped the braking cinch, turned himself head first into the wind and yanked the pin holding the last coupling. He lifted from the Floor, kiting in the hydrogen gale, oscillated widely for a minute and eventually stabilized feet-first toward the gap. The cable pulled out to its full taut.

"I did it and Pappa's a jerk!" he whooped.

"I beg your pardon, Mr. Hand."

"Pappa!"

"Yes, Mr. Hand. I see that you made it through the Gap. We were expecting you. Congratulations." Pappa could not express relief because he could not feel anxiety. He could, however, recognize accomplishment.

"I'm coming up, Pappa," replied Mike. "I'm not quite out of the Gap so don't start pulling yet or you'll scrape me around the edge. I'll let you know when I'm clear."

"On your mark, Mr. Hand."

Mike was securely hooked to the cable but he was suspended by his hand brakes against the pull of the wind. He eased himself along the cable, moving horizontally to the edge of the Gap. If he released the brakes completely, he would slide along the cable on past the wind-Wrapper interface at 90 kph. He would then whip on out from the Cube and swing back to collide with the side of the Cube. That could be very dangerous in spite of the low gravity so he eased himself along the line, slipping the brake carefully until he reached the edge.

He could feel the drop in wind pressure against his legs. A little more. The wind differential moved up his body. A little more and the wall of wind was full against his body, which now hung upright from above. The face of the hurricane stopped within a meter of the edge and formed a big pillow against which Mike now bobbed.

"Any time now, Pappa. I'm clear." Mike's words were professionally calm in spite of his euphoria. You're home free, he thought, relax and enjoy the view.

And he did, such as it was. The Cube was absolutely featureless, providing little esthetic improvement over the interior of the Gap and no clue to his progress. Turning around he found that the featureless Ball didn't help much either. When he must have been several kilometers up from the Gap he could see a more pronounced curvature to the horizon, so something was happening.

In his boredom Mike recalled an amusement park ride, a Ferris wheel or a parachute thing, whatever. The ride wasn't the image, it was the view.

He could see forever, down, out. The boardwalk shrunk as he watched, the people turning into little things as detail compressed with the altitude. Trees really did look like those toys on his model train set. And he could hear as far as he could see. No trees here, no people, nothing to gauge the height. A gentle tug of remembered vertigo alerted his stomach.

"How're we coming, Pappa?" Mild panic.

"We are coming just fine, Mr. Hand," replied Pappa. "You are lifting at ten kilometers per hour at the present time. As you near the Roof we will slow that rate somewhat. The transition to the Roof should occur in just under four hours. Can I do anything for you?"

"Yeah," he answered. "Get me a pizza and a pitcher of beer."

"I'll have it ready when you arrive, Mr. Hand."

"That's not what I had in mind. How about a little music down here. This is really boring."

"You got it." Aside from Pappa's penchant for the classical polka, the rest of the ascent was uneventful.

CHAPTER 13

DEBRIEFING

"Nice Work, Mike," said Jason with genuine admiration. "Let's get you out of that strappado. Nice work."

"Me too," chimed in Dac from the ship above. "We've got a party waiting when you get back up here." Strappado?

Jason and Fats Bic grappled with the straps and buckles while Mike struggled to disengage himself from the slingshot that was his home for the last five or six cycles. Fats yanked at a stubborn clip that gave way suddenly, sending them all sprawling on the Roof. They started giggling like kids in winter's first snowfall and made quite a sport of knocking each other down again, whooping it up like fools. The others, a little embarrassed for them, kept at their task, reloading the equipment for the ascent to the profit center.

"How did you manage to walk through the Gap? You can't even stand up!" prodded Fats with a roar.

"I didn't walk. I flew." shouted Mike, "Like this!" With that, he flipped Bic's legs out from under him, sending him into a slow-motion free fall to the Roof.

"Chirp."

They spun around on the roof and skittered into a tripod lamp stand which fell noiselessly. They struggled mutually to regain their composure, then immediately melted into a heap of merriment.

"Chirp."

"Hey you guys. Listen up!" Dac, minus the mirth.

Things settled down pretty quickly, but Jason and Bic and Mike had a little trouble with residual snickers on their way back to the shuttle hold.

"Pappa has something. Sounds like priority. I need your front line opinion. Pappa?"

"Chirp?"

Long pause.

"Chirp!" A statement expecting immediate attention. A subtle inflection that indeed caught everyone's instant attention.

"I detected a sudden change in the frequency of vibration of the Cube. It has added multiplexed overtones to the base frequency. The overtones are completely off the scale. A moment while I recalibrate."

"What does that mean, Pappa?" asked Mike apprehensively.

"The Thingy does only one thing that we know of, and that is to vibrate. The frequency of vibration has not changed since it was first detected, until now. A sudden change of this magnitude in a matter of nanoseconds indicates a profound alteration in the internal organization of the Cube. The new frequencies are consistent with altered dimensions with new resonant frequencies. It seems to be analogous to the piezoelectric effects preceding an earthquake, but in a structure with the elasticity of diamond."

"Are you saying we're going to have an earthquake down here?" asked Mike. "Or Cubequake, or whatever?"

"Oh no, Mr. Hand. Nothing like that."

"Then what's the problem," asked Jason, relieved.

"It's hard to say exactly, Mr. Fielding," responded Pappa matter-of-factly. "I believe the Cube is about to shatter."

"Abandon Cube!" shouted Jason. "Everyone on board! Cut 'er loose and leave that junk! Let's get out of here! Move it! Move it!"

They moved it as one and vacated the Cube in less than ten minutes. Scratch one slightly used antenna, thought Dac ruefully.

"Pappa! Keep track of all that equipment and plan on recovery if and when."

CHAPTER 14

SHATTERING

"Back her off to a half million clicks," ordered Dac as soon as the shuttle was securely in the PC. "I don't want to be anywhere near that thing when she blows. That sound far enough, Pappa?"

"Quite, Mr. Olson, although I'm not sure it was necessary to leave orbit. What did you have in mind?"

"What did I ... !? Dac caught his breath in surprise, checked their distance from the Thingy, and reiterated to Pappa, "I thought you said the Cube was going to explode!"

"I said it was going to shatter. I did not say it was going to explode. As a matter of fact ..."

"What in Hell's Thesaurus is the difference!?" Dac was trying to avoid sounding like a fool for abandoning the expedition unnecessarily. "Glass shatters. Bombs shatter. Ice shatters. And anything close gets hurt. Right?"

"Yes, Mr. Olson, if there is some outside energy added to the equation to impart velocity to the shards. In this case, the Cube will shatter but there appears to be no outside energy added; it will simply fall apart. I apologize if the completely accurate term I used caused distress."

"As a matter of fact," continues Pappa, "it has begun. If you will take a ..."

Dac spun around to his display console and hit external visuals only to see blank space. His fingers danced on the console to direct the receptors on the rapidly receding Thingy. Dac flipped a few toggles and adjusted a few movable things, looking for a clue. The rest of the crew, overhearing the conversation, fell immediately to their duties, air suits and all, looking for trouble on the Cube. Everything appeared normal, as alien artifacts go.

"What am I looking for, Pappa?" asked Dac with a little confusion.

"Whatever is happening has only just begun. At this range you cannot see it on your instrument, Mr. Olson. Let me bring up my analysis and I will construct a visual."

Pappa drew the standard line schematic of the Thingy as viewed from above its equator, which was limned in blue. The drawing looked like a spherical wire bird cage. Perpendicular to the equator were the purely arbitrary green lines of longitude Pappa had added for convenience, with the zero meridian centered on face one of the Cube. Superimposed on the globe were new lines Pappa had identified in red, running parallel to the lines of longitude from about 45 degrees north latitude to 45 degrees south. The whole structure rotated in real time and displayed something new; four red longitudinal great circle lines spaced equally around the Thingy.

"That's new," whistled Dac. "Any ideas? Survey?"

"Nothing yet, sir. Given the change in frequency, they could represent the nodes of standing waves on the surface."

"That's good, Bravo. Can you draw a conclusion?"

"No, sir."

"Geology?" barked Dac. "What have you got?"

"I confirm Survey, Mr. Olson," replied Mercedes Mead. "The surface is no longer a perfect sphere. It is slightly higher along a line between and equidistant from those red lines. The difference is increasing at an accelerating rate. Standing wave seems a sound preliminary analysis."

"Reconfirmed," intoned Survey.

"You're doing good. Keep talking. Anything else?" Dac paused to give everyone an opportunity to contribute. "Okay! Good job. Keep your eyes glued. Let me know immediately of anything, repeat anything that might be a threat of any kind.

"Pappa, I want projections based on the observed changes as a baseline for observations. That will be nominal. Notify me of any significant deviations from that baseline. I want formal reports on everyone's observations and experiences on record. This will all be compiled for our report to HO so make it pretty."

"Chirp."

"Now what!?"

"If you will watch your display, Mr. Olson," said Pappa, "you will notice the Cube. I have highlighted the points of interest."

While Dac watched, Pappa rotated the bird cage from the equatorial view to a view directly above the Cube. New lines bisected the Roof, cutting the square face into four smaller squares. The lines extended onto the Base as well and lined up with the four red lines on the Ball.

"Hell's Cheesecutter!" emitted Dac involuntarily.

"Indeed," replied Pappa. "The lines represent discontinuities in the surface vibrational frequencies, Mr. Olson. That is to say, the surface, and presumably the interior, does not vibrate at all along those lines. The width of the line is extremely small, on the order of about five centimeters. They appear to be fracture lines."

"I thought you said this was a glass," challenged Dac.

"Yes sir, that is correct," replied Pappa. "The Cube is fracturing just as any hard material can be made to fracture. The Cube is being made to fracture along these lines. The lines, however, do not represent crystalline planes. They are imposed on the Cube just as all of the other physical features seem to be imposed on the materials."

"Oh. And?"

"I have no more ideas at this time, Mr. Olson."

"Meteorology." It was a request for Dac's attention.

"What is it, Bic?"

"I don't know about the Cube exploding, sir," said Fats, "but the Wrapper is."

"Is what?" said Dac irritably.

"Exploding, Mr. Olson." replied Bic, calmly.

"Exploding!" said Dac, even more irritated. "What? The Wrapper? Hell's Bunghole! Can't these aliens make anything that lasts?"

"Yes, Mr. Olson," said Fats, uncertain as to which of Dac's comments his affirmative would be applied. "The Wrapper just, uh, popped, like a balloon."

"You said exploding, Bic," said Dac. "Is it burning?"

"No, Mr. Olson, the Wrapper is dissipating very rapidly under its own pressure," said Fats Bic, "but there is no chemical or other reaction. Whatever held the hydrogen on the Thingy just turned off, instantly. The leading edge of the hydrogen layer is expanding radially at 128 kilometers per second and accelerating. It will reach our present position in about three hours."

"Accelerating?" repeated Dac. "How can that be?"

"The hydrogen was … is under pressure," responded Fats Bic, "and the Wrapper was fifty kilometers deep at 2.2 Earth bars. The advancing front is still accelerating under that pressure."

"What's the velocity at impact," asked Dac as he reviewed his board to locate the front.

"Rough estimate," said Fats, "about two thousand kilometers per second. That's very rough, give or take twenty percent. I'm on it."

"Two thou … !" Dac paused to shift gears. "Pappa! Hazard assessment!"

"None whatsoever, Mr. Olson," responded Pappa instantly. "The gas will be quite diffuse when it reaches us."

"Bic?"

"Agreed, Mr. Olson," said Fats. "Nothing to worry about."

"Nothing to worry about!" fumed Dac Olson. "Then why all the fuss!?" He knew that was unfair as soon as he said it. Fats hadn't made a fuss; he was only doing his job. "Okay. Sorry about that, Fats."

"Yes, Mr. Olson," replied Fats apprehensively. "But the Wrapper isn't the problem; the Ball is the problem. The Ball may be right behind the Wrapper and the Ball isn't made of gas. The Ball is made of rock. A hundred kilometers of rock!"

"Pappa?"

"Actually, Mr. Olson," said Pappa, "it is more like a hundred and fifty kilometers of rock below any given point on the surface." Pappa whipped up a refreshed bird cage. The red longitudinal lines were more pronounced, deeper and broader. Pappa had added what looked like isobars to the surface of the Ball.

"What are … ?"

"I believe Mr. Bic is correct, Mr. Olson," said Pappa. "The Ball is definitely expanding rapidly, although I hesitate to use the word exploding. The contour lines monitor the bulging of the four lobes of the Ball. Each line represents a ten kilometer deviation from the mean diameter. Yellow is positive and red is negative. Whatever the process, it seems to be continuing in an orderly fashion."

"To what end?" asked Dac.

"Chirp," responded Pappa with a disquietingly terminal "Sputt".

"Hazard assessment, Pappa."

"The hazard is uncertain, Mr. Olson," said Pappa. "There are several countermanding factors. The Ball has apparently been released from whatever held it in place and it is expanding rapidly. The thickness of the Ball presents a considerable hazard at any speed, and so must be monitored closely.

"On the other hand," continued Pappa, "the Ball is not expanding under pressure as is the Wrapper; it is expanding radially as the result of inertial forces. At the equator the surface speed was slightly more than three thousand kilometers per hour. The speed of the Ball material at other latitudes graduates down to practically zero. The result will be an expanding disc of matter. In our polar orbit at this distance we will pass through the disc in about seven hours. We will probably suffer damage at that time. Extent unknown."

"Probably! Probably!?" Deep breath. Okay, calmly. "Recommended action?"

"Why, Mr. Olson," replied Pappa with a surprising amount of surprise in his usually inflexible voice. "Do not pass through the disc."

"Jason, take over," said Dac with an 'I'm-too-old-for-this' scowl. "You heard the man; don't hit the disc. I'll be in mess and then in my cabin if anything pops."

Dac released his console to Jason as the crew resumed their pursuits with renewed enthusiasm. He fiddled with a few maintenance decisions, checked the ship's status, checked the expanding bubble of gas.

"Snoon," he mumbled to Marcy on his way through the bulkhead.

"Sqweet," replied Marcy Phillips.

CHAPTER 15

BREAKUP

"Chirp."

"Chirp."

"Chirp."

"Dammit, Pappa!" Dac rolled over and viciously flipped on Pappa's channel. "What in Hell's OS *is* it!" Marcy headed for the head. "This had better be good or I'll erase a few of your gigabytes with a hammer!"

"Is this a bad time, Mr. Olson?" asked Pappa solicitously.

"Not anymore," resigned Dac. Grump. "What is it?"

"I thought you would want to know as soon as possible, Mr. Olson. The Ball is gone."

"What!?"

"The Ball is gone," repeated Pappa. "Or more precisely, the matter and structure of which the Ball consisted is no longer visible. I think you will be interested in the result."

"I'll be right up." Dac caught Marcy's eye as he reached for his clothes. "Sorry. You'll probably want to be in on this too. Not too close behind, okay?"

"Fine," she responded as she bounded out the door. "Give me two minutes head start."

"All right, what's all the commotion?" said Dac as he swept onto the flight deck. The crew was sure excited about something, thought Dac. The air tingled.

"Take a look here," said Jason as he rose from the command console to make way for Dac. "The dirt's gone and that's what's left. Can you believe it?"

"No," said Dac before looking. "I don't believe any of this whole Thingy business. It's just a bad dream. What's so ..."

Dac had to look at the display for a few moments to grasp what he was seeing. The screen showed the outline of a long four-sided prism, the proportion of a pen or a piece of stick candy, maybe ten or twelve to one. It looked to have an eraser at each end.

"Is this what I got out of ..." Dac reconsidered. "What is this anyway? What am I looking at?"

"That is the artifact, Dac. Without the Wrapper and the Ball." Jason couldn't take his eyes off of it. "This end here," he said, pointing to one of the erasers, "is the Cube. The rest of it was inside the Ball."

"The Cube?" Dac finally managed to shift his sense of perspective so that instead of looking at a pencil he was looking at a 500 kilometer long bar of metallic hydrogen with a Cube on each end.

"The Cube! That's the Cube? Then this," he said pointing to the middle longest of the three sections, "is the Base?"

"Right," confirmed Jason. "What we called the Base was really the end of the central part, barely sticking out of the Ball. Just like a candy apple on a stick. Now the candy and the apple are gone and all we have is the stick."

"There's a Cube and a Gap on both ends," paced Dac. "The other Cube was at the center of the Ball. That sounds important somehow. Are the Cubes identical?"

"As far as we can tell they are," replied Jason. "Obviously the Ball formed around one Cube but not the other, so they must be different somehow. Some sort of polarization maybe. No clue at this point."

"But Lordy! That must be, what did you say? 500 kilometers long!"

"I didn't say, but that's a pretty good guess," confirmed Jason.

"So what do we know now?"

Silence.

"What new information does this tell us?"

Silence.

"Chirp."

"Pappa? What's different from an hour ago?"

"The dirt has ..."

"I know! I know! But what's important we know now we didn't know then!" Dac wasn't angered so much as frustrated that his excitement had no focus. He wanted a handle. "Ideas? Anything?"

"I think we need a new name for whatever that is," said Mercedes Mead, Geology Associate. "I propose we call it the Shaft."

That brought a few snickers and a snort. Then Jason smiled, then Dac smiled, then they all smiled. Then a little genuine laughter.

"Okay. I deserved that," said Dac. "I was getting a little heavy. Okay. Anybody else?"

"The Ball. I think I know what happened to it."

"Let's hear it, Pete."

"Well, the Wrapper and the Ball weren't really things at all," he began. "I got to wondering how the Ball disappeared so quickly and I figure it was because the Ball was only partly there in the first place. The dirt was space junk pulverized by the vibration of the field that held it, that 11,000 Hertz. Any space debris that hit it just got ground into dust like Ross' helmet when he fell in. The Ball dust seemed to be finely dispersed and separated by empty space. That's why it disappeared so quickly, there were no big chunks. As soon as it thinned out even a little it became effectively transparent and cold as space. If we look, though, I think we can still find it. It was relatively warm so we should still be able to detect it in infrared."

"That probably explains the void in the center," added Bic, Meteorology. "The Ball wasn't really hollow because the Ball wasn't really there; it was just the shape of the field, made visible by the dust suspension."

"Okay," said Dac. "I like that. Now prove it. See if you can find that dust disc and let's go catch us some. It may tell us something. Marcy and anybody else, figure out what that Ball field was and how it was generated and what it did. Gimme some whys!" Dac was in his full-bore Commander CEO mode and crewones liked it. "Pappa. Take us back down to spitting distance. I want a good look at the Shaft. Now is good."

"Chirp."

What does it do? he thought, and why! Who put it here? When? Where's its daddy? And what, he thought with considerable apprehension, will HO think when they find out we broke it?

CHAPTER 16

BREAKDOWN

"That's the damndest! muttered Dac as he reviewed the orbitals on his display. "Is that the best you can do, Pappa?"

"That depends on what you mean by best, Mr. Olson," answered Pappa, probably not obtusely. "The Shaft is over 500 kilometers long. A polar orbit requires a rather long ellipse around two foci located on the Shaft at ..."

"We had a polar orbit before," snapped Dac. "Why can't we do it now?"

"We can, Mr. Olson, but the dirt Ball, diaphanous as it was, still held considerable mass in proportion to the Shaft. While the gravity of the Ball's mass was light, it was effectively spheroid. Now, however ..."

"Okayokay," interrupted Dac, still muttering. "Equatorial will have to do, but what is there to look at in the center of the Shaft? All the action is at the Cube."

Dac paused to reflect that there had been virtually no action at all on the part of the Thingy. We're the protagonists here, not the Thingy.

"If you will tell me exactly what action you expect to occur, Mr. Olson," responded Pappa with an undertone of solid state petulance, "I will set a proper orbit for your observations."

Dac almost lost it but managed to put a timely lid on it. Pappa is good but he can't rewrite the laws of physics, Dac admitted; the orbit was written by the aliens, not Pappa.

"All right, thank you, Pappa. Equatorial will do for now. If something pops, we'll adjust accordingly."

"Mr. Olson?" Pete Bravo, Survey.

"Yo," said Dac without thinking. He looked around sheepishly and was relieved to see only Bravo had heard, complete with a little smirk. Dac fixed Pete's eyes with his own and brought the smirk to an audible halt. "Yes, Pete. What is it?"

"Now that the Ball and Wrapper are gone," said Pete, "I've been able to get a much clearer picture of the Cube. I think I have a clue to what it does."

Dac belly-jerked upright in his recliner and spun around to Pete in one motion, expectantly. "Clue! All we have is clues! Do you have any answers?"

"Unh," restarted Pete, not expecting that kind of reaction. "Well, I have some firm data that may provide an answer, yes." Pete checked Dac's composure for permission to proceed. Go. "The Gap is radiating gravity waves. They are weak but they are very clear. They are probably associated with the oscillations of the Cubes on each end, but I'm not sure if the oscillations cause the waves or the waves cause the oscillations. Probably both, in a sort of resonance system."

"That's new but hardly surprising. All moving things generate gravity waves, don't they?"

"Yes, Mr. Olson, but most are so weak they are virtually undetectable," resumed Pete. "Our instruments are really geared more for rapidly orbiting binaries, for example, than little blocks of hydrogen like the Shaft. You know, prospecting applications. I wouldn't usually be able to detect them but out here in the Bubble there is practically no background clutter, we are very close to the source and the signals from the Thingy are exceptionally coherent and crisp. While they are very weak on an absolute scale, they are incredibly strong for the size of the object." Pete paused before taking his next leap.

"I think that is what the Thingy does; it makes waves," added Pete. "Or rather, it's an artificial gravity well whose operation generates waves."

"That's new," mused Dac. "And?"

"Well, and this is just a guess at this time, Mr. Olson," said Pete, protecting his butt, "I think the gravity waves are related to that hydrogen wind in the Gap and the hydrogen Wrapper."

"In what way? Are you saying the gravity emissions caused the wind?"

"Not exactly. Like I said, this is mostly a guess," again protectively, "but gravitons seem to be leaking from the Gap, and they propagate like any particle passing through a slit. I think the Thingy does something and the mechanism that does it generates the gravity waves as a by-product, like a machine giving off heat or noise. The Thingy might be intended to do just what it looks like it's doing, make hydrogen."

"Make hydrogen!! You mean making the hydrogen wind?" Dac had to stop and think about that.

"Why?" came to mind.

"Not a clue."

"How?"

"Well, we've looked at the possibility the hydrogen wind may be simply sublimating from the Cube itself but discounted it as upside down; where did the Cube come from in the first place and why." Pete paused for part two. "You know."

Yeah, Dac knew.

"There are only a few other possibilities. The first is the hydrogen wind was building the Cube somehow. That's consistent with Pappa's observation that the Cube is growing. The problem in that case is where does the hydrogen for the wind come from? The second possibility is the Cube manufactures the hydrogen somehow. Third, both."

"Both? Which both?"

"Well, the Cube makes hydrogen to build the Cube and building the Cube generates more hydrogen. Like a fast breeder reactor, or maybe more like a plant that uses chlorophyll to make its own food. I know that's pretty vague, but whatever the process is, it generates gravity waves." Pete squinted in apprehension. "That's just a guess, Mr. Olson."

"Good guessing, Pete. How about the rest of you? Comments?" Dac had noticed the others were conspicuously quiet during Pete's exposition.

Most of the crew had stopped their work and were listening intently to Pete's analysis. Pete was guessing here, admittedly, but he was a very sound scientist and his guesses had an uncanny pattern of validity.

"Gravity waves. And you say they're coherent?" Gerry Ast, Communications. "Could they be modulated, like some sort of signal? Maybe that's how the aliens are trying to communicate, either with us or somebody else. It would make a lot of sense because gravity waves propagate infinitely and nothing blocks them."

"I haven't looked into that, Gerry," replied Pete. "But that's a high probable. Let's get together on that."

"More?" prompted Dac.

"It may be a gravity well, but it was not strong enough to maintain the Wrapper," said Fats Bic. "Some other mechanism held the Wrapper in place and it was turned off. Or at least it stopped. The Wrapper field is gone but the gravity well is still there, so they must be the result of two different functions."

"That's true, Bic. Good. Conclusion?"

"…" Fats turned his palms and his eyeballs upward.

"More," said Dac. "We're on a roll here."

"Mike," said Mercedes Mead. "Didn't you say you found the pressure in the Gap was constant everywhere, even though the gas was moving outward and should have been losing pressure as it expanded?"

"Yes, that's right. No pressure variation at all."

"Well, the only way that could happen is if more gas were being introduced into the Gap as the gas expanded outward. Putting two and two together, the Cube must be generating that gas, just like Pete suggests."

"That sounds like a confirmation to me," confirmed Dac. "Any idea how it generates the hydrogen? Anyone?"

"Chirp."

"Let's hear it, Pappa."

"Based on your observations so far, there seems to be a reasonably valid working hypothesis: the hydrogen gas is assembled by the Cube in the Gap from its constituent subatomic particles."

"Can you be a little more specific, Pappa," coaxed Dac.

"A hydrogen atom is made up of an electron and a proton. Those particles are composed of an assortment of quarks and an infusion of energy. Perhaps the Cube facilitates the combination of these components into hydrogen."

"Okay, but that only begs the question, Pappa. Before: Where does the hydrogen comes from. Now: Where do the quarks come from?" Good question, that. From Dac.

"Of course, Mr. Olson," rejoined Pappa. "They come from nowhere is the only reasonable conclusion." Pappa seemed quite comfortable with nowhere as a reasonable conclusion.

"Of course," Dac looked helplessly at the crew.

"Mr. Olson," chimed in Mike Hand. "When I was in the Gap, at the dead center, I could feel the column where the gas radiated outward. I lived in that gas for a long time and I remember making that same statement to myself; the gas just seemed to come from nowhere and push itself out. I know that's intuitive at best, but Pappa's hypothesis rings true, it feels right."

"Okay," said Dac. "So the Cube takes quarks and stuff out of nowhere and makes hydrogen. Now can somebody tell me exactly where nowhere is?"

"Virtual particles!" said Ross Label suddenly, startling most, including himself. "The Cube makes hydrogen out of virtual particles before they get away!"

"Virtual particles?" From most of the crew, their sophistication in things physical reflected inversely in their level of surprise.

"Virtual particles?" Marcy.

"Virtual particles! Of course!" Mercedes.

"Virtual particles? What virtual particles?" Mike.

"Of course. Virtual particles." What in Hell's Textbooks are virtual particles? thought Dac, anxious to maintain his self respect, at least in his own mind. "Explain that, Ross."

"Sure," continued Ross with enthusiasm. "Quantum mechanics requires them. Particles pop into and out of existence constantly. The whole universe is a soup of virtual particles. More stuff than real particles! At least that's what I read."

"Quite right, Mr. Label," interjected Pappa, saving Ross just at his qualitative limit. "At any moment there is more matter in the form of virtual particles than in the real material with which we are familiar. The particles oscillate into and out of our realm so fast they have no impact we can detect at a macro level. However, they do play an important role in certain quantum reactions. The Thingy may harvest these particles, so to speak, and use them to make hydrogen out of nothing, for lack of a better term."

"All right," said Dac, still not convinced but willing to be open-minded. "When they disappear, where do they go? What's on the other side?"

"They go there," responded Marcy Phillips, on board now. "They come here and go back. Except when a Cube catches them, then they stay. I think Pete was right that the purpose of the Thingy is to make hydrogen, but we may need to be more subtle. The purpose of the Thingy may be to catch virtual particles to build itself. The fact that the particles also combine into gaseous hydrogen may be incidental, more or less by default. Or maybe it's simply the easiest method of many alternate ways to do it."

"I'm not sure I buy a word of this," said Dac dubiously. "This is a lot of speculation, and that's good mind you, that's what I want. But it's starting to sound like Alice in Wonderland. Can anyone give me something hard?"

"Chirp."

"Pappa, can you make sense of this?"

"Probably eventually. However, right now you may want to examine the Thingy on display, Mr. Olson. It is losing its structural integrity."

"It's what!?"

"It is falling apart!" interpreted Mercedes.

Everyone scrambled to their work stations in a flurry of flipped switches and visceral exclamations. Mike Hand's display was already tuned to Pappa and verified his assessment of the situation.

"Lordy. Now what!?" said Dac. "And I still haven't had my morning coffee."

The Gap had disappeared, that's what. Both ends, leaving a solid Shaft. As they watched in wonder, it was splitting lengthwise along the fracture lines Pappa had delineated and separating at the center, forming eight Thingettes identical in shape to the original Shaft but without Gaps. Pappa's bird cage drawings separated slowly, each spinning as the original Thingy.

"Chirp."

"Yes, Pappa!"

"We now have no practical orbit, Mr. Olson, or will shortly. We will drift in the general direction of galactic north. Your instructions?"

"Set a trajectory to follow the closest of the segments," ordered Dac. "Monitor the others as long as you can."

"Chi..."

"Now what!?"

Now what became obvious as Pappa refreshed the displayed bird cages with lines showing that each of the eight new Thingettes had fracture lines of their own, precisely dividing each into eight more subunits.

"Good lord!" Realization set in, "Pappa! How long until these, unh … offspring … split again into, whatever, 64ths?"

"That is difficult to predict, Mr. Olson. The data set is quite limited, that is, to only one event," replied Pappa. "I am reluctant to make a projection of any kind. I have no evidence that these one-eighth parts will also divide but the appearance of the same fracture lines as appeared on the original Shaft bodes another fracture cycle. The initial fracturing occurred less than an hour ago."

Dac wasn't sure why that was important, or for that matter what in Hell's Dictionary bode meant. He had a fight-or-flight reaction in his stomach that was too urgent to ignore. The replication of the Thingy was ominous, he imagined, even evil; it was about to take revenge on their insult. He couldn't take his eyes from the screen. Nor could anyone else.

"What's happening people! Everything's falling apart and I need to know which way to jump!" Pause for response. "Anytime."

"Mr. Olson?" Mead, Geology. "I think we broke it."

"Broke it!?" interrobanged Dac. "How could we break something that size? What are you thinking?"

"Well, maybe breaking is the wrong term," hedged Mercedes Mead. "I think our landing may have initiated some built-in breakup mechanism. Maybe a defense mechanism."

"Why do you say that, Mead?" That was a new thoughtline entirely, not to be discarded unexamined. "Go on."

"Well, in the first place, the breakdown of the Shaft is clearly too precise and orderly to be accidental," resumed Mercedes. "It didn't just shatter; the aliens intended that it come apart in that way. Secondly, there's not a chance in space the aliens knew when we'd be here to witness a planned breakup of the Shaft, and even less chance that it broke up randomly just when we were here. Our presence triggered it," concluded Mercedes.

"I was afraid someone would reach that same conclusion," replied Dac. "We broke it. Agreement?" A few nods.

"Disagreement?"

"Chirp."

"Yes, Pappa?"

"Mr. Olson, keep in mind that while this region of space is relatively empty, it is not totally so. The probability of a collision between the original Thingy and a piece of passing rock the size of the shuttle, for example, per 1,000 years is approximately 0.022 plus or minus 0.006."

"Twenty-two one-thousandths?" repeated Dac, struggling with his hyphenation. "That doesn't seem a likely chance of collision, does it?"

"That probability is highly significant in this context, Mr. Olson," opined Pappa in his mildly ingratiating tutorial but nonetheless irritatingly pedagogical mode. "The probability of one occurs at 45,454.55 years. The existence of ..."

"One?" inserted Dac in his tutoree mode. "One what?"

"A probability of one indicates dead certainty, Mr. Olson."

"You're telling me the Thingy will ... uh ... reproduce every forty-five thousand years?"

"Not at all, Mr. Olson. That is the probability of a shuttle-sized object striking a 500 kilometer long Thingy in 45,454.55 years. The observation that there are far fewer large objects floating in space than smaller, the probability of a larger object impacting the Thingy implies more years, for smaller objects fewer years. The amount of pulverized space debris suspended in the Ball probably confirms and is at least consistent with this estimate."

"Your point, Pappa?" probed Dac.

"It is extremely likely that the Shaft was hit violently many times by something far more intrusive than our landing on the Cube." Pappa paused for a reaction. Hearing none, he continued. "Given that our landing started a breakup, it seems reasonable that other more energetic encounters would have also initiated a breakup, assuming of course, that the Shaft was designed to break up in response to some intrusion as Associate Mead contends.

"Estimating the age of the Shaft by its observed growth rate," continued Pappa, "and given the probabilities of collision described, the shaft would have never had a chance to grow to the size we found. Therefore, I don't agree that we caused the breakup of the Shaft."

"Mead?"

"Pappa's reasoning is valid in terms of collisions," responded Mead immediately. "But as long as we're speculating, we might assume that the Wrapper was just that, a wrapper to protect the Shaft against the vast bulk of collisions that might break up the Shaft, and the Ball was a further mechanism to grind space debris into a second echelon defense," explained Mercedes.

"Whether or not that shielding effect was by design, that is the practical effect. I'd compare it to the tough skin on any live critter and the protective outer shielding on almost everything we make, from toasters to spaceships. The danger of collision would be greatly minimized and the growth potential enhanced proportionately.

"Another flaw in Pappa's reasoning," she continued, "is his assumption the Shaft would break up only in response to some mechanical intrusion. What if instead the shaft was set to break up in the presence of something indicating intelligent life, like radar, radio, EPR or X-ray radiation? Or any and all of the above? Or, for that matter, like walking right on through the thing?"

"Pappa?"

"I must concede all of Mead's points without ceding any of mine, Mr. Olson. It seems likely we were instrumental in the breakup, at least to the extent of its timing."

"That sounds like a qualification, Pappa," said Dac. "Amplify."

"It's obvious the breakup mechanism was designed into the Shaft. Therefore the Shaft would probably have broken up eventually upon any of a variety of predetermined triggers. Our intrusion probably had no impact as to whether it would break up, only when."

"Mead?"

"Agreed."

"Conclusions?"

"The Wrapper was just that, Mr. Olson," said Fats Bic. "Whatever the Wrapper and Ball were, they were no longer needed and were sloughed off. They may have been simply incidental to the Thingy and were released incidentally." Bic hesitated with a low 'unhh' to hold his place. He had more to say.

"Feel free to speak, Bic," encouraged Dac. "I want every idea right now."

"It might sound sorta' dumb, but if the Shaft was alive, I'd say it was molting. Or ... or reproducing."

"Reproducing!?"

Virtually everyone on the flight deck looked up at Edward Fats Bic, Associate, Meteorology. The possibility that the Thingy itself was alive had not been seriously considered and they struggled to consider it now. They had conformed, nominally, to corporate regs against intruding on an alien life form and put the matter out of mind in their excitement to explore the Thingy.

"Biology! Comment?"

"It may be reproducing but that's pure speculation at this point. I can guarantee it's not alive, Mr. Olson. Sir!" A little professional defensiveness there.

"Take it easy Ross," replied Dac mildly. Everyone's keyed up, he thought, and I am too. But there's no immediate danger and there's no need to let emotions interfere with brains. "Take it easy everyone. Right now it's just a big board game and we're trying to figure out who shot the butler. Okay?" That helped.

"Okay, Fats, what makes you think it's reproducing?" Dac used Bic's nick name deliberately to ease off the formality and encourage a little speculation.

"I know biology's not my field, but it's obvious that everything about the Thingy is deliberate." Bic paused to organize his thoughts. "Those fracture lines were not random; they're very precise, by design. Pappa says the Cube is going to fracture again, probably along those lines, and you have sixty-four smaller parts where there was one big one.

"We don't know what it is, but the Cube is obviously doing something," he continued, "and the small parts will probably do the same thing, or something else, but it's not likely the parts will do nothing. So you have small parts of the Cube that can do what the big one does. Did. That sounds like reproduction. At least in the Penrose tiles sense." Bic finished and looked wide-eyed at Dac, awaiting his fate.

"That's good, Bic," said Dac after a moment. "That's good. Don't know if it's right or not but I want to find out. There are lots of non-alive things that reproduce after a fashion. Viruses come to mind. Dust bunnies. Politicians. Maybe this one's just bigger than most. Biology, is that thing alive?"

"In a sense Bic could be right," responded Ross Label, "but I don't think life is a factor. The high degree of order associated with the Thingy indicates a deliberate program is at work. Life though? There's a big difference between reproduction and life. Any accepted definition of life requires some form of metabolism, sentience, growth, movement, memory, learning and adaptability in addition to simple reproduction by fissure. There are no signs of any of those other abilities on the Cube. Even if it fractures into neat little Thingettes, it may mean no more than simple entropy; it's falling apart, decomposing, unraveling. But I'm open on this. Criminitly, we're writing the book on this! Anything's *possible*."

"Thank you, Ross," checked Dac. Criminitly? "Rebuttals?"

The crew looked at each other blankly. Finally, finding no one would champion his position for him, Bic rejoined the fray.

"Okay," he said with a deep breath, "First of all, the metabolism. We can't expect aliens to breathe air like we do and eat steaks and veggies, so we can't expect our brand of metabolism. However, the Thingy is acquiring mass from its environment, like all creatures that grow by metabolizing ingested solid, liquid and gaseous matter. Some lichens even eat rock. The thing sure seems to be exhaling, or eliminating or flatulating or something.

"Sentience? We just decided that it chose this particular time to fracture, probably as a direct result of our contact. Movement? They sure move, and they seem to have a will of their own, or at least they don't move the way we would expect inert objects to move under the sway of classical Newtonian physics. Adaptability. Who knows; we sure don't know yet. But if the Thingy reacted to our presence we can reasonably assume it will adapt to it, in a way that it, not us, feels is successful. Maybe what they're doing now is adapting.

"I think all of the requirements for life are present," concluded Bic, "at least nominally. We should therefore assume it is alive rather than assume it isn't."

"Ross?"

"That could be a tentative default position," said Ross, "as a basis for decision-making. However, I think that's reaching a bit. A lot. It's not alive. Period."

"All right," said Dac. "Include the possibility of life as one of the valid alternatives in all of your work, until proven otherwise," directed Dac. "We don't know what we have here, people, so we don't know who's going to be the expert. Don't worry about stepping out of your field to pursue an idea. We need a little synergy on this. Whatever that fool word is.

"Keep in mind," Dac continued, "until we determine the Thingy is alive, assume that it is artifact, a thing that was made by something else. Its makers were certainly alive. Like any artifact, the Cube reveals the intent of its makers. The more we know about the Cube the more we know about the aliens themselves. Pursue every line of thought as far as it takes you. All of you. There are no dumb ideas."

"Anyone else?" he urged. "If not, then, let's get back to work on it. Whatever the mechanism, it seems we probably broke it somehow. I still want to get ..."

"Incoming, Mr. Olson," broke in Gerry Ast, Communications. "It's HO. They say to observe, repeat observe only and send a full status report. Plus ancillaries and coordinates, et cetera. A BE party will arrive in approximately 7,200 hours. That's, uh, about ten clock months, humping it."

"Great!" cried Dac in mock despair as he watched the eight Shafts break into 64 Shafts. "We just broke the damned thing and they want a status report! By the time they get here there won't be anything left!" Resigned pause. "Pappa, how long did that second division take?"

"Thirty-two minutes, Mr. Olson."

CHAPTER 17

DUST

"Thirty-two!?" Thirty-two? Hell's Litter! "Projection, Pappa!"

"At that division rate?" asked Pappa, effortlessly unperturbed.

"Yes," replied Dac, valiantly trying to also remain unperturbed in spite of this jarring realization.

"Assume that the Thingys will continue to fracture without a lower limit to their size?" narrowed Pappa.

"Yes," said Dac after a moment. "I want a profile on this."

"The cloud of Thingys will be effectively invisible in 13 hours and some. It will be transparent in a slightly greater period but this is very tentative, depending on whether the reflective qualities remain constant, our aspect angle, a few other …"

"What do you mean by effectively transparent?" asked Pete Bravo.

"At the present rate, the Thingys will be approximately 0.4657 millimeters long in about 14 more hours. Dispersal will average approximately one thousand Thingys per cubic kilometer at that time, making radar minimally effective and occlusion chancy. There is almost no ambient light here and the Thingys do not reflect what little light there is. They will be extremely difficult to see, Mr. Bravo."

"Fourteen hours!?" remarked Fats Bic. "That thing's 500 kilometers long! It will take centuries to break it down to a half centimeter."

"One-half millimeter, Mr. Bic. To be exact 0.4657 milimeter," repeated Pappa. "That should occur in 15.33 hours from the first division, about fourteen hours from now. Again assuming …"

"Hell's Math! That can't be right!" sputtered Dac, then adding plaintively, "*Can* it?"

"At a constant rate of 32 minutes per fission cycle, including the cycles completed, there will be thirty fissions in 15.33 hours, each multiplying the number of Thingys by eight and dividing their length by two. Two to the thirtieth power is just over one billion. 500 kilometers is 500 million millimeters. 500 million millimeters divided by just over one billion is just under one half millimeter. That's conservative, Mr. Bic."

"Conservative?" reflected Mike Hand. "You mean it could break down faster than that?"

"Yes, Mr. Hand, or more slowly depending on the cycle time. Keep in mind that is a very rough guess, assuming that ..."

"But it might stop dividing?" rejoined Mike.

"Yes, Mr. Hand, it might stop," conceded Pappa. "However, there is no evidence that it will stop and considerable evidence that it will continue to break down. In fact, if you check your displays you will note that it is already doing so, slightly more quickly than the previous cycle. I'll update each cycle if that will be satisfactory."

"This is going to look really good," mumbled Dac. "We find the first alien artifact in the known universe. Not just the first alien artifact, one absolutely gigantic, monstrous, un-loseable 500 kilometer long artifact. And we lose it. *I* lose it." Dac paused for a moment and added, "Anybody wanna be a vice president?"

"We haven't lost it yet, Mr. Olson," said Fats Bic. "In fact, this might work out even better than we could have hoped."

All eyes were on Fats, in disbelief.

"Unh," coughed Bic, embarrassed. "Well, it would be pretty hard to take the whole Thingy, Ball and Wrapper and all into town for analysis. Even if we could, we wouldn't because we don't know what it is or what it would do in captivity. And we probably shouldn't even if we could: it isn't ours, after all."

"So?"

"So now there are a billion of them, or will be, and once they're small enough to fit in a bread box, we can take as many home as we like. BE can have a bunch to play with to their heart's content. Nobody will miss 'em."

Dac brightened. Everybody brightened.

"Boit." Mamma, however, quickly interrupted.

"Yes, Mamma?"

"Over my dead body!" responded Mamma emphatically as well as metaphorically.

"Excuse me?" Dac startled at Mamma's uncharacteristically abrupt contrariness.

"You're not bringing those Thingys into my ship without complete BE clearance," clarified Momma quite necessarily. "Who knows what they've been into or what they'll get into."

"Yes, of course, Mamma," relented Dac with a smile. Then, thoughtfully to the others, "Mamma has a good point. How *do* we know what they've been into? Or up to. We have to be sure they're safe, and when it comes to a Thingy, we don't know what safe is."

"Biology and Geology, work with Pappa on that," Dac commanded. He thought for another moment and added, "Assuming they're safe, and assuming we decide to take a few along, how do we do that? Ideas?"

"What will we need to maintain a safe environment for it, if environment is the right word?" volunteered Mercedes. "Safe in both directions. Apparently its environment is empty space; could we just strap it to the outside, or tow it? That would keep Mamma happy."

"Yes it would, Mercedes," agreed Mamma. "Thank you."

"How do we contain it if it keeps on dividing into microscopic dust? Maybe we'd have to give the BE guys a vacuum sweeper." Mike Hand was only partly joking.

"Or for that matter," jumped in Marcy, "what if it's in containment and all that metallic hydrogen evaporates catastrophically? It could blow the place apart from the evaporative pressure alone. And if that gas ignited ... Wow!"

"All good points. Thank you for sharing." Dac hesitated a moment to re-evaluate his decision to lasso a Thingy. It still seemed like the only viable option from a corporate standpoint, so he continued. "Geology and Meteorology, I want you to get on that, too. Get engineering involved, figure out the contingencies, what we'll need, and make it happen. Just in case. Pappa?"

"Chirp."

"I want you to work with Fielding and Hand to track those Thingys. Keep us within hailing distance. Maintain observation on a reasonable segment of the cloud and track the dissipation of the rest." Dac paused to choose words for his rationalization.

"BE won't be here for nearly a year; the Thingys may be long gone by then. The only proof will be the ones we catch so be prepared to contain a sample and bring it on board if necessary." Dac considered for a moment. "We'll capture one if the length of the Thingy drops below, say, one meter. How long will that take, Pappa?"

"The length should be less than one meter in a bit over seven hours," said Pappa with an audible wince. Then he added almost apologetically, "The division rate is accelerating slightly, Mr. Olson."

"Seven hours!?" From pretty much everyone, followed by a few groans.

"And some," corrected Pappa. "Given that ..."

"No time for givens, Pappa. Let's make it happen!" More privately, "Snoon."

"Sqweet."

"What do you make of all this, Marcy?" mumbled Dac absently, snuggling inconspicuously to restore circulation in his left arm. "Do you have a feeling one way or another?"

"About what?" replied Marcy, alarmed. "About us!?"

"Oh, No! No," returned Dac, perhaps a bit too quickly for good taste, considering the circumstances. "I mean the Thingys. What do you think is going on?"

"The Thingys? Oh, right," said Marcy, relieved. "I thought you were starting in on ... Never mind." Pause. "I don't have strong feelings, Dac. Thingys are just that, things, so I haven't gotten emotionally involved. They are extremely interesting technically and historically of course. I'm as excited as anybody about what the deal is but I really don't have a feeling, as you put it." Snuggle. "But I think it's troubling you. Want to let me in on it?" Snuggle.

"I guess you're right," replied Dac. "Well, no, that's not right. It doesn't trouble me, it bothers the Hell out of me. It *really* bothers the Hell out of me. I think they're basically evil."

"Evil?" reflected Marcy. "It's just a thing, how can it be evil?"

"You know what I mean. Sure, the Thingy is probably just a machine, and at heart it's probably just a very good-natured simple-minded machine." Dac paused to pull his thought together. "But the whys scare me. Why is it there, why is it making hydrogen? Why was it growing and now why is it breaking up? Why did the aliens make it? What's going to be the ultimate result and do we care, or need to care?"

"Whew!" whistled Marcy. "I'd *say* you have some feelings on this. I think everyone is thinking the same thoughts, Dac. Good Lord, it's the biggest event ever, how could you not think about it? Is this starting to, you know, affect you somehow?"

"No. I guess I just ..." Dac broke off to pense a while, enjoying the comfort. Presently, "Did you ever wonder about what's left after we're gone?"

"Nice segue," said Marcy, sitting up to get a clear view of Dac's face. "Now you're into death? You really know how to put a girl in a romantic mood."

"Death? Ah!" said Dac with a chuckle. "No, I don't mean us, you and me, being dead. I mean everybody, civilization, our culture, 473 worlds or whatever it is now. It won't last forever, you know."

"Nothing lasts forever. Is there something here I'm missing?"

"Just thinking," thought Dac. "You know about the Big Bang, don't you?"

Marcy looked at Dac, apprehensively. "I thought we just ..."

"I mean the origin of the universe," explained Dac quickly, keeping an eye on Marcy. "The expanding universe? Inflation theory? Any of this sound familiar?"

"Oh, right," said Marcy with mock relief. "Sorry. I was still working on the afterglow."

"No, I'm the one who should be sorry." Snuggle. "It's just that damned Thingy. I keep getting the feeling there's something cosmic and sinister about it. Something with eternal implications. Know what I mean?"

"Yeah," murmured Marcy Phillips, Electronics Engineer. "You need a little less theory and a little more inflation."

✦ ✦ ✦

Geology, Biology, Mechanical and Jason Fielding bumbled into Dac's small office to report on their plans to capture a Thingy. Jason sat in the only other chair, Mike Hand stood opposite, with Mead and Label tucked in behind. Jason shuffled a sheaf of papers while Ross Label cleared his throat.

"Let's hear it. Who's first, Jason?"

"The Thingys," began Jason, "continue to divide at about the original rate, Mr. Olson, in fact, a little faster each division. It's been five hours since the first division and they're down to less than 500 meters long now, with no sign of stopping. There are over one billion of them, all over the place. They are dispersing rapidly, far more quickly than the original angular momentum would allow. They are self-propelled somehow, or mutually repulsive. At any rate, we're moving alongside a small cluster of a few thousand that seem to be headed somewhere. We have notified HO and the incoming BE of rendezvous coordinates."

"A billion!? Already?" exclaimed Dac. "I thought there wouldn't be that many until, what, at least sixteen hours. Pappa!"

"Chirp."

"Straighten me out on this, Pappa."

"You're confusing the effect of the Thingy's division on the number of Thingys with the effect on the length of the Thingys. There have been ten divisions so far. At each fission, each Thingy divides into eight new Thingys." Pappa paused for a reaction. Getting none, he continued. "Eight to the tenth power is just over a billion Thingys."

"However, at each division the length of the Thingy is divided by two. Two to the tenth power is just over 1,000, and one thousandth of 500 kilometers is 500 meters."

"Got it," said Dac, who really did get it. "How many will there be when they get down to one meter long?"

"Pappa?" pleaded Jason.

"Chirp. 144,115,180,000,000,000. Chirp."

"A hundred quadrillion!?" Generalized stunned disbelief.

"Chirp. Actually, Mr. Fielding, 144,115 ..."

"Okay. Okay. A bunch," concluded Dac. "Go on, Jason. How are you going to lasso those things?"

"We knocked around a few ideas and we always came to the same point; the Thingys, no matter how small, are too dangerous to bring inside the ship."

"Dangerous? How is that?"

"We have no idea how far they will divide," replied Jason. "We have seen nothing to indicate a lower limit on their size so we have to assume they could eventually get to be microscopic. The last thing we need on the ship is a few hundred billion microscopic alien machines. Even if they were completely inert and benign, they could raise havoc just by getting into the works. They could even be poisonous if inhaled."

"Or explosive," added Mike. "Imagine a dispersion of microscopic crystals of metallic hydrogen in our oxygen atmosphere! Even if they didn't explode chemically as crystals, they could all vaporize simultaneously with the same results. And then explode as hydrogen gas!"

"Is it possible," said Mercedes, "that is what the Thingy is designed to do? Maybe it's a weapon of some sort, a bomb. It disperses, infiltrates, and then explodes or contaminates or infects."

"To what end?" asked Ross. "It would be a great weapon in the right military situation but we're not at war. Are we?" Ross got a variety of really apprehensive looks at that observation. "I mean, maybe they could be used to clear a planet for development. Or as a defensive device against an invasive species. Oops."

"You mean like us, for example," concluded Jason. "My guess is that you're probably right."

A shrug from Mercedes and nothing from anyone else.

"Okay, good safety rule," agreed Dac to get back on track. "No Thingys on board."

"Boit! Thank you," said Mamma gratefully.

"Yes. Well, the trick," continued Jason, "will be to put one in a container that will maintain a space-like atmosphere, if you'll excuse the oxymoron, and contain them if they continue to break down to microscopic size."

"Such as?"

"We need something big enough to hold a dozen Thingys with mobility to catch them, windows for observation and hermetic sealing to prevent contamination. The only thing like that on board is the shuttle or one of the escape pods."

"Contamination?"

"Yes, in both directions. We may have broken the first one. We don't want to break any more or change any properties until they are studied completely. On the flip side, we don't want microscopic alien artifacts getting into the ship's innards. Period. A pod makes the most sense, cold and evacuated, of course. We can assume a pod is available?"

"Available?" Dac looked from face to face. "You mean expendable, don't you?"

"Unnh... Yeah, I guess." Sheepishly. Jason was rarely sheepish about anything except maybe women. "But only if absolutely necessary."

"And who decides on this alleged necessity?"

"You do, Mr. Olson. Absolutely!"

Dac carefully considered how to explain to corporate the loss of not only the Thingy but also a near-new and unused first-class Associated Safety Systems Survival Pod, SKU 378583-77. And whether he wanted to take the personal financial hit since its loss would come directly out of this voyage's bottom line.

"Okay. Agreed. But just one. What else?"

"We have stripped a pod of all non-essential gear and padded any sharp corners that might provoke a Thingy. We ..."

"Wait a minute!" Dac interrupted. "I thought I heard you say, and I quote, 'We *have stripped*'" That's past perfect tense, isn't it" He wasn't sure about the past perfect bit but nobody was willing to challenge the point. "That sounds a little presumptuous to me. How does that sound to you?"

"Presumptuous! Mr. Olson, Sir!" In unison. Dac had to admire them for *something* at that. Chutzpah came to mind.

"Proceed." Dac wasn't sure about proceeding but he was already all in.

"Unnh ... We'll capture Thingys by pushing the pod attached to the shuttle," resumed Jason. "Pappa will monitor the fission cycles and set a trajectory to intercept them as soon as they divide so we'll have the full 30 minutes to chase them. After that the Pod will be mounted on brackets being installed on the aft hull, at the end of standoffs 100 meters long."

"Good, I think," said Dac. "You have three more hours to get ready. Will that be enough?"

"Yes, I think so. There is one thing, Mr. Olson."

"That is?"

"Once we catch them ... Uh ... what do we do with them?"

"Lordy! Jason! Who knows!? I sure don't know," grinned Dac. "Do you know? We'll let HO worry about that. I can tell you one thing; I'm not going to lose them. I don't want to be caught empty-handed when BE arrives. Once they take over it's their problem. Just make sure you don't lose them, Jason, or it will be your problem, too. Biology?"

Ross Label jumped to attention, fumbled for his notes and shouldered his way around Mike Hand who struggled to leave with Jason Fielding.

"No, stay," said Dac. "I want everybody to know who's doing what to who." Whom? Hell's Syntax! "Ross?"

"This should be short, Mr. Olson," began Ross Label, Biology. "There are still no signs of any biological activity of any sort. We are tracking a cluster of Thingys that Pappa selected. He worked their trajectories backward and found Thingys that came from the center of the Shaft so they weren't contaminated by us, the junk in the Ball, or anything else."

"Good thinking, Ross." It was. "And all of these Thingys are identical? There is no internal structure coming to the surface as they divide?"

"Good question, Mr. Olson." Corporate kissass has its purposes, thought Jason, grudgingly. "No. Either there is no internal structure, or it is reorganized before splitting so that nothing is exposed. I suspect the latter but there are no observations to support that."

"Go on."

"Since we won't be bringing anything on board," Ross asserted, "the risk of contamination will be minimal. We have been over the shuttle any number of times since we returned and have found nothing. And I mean nothing. If anything was going to grow it would have by now. Every external surface of the shuttle is completely sterile.

"To be certain," Ross continued, "no person will actually touch a Thingy, and anything that does will be jettisoned. We will use standard sanitation procedures on all EVAs. We'll abandon the pod to BE unopened. Biological hazards are their specialty. I don't think there will be any sort of contamination problem. In fact," paused Ross, distracted a little, "even my pressure suit is completely clean. The one I took a bath in."

"A bath?" said Dac, puzzled.

"Yes. When I fell into the Ball. The Ball was nothing but super fine space dust. It should have clung to the suit like talcum powder, or at least gotten wedged into cracks and places. But the suit was completely clean. I imagine it was some electrostatic process, but it's still a little preternatural."

"Preternatural?" straight-manned Dac.

"Well, extraordinary then. Whatever, we don't need to worry about contamination."

"I see," replied Dac. He didn't. "Anything else? Mead?"

"We managed to collect some of the dust from the Ball," said Mercedes Mead, holding up a stoppered vial. "Ross is right. This stuff won't stick to anything. As you can see, it's still in suspension, it doesn't settle out at all. I centrifuged it and it sprang right back into suspension. Spectral analysis shows nothing but space junk, mostly rock with a smattering of iron, water, ammonia, methane, standard space stuff in standard space proportions. I'm certain that it is not really part of the Thingy. The aggregate is extraordinary, however."

"Extraordinary? How so?"

"Well, preternatural actually," replied Mead with a straight face. "Each particle of dust is a perfect sphere, and all of the spheres are exactly the same size except for a small percentage that is extremely irregular. Those may be new infusions that had not yet been, uh, processed. The entrained gases don't sublimate at laboratory temperature, which is impossible. Those spheres should be exploding like popcorn, just like a comet approaching the sun, but they don't. Everything has been thoroughly impacted somehow, and the result is permanent. So far."

"Any ideas as to how, or to what purpose, Mercedes?" asked Dac.

"No, not really, Mr. Olson. They remind me mostly of hairballs. They are probably just an accident of whatever sustains the Ball itself."

"Hairballs?" prompted Dac with a straight face, deliberately setting himself up.

"Yeah, hairballs." No punch line.

"Well, that's all good," said Dac after an embarrassed moment. "Good work." Dac checked his watch. "We have about three hours so take advantage of it. Down shift."

The crew left one by one as they wrapped up their work for the night. Dac lingered behind to catch up on some work undisturbed. He turned to his desk, kicked off his shoes, sorted a few things and settled down to his reports for HO and BE. "This will be good," he thought as he picked up the stylus. "They'll come charging out here to find the greatest discovery of all time and I'm going to hand them a pod full of dust. Why does this have to happen to me? I never ..."

"Chirp."

"Yes, Pappa," said Dac, dropping the stylus with resignation.

"I have new information you may find interesting, Mr. Olson."

"Oh?" Pappa's propensity for understatement was legend and Dac's nap hair bristled. "I'm very busy, Pappa. Is this important?"

"Yes, it is, Mr. Olson. The Thingys are not here."

CHAPTER 18

DROPOUTS

"They're gone?"

Dac leaped from his desk to the console in the center of his office. Stocking footed as he was in his leisure, he skidded on past and bumped his swivel chair. The chair swiveled about and bumped him in the behind. He didn't notice.

"Where did they ...!"

Dac stopped mid-thought as he realized the console still displayed a cluster of Thingys spinning merrily off the port warehouses. He checked the clock to verify real time mode and adjusted the display pointlessly. Range? Nominal. All within one hundred kilometers.

"Hell's Bits and Bytes!" Dac relaxed enough to swear at Pappa, who probably deserved it this time. "Don't do that to me, Pappa! I almost passed my stomach!" Dac took a few moments to subside. Then, somewhat more professionally, "What are you talking about, Pappa. They're right there!"

"Actually, Mr. Olson, those are only illustrations based on ..."

"Pappa! I know what they are!" Dac took a breath to reign in his irritation. "You put those drawings there and now you say they aren't there. Who's right?"

"Neither," responded Pappa after a moment to sort out his role in Dac's question. "The illustration is a one-to-one mapping of the physical characteristics of the Thingys and accurately depicts the data our sensors pick up, within the range of precision indicated on the display. However ..." Pappa paused, long enough for Dac to pick up on the pausal undertow.

Pappa rarely paused, and then only when caught between a culpable lack of information and an irreconcilable mandate. Dac, who was rapidly losing patience with the tin man, recognized the dilemma, reversed himself instantly and tuned in to Pappa's uncertainty.

"However?" A mild socialized coded prompt that tripped a few of Pappa's social chips. Dac could almost hear Pappa's relief.

"They are not gone, Mr. Olson. They are not *here*. At least they are not here in the sense the word usually means. I do not know what to make of it, but something strange emerged as I analyzed the records since the Thingy was first discovered. It is standard procedure to consolidate data for compression and storage. There were a few ... anomalies."

Pappa didn't pause; he stopped, evidenced by the complete absence of the irritatingly buzzy carrier wave in the aging speaker. Dac understood that Pappa needed authorization to speculate if necessary.

"*Everything* is strange, Pappa," soothed Dac. Pappa's human emulators would respond to certain formula expressions of human empathy and adjust Pappa's fuzzy logic several clicks toward loose. "Don't worry about making a mistake, Pappa. I want to hear all of your ideas."

"Thank you, Mr. Olson," replied Pappa, sincerely. "I am embarrassed I didn't identify this earlier, but the data is obscure and contradictory. As you know, radar and light frequencies barely reflect from the Thingys when they should have reflected off the flat metallic hydrogen as if from a mirror. I was trying to determine why I could not see the Cube when we first approached the Thingy. Optics could see it but I could not, until I found an extremely high frequency of radiation that would illuminate the Cube.

"I finally analyzed the returning photon stream itself, to see what I was missing," said Pappa. "Perhaps ... I don't know what I was looking for." Pause. "It is extremely difficult to speculate on the basis of the limited data I have at my disposal, Mr. Olson."

Pappa was in genuine agony at his perplexity, but it wasn't an emotional reaction. Pappa's responsibility was reliable information and he could not function below a given confidence level without administrative release. Dac intervened to loosen Pappa a little more and cut the recorders with a flourish.

"This is not on record, Pappa, NORDO-58 . Okay?"

"Yes, Mr. Olson. Thank you. The reflected photons had been processed somehow. They were received at a far lower energy, which is why they were not being detected. The Thingy was effectively converting them to a far lower frequency."

"That's not too strange," responded Dac mildly. "I'm a long shot from being a physicist, but most substances absorb photons and emit them at a different frequency." Then he added doubtfully. "Don't they?"

"Yes, that is largely true," affirmed Pappa. "The strange part is in this case not all of them are reflected or re-emitted. There is a seemingly irregular pattern of dropouts, very brief intervals in which no photons are reflected at all. The returning intermittent pattern of photons is interpreted by System Analyticals as being a much lower frequency, although a modulated one."

"Can you be a little more specific?" coached Dac. He had a thrill-ish feeling he really needed to know what was coming.

"We sent a continuous stream of radiation at one frequency," translated Pappa, "but we received a modulated stream at a different frequency. Individual photons are reduced in energy and the photon stream itself seems to be modulated."

"Modulated? You mean like a radio signal!?"

"That is a close analogy. However, the modulation is more like telemetry than radio, an intermittent stream of bits like a very discrete on-off digital transmission rather than a continuously variable composite of sine waves."

"You mean it's talking," Dac almost choked. "To us!? What in Hell's DJ is it saying?"

"I am not sure it is saying anything, Mr. Olson," replied Pappa, "and certainly not to us. I wanted to clear this with you first. Further investigation would involve extensive work by others of the crew and that is your responsibility. I did not want to unnecessarily divert the crew to possibly unprofitable activity."

"Unnecess ...?" Dac started. "Hell's Pups, I'm getting everyone on this. Now!" Pause. "Nice work, Pappa. Don't worry about a thing. That was great work!"

It was, indeed.

"Thank you, Mr. Olson."

Sputt. "... SHUNS!" Sputt.

"Christomity!" expleted Gerry Ast. She bounced forward in her chair and jabbed for the volume control in one jerk. Coffee splashed over the dinner she had just set out fresh and hot after a long watch and instantly rendered her newspaper limp and transparent. "Dammitall!"

"Communications! Ast, are you there!" It was Dac Olson, apparently out of control. Again. Now what? "Get down here immediately!"

"Where's here, Mr. Olson?" muttered Gerry as she fumbled for a rag. "I'm a little busy right this second."

"Get down to Conference XII, Ast! Grab everyone you see. Drop everything!"

"Got that part right!" mumbled Gerry as she mopped the table. She shoved the sodden mess into the wastebasket, mug and all, took a few quick swipes at the visible and/or sticky stuff and headed for the door. In the corridor Gerry bounced off the commotion heading for Conference XII.

"He must have called down everyone except Maintenance," said Ross Label in passing.

"What?" answered Freddie Meyer, Maintenance.

"Never mind." Ross.

"God bless the Federation!" Somebody. "Now what!?"

"Man! I was just getting ..."

"Where's my shoe? I lost my shoe!"

The mob crunched around a few corners and through the narrow doorway to find a place in Conference XII. Twelve crewones were crammed into a room built for a comfortable five or a tight ten. A few sat but stood to take up less room. General but professional hubbub.

Gerry Ast noticed most were also in various states of undress or ununiform under the same urgency. Dac stood to one side of the large display panel, intent on a scroll of printouts. The last crewone squeezed in and the racket settled expectantly. Dac's excitement was visible.

"That's everyone?" surveyed Dac to no one in particular. "We can get started. Pappa has come up with some ideas, some extremely important ideas, and I want all of you involved. Pappa, tell everyone what you just told me. Don't leave anything out and don't be afraid to speculate."

ing.

Pappa left nothing out. Fortified by Dac's earlier encouragement, Pappa had reorganized his thoughts and presented them to the crew without his previous hesitation. He reviewed his discovery of the modulation in the radar echoes, the intermittent dropouts in the reflected radiation, the high-frequency component wave form, everything. Nice visuals too, supported by references to current research into each aspect of his findings. Pappa finished, the blank screen reflecting the stunned faces of the crew.

"Questions?"

The crew, stunned and struggling to assimilate Pappa's revelations, was slow to react. Finally, Marcy Phillips, Electronics, put her thoughts together.

"Yes!" said Marcy. "Can you describe the wave form?"

"It is a perfect square wave form, Marcy," replied Pappa, Dac's previous loosening of protocol evident. "The positive phase is perfectly flat, as is the zero phase. There is no negative phase."

"It can be parsed into at least two components," continued Pappa. "One is an absolutely regular dropout of the radiation. It turns on and off at perfectly regular intervals, on the order of ten to the 46th Hz."

"That's an odd frequency, Pappa" Marcy follow-upped. "How did you find that?"

"I examined this frequency because it matches the oscillation rate of the gravity waves observed earlier," responded Pappa. "It is one of several million I have examined so far. There may be other ..."

"What exactly do you mean by dropout, Pappa?" asked Marcy.

"The reflected radiation stops instantly completely and cleanly," responded Pappa, "then starts cleanly, instantly. Some reflections are on the order of only two or three photons. The intervening zero phases are not reflection components but rather a complete absence of any reflection at all."

"Which Thingy is it coming from now?" asked Pete Bravo, Survey.

"Why, from all of them," replied Pappa incontrovertibly. "The reflections are perfectly coherent in that respect, Pete. All of the radiation from every one of the Thingys start and stop simultaneously."

"You mean they're coordinating with each other!" remarked Pete. "They're talking to each other?"

"I said nothing of the kind," stated Pappa flatly, obviously stating what was, to Pappa, the obvious. He conveyed a mildly indulgent surprise by a certain impatient tininess. "They are doing whatever it is they do simultaneously, just as they fracture simultaneously according to some program. Execution of the program is apparently extremely precise, but its simultaneity does not necessarily imply coordination, much less speech."

"Oh."

General thoughtfulness while each reviewed hisser next question to minimize their own exposure to ridicule.

"Let me get something straight," interjected Dac to get things going again. "It sounds like we're talking about two different things here. You say the frequency of dropouts in the reflected radiation is the same as the frequency of oscillation of the Thingys. And ... unh ... three things, the same as the frequency of the gravity waves. Do I have that right?"

"Quite so, Mr. Olson." There were limits to Pappa's relaxed formalities. "It makes sense that the gravity waves and the oscillation of the Thingy should correspond, but the dropouts would not be expected to match. They would be expected to vary in frequency with the oscillations; that is the basis of all simple Doppler effects."

"But you're not talking about Doppler effects. You're talking about complete dropouts." Marcy.

"Yes."

"And?" she encouraged.

"I tried to compile a theory to describe some manner of oscillation or movement that would generate gravity waves and reflected dropouts at the same time. The problem is that the Thingy's gravity waves are quite strong. Because gravitational force is extremely weak, this implies the involvement of considerable mass, which in turn makes the extremely high frequency unlikely. In addition, movement of mass would induce a Dopplered frequency variation, not intermittency.

"On the other hand, a mechanism that produced complete dropouts, such as turning the surface reflectivity of the Thingy on and off, probably wouldn't generate gravity waves because there is no need for large scale mass movement, only surface fluctuation."

"And?" continued Marcy persistently.

"There are only a few possibilities. The first is that the oscillations that cause the gravity waves somehow also cause simultaneous changes in reflectivity, but I have no idea as to the mechanism, nor any evidence. A second possibility is that some third system causes both, again with no evidence or clue to the existence or nature of the device. But there is another ..." Pappa hesitated meaningfully.

"Go on, Pappa," urged Dac after an unusually long moment.

"Gravity waves can be caused by movement of mass relative to the observer," continued an obviously relieved Pappa. "At least all observed natural sources of gravity waves are of this sort. Theoretically, however, they could also be caused by the instantaneous creation or destruction of mass, with no relative movement necessary. Theoretically, I emphasize, gravity waves of this sort have never been observed outside of the laboratory."

"Until now, I take it?" concluded Dac.

"Until now," repeated Pappa. "Intermittent existence of mass is only a theoretical explanation. That is why I was reluctant to speculate in the first place; it is one thing to state a null hypothesis and quite another to prove it.

"There is other supporting evidence, however," continued Pappa. "I described the nature of the photons that are reflected and the existence of the high-frequency dropouts. We have not discussed what the dropouts themselves consist of." Pappa paused for evidence of understanding.

"Wait a minute," said Marcy after a moment of understanding. "If there's nothing in the dropouts, what can they consist of?"

"I said there is no reflected radiation in the dropouts, Marcy. I did not say there was nothing in the dropouts."

"If I hear you right," suggested Gerry Ast, "you're suggesting the gaps in the reflection, non-reflections if you will, have, uh, reflections?" Ast wasn't sure what she said either.

"Yes, Gerry." Pappa was deliberately allowing the crew to sort things out one step at a time. "Except for the reflections part."

"Again?" Mercedes.

"The non-reflection components, as Marcy described them, are not empty but they are not reflections." Pappa thought that covered the point adequately.

"Then the Thingys are transmitting information to us after all!"

Apparently not.

"No, Gerry, I did not say that either," responded Pappa patiently, giving it another try. "The radiation I detected in the gaps in the reflected signal is from natural sources, generally indistinguishable from normal background radiation. As far as I can tell, it is completely random and devoid of meaning."

"So you're saying that when the radiation stops," concluded Fats Bic, Meteorology, "the background radiation starts, and vice-versa? Star light and gamma rays and X-rays and stuff?"

"That is correct, uh, Mr. Fats," replied Pappa, with a lingering reluctance to resort to intimate nicknames.

"Conclusion, Pappa," ordered Dac. "Can we tie this up?"

"There are two observations leading to the same conclusion," summarized Pappa. "The first is the gravity waves are directly related to the dropouts, but Thingy movement would cause frequency variations, not dropouts. This suggests the gravity waves result from the creation and destruction of mass rather than movement of mass.

"The second is the fact that natural random background radiation fills the dropouts in the reflections, suggesting that there is nothing to block the background radiation during the dropouts.

"This is highly hypothetical at this time," said Pappa reluctantly, "but if my observations are correct, Thingys exist and then don't exist rapidly and instantly."

"All of them?"

"All of them, Mr. Olson. Simultaneously, precisely in synchronization with the fluctuations in gravity waves."

"And?" Several of the crew simultaneously.

"And most of the time they are not here."

"Not here!? You mean part of the time they are here and part of the time they are somewhere else?"

"I cannot hazard a guess about somewhere else, but if their existence coincides with the existence of reflected radar signals, most of the time they are not here. They may be nowhere."

"You'll have to fill me in on nowhere, Pappa," interrupted Fats. "I flunked Nowhere 101."

"Of course, Mr. Fats," said Pappa understandingly. "As I understand it, many humans find the term 'nowhere' disturbingly insubstantial."

"Fats is Okay, Pappa," urged Fats. "Just Fats"

"Thank you, Mr. Just Fats. We ..."

"No Mr. No Just. Fats!"

"Got it, Fats! We have a great deal of evidence suggesting that our idea of reality is only one phase of an indeterminate number of co-dependent realities. Witness virtual particles, black holes, white holes, EPR effects, tachyons and the like. Theories, speculations really, even suggest alternate or parallel universes but there is no supporting empirical evidence for them.

"Virtual particles, for instance, are not real but there are such entities." Pappa paused to let the crew accommodate *that*! Noting a quorum of affirmative nods, he continued. "However, they do not exist all of the time. Part of the time they are not 'here' in the usual sense of the word; the laws of quantum mechanics do not operate on them completely. That is why they are not real.

"When virtual particles are not here, we really have no idea where they are." Pappa ran another quick nod check. "It may be they are in no *where* in the sense they exist in some space-occupying geographical place, if you'll excuse my loose analogy. It may also be true that they never actually leave; they may only manifest themselves intermittently, with their apparent non-existence being simply a function of our limited time-dependent senses. Whatever, as we commonly define reality and to the extent that we monitor reality, Thingys sometimes do not exist, hence they are not here. Not always," an addendum Pappa felt compelled to add for clarification.

"Thank you for sharing, Pappa," said Fats.

"You're quite welcome, Fats!"

"Questions?" prodded Dac after another few seconds.

"Pappa?" Gerry Ast. "If I recall, you said the original modulation in the reflections was irregular. Is that right?"

"Yes, Gerry. It is still irregular."

"And you managed to extract a regular signal from that modulation. Right?"

"No, that's not quite right," replied Pappa. "Your use of the word signal implies meaning and intent where there is probably neither. The irregular dropouts in the reflections have at least two components. The two components can be thought of as wave forms that combine additively, the result being one irregular pattern of intermittency.

"I did resolve this pattern into two wave forms," continued Pappa "One of which is a square wave at an extremely high frequency corresponding to that of the oscillation of the Thingy and to the frequency of gravity waves from the Thingy. It is not a signal in the sense that it conveys information, but it does admit to wave form analysis. It is a mathematical construct, probably with a corresponding physical adjunct."

"Yes," paced Ast with a little frustration. "I understand. In a way this, uh, wave form is incidental to what's going on. That is, it's a result of something else, like your proposed intermittent mass."

"On the basis of the data I have at this point, that seems most likely." Pappa's voice somehow conveyed heightened interest in Gerry's line of questions, as though his transistors found these electrons more significant than others. "Your conclusion, Gerry?"

"No conclusion yet, Pappa, just another question." She paused to formulate another question. "You resolved the pattern into two wave forms and gave us a rundown on one. What happened to the other?"

"I beg your pardon, Gerry. Nothing happened to it."

"What did your analysis of the second wave form reveal?" Dammit, Pappa!

"I have not analyzed the other wave form, Gerry."

"You haven't? Why not!?" asked Gerry sharply. Double Dammit!

"One moment, please, Associate Ast." Pappa paused to appraise the threat in Gerry's voice. Dac noticed Pappa's use of Gerry's formal title, as did most others.

"Work on the second component," resumed Pappa, "was deferred pending analysis of the first component which was far simpler and promised to clarify the physical nature of the Thingys more readily. Analysis of the second component was further delayed by Mr. Olson's order to '*drop everything*' for this conference."

Everyone looked at Dac who shrugged palms up.

"Pappa, can you give us anything on the second component?" asked Gerry Ast, chagrined.

"I can only give you an overview at this time," replied Pappa. "As I said, I have not analyzed it thoroughly."

"Go for it. Uh ... Please." Dac was not certain of the code phrasing needed to allow this level of speculation. "Try a good overview, Pappa. Do your best. Now."

Pause. In fact an inordinate pause as Pappa goes.

"The second wave form was first recorded when we approached the Thingy, at a distance of approximately ten days extant."

Pause.

"It is a sequence that repeats every 473 minutes."

Pause.

"I have prepared a composite of the thirteen complete sequences recorded so far to eliminate ambiguities."

Pause.

"Certain sequences within the main sequence repeat quite often, others more or less so."

Pause.

"The ..." Pappa stopped.

"Please go on, Pappa," encouraged Gerry mildly.

"The second component almost certainly ... indicates intelligent intervention."

The result, understandably, was a bombshell. Everyone reacted at once. Questions fired at Pappa like opening day of duck season. Pappa overloaded at mashed verbalizations and flashed confusion. Dac stepped forward, arms upraised in the universal appeal for order, and imposed it with his eyes. After a moment Dac nodded to Ast to continue.

"What does it say?" asked Gerry Ast obviously.

"I have no idea, Gerry. It may be saying nothing, to us or to anyone."

"How can it be language if it doesn't say anything?" she pursued.

"I am certain I did not use the term language." There was a momentary pause as Pappa checked his registry to be certain that he did not use the term language. Satisfied, he continued, "The repeated sequence indicates a discrete body of data with a beginning and end, usually associated with language but not necessarily so. Computer programming will display these characteristics, as will simple mechanical operations and even non-intelligent life cycles. The wave form, therefore, may reflect intelligent intervention but it may not be communicating in the sense that an intellect is deliberately conveying ideas intended to be apprehended by another intellect."

General silence. Everyone.

"Unh. We need a little help on that, Pappa." Dac hesitated to form a neutral un-leading question. "Can you give us an example of a repeated sequential pattern like this that doesn't convey some sort of ideas or language?"

"Yes, Mr. Olson. A good example might be the recurring cyclical noise from that oscillating fan in the corner. If it is analyzed and reduced to its composite sine waves, it is extremely complex and repeats consistently. To a naïve subject, one who had never heard it before, it would definitely draw attention and imply something intelligently designed, as opposed to a natural phenomenon such as random forest noises. But the noise is not language in any sense; it is an accidental combination of the fan's design and worn bearings. That noise can provide useful information for repair technicians who need to know and know how to interpret it, but it is not language.

"We may be simply listening to the internal programming of the Thingys," Pappa continued. "After all, Thingys are of intelligent origin, and they are doing something right now. One would expect they are following complex instructions imbedded in some physical media. This signal may simply be concomitant incidental noise, as it were."

A disappointed hush fell over the room, the aftermath of the crushed expectation of social intercourse with the gods themselves. Darn it!

Dac looked at the flat, probably disappointed faces around the room. I can understand their disappointment, he thought. I expected, no, hoped for a reception speech and the keys to the Thingy. Instead all we may get is a squeaky wheel. That's the arrogance of humans at work; we've been the only guys in space so long we think everyone else marches to our drums, thinks the way we do. The aliens probably wouldn't give us humans two squats in a banana patch.

"Look, I don't care if it's the label on a can of dog food," said Dac suddenly, with feeling. The crew's startled funk was audible. "It's intelligent and I want to know what it means! If it's a program for the Thingy, that's important! That will tell us what they're doing and how they're doing it.

And just maybe why. I want to know that!" Dac fixed each crewone with his eyes, reinforcing what he had just said.

"Remember the Rosetta stone? That was just a grocery list or something, but it opened up all of ancient language and history. And think of all those garbage pits the archaeologists sift through to piece together the Trojan War. History isn't going to judge us badly because all we found was an alien thermostat or classified ads. They *will* judge us badly if we blow it and somebody else translates the classified ads first. If they remember us at all!"

One more scan of the crew.

"Now," said coach Dac, "if there are no more questions ..."

Scramble.

CHAPTER 19

ROUNDUP

"They stopped?" asked Dac Olson.

"Yes, Mr. Olson. In fact, they have stopped twenty times so far," replied Pappa incontrovertibly. "However, if you meant to ask if they will eventually divide again, I have no idea. They have divided at a slightly accelerating but predictable interval averaging twenty-nine minutes. They are now somewhat out of pattern. There has not been a fissure for just over an hour."

"How big are they now?" asked Dac.

"47.68 centimeters, Mr. Olson," said Pappa, "and holding."

"A half meter," Dac mumbled to himself. "And they still have that same signal?"

"Do you refer to the sequence of dropouts in the reflected radar scan?" Pappa needed to clarify another of Dac's distressingly imprecise questions.

"Yes."

"Yes."

"All of them?"

"Yes, Mr. Olson," replied Pappa patiently. "All of them."

"And they're all precisely synchronized?"

"I assume you're referring to your alleged signals." Pappa turned up his human tolerance a tad, which was in turn reflected in his slightly sing-songed, and to Dac a tad more irritating voice.

"Yes!" Dac had to adjust his Pappa tolerance a tad too.

"No, Mr. Olson." Pappa paused, expecting the obvious question. Not hearing it, Pappa continued anyway. "Synchronicity implies that the shafts are in some kind of communication or linkage with each other, with perhaps some level of self-adjusting feedback loop. There is no evidence that suggests that is the case. The shafts are, however, doing the same thing at the same time, if that is your question. Yes, precisely."

"What in Hell's Stopwatch is the diff ..."

"For example," interrupted Pappa unintentionally, "if you divide a sample of a radioactive substance, the two parts emit particles at precisely the same rate, without any interaction between the two parts."

"Unh, OK. Thanks, Pappa."

Dac studied his control board and the motionless illustration of the shuttle. As they talked, the shuttle/pod, crewed by Mike Hand, Jason Fielding and Fats Bic approached the chosen Shaft and prepared to capture it. Jason waited for Dac's approval to proceed, pending Pappa's navigational concurrence.

"Excuse me, Mr. Olson." Pappa, in his most businesslike mode. "The shuttle will be at capture proximity in seven minutes. Shall we proceed with the capture?"

"A half meter," said Dac pensively to no one in particular, ignoring Pappa. "Five hundred kilometers down to a half meter! Without change in the basic structure. What can do that?"

"What's that?" asked Mercedes, looking up from her workstation.

"Oh, nothing, Mead," replied Dac. "Just mumbling to myself." Then after a moment he continued, needing the sounding board Mercedes provided. "I'm trying to understand how a machine can divide down like that, by a factor of billions, and still retain all of the qualities of the original machine. At least as far as we understand them. Nothing else in nature can approach that, except massive accumulations of simple homogeneous matter like a lake full of water."

"I know," replied Mercedes. "We've all wondered about that a thousand times. There's something behind it, some intelligence obviously, with some motive. But why they do it is a completely different problem from how they do it."

"Yeah, and it can't be done," chimed in Gerry Ast. "The scale is just too fantastic."

"Any new ideas?" asked Fats. "Anything!"

"Are we missing something here," asked Marcy Phillips tentatively. She had been listening, like everyone on the deck, and had thought the problem through a thousand times, like everyone on the deck. "Maybe we're looking through the wrong end of the telescope."

"Go on, Marcy."

"Well, we're all assuming this is a machine," said Marcy, "and we're trying to figure out how it works and why. Maybe it's not a machine, and it doesn't work. At least not in the sense we use the word. Maybe it's analogous to, say, the frost in a food freezer, or the exhaust from a motor, or noise from a jet engine, or the heat from a light bulb. Or, or something that's just incidental to the real machine. A byproduct or scrap or … or …"

"Or maybe it's only a vehicle or medium, like the refrigerant in a cooling system!" said Bic, picking up on the idea. "Or … or …"

"Or maybe a part of another remote machine, like a radio receiver is only part of the radio system," said Fats. "Or like a standing wave is part of a musical instrument."

"Or maybe it's garbage," said Mike Hand, seriously.

"Or, or, or," said Dac with a smile. "Let's get all the ors in the water. Let me see if I understand what you're saying. Marcy, you think the reason Thingys can break down to such a small scale and still function as a machine is that they may not be machines after all, or at least not complete free-standing machines; they may be only a part of something else. And as such they don't have a complex structure to breakdown and rebuild every thirty minutes. Am I tracking on this?"

"Yes," said Marcy, looking around for encouragement from the rest of Unit One. "The apparent structure may be no more essential to their function than the complex structure of a snowflake."

"And since they don't have a complex structure to replicate," continued Mead, "they can divide down to almost any degree."

"In that case," asked Dac, "if there's no complex structure and the little ones are just like the big ones, why divide at all?"

Silence for a moment.

"The most obvious reason is just what we're seeing," responded Mercedes. "Dispersion."

"Dispersion?" said Dac. "Like sugar in coffee?"

"Well, yes," replied Mercedes. "Maybe more like broadcasting seeds, or seeding clouds. But maybe with some intent such as to limit the local environmental impact, like spreading manure."

"Or maybe," concluded Dac, "to maximize the impact. Like biological warfare."

The crew glanced at each other apprehensively. No one liked the direction of the conversation. The possibilities were vast and admittedly speculative, but the conclusions were starting to fall into a few large buckets. The Thingys were mindless, controlled by something else and someone else, from somewhere else. The intent was unknown, maybe unknowable, and probably totally indifferent to humans. Good, bad or indifferent, the impact was potentially, probably vast.

"Okay, this is all fun speculation," said Dac. "But does it help us? How do we follow up on those ideas? Where's the other part of the machine? What do we do now?"

"We could start with that Shaft out there," said Mead, nodding to Dac's display board. "It seems stable. Shall we proceed with capture?"

"Hazards, Pappa?"

"No immediate hazard, Mr. Olson," responded Pappa ambiguously. "Everything is nominal."

"Thank you, Pappa," said Dac mechanically. "All right, let's do it! Proceed as planned." We have to have something to show for our troubles, he thought to himself.

Jason maneuvered the shuttle up to the Shaft at a snail's pace, a few centimeters per second. The modified escape pod was secured to the nose of the shuttle with its open hatch forward, aimed at the shaft of the mini-Thingy. He studied the display panel carefully, aligning the construct of the shuttle/pod with the glowing sliver representing the chosen Shaft.

Live, the Shaft, less than half a meter long and four centimeters thick, was all but invisible. Jason looked for it through the view port anyway.

He could not see the Shaft as such; he could only locate the Shaft through the heads-up display. Only an occasional star winked out as the Shaft, viewed end on, passed in front of a prominent star. He was at the mercy of Pappa's navigational data, flying on instruments, and unconsciously looked over to the ship for reassurance. The ship paced alongside the Shaft's trajectory, three kilometers off to one side. It was huge, even at this distance, and ugly. It always reminded Jason of an old steel mill, but it was home.

"Looking good," said Jason mechanically to Mike Hand. "I have it at two meters."

"Agreed," replied Mike as agreeably as circumstances allowed.

"Alignment looks good, maybe low," said Fats. "Can we bring her up a tad? Make that two tads."

Edward Fats Bic, meteorology, was in the pod for a close-up look, to talk Mike onto the Shaft and secure the Shaft in the pod so it wouldn't rattle around. His visual confirmation of computer navigation was essential, particularly after the Shaft entered the pod and the ad hoc visual systems became useless. Fats would ride with the Shaft in the pod back to the standoff on the ship and verify that everything was safely battened down before leaving the pod unattended.

Mike was responsible for co-piloting the shuttle/pod. He monitored the shuttle's navigational system, cross-checked with the pod's limited but accurate system, and provided audio feedback to Jason who flew by Pappa's far more powerful system. Pappa was able to scan the Shaft with hundreds of frequencies simultaneously and correlate its location with his projections based on the Shaft's trajectory, a hundred thousand times a second. The shuttle's systems were accurate enough, but simply did not have that kind of power.

"You got it, Fats," replied Jason with a tweak. Then in a few seconds, "You have the helm, Mike."

The shuttle's navigational system was useless once the Shaft was close to the pod, and Pappa's system would cease when the Shaft was inside. At this point, Mike took over navigation visually, assisted by Fats.

The interior of the pod was brightly lit. Once inside the pod, the otherwise invisible Shaft would show up clearly as a silhouette against the inside walls of the pod, prepped to mostly white. Hopefully Mike could see it by video but their experience illuminating the Thingy with vanilla light sources had proven unprofitable. Fats was the on-site eyeballs. At least that was the plan. Radio silence was tense as the shuttle inched in.

"The leading edge of the pod's hatch is flush with the end of the Shaft," said Fats in that flat machine voice that seems to take over when humans function as machines. "Good shot, Mike. Dead center. No problem. Keep moving in."

Mike didn't respond, confident in his ability and busy monitoring everything. He was motionless as he studied the monitors, watching the Shaft slip into the glaring white interior of the pod. In spite of its small size, the Shaft was awesome; it was alien and it was here and you could see it! One minute passed as Mike worked the pod over the Shaft. Two.

"She's in the pod," said Fats flatly. "Everything's nominal. Give it a little more clearance before you shut the hatch."

Several more quiet interminable seconds.

"That's it," said Fats finally. "Put a lid on it!"

A mild clumpy-clang confirmed the hatch had closed and locked. Mike leaned back and straightened, looking to Jason. Jason nodded and upthumbed Mike for the job well done.

"Okay, Mr. Olson," said Jason. "We've got your Shaft all gift wrapped. We're bringing it in!"

Back on the ship the crew relaxed visibly at the news. A generally good-natured hubbub celebrated the completion of the capture. Somehow, putting a lid on a little Thingy evoked a feeling of control over the big Thingy that had been so completely beyond their control. Dac smiled at the released tension and turned to the crew.

"Nice work," he began. "You all did a fine job on ..."

A loud low-frequency bang thumped over the intercom, bringing the celebration to an instant stop. The sound was solid and gut-wrenching, like the impact of a large and heavy iron maul on a stump, the kind you feel through your feet. Silence for an intense ten seconds.

"We have a problem, Mr. Olson," said Mike Hand, his voice obviously strained.

"Hell's Worms!" said Dac impatiently. "Now what!"

"I don't know," replied Jason. "We ran into something!"

"Ran into ..." Dac was terminally incredulous. "What can you run into!? There's nothing out there but ... Ohmygod! No!"

"The Shaft!" said Fats through his teeth. "The Shaft. We hit the Shaft!"

"What!?" said Dac still unable to believe. "Repeat! I thought you said you hit the Shaft!"

"The Shaft," said Fats. "After we closed the hatch on the pod we were still moving. The Shaft hit the back of the pod. Or we hit the end of the Shaft."

"We just bounced off!" remarked Mike, in better control but equally unbelieving.

"What's your situation now?" asked Dac urgently.

"Everything's stable," said Jason after a few seconds. "No damage. No injuries. All systems are nominal. The Shaft is in the pod, stationary, against a bulkhead."

"That's one heavy slug," said Mike with a whistle. "I'm glad my old flight instructor didn't see that rendezvous. That was really smooth!"

"No problem," said Jason with a smile. "I'm taking the helm, Mr. Hand. Let's bring her in."

Jason activated his board and requested navigation to set a course back to the ship. Satisfied, he turned the shuttle towards the ship and fired thrusters.

The shuttle moved forward slightly and then swung violently to the side. Several loud thumps rang through the structure, along with a few shouts and a gurgling grunt from Fats inside the pod. Jason controlled the shuttle quickly, stabilized it.

"Heavy is right!" said Jason, exasperated. "It doesn't budge. Hang on, Mike. I'm going to punch it!" He did.

The shuttle lurched and seemed to move. The structure creaked as the strain of the thrusters distorted the superstructure microscopically and twisted the mounts to the pod. Then a screech of tearing metal ripped through the shuttle. A terrible screech of pain ripped over the intercom.

"Abort!!" shouted Mike. "Release the Pod! Now!"

The crew on the ship's flight deck heard what sounded like a cannon shot in the background. Dac, everyone, flashed to their boards to see what they could. They heard metal tearing and the static discharge of electronic circuits ripping. They saw the pod and the shuttle separating. They heard a great deal of shouting, mostly non-regulation epithets. They saw fragments of the craft spinning into space. Then they heard nothing for a long minute.

"Mike? Jason?" called Dac anxiously. "Talk to me, Shuttle. What's happening?"

Nothing.

"Pappa?"

"The shuttle is intact, Mr. Olson," replied Pappa. "No apparent structural damage. All shuttle life support systems are functioning normally. No radio contact. The pod, however, has lost structural integrity and has separated from the shuttle. The Shaft has separated from the pod."

"Sputt."

"Dac! Are you there!?" Jason Fielding, cool but urgent. "This is shuttle, Dac. Do you read me?"

"I read you, Jason," replied Dac. "What happened?"

"I don't know yet," said Jason, frustrated. "We had that little devil, Dac. But when we turned back to the ship the shuttle just spun around like crack the whip! When I fired to start back to the ship, things came apart. I don't know what happened exactly but the shaft just went right through the side of the pod! Took off like a shot and ripped all holy bejeebers out of it! The antennas went with it. I'm on backup now. Did you see what happened?"

"Is everyone all right?" asked Dac anxiously. First things first.

"Yes, Mr. Olson," replied Mike. "Nobody hurt. The shuttle is okay but the pod is loose. It's probably scrap but we can retrieve it. Fats is still in the Pod."

"We saw things come apart," replied Dac. "Do you know what went wrong?"

"I wish I knew," said Jason, "We moved in at a crawl, only a few centimeters per second. We approached the Shaft end on, slipped over it and closed the hatch. Then bang! It felt like we ran into a solid brick wall. It must have been the back side of the pod hitting the Shaft. Like I said, it felt like we actually bounced off it!"

"Are you telling me that little hunk of hydrogen is heavier than the shuttle and pod combined!?" asked Dac.

"That's what it felt like, Mr. Olson," said Mike. "Bang! Like hitting your head under the sink."

"Pappa! Is that possible?"

"No, Mr. Olson."

"Amplify."

"The Shaft's volume is less than one thousandth of a cubic meter. If that is solid metallic hydrogen, it should not have that inertial mass. On the other hand, if the apparent mass of this small Shaft indicated by the result of this collision is extrapolated to the size of the original Thingy, it would have had a gravity well equivalent to Earth's. That was obviously not the case; the original Thingy's mass was consistent with metallic hydrogen, so the observed instant phenomenon is not possible."

"Then what happened out there, Pappa?" asked Dac. "Did the shuttle bounce off that hydrogen Shaft or not?"

"Yes, Mr. Olson."

"Yes what!" Grumble.

"The shuttle and pod were deflected from their path upon impact with the Shaft, Mr. Olson," replied Pappa. "The Shaft did not move. Or more precisely, it did not deviate from its trajectory as a result of the impact. In fact, the Shaft is still moving precisely on its previous trajectory."

"Mike?"

"Like I said, Mr. Olson," responded Mike. "I don't think it's the mass of the Shaft. I think the Shaft has a mind of its own. It's going somewhere."

"What do you mean?" asked Dac.

"Just that," responded Jason. "It doesn't want to move. When we started back to the ship we just stopped dead and swung like a rock on a string, like we had one foot nailed to space. The shuttle couldn't budge it. We went to one quarter power but it wouldn't budge. That's when the pod gave away."

There was an excited exchange of words in the background and Mike returned.

"My God!" said Mike, some emotion tearing at his voice. "It's Bic! He's ... He's dead. I just saw him in the monitors. The Shaft cut him in two when it went through the side of the pod."

Dac pondered events for a long moment. Everyone pondered.

"Bring Edward home," said Dac simply.

CHAPTER 20

TURNABOUT

"Everything?"

"Yes, everything!" muttered Dac in frustration. "Tell them everything. I want all of your reports on Gerry's desk in one hour. Make them pretty but make them true. No BS."

"Pappa?" added Dac. "That goes for you too. Send everything you have to HO. I want a complete information dump, understand?"

"Yes, Mr. Olson."

"Pappa," said Dac after a thought. "How many of those Shafts are you tracking?"

I have precise locations and trajectories on the closest thousand, Mr. Olson," replied Pappa. "Beyond that the data is somewhat probabilistic, with reliability deteriorating inversely by distance. The sheer numbers ..."

"Mr. Olson. If I may." Jason inserted himself into what was obviously CEO Dac Olson fulfilling his responsibility, a delicate interruption at best.

"Yes, Jason," a little shortly, making a mental placeholder.

"I have an observation you may want to consider before making your report."

"Let's hear it, Jason," said Dac in only a second. Dac knew Jason well enough to respect his input implicitly.

"Before you send your report, there's a question I have about Bic's death. That whole mashup," began Jason. He paused to get his thoughts together, not from any confusion or doubt but from a little anxiety and maybe even fear. That was a new awareness in Jason and he didn't like it.

"I guess my concern," he continued, "at least for your report, is that we know how Fats died, but not completely *how*. I mean, there are only two possibilities; either the pod moved or the Thingy moved. If the pod moved then the Thingy stayed put and I dragged the pod and Fats right on through it, past it and through Fats. If the Thingy moved, then somehow, out of the billions of little Thingys out there, that one shaft knew to slice through Fats at just the right time, in just the right direction. Either way is scary."

Dac looked intensely at Jason, as did the rest of the crew. They had all thought much the same thing one way or another but Jason made it all more real by verbalizing it.

"Yes. You're correct on both counts, and you're correct that we don't know which is right. What really *happened*. I'll include your observations in the report. I … we have to."

"Mercedes. Work with Jason on the wording for that," said Dac. "Get input from anyone who wants to add anything, and consolidate it. I expect everyone in the known universe will want to know, should know about the problem." said Dac, adding hopefully under his breath, "Maybe they'll find their own Thingys and leave us alone."

Dac swiveled back to his console and pondered the Shaft displayed on his board. Pappa assured him that it was the same Shaft that punched a hole in Fats Bic but it looked like all the others. They couldn't really see it, of course, it was just another of Pappa's constructs, but it was real enough.

Real enough to stop a thousand kilo shuttle in its tracks and wreck a pod and rip up one damn fine scientist! Hell's Grinder, he thought, what if we had actually gotten one into the ship! That would be a report to send back to HO! Lost, one heavyweight profit center, slightly used, last seen ripped to shreds in the Bubble!

"Pappa!" said Dac in a bark that surprised most of the crew and probably Pappa. "I want to talk to that Goddam Thingy out there!"

"I beg your pardon, Mr. Olson," replied Pappa uncertainly. "It has shown no inclination to talk to anyone."

"I didn't ask what the Thingy wants, Pappa," said Dac with a merry but unsettlingly demonic gleam in his eyes. "I'm telling you and I'm telling the Thingy and I'm telling the aliens. We're going to bang on their doors until somebody answers."

The crew sat stunned and slack jawed at their workstations. Jason swung around to face Dac, glanced across the deck to Mike Hand and back to Dac.

"Take it easy, Dac," he said calmingly. "We're all upset about Fats. That sort of thing is never easy but we've got to ..."

"Hell's Farts!" exploded Dac. "We have a problem. Right here in River City, Jason, and I'll tell you what we gotta!"

Dac stopped to calm himself, looking from face to face as he forced himself to breathe deeply.

"Sorry, Jason." Heartfelt.

He could see the pain in their faces, pain at the death of Fats and pain at the sight of their superior officer losing it. Well Dammit, he reaffirmed to himself, I'm not losing it. I know what to do but I need a working team; a temper tantrum won't help. Slow down. Easy. Smile. Relax the vocal chords. Make deliberate calm motions, no nervousness. Okay, now say something intelligent. And make it good!

"Pappa!" Pappa's motherboard jumped. Why wait, thought Dac. "Take us out a hundred thousand kilometers beyond the leading edge of the Shafts and maintain that margin. Immediately, but with extreme, repeat extreme caution. Jason, I want to see you and all team leaders for units Two, Three and Four in my office in ten minutes. Pappa! Donuts and coffee." Dac stood, slowly fixing each of the crew with his eyes. "Condition Three," he added simply. "Now!"

Dac walked calmly off the flight deck. As soon as the door closed behind him, everyone jumped for their SOP manual to figure out what in SOP Condition Three meant.

Condition Three: first level of alert in case of hostile conditions. Emergency channels opened. Power conservation procedures implemented. Computers reconfigured for military action, defensive programs loaded. Critical structural nexi secured. Provisions dispersal plan initiated. Life support backup on line, strategic units isolated. Emergency backup grids up. Weapons loaded and on standby.

None of the crew had ever gone to Condition Three on active duty and had taken what little battle training they were given largely as a joke. Defensive training was mostly in case of pirates and process servers, neither of which had any of them ever seen or heard tell of. They had to read it several times over to believe it. As the magnitude of Dac's command registered with the crew, they each looked up at Jason in turn. In disbelief.

"You heard the man," said Jason calmly but with authority and a smile he didn't feel. "Move it!"

"You can't be serious, Dac," said Jason, almost shouting. "You're going to declare war on the aliens!?" The summoned staff had hardly entered Dac's office but Jason couldn't restrain himself. He wasn't shouting, at least on the outside, but he was intense, more than usual. Dac was the boss after all.

"No, of course not," replied Dac calmly. "But they might declare war on us and I want to be ready." Pause. "In fact they may have attacked already."

Jason grudging conceded the point by his silence. Okay, he thought, I'll listen.

Dac took another swig of better than usual coffee while the rest fumbled in behind Jason. Everyone found a seat. There were enough seats for everyone around the office, including for Dac, but he deliberately remained seated at his desk. Nobody had ever seen Dac at his desk for more than a moment as he preferred a more casual atmosphere, even for tense situations. Especially for tense situations. Now, however, he sat almost imperiously. He motioned offhandedly to the side table with refreshments. No takers.

"Now what makes you think the aliens will declare war on us!" said Alex Castell, fuming. Alex had long since earned the right to a little up-frontedness.

"We did break their Thingy, you know, Alex. And because I'm ... we are going to jerk some chains and rattle some cages and kick some ass!" said Dac coolly. "That's why!"

Dac looked at each of his stunned team leaders in turn, trying to instill in them his own resolve while at the same time trying to read their thoughts. Jason will do what I tell him to do. He may not like it, and he won't hesitate to tell me so, but he won't hesitate to do it.

Alex Castell, Unit Two, probably the same as Jason; solid, reliable, will follow my order unquestioningly, but he will question me up to the point I make it an order. Sometimes too many questions.

Uni Farber, Unit Three, unknown. She's experienced, tough. She wouldn't be here if she weren't. But I've never had to rely on her when the chips were down. That's not a negative, just a statement of fact.

Max Berkley, Unit Four. Smart, aggressive, a hard-charging bite-em-off-and-spit-em-out son of a bitch. But good, very good, smart and savvy. He'll command someday. The only problem is his impulsiveness in what he sees as a black and white world. Needs a little seasoning, more awareness of the grays. A damned fine team, if they all buy in.

"Okay," began Dac. "We need to ... I need to make a few decisions. When I make those decisions I need to have your complete commitment. This has never happened before so there are no guidelines. HO has a manual for everything but this, so we're breaking ground. Just hear me out. Then I want your honest input. Okay?"

Nods and mumbled affirmatives. Max reached for a cup of coffee.

"First of all," began Dac, "there is a distinct danger to the ship and crew. Right now there are ... Pappa! How many of those Shafts are there out there right now?" Dac knew the answer; a *bunch*. But he wanted the point for effect, a shot across their collective bow.

"1,152,921,500,000,000,000, Mr. Olson. That figure assumes ..."

"In English, Pappa. Please."

"That is in English ... Oh, yes Of course. That is something over a quintillion, Mr. Olson. A thousand thousand thousand billions. Will that do?"

"That will do nicely, Pappa. And how long since they started to divide?"

"About 10.5 hours, Mr. Olson," replied Pappa. "Is there a conclusion you want to draw? Perhaps I could ..."

"Thank you, Pappa," continued Dac with a wink to the others. "And what's the maximum dispersion rate for that cloud of Shafts?"

"The eight Shafts from the original Thingy separated at approximately ten kilometers per hour, due to the rotation of the original Thingy. At each subsequent division, the subdivided shafts separate at a velocity inversely proportionate to the size of the new generation of Shafts, with an incremental factor slightly greater than one. The leading edge ..."

"What in Hell's Buckshot does *that* mean?" Probably Dac, but everyone thought it.

"They accelerate at each division, Mr. Olson."

"That's impossible!"

"Quite." Pappa paused expecting another of Dac's disconcerting statements of the obvious. Getting none, he continued. "The leading edge is now traveling at approximately 24,266.1 kilometers per hour from the center of the cloud. In fact, the ..."

"How big, Pappa?"

"The cloud itself is expanding but individual Shafts move in a spiral around the center. An interesting feature of the geometry of the ..."

"How BIG!?"

"The cloud is roughly disc shaped, 21,720 kilometers thick and 119,320 kilometers in diameter, approximately 77,300,000,000,000 cubic kilometers total volume, Mr. Olson." Momentary break in pace, enough to be noticed. "If you would tell me what you are about, Mr. Olson, I might be more helpful."

"I don't know what I want, yet," replied Dac. "I'm still fishing. Pappa. How many Shafts per cubic kilometer?"

"They average about 14,915 per cubic kilometer, Mr. Olson. Some areas are somewhat more densely populated than others, ranging from nearly a million per cubic kilometer at the center to around 200 out here at the edge of the cloud."

"How far apart are they?"

"The mean distance between Shafts is 144 meters, Mr. Olson," replied Pappa instantly, now that he saw where Dac was going. "The range is almost zero at the center up to hundreds of kilometers in our vicinity."

"Thousands of those things per cubic kilometer," reiterated Dac. "Millions! The same little slivers that just ripped Fats' guts out and destroyed one industrial strength emergency pod. This ship's made out of the same stuff the pod is made of, and you're made out of the same stuff as Fats. Anybody still think they're not a hazard."

"Well, yes, they are right now," said Alex, "but they're dispersing. In a thousand hours the cloud will have the average density of a comet's tail. In a year they will be no more hazardous than random meteors. We've already flagged HO. They can divert traffic from the area and that's that."

"Except for a few details," rejoined Dac. "First, these aren't meteors. They have an apparent mass greater than a shuttle. Maybe far greater. You found that out, Jason. Pappa says that Shaft didn't so much as budge. It should have moved to a degree proportional to the relative masses of the shuttle and Shaft, at least a little. It didn't move at all. Therefore its mass must be considered mathematically infinite, at least for the working moment. We're sailing through uncharted waters with reefs and shoals that can tear the belly out of this ..." with a rueful smile, "... profit center."

"Second, space junk, and particularly comet stuff, will break up on impact, pulverize. That's why everything is double-hulled with heavy tinfoil and redundant as Hell's Toenails. Which is usually enough. Maybe the mini-Thingys break up at high velocities, and maybe not, but our experience is that they shatter only when and if they want to. Imagine hitting a few million of them at Bubble speed.

"Third." Dac thought for a moment. "Third, if, as seems likely, they are going somewhere and are locked to some other device, they are controlled. Think of the magnitude of a weapon like that! A controlled fleet of trillions of indestructible invisible flechettes, each with infinite mass. These crates we call home ain't exactly armor plated; the hulls aren't as strong as a Ford truck back home. Those little devils could tear up the whole corporate fleet like a shotgun blast through a carton of eggs.

"Fourth," he continued. "While they are dispersing now, they may not disperse forever. Pappa found that they are accelerating in defiance of the laws of conservation of energy and angular momentum. That means something is adding vectored energy to them. They do what they Goddam want to do and go where they Goddam like. It is completely unreasonable to assume that they will simply float mindlessly away into space. And whatever is going to happen someday, today it's a bloody mine field out there!

"Fifth," said Dac with finality. "They don't know we're here, or they don't care. They're as indifferent to us as an avalanche or earthquake. That makes them extremely dangerous completely aside from all other considerations, like a car on a freeway squashing an ant on the pavement.

"That's what I want to fix," said Dac, his tone changing from assertive to earnest. "And that's where you come in. I want to get their attention."

"But why the Condition Three, Dac," said Alex. "You just want to ring the door bell, don't you? Not storm the ramparts."

"You're right, Alex," replied Dac. "But they may not make that distinction, at least not the same distinction we make. They may misunderstand the intent and strike back inadvertently, like you might slap a mosquito that just dropped by for a friendly drink. History's full of cultural clashes that resulted from misinterpreted social initiatives. I want to ring the door bell but I have to be ready for war. Or the equivalent of defensive war."

"I see," said Max. "So far we've just been looking and listening. Now you want to go on the initiative."

"Yes, Max," replied Dac. "That's where you come in. I want you to tell me how to do that."

"Now wait a minute," said Uni. "Why now? Why us? Why not let HO send in an armada."

"The simple answer," responded Dac, "aside from there being no armada, is standing order No. 1. You know."

Yeah, they knew: Upon identifying intelligent alien life, secure the area, contact the HO, the aliens and maybe the Feds, in that order.

"So our orders are to contact the aliens," concluded Dac. "Besides, we didn't know about their extreme mass until now. That changes the equation. And we didn't know they had direction, which may be the same thing. But that's also new and changes the urgency. And we didn't know they would stop dividing at a hazardous size. If they divided down to powder we could forget about them. Maybe. They didn't so we can't. Things are different from a day ago."

Dac paused thoughtfully. The others, sensing he was not finished, waited.

"And they're getting away from us, you know?" Dac was in a little pain at that. "We may lose them. We sure can't catch them. Hell's Pox, we can't even see them. The biggest find imaginable and we may be the ones who lost them. You just suggested that by the time BE gets here they will have the density of space dust. And they'll be as hard to find; if they're spread so thin they pose no hazard, they'll be so dispersed they'll be impossible to find. So we're going to ring their bell." Dac seemed to have finally convinced himself, and it showed.

"What about the 'don't touch' part?" asked Uni.

"I wondered about that too," said Dac. "How do you contact the aliens without touching them, or something?" Dac paused to review his own words. *These* aliens, as opposed to all other aliens? "What are the rules for contacting Cubes and Thingys and Shafts that pretty much ignore us?"

"Well, none, I guess," said Uni. "But that's a fine point, Dac."

"Yes, it is," he replied, "but it's a fine point because we've never seen an alien before; the rules are necessarily broad and vague. Another fine point; we haven't actually seen or touched an alien yet, only their Thingys, which is like finding a Coke bottle on a new moon but with no one in sight. Is it touching whatever put it there if you pick it up?"

Dac wasn't completely comfortable with that but a survey of faces indicated buy in. Close enough!

"I don't intend to walk up and hit one in the chops. Look, what if you met an alien that talks only through touch. Just about every animal back home communicates through touch, or can if it wants, but not all of them talk like we do. Do you think the rules say you can't talk to it just because you aren't supposed to touch one?" Dac continued with a little energy. "Or one that likes to hug. Or one that hits you in the chops to show affection. I think the touching rule simply means don't do something dumb and muddle things up."

"So you're going to ring their door bell," said Alex, "knowing there's a chance you might muddle things up and start a war?"

"That's not quite how I'd say it," said Dac. "But that about sums it up. Yes."

"All right, Dac," challenged Jason. "How would you say it? How are you going to ring their bell?"

"I don't know," said Dac after a moment to see if the others were ready for the next step, "but try this for size. First we're going to learn their language and translate the signal Pappa found. That's our USDA choice number one priority. And while we're doing that, we need to figure out what to say to them."

"That's what we've been doing, Dac," said Jason. "Gerry Ast has spent every minute she can spare on ..."

"That's old," interrupted Dac, ignoring Jason's protocol slip for the nonce. "This is new. I want a team made up of the communication officers from all six units on this full time, reporting directly to Uni Farber. They're to do nothing else. They'll have highest priority on Pappa's time as well. In addition, Uni, contact HO and get their experts on it. It will probably require a lot of number crunching and I'm sure they'll give it all the capacity available. Let me know your plans and what you need as soon as possible."

"You got it! Mr. Olson," said Uni Farber, maybe too enthusiastically, with a grin.

"Jason," said Dac with a firmer command in his voice. "I want your team to prepare a series of graduated non-language intrusions."

"Excuse me!?"

"Uh, ring the door bell," said Dac, "knock on the door, bang on the door, throw a pebble at the window, throw a rock through the window. Et cetera, et cetera and so forth."

Jason looked at Dac through narrowed eyes, then wide-eyed the others for help.

"Don't bother looking at me like I don't know what I'm talking about, Jason," said Dac jovially. "I don't. What I want is how to get their attention if we can't talk to them. We seem to have a general feeling that the Shafts are only a piece of something else, like we're fish looking at an oar in the water. What I want to do is nudge the oar enough so somebody on the other end will say 'Hey! What's that?'

"The first thing to do is the mildest kind of intrusion you can come up with. Then the second mildest and so on. You can pound on it with a hammer or squeeze it or X-ray it. Whatever. I just want a plan, what to do and how to do it and in what order."

"Any top end limits?" asked Jason, mollified.

"No ..." replied Dac, thinking. He hadn't considered that, how far can we go? "At least not in planning. But we don't actually *do* anything without my approval and probably HO approval. Include everything you can think of. We'll worry about how far we actually go later. HO will probably be control on that anyway. Give me a plan first. Let me know what you need."

"Well. Personnel for starters." Jason sounded like he was getting into it.

"Use the engineers, geological and meteorological officers from all units," replied Dac. "Include Five and Six as needed. They're yours. If you need anyone else, just ask. Very high priority, Jason, but Uni's translation team overrides if there's a conflict."

"No problem," said Jason. "I understand. We'll send a pre-approach letter first. If that doesn't work, we'll knock."

"Right on, Jason," confirmed Dac. "Alex, I want you in charge of defensive preparedness. Everything's in the book and you know what to do. Questions?"

"No, Mr. Olson," replied Alex. "Not yet, anyway. The first step will be to confirm that we're up to Condition Three. Then I'll begin review training for Condition Two immediately."

"Yes, Alex," said Dac. "By the book. But I want you in on everything Jason does and plan for contingencies accordingly. Understood?"

"Yes, Mr. Olson." "Understood." From Jason and Alex simultaneously as they nodded to each other.

"Max," said Dac looking directly and deliberately at Max. "This may be the most impossible job but it's probably the most important. I want to know what those things are and what they're doing and how they're doing it. We've been throwing around a lot of half-baked speculations so far; nothing was riding on speculation. Now I want something firm I can act on! Give me a few of the most likely scenarios, two or three or whatever. Make them tight, tight enough to act on quickly if one proves correct. You get everyone who isn't spoken for. Uni has priority and Alex has priority. Work closely with Uni's team; if they translate Thingy talk they may be able to tell what you need to know. Work with Jason; your conclusions may give him clues to what aliens react to. Okay?"

"I understand," said Max, smiling. Grinning. Max was a physicist and this was the opportunity of a lifetime. A universe of lifetimes.

"Chirp. Mr. Olson?"

"Yes, Pappa."

"What about everything else?"

Everything else was maintenance of life support systems, environmental research, traffic control, manufacturing industries, inventory control, educational programs, marketing, compilation and research on the last several planetary encounters for exploitation opportunities, astronomical and scientific experiments hitching a ride on the profit center. Hundreds of big jobs and little jobs that accompany a profit center, which was essentially a self-contained and self-supporting factory town.

"We'll just stop doing anything that doesn't support life or the systems needed for the activities I just ordered. Let me know where there are conflicts, with your recommendations. All of you."

"Yes, Mr. Olson."

"And Pappa?"

"Yes, Mr. Olson?"

"Monitor everything and stop me before I do something really dumb and muddle everything up."

"Then I think there is something you should know, Mr. Olson," said Pappa.

"What's that, Pappa?" Hackles up!

"The Shafts are growing again."

CHAPTER 21

🕉 ☸

FIRST DOUBT

"Growing!"

"Yes, Mr. Olson," said Pappa matter of factly. "The growth is barely detectable but real. I have high confidence in my data."

"How fast are they growing?" asked Alex, grasping the situation immediately.

"It," corrected Pappa. "I am able to monitor only one shaft with any precision. The previous reliable measurement is 17 hours old, just before we attempted to capture it. Based on that measurement, the Shaft is now approximately 0.001 of a percent longer than it was at that time."

"It grew a thousandth of a percent?" reflected Dac, relieved. He mentally discounted the significance of Pappa's discovery, placing it somewhere below 'get laundry done.' "Is that a problem?"

"I don't know that it's a problem, Mr. Olson," replied Pappa, "but there are certain aspects of the situation that concern me. I have no idea when it actually started to grow so I cannot determine its actual growth rate accurately at this time. However, assuming every Shaft grew simultaneously at the same rate, they have together acquired a total of approximately 8.796 cubic kilometers of metallic hydrogen."

"Nine cubic kilometers of solid metallic hydrogen in 17 hours!" exclaimed Uni. Then in realization, "Oh my God." It wasn't an exclamation; it was a prayer.

"Yes," confirmed Pappa. "There are, after all, over a million trillion Shafts. A thousandth of a percent of each adds up to a significant total. I thought you would like to know."

"Thanks, Pappa," said Dac ruefully. Yeah, I really wanted to know that! With everything else to worry about here was one more unknown. Then he softened. "Thanks. I do need to know that. Someday, but not right now, okay?"

He looked over to his board at the outline of the Shaft that had killed Fats Bic. There was something new but it took Dac a moment to realize what it was. The previously monolithic Shaft now had erasers; it had turned back into a Thingy with a Cube and a Gap on each end.

"Pappa," said Dac apprehensively. "When did the Gaps come back?"

"The Gaps first reappeared two hours ago, Mr. Olson," replied Pappa.

"If these Thingys create hydrogen in the Gap," speculated Dac, struggling to recall the discussions about the purpose of the Thingys, "then the growth probably started two hours ago along with the new Gaps, not 17 hours ago."

"That seems reasonable, Mr. Olson."

"Then all of those Thingys," concluded Dac, "may have created nine cubic kilometers of solid matter in two hours."

"Yes, Mr. Olson," replied Pappa, "based on those assumptions. However, the problem is somewhat more complex than that."

"Amplify." Dac considered *everything* was more complex than that.

"The figures I gave you," said Pappa, "are based on the growth of the Shaft in only one dimension, the length. That is the only measurement I have been able to confirm at this time. It is reasonable to assume, however, that they grow proportionately in all dimensions."

"Why is that, Pappa?"

"Because that," said Pappa stiffly, "is the ratio in which they divided. The dimensional ratio has been constant at close to 11.92:1:1 throughout the division process. It is reasonable to assume it will continue to remain constant in any growth pattern."

"Okay," said Dac, chastened. And bless your little neural network too, he added to himself. "Go on."

"You will recall that the original Thingy was growing when we found it," continued Pappa.

"Yes," said Dac slowly, not certain he wanted to hear what was coming. "You didn't make much of it at the time, if I recall correctly."

"Yes, it was an isolated fact at that time. Now that the division process has apparently reversed, however, it is reasonable to assume," assumed Pappa, "that each of these half-meter long Shafts will eventually grow into a full-sized Thingy."

Pappa paused to correct himself, realizing that 'full-sized' was an unwarranted deduction. Who knew what a full-sized Thingy was.

"That is," he qualified, "each Shaft will grow to at least 500 kilometers in length, or 882,000 cubic kilometers."

"Each!?" Dac choked.

"Each," confirmed Pappa with a ring of certainty. "In fact, assuming ..."

"Wait up, Pappa. This is getting out of hand." Jason tried to squelch a crooked I-don't-believe-a-word-of-this smile. He rubbed the back of his neck with his left hand while he thought, then the bridge of his nose with his right. "Let me see if I've got this straight, Pappa. You're talking about 882,000 cubic kilometers per Big Thingy, times a million trillion Little Thingys. Right?"

"Yes, Mr. Fielding," replied Pappa. "More or less."

"And that equals what," asked Dac, now very interested in the course of the conversation. "In, say, earth volumes?"

"Approximately 1,247,570,000,000 earth volumes," answered Pappa immediately. "You can understand why I felt you should be informed."

"Yes."

"Actually," hedged Pappa, "that figure may be a little misleading because of the difference in density between metallic hydrogen on the one hand, and earth's rock mantle and iron core. Earth is quite dense as such things go. A comparison to the Sun would be more appropriate as the densities are roughly equivalent."

"Okay, Pappa," said Jason. "Make it solar volumes."

"The approximate total accumulated growth, assuming each small Thingy eventually grew to the size of the large Thingy we first encountered," rephrased Pappa, anticipating disbelief born of misunderstanding, "would be 958,947.2 solar volumes, and roughly that same number of solar masses."

"That's almost one million suns!" said Uni weakly on behalf of the others, in disbelief born of understanding.

"However," qualified Pappa, "that figure does not take into account the additional matter that may accrue in the Wrappers if the ultimate Thingys have Wrappers like the first. That could nearly double ..."

"Okay," said Jason. "I get the picture."

"Pappa?" inquired Alex. "You keep saying approximately. Just how approximate is your projection?"

"The number of Shafts is very accurate," Mr. Castell. "The rate of growth is only a guess at this time, but that's irrelevant. We know the size of the original Thingy; that is very hard data. I assumed every Shaft ultimately becomes as large as the original Thingy, an admittedly highly speculative but reasonable assumption in light of the observation that the original Thingy was growing and the present Shafts are growing. On that basis, the estimate of one million solar volumes is highly valid, with a margin of variability of perhaps as much as plus or minus one hundred per cent."

"One hundred per cent!?" One hundred per cent? thought Dac with a flare of incredulity, overmatched by most other crewones. "One hundred per cent!?"

"Yes. This is all highly speculative, Mr. Olson. I could be completely wrong on all assumptions, except for the current number of Shafts," qualified Pappa, for the record, of course.

"Okay, Pappa. We all understand the fuzzy numbers bit, but what do you *think*?" Dac mollified Pappa to get something with a handle on it. "Give us your best reasonable working estimate. How many solar volumes?"

"I am comfortable with my original projection; One million solar volumes."

"Hell's Spatula!" said Dac. "If only one out of a thousand Shafts turns into a Big Thingy, that still works out to one thousand new suns-stuff!"

"Quite, Mr. Olson."

"Okay, Pappa," said Max. "Big question. How long is this going to take? Are we talking a million new suns in what, a billion years? That's not a lot to get excited about before I've had my lunch."

"At a constant one thousandth of one percent rate of growth compounded periodically?" asked Pappa.

"Sure," said Max. "Whatever."

"Assuming a compounding period of two hours or seventeen hours?"

"Give me a range," said Max with a little smirky aside to Alex, as though this was too esoteric to fool with.

"That works out to between 23,486,000 and 2,763,000 hours, Mr. Berkley," said Pappa. "And some."

"See," gloated Max. "Millions. I'll leave a wake-up call."

The rest in the room followed the transaction with considerable interest. Most resented Max's cavalier attitude but had to admit that it didn't seem to be a serious problem. Or at least not an immediate or urgent problem.

"Wait a minute, Pappa," said Dac intently. "You said hours. What's that in people talk, like years?"

"Each Shaft," replied Pappa, pronouncing his words carefully to avoid further misinterpretation of the nature of the problem. "will be 500 kilometers long in somewhere between 2,680 and 315 years."

"Three hundred years!" That was Max, his attitude newly and dramatically sober. "You're saying there could be a million new suns in the immediate vicinity in three hundred years!"

"I did not say suns, Mr. Berkley," corrected Pappa gently. "I said approximate solar volumes or mass equivalents. There will be that much matter but I have no idea whether it will be in the form of suns or Thingys. I also have no idea whether it will be in this immediate vicinity in three hundred years. Relatively speaking, however, at the present maximum Shaft velocity, the mass will be quite concentrated."

"Yeah, but still," said Uni. "A million trillion new Thingys!"

"I did not say new," interrupted Pappa. "We have yet to determine from whence Thingys come. It may or may not be new mass. They may simply be a reconfiguration of existing mass." That ought to do it, thought Pappa.

"Your assessment, Pappa," said Dac. "I'm asking for your personal opinion. Are the Thingys made of new matter that wasn't here before there were Thingys? Are they creating new matter out of nothing?"

"Of course, Mr. Olson." Mathematical calculations and logical deductions were one thing; personal opinions something else. "That conclusion is all but inescapable."

"Then you think it's likely there will be a million solar masses, in the form of a million trillion new, repeat new 500 kilometer long Thingys, in the immediate vicinity in as little as three hundred years." Dac was making a conclusive statement for Pappa to confirm.

'Oh, no, Mr. Olson," replied Pappa. "That is not at all possible."

"Not possible!" exploded Dac. "Then what in Hell's Spits are we talking about!?"

"I am not certain what *you* are talking about, Mr. Olson," replied Pappa coolly. "*I* am talking about a black hole. A very large black hole."

"Ah!" in one form or another, from everyone except Uni Farber who said, "All right!"

"It's probable," continued Pappa, "that unless they are very widely dispersed, a confluence of mass that large will collapse long before the Thingys reach 500 kilometers."

"I see what you're saying, Pappa," said Uni. "But even in that case the mass will still be present, in one form or another."

"That's true," replied Pappa, eager to talk to someone who seemed to have a grasp of the situation. "But when the Thingys collapse into a black hole they will probably stop growing. The black hole will only grow through accretion of local matter, which, of course, may well include additional growing Thingys."

"But in that case," observed Uni, "The total mass will be far less than it would have been had the aggregation not collapsed."

"That is correct," replied Pappa, "or at least probable."

"Then can you adjust your projection," asked Uni, "taking into consideration the collapse of the Thingy cloud into a black hole at their earliest opportunity?"

Pappa worked at the problem for a considerable time, far longer than he typically needed for anything. Past a point he would usually indicate there was no possible answer and ask for guidance.

"Pappa?" prodded Uni.

"There are a surprising number of variables." said Pappa deliberately, as though assembling each word one at a time after listening to his last. "Some of the rigorously logical solutions I derive do not make good sense. Others are trivial. It seems like a straight forward problem but ... there is something else."

"Look, Pappa," interrupted Dac, realizing Pappa had committed so much of his capacity to the problem that processing it was retarded. "Take your time with this. That solution is not a high priority right now. We've got other more important things to worry about."

"The solution seems to involve a much more complex set of parameters than I first assumed," replied Pappa apologetically, ignoring Dac. "And there may be far-reaching ... cosmic ... ramifications." That got their attention.

Pause.

"The cloud of Shafts is under the influence of ... part of ... something else. A larger body. A vastly larger body."

Pause.

"A significant factor in the problem is the shape of space. It is a variable."

Pause.

"I cannot derive a solution, Mr. Olson," said Pappa finally, back to his usual diffident but cheerful frame of mind. "That is all I can tell you at this point without more accurate data."

Dac was almost afraid to ask. Almost.

"What do you need, Pappa?"

"I need precise measurements," answered Pappa quickly, urgently. "More precise measurements than I can make from here, on a statistically valid sample of the Shafts."

"You want me to bring one in for a fitting?" said Dac sarcastically. "Or maybe I should send out a few of the guys with yardsticks."

"Yes. Thank you, Mr. Olson," said Pappa. "That will do nicely."

CHAPTER 22

※◎ ◎※

PERIOD

Dac swept busily into the conference room and stopped in surprise. "You've been busy," he said with a smile and sweep of his hand at the walls. "Something happened!"

The conference room looked busy indeed. It was plastered with large sheets of scribbled newsprint and long ribbons of neatly printed program output, taped to the walls in some kiltered order obvious only to Uni Farber's translation team. Auxiliary display boards flickered moment by moment, monitoring Pappa's work. Stale debris cluttered the table from on-the-fly feedings, ossified evidence of their progress. The team, everyone, referred to the room as Spook Central.

"Is it War and Peace," he asked happily, "or the classifieds?"

Dac moved around the conference table to an open seat, flopped an armload of file folders onto the table and shoved everything forward to make room to write. He reached for a donut and napkin from the platter in the center of the table as someone passed him a cup of coffee, black. Settled, he looked around at the five intense faces looking back at him. "Not funny, hunh?"

The translation team: Uni Farber and the communications officers from the six management units. All highly skilled in the technical tools of the trade, and each with hisser unique assets.

Winnie Logo, Unit Two. Speaks six languages expertly and understands Lord knows how many others, specializing in those with Indo-European roots. She had diplomatic corps experience on three planets, four years with the corporation, two on the Jobs.

Bill Stewart, Unit Three. The oldest of the team, with vast experience in industrial espionage and executive security. He was well traveled from chaperoning the top brass throughout its holdings, and familiar with social customs everywhere. Bill was a very intense personality and acutely aware of subtle interpersonal nuances in dealing with foreigners. In this business everyone was a foreigner, thought Dac.

Ad Blanker, Unit Four. The youngest but the most experienced in his narrow technical field. Mostly a technician, he was learning the human side of the business fast. He was a master at statistical analysis and kept Pappa humming exploring the blizzard of space radiation they plowed through, looking for anything unusual. His intuitive analytical sense rivaled Pappa's computational power and they made a formidable team.

Pat Grey, Unit Five. Easily the largest of the team. Pat was a first-class technician, but intellectually not as powerful as the others. He made up for that in hard work and a good-natured homey intuitiveness that was legendary in usually being right. He was a two-legged Occam's Razor and the unofficial referee in many things disputational.

Jimmy 'FAX' Klein, unit Six. An incredibly powerful mind with a closed quiet introverted personality. His nickname, never used to his face, meant he was a facsimile of a person, a paper cutout. He knew more trivia about more subjects than anyone on the Jobs. The only social activity in which he was comfortable was taking on the whole crew in Trivial Pursuit. He was recognizable by being the only crewone nobody knew.

"Neither," answered Uni. "We've been busy, but I'm afraid not very productive yet."

"I didn't expect miracles, Uni," said Dac mildly, realizing he had unfairly put Uni on the spot. "Go on, please."

"As you know," replied Uni, reassured, "we dumped everything to HO a week ago, thirty-two cycles of the complete signal. We got their first response late last night and we're just now getting into it. Seven-day lag times make conversation a little slow. Tedious too.

"They haven't had time," she continued, "to set up a team of language experts and cryptanalysts. At least not before they sent out their initial response. They are running some basic statistical analyses for us. Pappa is reviewing them now. They uploaded some software so Pappa can do anything they're doing, but they still have more capacity to do it far faster, even allowing for the delay. Mostly they confirmed our preliminary findings. They will upload their results daily." Uni paused to position her next comment.

"We do have a few very tentative conclusions, Mr. Olson. Not language, mind you, but deductions about their language."

"Great!" said Dac, genuinely intrigued. "What have you got?"

"First of all," she began, glancing to the others on the team for support, "we feel the sequence is language rather than machine programming or something else."

"That's Big!" enthused Dac. "How did you guys figure that?"

"The signal shows no correlation with the observed activity of the Shafts," replied Uni. "Admittedly, the Shafts didn't do much, just divide, so there isn't a lot of activity to correlate with. But the full sequence is 7.88 plus hours long which spans fifteen complete divisions, so the sequence is probably not directly related to the shaft's breakdown. Breakup? Whatever.

"The sequence was recorded thirteen times prior to their dividing and several times since they stopped. As far as we can tell, there has been no change in the sequence when it started to divide, while dividing, or when the pieces started to grow."

"So you have a complete … uh … book to work on?" Dac was getting a little excited about their progress. "That's great!"

"However," cautioned Uni, "we can't be completely certain about that. The recordings of the sequences are not all perfect. We're missing a lot of pieces throughout the sequences and each sequence is missing thousands of little parts, different parts each time. There may be extremely subtle signals we missed. Taken as a whole, the conclusion that this is a language is of mixed value at this point."

"How so?" prompted Dac, a little puzzled and let down.

"If the sequence were completely mechanical like a computer program," she replied, "it would probably be far easier to translate but less informative. If it's real alien talk, it might provide a wealth of information, but it will also be that much more difficult to translate. It's the difference between computer machine language and, say, your War and Peace."

"Fair enough," said Dac. "What else?"

"By making a composite of all thirty-two recorded sequences, we have what we feel is one fairly accurate sequence, probably three to five per cent accurate. As a result ..."

"Excuse me, Uni," interrupted Dac. "Only three percent?"

"Yes," replied Uni. "It may actually be far better but Pappa's not completely comfortable beyond that level. The problem is the mass of data, the degree of compression and the rate of transmission, if that's the right word."

"You'll have to explain that, Uni," prompted Dac. "Is it alien speak or not?"

"Ad, that's your thing," said Uni with a nod to Ad Blanker.

"The sequence isn't really being transmitted, Mr. Olson," began Ad. "We're just listening in on it and it may not all be the same sort of stuff. Probably not. The sequence can be thought of as being carried on a wave with a frequency in the neighborhood of 2.5 X 10 to the 46th. Extremely high, almost too high to record individual Hertz with our equipment. Our recordings aren't always clean; lots of spurious nonsense in there.

"In addition," he continued, "signal strength is not exactly overpowering, something on the order of one millionth of the ambient gravitational clutter. The random clutter in our system, particularly at high gain, interferes with the highly compressed signal. A barely detectable static pop might wipe out a few trillion bits of data. We're trying to develop filters to give us cleaner signals, but for now we have a lot of trash in there."

"Is that going to be a problem?" asked Dac, sensing a problem.

"No."

"Uh ..." How's that? thought Dac.

"How's that, Ad?"

"There is so much data," replied Ad, "that we could probably work out a good working vocabulary and grammar with one or two percent of the sequence. Like having only one volume of a very large set of encyclopedias; it's not really a problem. Once we have that, the rest is downhill."

"Okay," said Dac, relieved. "Great!"

"Another reasonable conclusion," rejoined Uni, "is that it was meant to be read, and therefore has probably been composed to be read, and probably read in the order presented."

"How do you come by that?" asked Dac. "That sounds like mind-reading."

"Well," said Uni cautiously, "if the first conclusion is valid, that it's not machine talk, it is probably intended for other aliens, or somebody."

"Okay, but how does that help us?"

"I don't know if it helps us translate," replied Uni, "but it's a good sign. If we assume the aliens acquire information in a more or less linear fashion like we do, the sequence is probably meant to be acquired the same way, linearly. We can see a whole photograph or a sunset simultaneously but we can't listen to all of a symphony simultaneously or read a book all at once; we have to take it one piece at a time. We're proceeding on the assumption that this information is linear. At least major elements are.

"This also implies," she continued, "that there is some order to it. Even if it is classified ads, or especially if it is classifieds, the order should become apparent and that should give us clues to what it is, and then what it says. If you look at, say, a parts manual for the first time, you have to study it first to get the lay of it. But once you do, you can find your way around quickly. That's what we're looking for, the system."

"What if it's just the alien equivalent of static?" said Dac in jest, "Or a squeaky wheel?"

They all looked at him as if he had suggested outlawing pizza.

"That's possible," replied Uni suspiciously, unamused. "However, we prefer not to consider that alternative."

"Uh, okay. Sorry." Sheesh, he thought, professional temperament already. "Anything else?"

"Yes!" said Uni, happy to change the subject. "We think we may have actually translated something!"

"All right!" said Dac, just as happy to change the subject. "What?"

"We're sure we have their period."

"Period?" Did she just say period?

"You know," urged Uni. "Like punctuation at the end of a sentence. So far we've found something over three hundred thousand chunks that end with the same short sequence followed by a significant interval with no signal. Probably a period, or something like 'end' or 'return' or 'page number' or 'prompt for input.' Some sort of deliminator in a set of instructions."

"That's it?"

"Yes," said Uni, beaming. "We have a lot of guesses," she added with a wave around the room, "but the period is the only sure bet so far."

"Okay, good work!" said Dac, and he supposed it really was. "Same time tomorrow?"

CHAPTER 23

A LOOK BACK

"Maybe Thingys need to kill."

Jason Fielding struggled with his life suit, banging a stuck buckle with the heel of his right hand. He and Mike Hand bumped into each other in the cramped prep room and rattled other equipment as they prepared Vlad and Ross to EVA to measure a Shaft or five for Pappa.

"Need to kill?" answered Mike Hand with an exaggerated look of horror. "You think they wander around space looking for victims, like sharks driven by some primordial urge? Shades of Dracula!" Mike made the motions of a joke but looked askance at Jason, assessing his sanity. Was he serious? He sure looked serious.

"Are you serious?" he asked.

"Yes," replied Jason with a rue smile. "But not like that. I mean maybe they're programmed to react at some trigger. And kill in self defense if necessary."

"Now how could aliens program a Shaft to kill Fats!" said Ross Label, Biology. "That's really been getting to you hasn't it."

"Yes," admitted Jason. "It bothers me because I did it. I know it was an accident, but nobody else did it, *I* did it." Pause. "I've seen death before, and I've even had to kill before. I don't like it but I don't wallow in it either. Fats is dead, that's that. But maybe there's a lesson in there somewhere."

"Like what?" asked Vlad. Vlad Svoboda, Unit Two geology officer.

"I can't imagine they are programmed to kill." Jason added, "Knowingly. But maybe the Thingy was programmed to defend itself in the only way it can, using what it does naturally anyway. You know, like a coral reef defends itself by growing around its attacker because that's all it can do. Or even just a land mine or sea mine; it's built to explode if it gets touched hard enough. No thinking necessary."

"Okay," said Ross slowly, conceding the point for the sake of the discussion. "Then what?" He slapped something on his belt that wouldn't cooperate and grabbed at a tool.

"Well," continued Jason, "everyone agrees that we triggered the breakdown by interfering with it. It was programmed to break down, that's obvious, but we probably started the process somehow. Then maybe we also triggered the growth when we tried to capture it. Or maybe the growth is just an automatic continuation of the division process. The Thingy needed a trigger to start dividing, and the Thingettes needed a trigger to start growing.

"Whatever," he concluded, "I can see the process as a purely automatic defensive reaction. Any contact with intelligent life triggers the defensive reaction; it divides into billions of pieces and disperses, making it effectively invisible. The pieces grow to the point that some collapse into a black hole and take its assailant with it, the rest survive to keep the cycle going. Slow but effective, and no traces."

Mike looked hard at Jason. Ross looked away, slightly embarrassed for Jason.

"In fact," Jason added, "the same thing might happen if a Thingy ran into a moon or a planet."

"Okay," said Mike. "I'll buy this defensive reaction bit as possible but it sounds like something for Max' team to worry about. Right now we have to chase down a few of those little killers and put a muzzle on 'em."

"What are we looking for anyway, Vlad?" said Ross. "I mean I understand what we're doing right now but I'm still a little fuzzy on the mission objective here. What are we looking for?"

"Beat's me," replied Vlad. "Something different, I guess. Anything out of pattern."

"What's the pattern?" said Mike. "All they do is spin."

"Well, that's true enough," said Vlad. "They spin, their axes all pointed in exactly the same direction. They also grow in three dimensions maintaining perfect proportions. And they vibrate at an incredible, absolutely constant frequency. And each one is moving in a straight line.

They're accelerating predictably, completely contrary to the laws of physics. And the message from them has been precisely the same, repeated over and over, by a billion of them simultaneously. Outside of that, I guess there's not much of a pattern."

"All right, all right," muttered Mike with a cheerful gotta-job-to-do attitude. They each cross-checked the other's equipment and life suit. Standard EVA triple-check. "Let's do it."

Mike flipped the lock latching the helmet to his life suit and tapped his monitors to check vitals. He wrestled the mesh bag of instruments from the storage rack, jangled it once to compact the mass and snapped the tether to his utility harness.

Jason's 'non-language intrusions' team had designed an array of simple but extremely sensitive devices to attach to the shafts; Ross and Vlad had duty.

The instruments would measure whatever reaction the Shafts might have to their assaults. Reflective panels to monitor rotation and assist radar in tracking movement. Transducers to monitor the rate of oscillation. Transmitters and receivers. Devices to knock on the door, to apply sound waves, pressure, heat, radio waves and a variety of other forms of energy at a variety of intensities and frequencies. Heavy brackets for towing. Bull's-eyes for targeting.

Vlad looked thoughtfully at the net sling full of instruments like it was a bag of junk from the attic.

"Transducers," he mumbled.

"Huh?"

"Transducers," repeated Vlad. "The weak link. You know."

"What are you talking about? This stuff?"

"These are all transducers," confirmed Vlad. "Things to convert one energy form into another. That's always the weak link in any system. Just like your stereo; the microphone that recorded the music and the speakers that reconstruct it are the most critical."

"Yeah. Okay," muttered Ross as he fumbled with the sack. "So why's that?"

"Because the difference between the mechanics of sound waves and electronics are so different." Vlad paused to grunt a gizmo into place. "Because mechanical things have their own resonance frequencies and their own inertia. Because things are heavier than air and electrons. It's

202

too hard to get there from here and back; there's too much slippage in the translation."

"If I get your drift," said Ross, not at all certain he had, "you think these, uh, transducers won't work?"

"Oh, they'll work all right." He paused. "It's just the irony of it, I guess. This thing here, for example. It's supposed to measure any change in size. It's very precise, but the technology is basically the same as ol' Piezo worked out back when. It uses principles not much more sophisticated than Edison's first talkie. And we're using it to see if banging on these artifacts will get their attention! If it does," Vlad added, "they'll take one look and think we're out of the Stone Age. Theirs, not ours."

"Right."

Jason upthumbed the technician through the camera. With a final nod to Vlad and Ross through the airlock window, Mike turned to the hatch and waited for space.

"Okay, how many *is* a valid sample?"

"Come on," urged Ross. "Guess."

Vlad just grunted. A statistically valid sample of a million trillion Shafts? He thought to himself without really thinking about it. He was too busy right now, wrangling a Shaft and hog-tying it. He smiled at his metaphor; putting Pappa's instruments on a Shaft wasn't exactly cattle rustling but was a wrangle.

A million trillion! Vlad had visions of spending the rest of his natural life out here sticking micrometers on a billion Shafts. One at a time. Grumble. Why was he out here when there were plenty of Fives and Sixes for this kind of grunt work? That's what they're here for isn't it, to get practical hands-on experience? He grumbled again as he put his hand on another micrometer from the case tethered to his life suit.

"Five," said Ross Label, as though pulling a rabbit out of a hat.

"Five?" said Vlad dully, still miffed.

"Five Shafts. That's all it takes for a statistical sample." Ross turned to Vlad as though that would get his attention. "Pappa says that's all he needs for his projections."

"What? Oh, yeah," replied Vlad absently, busy. "Dammit!" Vlad still had a problem with the Shafts.

They rotated in space like any free-floating flotsam, but they were stuck in space like Ayer's Rock. At first contact he expected the Shaft to bounce away at his touch. It took a little time to adjust to its solidity when it didn't.

Once he got down to the fine work, he found the rotation of the Shaft and its almost complete lack of surface friction made attaching the instruments extremely difficult.

"Damn!"

It slowly slipped from his glove-encumbered grasp like a wet bar of soap or a fresh cantaloupe seed. The slightest touch would knock the instrument off, pushing his attempts at the fine adjustments beyond frustration. After the first few aborted attempts to attach instruments, they went back to the drawing board.

"Tell me again what the problem is," said Monk McIlhany, mechanic extraordinaire.

"Those fool things, excuse me, Thingys, are too darn slippery. And rotary. I have to hang on with one hand and work with the other. That rotation is just fast enough to keep you whipping away! Too tricky for fine work."

"Show me."

"Like this." Vlad held up a hand like he was holding a tumbler of water or a bouquet of flowers and pantomimed fiddling with a screwdriver against the imaginary object, rotating it as he did so.

"Try this," said Monk, handing Vlad a set of old reliable box-end Crescent wrenches. "They should help."

"Uunnh ..." Vlad was stumped at that. "I don't think I can stop them with a wrench!"

"You don't stop *them*. You start *you*." Monk poked a random piece of bar stock directly at Vlad's nose. "Find a wrench that fits and hang on. You will rotate with the Thingy. Find your center of gravity," he added moving the bar down to poke Vlad's belly, "and then you are relatively stationary."

"Hey! It works!" exclaimed Vlad back on the job. "HO bless Monk! Give that man a raise and a promotion!"

Monk and crew had also devised a harness which simplified installing the instruments enormously but it was still tricky and delicate. Vlad fiddled with the last adjustments to the micrometer, setting the sensor plates to precisely two grains pressure, two opposing plates per dimension, six to a Shaft. The Shaft rotated at almost one revolution per hour, just like its big brother, or daddy, making the final fine adjustments dicey.

"Okay, done. Check out the readings," Vlad mumbled to himself. "Okay, right on. Set baseline. Pappa was right; each of these devils is exactly the same size as every other. So far."

"Okay, micrometers installed. Remove the harness, check the readings again and number five is done." More mumbling. A blinking amber indicator light confirmed the instruments were on line.

"Looks Good," announced Vlad. "Back to the shuttle and it's Miller time. What were you were saying, Ross?"

"Never mind."

Dac watched his board as number five came on line. The readouts jumped excitedly as Vlad made the final adjustments and removed the harness. Another jump, then the readings settled on one number. Dead rock solid, without fluctuation, exactly the same as the other four Shafts to six decimal places. The five Shafts were exactly the same size, to a millionth of a centimeter. Pappa was right, he thought; five Shafts probably *is* statistically valid.

"Will that do it?" asked Dac of the board.

"That will do nicely," answered Pappa. "Thank you."

Dac looked at the board in a mild funk, uneasy about something but not sure what. Hell's Boils! He knew what it was; it was these Thingys, that's what. He just didn't know what about them that bothered him; he didn't have a comfortable level of specificity about the problem. So far they hadn't done anything dangerous, except kill Fats Bic, but we're just as guilty for that. Or dumb. He still didn't have a focus for his funk. What's behind them!

"Pappa!" said Dac suddenly. "Where do these things come from?"

"Things?" responded Pappa. Pappa scanned Dac's eyes and found them focused on the bird cage illustration of the Shaft that had killed Fats Bic. "If you mean the Shafts, they came from the original ..."

"I know," interrupted Dac. "I mean where did all of this come from, the Thingys, the Shafts, everything."

"Our current working hypothesis," answered Pappa, uncertain of Dac's direction, "is that they somehow capture new matter in the form of transient virtual particles ..."

"That's not what I mean, Pappa," said Dac, frustrated at his limited Thingy-ish vocabulary. He wasn't sure what he did mean, but it wasn't that. "I guess I mean how it got here. Where did it come from in the sense of, where was it before it was here?"

"If I understand you," responded Pappa, "you want to know its previous coordinates and vector?"

"Yes!" said Dac, almost shouting. "Where did that first Thingy come from and where was it going!"

"One moment." A moment. "When we found it," Pappa took an extra moment to assess Dac's emotional status, just in case, "the original Thingy was moving towards Lacerta, roughly parallel to our own trajectory. Its velocity was approximately 80% of our own, about .0012 percent of light speed. The details are on your board now, Mr. Olson."

Dac studied the information displayed. There it was in the middle of the Bubble where there was nothing before, nothing known. Going like Hell's Bullet from somewhere to somewhere. Now it's going like Hell's Buckshot, he thought.

"So it came from where?"

"Assuming," Here we go again, thought Dac, "the original Thingy was moving in a straight line," answered Pappa. "It came from the general direction of Hydra. But if it was in space as long as it seems to have been, and moving at that speed for all of that time, it may have originally come from anywhere. You will observe that the derivative Shafts are moving in virtually every direction even now."

"Can you give me a vector for the whole cloud of Shafts?"

"Yes, Mr. Olson," replied Pappa. "The cloud is moving as a whole in the same direction as the first Thingy, but dissipating rapidly. Please check your board."

"Looking at the center of mass of the cloud," followed Dac, "does it have the same vector as the original when we found it?"

"No," replied Pappa. "The cloud is accelerating slightly, but in the same direction."

"Accelerating!?"

Dac pondered that for a few seconds, adjusting for the scale. The Shafts in the cloud were also accelerating, deliberately dispersing, he thought, excusing the anthropomorphism. The concept of the expanding universe pushed to the surface, from some long ago and mostly forgotten physics course. Did these things push each other apart, or inflate like the surface of the classical cosmic balloon? Or was that a raison cake?

"The whole cloud?"

"The center of mass of the cloud," corrected Pappa, "as you requested. Individual motions are distributed in a highly symmetrical manner, with a range of proper motions in a largely ecliptic plane, if you will."

Dac then took a different tack.

"Just how long do you think it has been in space?" asked Dac. The question hadn't really come up before, at least not in any serious discussion.

"Assuming ..."

"How long!" barked Dac. "Make a Goddam guess!"

"At least 315 years, Mr. Olson," replied Pappa instantly, his emulators abuzz, "for the one original Thingy, but probably more like several thousand years. However ..." Pappa paused on his own initiative.

"However what?" responded Dac apprehensively.

"The original Thingy may have been ... probably represents only one derivative cycle of previous fission and growth cycles such as we now witness."

"Translate that, Pappa," said Dac, reasonably sure he knew what it meant.

"We have seen the Thingy break down into many small Shafts," explained Pappa, "and start to grow again. Each Shaft will probably grow into another Thingy the size of the original. That is one cycle. The number of previous cycles cannot be determined, Mr. Olson, but if they are regenerating from the inexhaustible supply of virtual matter, they may have repeated the cycle any number of times."

"Any number?" asked Dac. "Like a thousand times?"

"Yes."

"A million times?"

"There is no apparent reason why they could not have completed a million cycles, Mr. Olson."

"Is there an apparent reason," probed Dac, "why they could not have completed, say, a billion cycles?"

"Yes, Mr. Olson," said Pappa. "With a minimum cyclic period of three hundred years it would take three hundred billion years to complete a billion cycles. Our best estimates place the age of the universe at around fourteen billion years, plus or minus ..."

"Give me a practical maximum number of cycles then," said Dac.

"Anything up to a million cycles," answered Pappa, "is possible and reasonable. Given an average of one thousand years per cycle, that would take a billion years." Then after a moment, "That is wildly speculative, Mr. Olson; I cannot defend that figure and I am not sure I would be comfortable leaving this conversation on file without qualifiers."

"Okay," said Dac, agreeing completely. He wasn't sure he wanted that on record either, but it was no more irrational than anything else. "That's off the record, Pappa. Queue it for trash."

"Thank you, Mr. Olson. Is there anything else?"

"Yes. Where did they come from? We didn't settle that."

"Why, Mr. Olson," said Pappa, "they probably came from the direction of Hydra or Centaurus."

"Okay," said Dac sheepishly. "I knew that."

Dac studied the lethal Shaft on his board, lingering as though sheer persistence of eye fix could solve the mystery.

"Pappa, look back where the Thingy came from," he said, finally putting two and two together. "I want you to find something that looks or feels or smells like a million Thingy cycles!"

CHAPTER 24

THE KEY

"Bingo!" sang Uni, with her unflappably normal "Of course" mien.

"Gotcha!" said Pat Grey exultantly with the classically triumphant weightlifter's curled arm and clenched fist.

"It's a bloody book!" said Winnie Logo in disbelief. "Can you believe it?"

"Book nothing!" challenged Bill Stewart. "That's a whole library!"

"I see it and I believe it," added Uni, visibly impressed. "I hope I live long enough to read it! How long do you suppose it takes to say 'Hi'?"

"How long?" said Ad. "Bill's right; it's a library full. A full 0.0020-second word delivering data at something over two times ten to the 40th bps is ... well, a bunch. You could transmit everything in the Library of Congress in that one word."

"Well folks," said Uni with immense satisfaction. "You should be proud. All of you. I think we finally have the key. Bill, get Dac and whoever down here. And break out some Champagne!"

"War and Peace!" exulted Dac as he hustled into Spook Central with a grin and a sense of excitement. He looked expectantly at Uni and each of the others on her team, at the walls dripping with scribbled ideas, and back to Uni. 'Results!' was all he could think, we're finally getting somewhere! He scanned the room like he thought the results would be in a neat pile somewhere with a label pinned to them proclaiming 'The Theory of Everything According To the Aliens'.

"Right?" prompted Dac expectantly.

"Not quite, Mr. Olson," said Uni. Big grins all around. "But close. We feel we have found the basis for their vocabulary, the mechanism they use to build words. And we may have actually translated something! We have to give credit for the breakthrough to Ad. He made the first connections."

"Great!" enthused Dac. "Let's hear it, Ad."

"This is really something," began Ad, smiling to the others shyly. "Their words are built up of sequences structured like Army nomenclature. You know, 'Meal, ready-to-eat, beef, ground patty, with bun, one only.' Inside out from the way everybody talks. But the aliens are far more sophisticated than that. Complicated is probably a better word," he corrected, looking to Uni. "It's incredibly wasteful and redundant by our standards, but extremely precise."

"Give me an example."

"Take a word like, oh, wood," he continued. "That word implies a vast amount of experience in order to understand it precisely. And when we hear the word, or read it, we usually don't understand it precisely the way it was meant, we just get close enough to get by. If we need to be more precise we use a lot of adjectives and questions and answers and trial-and-error. Okay?"

"No," said Dac. "At least I'm not sure where you're going with this. Go ahead and I'll stop you before it hurts."

"All right," said Ad. "It appears that each alien word is a complete description of everything about that concept, structured like that army hamburger from the general to the specific. Their word for 'wood' might list concepts like living stuff, chemical composition, species and genus and phylum and whatever. What part of the tree it came from, who cut it and who processed it, the color, finish, size, everything you can imagine. It's as though they always add on to a word as it evolves without ever removing anything. The result might be a million distinct words for wood."

Ad stopped for some sort of registration or connection to Dac. Nothing, but at least tacit permission to continue.

"Take your War and Peace for example," continued Ad. "That title means a lot to anyone who read the book and understands the political and economic setting. It also usually means 'big hard-to-read book'. You assume all of that whenever you refer to the book by name, and if your listener doesn't understand all of that, well that's okay too. The aliens, however, seem to include all of that background in the word for the book; the equivalent of the whole book is the word, along with the history of the period and maybe several literary critiques as well. They don't imply or assume anything, they include it all! And the incredible part is that every time they use the same word they repeat the whole blooming sequence!"

"Now it *is* starting to hurt," said Dac, eager to get to the good stuff. "But go on. I like pain."

"Okaaay," replied Ad skeptically. Was that a joke?

"It's similar to our information management systems to organize data," interjected Pat Grey, "but using hundreds of echelons of subdirectories, with the final subdirectory having only one piece of information in it. Their word for that piece of information would be the equivalent of the complete path for that subdirectory."

"That's a good way to describe it, Pat," said Uni. "And the complete path is repeated each time the word is used. Remember that first translation that we thought was a period?"

"The sentence ending sequence?" replied Dac. "Sure."

"Right. Well we struggled with that for a long time because it was such a big period. One of their periods fills the same amount of memory as your ship's log to date, almost two year's entries!" Uni paused to check that Dac was keeping up. "We thought there had to be more meaning in a sequence that long but there isn't. It's just a period. But that period has everything there is to know about periods, which tells us a Helluva lot about their punctuation rules. Or it will eventually."

"Hell's Jots!" Dac blinked, contemplating his own apparently limited understanding of the mundane period. "How do you suppose they came up with this lingo?"

"I like to compare it to how our own genes and chromosomes developed," injected Ad. "We humans share a lot of genetic coding with all other animals, even down to amoebas. The theory is that as animals developed and evolved, chromosomes just kept adding more and more genes while keeping the original coding. Life even turns some of that coding off when it's no longer needed but life doesn't seem to delete it. It just keeps adding on." Ad stopped, feeling correctly that he had provided more information than was needed right now. "At least that's what I read," he finished mildly.

"I think I'm getting the idea," said Dac. "At least as much as I need right now. How did you manage to figure this all out?"

"Well, we didn't do it all by ourselves," said Uni, understating things a bit. "We had a little help. The process is simple enough but extremely labor intensive. You just look for identical strings in the sequence and compare them to near-identical strings. The differences are the keys to meaning. With their military style nomenclature, there are major, major strings that are identical with only the very last elements differing. The opening sequences group the words into general subjects; the endings specify the exact meaning. To make manipulation easier, we assign a short code to each long beginning sequence, making words and sentences much more manageable."

"Can Pappa do that?" asked Dac. Pappa was good but he had physical limits.

"The process takes massive computing power, far more than we have here. Most of the grunt work is done in the HO," answered Uni. "And even they had to borrow processing time. They assembled a consortium just for this project. It draws on computer capacity contributed by interested industries. They feed their results to us in real time, delayed three days, but in practice it takes several weeks to get responses. Then Pappa works primarily with our coded system to conserve capacity. We're the primary source of data so the final compilation is done here. Pappa compares their results with his refined recordings of the sequence to eliminate errors, and the whole mess is recycled."

"They're doing all that?" remarked Dac, recalling of the frustrating teeth-pulling he had to do for even minimal amenities for the ship. "Who did you have to … How did you get those crats …" Then after a moment contemplating his need for perceived professionalism, "When can we start talking to the aliens?"

"I don't think you completely understand, Mr. Olson," replied Uni patiently. "It's similar in scope to the original mapping of Ad's human genetic code, but for every person on one planet. The vast bulk of the codes are the same for everyone but each one is slightly different. Translation is a matter of finding those differences; the differences define the individual. A sentence is the equivalent of a row of people standing in a line. Alien writing is the equivalent of recording the genetic codes for everyone in that line of people. The aliens use the whole code; we're just going to use their first names."

"Wow," said Dac with a surprising lack of emotion; he was more stupefied by the scope than amazed. "Why do they write that way?"

"That's an obvious question, Dac," answered Jimmy Klein, using the informal first name in his excitement. Nobody noticed or cared. "We knocked that around a lot. We think the reason is precision; there is only one way to understand each word. Once we translate it there is probably no way we can mistranslate it. They must have no limits on storage capacity, or time for that matter."

"Or this message is extremely important," added Bill.

"But can we talk to them?" asked Dac.

"In a word," said Uni, "No. Not yet. It's like somebody took the covers off of all the books in a library and stuck them together into one big book a mile long. At this point we think we have broken that big book back down into the original books and we can identify chunks we'd call words. But that's all we have so far, the structure of the units. We don't know what the units mean. We need the key."

"What key?"

"We're looking for a Rosetta Stone," said Uni. "Remember the Rosetta Stone? For years archaeologists were unable to translate hieroglyphic writing, whatever that ancient Egyptian language was. Even the Egyptians couldn't translate it. Then they discovered the Rosetta stone. It had a message written in three different languages, hieroglyphics and Greek and something. The same message in all three. That was the key. That's what we need, something to give us an unambiguous meanings for a threshold number of words. Then the rest will happen."

"Uh, okay," said Dac, understanding in spite of his disappointment. "This has been a huge project. How did you pull all of it together so quickly?"

"I really didn't have to do it all," said Uni. "It just took off by itself. This has taken the corporation by storm and is spreading to the other planets as well; there must be some money in it somewhere.

"Apparently it will take most of a year to get a team out here," she continued. "Since they wouldn't be able to do much more than what we're doing anyway, right now we're the only game in town," added Uni.

"They're giving us anything we want in the way of technical support. In fact, they're throwing it at us. The clutter is starting to interfere with our work.

"I think every computer in the Peters sector is in on this, including all the washing machines and half the thermostats." Uni seemed a bit embarrassed at her unintended humor, but rolled with it.

"You said you had actually translated something?" said Dac, still considering thermostats. "More than the period, I hope."

"Yes," said Uni proudly. "That's one thing we can take full credit for. We're almost certain about the first word in the whole sequence."

"And that word is?"

"The first word is Hello."

"Hello!" mimicked Dac in uncontrolled Glee. "Months working with all the washing machines in the bloody universe and all we get is Hello!" Dac giggled himself to tears while he slipped limply from the sofa.

"Well, they're doing their best, Dac," said Marcy, put off by Dac's untypically mocking attitude about his own crew. "I mean, who's doing any better? At least it's something."

Dac picked up on Marcy's turned-off tone and instantly adjusted his own. His face actually creaked at the sudden stop.

"Look, Marcy," he began, massaging the back of her neck. "Sorry. That was uncalled for. I just get so full of this business I ... I don't know." Vulnerable mode. "I guess it's because we're making so little progress and everything is such a mystery. Every little detail becomes important, every little straw, and sometimes I just need to get away and blow the tubes out. You know what I mean?" A little smirk remained, however.

Marcy caught the smirk and the tubes bit and pushed herself gently out to arms length.

"Now come on!" said Dac with a devilish leer. "You know what I mean."

"Yeah, I know what you mean," said Marcy. Dac wasn't fooling anyone.

"Look, Marcy," said Dac, trying a diversionary tactic. "Tell you what. How about a pizza and a pitcher of beer down at Dino's, then we hit the drive-in. A couple of those awful midnight slasher or bikini things, with the top down. The convertible top. Then we make mad passionate love all night and rip holes in the sheets. Okay?" Dac put on his best spanking fresh BMOC pose, but with tongue hanging out to one side, panting.

"It'll take more than a pizza to mummpf nee mlorg."

"I'll get the lights," he said coming up for breath.

"Three," said Ad. "Definitely three."

"I agree," said Bill Stewart. "And I'd bet my pension the first is their history."

"That's a pretty safe bet," agreed Ad diplomatically. "That would be the most likely subject to open a message to another culture like us." He paused diplomatically. "There's only one problem."

"What's that?" asked Pat Grey, still a little wide-eyed about it all.

"Bill assumes it's a message to another culture like us. It could be a parts list or stage play for all we know." Ad scratched his chin stubble ostentatiously. "Bill, did you ever see a parts list open with a history lesson?"

"No," replied Bill grudgingly. Then brightening. "Well ... yes, as a matter of fact. I've seen plenty of catalogs that open with a blurb about what a fine company it is that makes these fine frannistans for the good of mankind and their wonderful people whose philosophy of hard work and craftsmanship produced such a success story and how old George Frump started the company on a shoestring back in blumpty-dump and now it is the largest ..."

"Okay. Okay," said Ad. "Maybe you're right. Let's assume the first part is some sort of history or background or overview or stage setting summary. That's as good as any working hypothesis right now and better than most. What about the other two parts?"

Three parts. The 473 minute sequence has three major sections each distinguished by the extended sequence that began each 'word' in that section. Each section seemed to be on a different subject, or directed at a different audience, or written in a different mode. The distinctions were not clear as to what they actually were, but they *were* distinct.

"Well, it seems likely that one of them would refer to the Shafts somehow," said Winnie. "How it works, a parts list, how to operate it, how to fix it, that sort of thing. After all, the message is built into the Shaft; it probably refers to the Shaft somewhere."

"That's not likely at all," said Mercedes bluntly. "We put all kinds of recordings in all kinds of media. When was the last time you bought a recording of a symphony that had the technical specifications of the disk recorded on the disk? Or a book with the bookbinder's manufacturing process printed in the book?"

"Yeah, maybe, Mercedes. But you're arguing a priori," rebutted Winnie, with fervor. "You're assuming it's a message about something other than the Shafts to prove that it's not about the Shafts. What if the message is the Shaft's operator's manual. Did you ever buy a car or any major appliance without an operator's manual!?"

"Okay. That's settled," moderated Uni. "The message, all or part, is either about the Shafts or it isn't. Good. We're making real progress here. What else have we got?"

"Chirp. Excuse me."

"What is it, Pappa?" said Uni. Just in time, she thought; those guys looked about ready to throw donuts.

"I believe Winnie Logo is correct," said Pappa.

"Since when are you choosing sides!" said Mercedes, only partly in good humor.

"Sides?" replied Pappa, confused. "Ah. There is a point of contention between those holding opposing opinions. May I ask what that point is?"

"We were just *exploring*," said Uni, with heavy emphasis on the word *exploring*, "the likelihood that information in the sequence concerns the Shafts as such. I would not call it a point of contention; we have simply not yet reached consensus. Now what is it you want, Pappa?"

"That is why I called," replied Pappa. "Part of the sequence does concern the Shaft itself. There is a sequence in the third part with structural characteristics consistent with certain physical qualities of the Shafts."

Spook Central was quiet as an undiscovered tomb. An electrostatic click betrayed Pappa verifying his link to Spook Central was still open. Satisfied, he continued.

"At one point there is what appears to be a series of three numbers in base twenty-six. The ratio of the three numbers is precisely that of the three dimensions of each Shaft."

"You're sure about the ratio?"

"That ratio," said Pappa, "has not changed in the slightest from the original thingy down to the smallest Shaft and at present as they continue to grow. The ratios are precise, to beyond my ability to measure. The probability of chance coincidence is virtually non-existent."

"And you're sure about the numbers?" checked Uni.

"I would not be sure about the numbers but for the precise match of their ratios with observation."

"That's a yes?"

"Yes."

"Probability?"

"One."

"One?"

"Complete certainty, Uni," translated Pappa. "There is no possibility of error."

"Bingo!"

"Chirp."

"Chirp."

"Chirp!"

"What is it, Pappa!" barked Dac, throttling a primordial rage born in that most profound of all frustrations. Dammitall! Do they have to call me about every hangnail and flyspeck! "This had better be good or I'll have your canastas!"

"Canas ...?"

"Never Goddam mind!!" Dac grabbed for his emergency mood enhancers. "Hell's Interruptus! What *is* it!"

"I believe, Mr. Olson," said Pappa proudly, "that we have found the Rosetta Stone."

"Don't forget the lights," shouted Dac over his shoulder.

CHAPTER 25

SOURCE

"The Great Attractor."

"The what!?"

"The Great Attractor, Mr. Olson," said Pappa, talking slow. "You asked what lies in the direction opposite to the vector of the Shaft cloud."

"I did?" said Dac, still distracted by the hassle with the breakdown of the water recovery plant precipitated by the breakdown in the sewage treatment plant. "Why?"

"I believe you felt a need to know the source of the Thingy, Mr. Olson," replied Pappa.

"Oh. Right." Dac terminated the vitriolic memo to HO about the shoddy equipment he was forced to work with, a mostly therapeutic exercise that would never make it to HO. He stretched his back and shoulders, arm wrestling himself behind his back.

"Okay, Pappa. What have you got?"

"The Great Attractor, Mr. Olson," repeated Pappa patiently. "It lies roughly in the direction of Hydra and Centaurus, as you specified."

"I thought that was just a theory, Pappa." He reconsidered. "Is there really something out there?"

"The evidence for the Great Attractor is circumstantial at best, Mr. Olson," said Pappa. "When the various component vectors for galactic motion are accounted for, there is always one indicating a gravitational influence roughly at a right angle to the overall expansion of the universe, towards Hydra. The assumption is some extremely large gravity well lies in that direction. It is thought to be a large concentration of dark matter or black holes. The object is beyond the range of present observational techniques. It will probably remain unobserved because of the Wall and the general interference of interstitial debris. There has been practically no hard research on the matter, Mr. Olson, as it has no practical value."

"No research?" responded Dac. "It seems like a profitable subject for research."

"That is true in the sense that research would likely provide some insight about the nature of things," agreed Pappa. "However, the subject is probably not profitable in the monetary sense. That particular line of study has no unique practical value over and above far more accessible venues. There apparently is little incentive to pursue it. My review of recent literature shows almost no direct studies, only incidental references, mostly tangential at best."

"Until now," observed Dac.

"Quite."

"The Great Attractor," repeated Dac. "It has a nice ring to it, doesn't it? Like some old movie star."

Pappa lost that track and was about to ask for clarification when Dac continued.

"Is it big enough?"

"Is what big enough for what, Mr. Olson?"

"The Great Attractor. There must be some estimate of size or mass or distance if they were able to identify the vectors pointing to it. Would it be anything like a million years of Shafts regenerating?"

"That's why I mentioned it, Mr. Olson," replied Pappa. "You did ask."

"Unh, right. And?"

"The mass of the alleged Great Attractor is very large but has been estimated to within a reasonable range, Mr. Olson. The possible mass of the postulated Shaft source is speculative at best, but given a range of assumptions I can project a range of possible masses back in time and space in the direction of the Great Attractor. Those two ranges overlap considerably at intersection."

"Is that a yes?"

"Yes, Mr. Olson." Dac had asked that question of Pappa a lot lately. Pappa made a note to examine the matter in depth.

✦ ✦ ✦

"Somewhat more than 200,000,000 light years, Mr. Berkley," replied Pappa. "Although you must understand that is only accurate to perhaps plus or minus 40,000,000 light years."

"Two hundred ..."

Max dropped the sheaf of papers to his lap and cast his eyes heavenward. He looked from Dac to Pappa, manifest in the display board, and back to Dac. They were serious, he thought. Serious!

"Let me get this straight," said Max with a not too well concealed derisive snort. "Mummmpf. You want me to chase all over the galaxy looking for Thingys millions of light years away." It was not a question.

"Yes," replied Dac, seriously. "Well, that's not exactly the way I would put it, Max." Dac looked at Max while he thought of a way to put it. Max looked back at him as if he had just asked Max to lasso a rainbow.

"Look, Max," he began. "One big Thingy is a curiosity. A million trillion tiny Shafts in a cloud is a hazard at best, but avoidable. A million trillion big Thingys a thousand years from now is serious."

"But," continued Dac seriously, "if our Big Thingy was only one pup from a previous cloud, and that cloud a pup from another previous cloud, back generation after generation ... Well, a trillion here and a trillion there, pretty soon you're talking serious mass."

Max was still wary of a wild goose chase but had to admit the magnitude of Dac's hypothesis commanded attention. They hadn't investigated the Thingy's provenance at all, its present and future realities being formidable enough to occupy their resources fully. And the idea of being the man who discovered the Great Attractor held a certain charm. It would certainly make his reputation as a scientist, he thought. And open who knew what doors. That sounded like upside all around.

"Okay," he said finally, mellowed somewhat. "But why me and why now? My team was charged with figuring out what they are and how they work, not where their daddies came from. What's the connection?"

"I don't *know* that there's a connection between where they come from and what they do," replied Dac, pronouncing his words carefully for effect, "But there *may* be a connection."

"May?" replied Max, trying hard not to sound sarcastic and largely failing. "There *may* be a better connection to the direction they're going. There *may* be a connection to the direction the axis of rotation is pointed; they all point exactly the same direction, you know. There *may* be a connection to their shape or rate of vibration or what they're made of or any of a thousand things we don't understand about them already!" Oops, he thought, I may have overstated my case. Go for broke. "Which one is first?"

"Good points," said Dac, noting Max' penchant for overstatement but reluctantly conceding that he had indeed made good points. "Maybe your team should pursue those as well. But ..."

"We *are* pursuing them," said Max flatly. "And others, of course."

"Of course," said Dac. "Then you understand why I think we should pursue this possibility as well, at least as part of your other efforts." Then in a milder tone, "I get this image, Max, of an iceberg in the middle of a sea. The first guy who saw one probably had no idea what it was, but finding out where it came from would have told him a lot about it, like if he travels in that direction watch out for more of them. Like there's a whole new land to explore and conquer. Like glaciers and ice ages and icemen."

Dac stopped, a little embarrassed at revealing his philosophical side. Max studied Dac, fascinated by his philosophical side. Maybe Dac wasn't just another crat he thought, sticking his nose into places that exposed his complete amateur status. Maybe he really wanted to know. Max had to admit, he did, too.

"All right," said Max. "But give me a priority on this. There's not a lot of computer time available, you know."

"Yes, I know." Everybody was screaming for more time because of the vast amount of computer capacity dedicated to the translation project. "Give it equal footing with any other promising line of inquiry, Max. Use your best judgment. Pappa? Have you been monitoring?"

"Yes, Mr. Olson."

"I want you to give Max all the help you can on this, consistent with other activities and priorities. Max has conflict resolution priority."

"Yes, Mr. Olson," confirmed Pappa. "Mr. Berkley, I think I can help you with this project."

Max looked at Dac and Dac looked at Max.

"What kept you?" said Max first.

"I beg your pardon?"

"Uh, what do you have for us, Pappa?" said Dac with a wry smile toward Max.

"Scan the sky in the direction of the Great Attractor for gravity waves at 2.4754 times 10 to the 46th."

Max recognized the frequency immediately, the vibrational frequency of the Shafts, the carrier wave frequency. It was also the frequency of the weak gravity waves emitted by the Thingys and Shafts. The possible connection to the Great Attractor was obvious, *now*. Max winked at Dac.

"If we do that, Pappa," asked Max slyly, "what do you expect we will find?"

"You will find a strong source of gravity waves at that frequency in that direction, Mr. Berkley."

"And why do you say that, Pappa?"

"Because I found a strong source of gravity waves at that frequency in that direction, Mr. Berkley."

"And why didn't you tell us that before?"

"Before what, Mr. Berkley?"

"... " Max was momentarily stumped.

"Never mind, Pappa," said Dac. "But how did you know to look for gravity waves?"

"The only evidence for the presence of the Great Attractor is its being a gravity well. In fact, Mr. Olson, I believe that is the reason it is called the Great Attractor. Gravity waves are very weak, as you know, but they travel an infinite distance, certainly far enough to encompass the Great Attractor. The mode of search was obvious."

"Okay," said Dac. Yes it was obvious, *now*. "Anyway, you found the source of the Shafts?"

"I did not say I found the source of the Shafts, Mr. Olson," said Pappa incontrovertibly. "I said I found a source of gravity waves at 2.4753 times ..."

"All right!" barked Dac. Hell's Obtusey Farts! "Close enough! Max?"

"Close enough," he agreed with a grin. "I'll take it from here."

CHAPTER 26

PRIMER

"You were right," said Uni. "It *is* a parts manual."

"Well, a numbers manual anyway," replied Winnie. "Look at this string!" Winnie flipped open several fanfolds of printout and ran her finger down a series of numbers. The file was one of dozens neatly stacked on a work table at the end of the room. "We had to reconstruct the numbers in base 128 to keep them manageable."

"Yes," confirmed Uni. "Mersenne primes. There are reams of number series like that. Look here, Fibonacci numbers to ... to ..." Flippity flip. "Lordy! Vinogradov to Lagrange to Thingy knows what."

"Do you think they mean anything," said Bill, leaning back in his chair. "I mean, other than just what they are?"

"There may be some connection to the rest of the message, Bill," replied Uni. "But I agree with the rest of you; this is probably a primer to help the reader do just what we're doing, read the message."

"Well, it certainly helps translation," said Mercedes. "At least it's starting to look like English, but it's not very enlightening yet. Mostly just childish babbling. Mr. Olson will have to wait for his War and Peace."

There were a few polite chuckles around Spook Central. Translation so far positively revealed thirty-six unique characters and potentially hundreds more. Pythagoras only knew how many there were in their number system. And mathematical terms for basic binary operations, maybe.

Non-math words developed far more gradually but randomly. Long strings that appeared to be 'sentences' might have only one or two translated words in a hundred or a thousand. The work proceeded methodically but slowly.

"I'll settle for War," said Dac as he slipped into the room. "Peace can wait. How're we coming?"

Dac stumbled a little to a stop and looked around the room in mild but pleasant surprise. The room was transformed, much more orderly now that they were making real progress. The trash disappeared. The walls displayed only a relatively few neatly printed flow charts outlining the structure of the message. The conference table in the center of the room was clean, bearing only current and apparently well organized work. The ubiquitous donuts were relegated to their proper place on a side table alongside the fresh coffee. Napkins were again in neat stacks, the pencils all sharpened. Dac looked around approvingly, and nodded to let them know he appreciated the improvement.

The team had progressed from the frantic guess-and-error stage that generated piles of half-developed and quickly abandoned ideas to a laid-back 'watch the monitor and see what the computers do next' mode. New words flowed from the HO consortium by twos and threes.

"Come on in," said Uni. "We were just discussing these number series. It seems the aliens meant to help us translate the message."

"How do you figure that," asked Dac with a little mock surprise. "I'm sure we didn't tell them we were coming."

"I'm sure they didn't expect us, Mr. Olson," said Uni. "But they apparently expected somebody who could not read Thingy-ish."

"Like who?"

"Like children," said Bill.

"Oh." Dac considered that. "How long do you think it takes the kids to recite their ABCs?"

"Take these number series, for example," continued Uni, ignoring Dac's comment. "If the numbers are actually functional, they wouldn't list them all; they would just record the formulas, the descriptors, the operators. That's the way a programmer would do it, write a subroutine to generate a number when needed. The listings take up massive space, and they're far longer than necessary to establish the series. The lists must be there only as a reading exercise or a drill."

"Or something like a test routine to trouble shoot the Shaft's function," suggested Ad, "which amounts to the same thing."

"Okay," conceded Dac. "It's a training course or something?"

"Not something," said Uni. "A training course."

"Okay. But how does that help us?"

"That's a big advantage," interjected Bill Stewart. "We can make a few assumptions that help direct our search."

"Like what?" asked Dac, actually engaged.

"Well," said Bill after a thoughtful moment, "we can assume they don't assume too much. Looking at the thorough way they do things, they probably don't assume anything. Just like these number series. Three or four series might have been enough to describe the basics of their number system, but they included over a hundred that we've found so far. They may be for their equivalent of memorizing the times tables. If it is designed to teach, then we can look for other exercises like this."

"Do you believe these guys actually expect their kids to recite these long lists of numbers?" said Dac. "That seems downright pointless and punitive."

"I agree, Mr. Olson." Bill looked to the others before continuing. "I'd bet that after a few numbers in a list, the student might be expected to actually calculate the numbers as an exercise. In that scenario, the lists would amount to answer sheets."

"Yes. Even more important," said Winnie, "the exercises should be cumulative. You know, present a simple concept or word, apply it, and then build on it logically in a pattern. When we find the pattern we can leap-frog from there. We can also expect the information on a given subject to be comprehensive instead of just bits and dabs, hopefully with cross-references."

"We can also assume," said Jimmy Klein, "that complex concepts have a description somewhere, like a glossary of terms or a help program, or an index. In fact, that's what I'm looking for right now, the index. It's almost inconceivable that a body of information this size wouldn't have an index or glossary of some sort. If it's a training course, those should be certain."

"That all sounds good," responded Dac, thoughtfully, "and I don't want to be a wet blanket. But aren't you assuming that they're very much human?"

"Yes, you're right," said Uni. "We are. But it's been possible to learn the language of many different species of animals on earth and elsewhere by making some very human assumptions.

"Some things," she continued, "like survival instincts, hunger, comfort, safety, fear, pain and many more subtle psychological characteristics are common to higher animals on any planet. We sorta talk, after a fashion, to dozens of reasonably bright animal species; I think it's valid to assume at least that much commonality with the aliens."

"What's the position of HO on the humanity of the aliens?" asked Dac. "Do they concur?"

"They concur," replied Uni, "in the sense that we have to start with some assumptions and human thought patterns are as valid as any of the other seventeen they are using in their databases. Since the experts on the other non-human species thought patterns are there and not here, they're letting us concentrate on the human approach. With guidance and control, of course."

"Of course." Dac pondered the discussion. "Are they human? I mean, I know they're not *human*, but do we have to treat them as human under our concept of the ... our law?"

"No."

"No? Unqualified no? That's kind of a conversation stopper."

"Yes. Not much room for discussion on that HO position."

Dac and Uni looked at each other thoughtfully. Uni gave in first.

"Keep in mind, Mr. Olson, that we aren't actually talking to the aliens; we're only listening in on what they wrote who knows when or how or why or to whom." Uni paused to formulate an example. "It's a little like the first explorers who found those big heads on Easter Island. They were obviously made by someone, and probably by humans but the stone statues themselves were only stone, not human, with no legal rights."

Dac seemed doubtful but satisfied, for now.

"So far we are getting some results," said Ad Blanker. "But there is a nagging translation problem. Humans are pretty sloppy with language. We can use a word loosely any number of ways. Take 'fix' for example, or 'do' or 'thing.' Those words have entirely different meanings in different contexts. Hundreds of meanings, sometimes even contradictory meanings. In the alien message, each context would be a completely different word, coming from entirely different roots."

"Yes, I see that," said Dac. "But we have plenty of alternate words for those contexts. Can't you just translate into those 'us'-specific words?"

"Yes!" blurted Ad, "If we could find them! That's the problem; the long general-to-specific opening sequence for each word may be completely different depending on context. The alien mathematical term 'is' isn't a generic concept-word for 'is more or less the same as, depending on the context' that we can look for. At least not one we can find. Translating one does not lead to finding other words meaning some sort of equivalency.

"Similarly," he continued, enjoying the opportunity, "the counting number 'one' used as a digit in a number is a different word entirely depending on its place in the number, or when used as an adjective, as in 'one potato.' Or worse yet, as in 'one shouldn't throw stones'.

"Our words are context sensitive," he concluded. "Theirs do not appear to be. If the meaning is shaded by context, they seem to just invent a new unrelated word for it, as if they just took the next number out of a box and added an appropriate opening string to categorize it. If there is a system, we sure haven't found it. They probably do not have synonyms, two words with the same meaning, or one word with two meanings, whatever you call those."

"I see," said Dac, beginning to see the magnitude of the problem. He reached for a donut. "You have a little problem there, don't you. But that sure seems like an incredibly wasteful way to do things. Does this actually make sense to you? Do they really talk this way?"

"My guess," said Ad, "is there's no way they could talk this way, or however they communicate. Take our digital sound recording systems; the recording is made by sampling the original music some hundred thousand times a second but the replay might only sound a one-second note. They write like the recorder but maybe only talk like the playback. What we're seeing is formal and technical. Nobody here talks like a dictionary. They don't either." One second. "Probably."

"I think of it as one of our spoken words, for example," chimed in Uni. "Take any spoken word along with all of the thought processes going into choosing that particular word and the sequence of nerve activity required to generate that word and the neural-muscular activity to make that sound and the physical accoutrements to that speech, like looking at someone with a smile or a frown or a wink. That's a lot behind every word."

"That's right, Uni," added Ad. "Plus body language is part of a word, too. Facial expression, posture, gesture, slouch, speed of talking, lisp, regional accent, disabilities in each person. How about interpersonal relationships; a word can mean completely different things depending on whether you're talking to your boss, or spouse or child or adversary."

"So if you want to be completely unambiguous to someone who can't see or hear you and doesn't know who you are," concluded Uni, "you have to include all of that. That would make our words pretty hefty, too."

"That's right," said Jimmy, "Their structure makes sense if you assume it's extremely important to totally eliminate ambiguity, at least in this application. We have all kinds of situations like that; they probably do, too.

"Remember the first computer program you wrote?" he continued. "You probably tried to tell the computer what you wanted instead of telling it exactly what to do. You had to break each operation down until there was no possible way the computer could get it wrong."

"And then it always got it wrong anyway," said Dac truthfully. "That's why I'm not a programmer."

"The same thing happens in speech," continued Jimmy. "How many times do you say something that's misunderstood? Then somebody has to ask questions to get it right, and you have to straighten them out, then they write a memo to confirm it, and you have to correct something in the memo, and so on. Well, the aliens just put all of that hassle up front into one long word that cannot be misunderstood."

"It's like two ways of doing business," interjected Bill. "One company ships every part they make without quality control, knowing some are defective and will be returned for repair. Another company tests each part to make sure it's perfect and won't be returned. Which way costs more in the long run; the cost of eliminating errors up front or the cost of repairing defects? Deming would love these guys!"

"I'm beginning to like them myself," agreed Dac.

"But!" said Mercedes in a passion. "There is one tremendous advantage to the alien vocabulary. Word structure relies on the fundamental principal of mathematics: each number, and each alien word, has one and only one unambiguous meaning. Once translated, the meaning of the word cannot be mistaken."

"I take it," said Dac, "the aliens have no word for pun."

CHAPTER 27

PUMPS

"They're pumps."

"Pumps?"

"Right," repeated Max. "Pumps."

"Pumps."

Max noticed Dac's change in inflection and assumed he had internalized the proposition. He could sympathize with Dac; he had trouble with the idea himself.

"What do they pump?" asked Dac, a little embarrassed feeling that Max assumed he knew what Max was talking about, but satisfied his was a reasonable question.

"Mass," replied Max, enjoying Dac's discomfort. "They do just what it looks like they're doing."

Dac managed to come to full attention as he pushed aside the stack of new work orders for the maintenance crew. He reached for the cold cup of coffee on the stained stack of completed work orders. I'm losing ground, he thought, comparing the relative thickness of the stacks. This bucket had better hold together for another year or we'll be walking home. Maybe he could get some decent equipment from that ship HO was sending to look at the Thingy. What's left of it.

"They pump mass," returned Dac to prove he had been paying attention. "Put that together for me again, Max."

"Okay," said Max, starting over. "You wanted our best analysis of what the Shafts are and what they do. The facts are they divide and multiply and then grow,. They produce hydrogen apparently from nowhere. They vibrate at an ungodly frequency that just also happens to be that of many flavors of virtual particles. And they are somewhere else most of the time. Plus a lot of other little facts that are consistent with our conclusion, or neutral.

"The best hypothesis," concluded Max, "and really the only one that fits all the facts so far, is that the Shafts pump mass into here."

"Whatever for?"

"Again, for the obvious reason," replied Max. "To take it away from there."

"Where's there?" said Dac, just as obviously.

"There is where the aliens are," said Max irrefutably. "They pump mass out of there."

"At the risk of being redundant," said Dac uneasily. "Why?"

"Because," replied Max, "they must have too much mass and want to get rid of it."

"What is this?" said Dac, suddenly dubious. "Garbage or toxic waste or something?"

"Now you're getting it!" said Max. "The mass is a problem of some sort, like toxic waste or ozone or free radicals or cosmic rays. In fact, very much like cosmic rays. They are disposing of it by pumping it out of there."

"To here." finished Dac uncertainly, feeling like the stooge in a 'Who's on first' routine.

"Right!" rejoined Max brightly.

"They must consider it a serious problem," commented Dac, "based on the magnitude of the, uh, pumps."

"That's one of the reasons we feel it's a problem for them," agreed Max, "and not a by-product of some construction or industrial activity; too much hassle compared to simpler ways to get matter out of the way. The problem must be serious to them to cause that scale of investment. We might compare it to building the Great Wall of China or that fool Ringworld."

"Wait a second, Max," paused Dac. "How do we know what their scale is? I mean, assigning the whole Thingy/Shaft construct as a large scale project is measuring it by our stature. They might be giants, figuratively speaking, too."

"Good point," conceded Max. "In fact, we considered that and some other puzzling factors. One is the question of where did they start? Like, did they first build a big 500-kilometer Thingy that breaks down or a little one-meter Shaft that grew up? Starting with a little Shaft and turning it loose on autopilot made the most sense, from their point of view. Very little upfront investment. But we really don't know which and it really doesn't matter."

"And what did you guys decide?"

"It came down to the pump idea, Dac." Max shifted a paper while he checked. "Given they are pumps and given the observed fact that, however they started, they grow very big. The whole structure was designed to have a massive impact, both on our end and on their end. Why they want that impact is speculative; the fact of the impact is incontrovertible."

"Hmmm. Okay. What else?"

"Well," said Max, "that's what they do, pump mass. We also have a working theory about how they do it. Pappa is certain the Shafts aren't here in our space-time most of the time; they're only here intermittently. They oscillate between here and there, popping into and out of existence slightly out of synchronization with virtual particles. This unsynchronized vibration is enough to alter the frequency of the particles, slowing them just enough to let them remain here a little longer. Just enough longer to interact and become permanent, real. So they don't go back where they came from. That process happens in the Gap where the effect is probably focused. The result is the wind in the Gap, coming literally out of nowhere.

'Ahhh." Dac was finally making the logical connection among all these disparate parts. "Ahhh."

"The Shafts are probably only a part of the whole machine," Max continued, seeing Dac's enlightenment, "analogous to maybe ... say a deep well drilling bit. They are attached to something there that doesn't come here; we only see the part that dips into our space momentarily. That's why they cannot be moved. In effect, we were trying to move the whole machine on their end by pushing on our end, and for only a fraction of the total time. Their end is bigger."

"What kind of machine?"

"No clue," said Max.

"Where do the particles come from?" asked Dac.

"From there," said Max. "Of course."

"Where's there?"

"We considered every possibility," replied Max. "Alternate universes, future or past times, parallel universes, whatever. We finally just used Occam's razor. We figure the aliens are somewhere else in our own vanilla universe, but probably very far away. The simplest place for virtual particles to go to when they leave here is somewhere else in our space; there are too many contradictory hypotheticals to justify any other conclusion. Their physics seems to be the same as ours, the math, everything except their technology which is far more advanced.

"In effect," he continued, "someone somewhere, some perfectly ordinary critters, are excavating their region of space and dumping the dirt here. There may be relativistic effects involved so they may not be in our time, but that's incidental, and probably indeterminable. The point is that the aliens live in our universe."

"Those particles, Max," reiterated Dac to get it straight. "You say they vibrate back and forth between here to there. And the Shafts also vibrate back and forth between here to there."

"Right." Max mumphed his response, caught with a donut in his mouth. Swallow. "Well, we have no idea where virtual particles, uh, live. The particles that leave there may not be the same particles that happen here. As I understand it, they can't be the same. But the *net* flow is probably from there to here." Max washed that down with a slug of coffee.

"And the particles and Shafts are out of sync," continued Dac, "which interferes with the particle's cycle?"

"Yes," said Max, pipes clear. "The result is a drag, manifested in time."

"So the particles have time to say 'Hey, what's going on around here?' and decide to stick around, get married and settle down."

Max looked intently across the desk, not certain Dac gave the matter the weight it deserved. Dac seemed to be in control of his faculties so Max figured it was safe to continue.

"Uh, right," confirmed Max. "In so many words."

"And the result is more mass here and less mass there," concluded Dac. "Wherever in Hell's Void *there* is."

"Right," said Max again.

"The rest of you concur in this?"

General smiling nods throughout the room. Vlad Svodoba, Unit Two meteorology. Clyde Rupp, biology. Tony Wong. Sci User, new face, thought Dac. Nraa Post, old hand. Penny Ash, God! Vera Scott. Vera Scott? Who's she? All fresh and sincere and hard-working and probably as right about this as I'm going to get today. Is this what I need to know to make decisions? Close enough for now, he concluded, if things don't get dicey.

"Home Office?"

"Yes, Mr. Olson," said Max. "They have been involved throughout. There are many more details, of course, but that's the gist of it. The preliminary report is on file. We'll download it to HO when you approve it."

Dac high-signed Tony Wong who was closest to the coffee. A fresh cup was passed back to him, black with sugar. Real sugar for the occasion.

"One more thing," resumed Dac. "If I have this right, the aliens have a problem with mass and they are pumping it here. To us. Right?"

"Right," said Max. "Well, probably not to *us* specifically, but here in general. We just bumped into it."

"And you all agree their problem is too much mass. Right?"

Right again, Dac concluded from the general but thoughtful lack of negatives. He sensed an undertow of uncertainty.

"That means now we have a problem with too much of their mass. Right?"

"Uh, well," began Max uncertainly. "Yes, assuming we have too much mass, and assuming it's a problem."

"Those are the same thing, Max," said Dac. "If there's *too much*, by definition it's a problem."

"Well, yes. But ..."

"But nothing!" said Dac directly enough, "Let me know when you can tell me what *our* problem is."

"I guess I was a little hard on them," admitted Dac. "But I need some basis for making problem-solving decisions and I can't solve a problem if I don't know what the problem is!" Pause. "*Can* I?"

"No, I guess not," said Marcy. "But you may have created a few problems."

"How's that?"

"It's all over the ship," she replied. "They were pretty proud of their work, and they thought you rejected it completely out of hand. Without even reading it all."

"Yeah, I think maybe I did."

"What are you going to do?"

"Well," replied Dac, pulling Marcy closer, "I thought maybe you and me ..."

"I mean about Max' team!"

"I'll take care of it."

"When?"

"Later. Okay?" Dac looked at Marcy and Marcy looked at Dac. Dead silence.

"What!? Now?"

Dac recognized that tone of silence. Yeah, right now.

"Okayokay," he conceded. "I'll read the report. How's that?"

"When?"

"What!? Now?"

Yeah, right now said Marcy's eyes and posture and tone of voice and fingertips and toes and hair.

"Okay. Fine!" Grumble, not too loud. "No problem." Yes problem!

Dac reached for the console and called up the "Shaft Resolution Task Team: Analysis and Commentary Thingy Functionalities. Recommendations for Executive Action and Further Study." Hell's Inkwell!

"Now?"

Marcy hadn't moved.

"I have to apologize, Max," said Dac, genuinely apologetic. "And all of you. You did a fine job on your report. I guess I was a little abrupt."

The team averted their embarrassed attention to nits and motes, pleased at Dac's remark but not sure how they should react. Gloating was out, but a sideways smile was appropriate. Dac allowed that it was.

"But I do have a question," Dac continued. He flipped through his printout of the report, hunting for a certain passage. "Ah. Here it is:"

"Inasmuch as the intended consequence of the function of the rotating prisms is, or is assumed to be for purposes of this study," he read, "the transmittal of sufficient mass from the immediate environs of the fabricators of the devices to effect a physical impact on those environs, it can and should be concluded that a concomitant and proportionate impact is effected on the immediate vicinity into which the transmitted mass is injected.

"Assuming further," he continued, "that the, by our standards, massive investment in design and manufacture, and probably on-going operating functions, is proportional to the motivation of the aliens for fabricating the prisms, it can and should be further concluded that the fabricators are impelled by what, to them at least, is a problem of considerable magnitude."

Dac took a well-earned breath. Hell's Bombast! Do they think I pay them by the word? He read on:

"Taking the simple presence of mass (as opposed to the qualitative nature of the mass which, for reasons of succinctness, will be explored later) as the vehicle for the fabricator's motivation, along with the sheer magnitude of the amount of mass involved, the primary effect to be achieved by the function of the prisms is the controlled adjustment of the value of the cosmological constant (which value has been strongly but, until the present, only theoretically proposed as being dependent on the quantity and density of mass in the space in question) in their general region of space in a, to the fabricators, favorable manner."

Deep breath. Marcy's going to pay for this!

"The presence of a like quantity of new infused mass into a sufficiently constrained targeted region of space can be expected to result in a proportionate but inverse alteration in the cosmological constant in the region of space into which the mass is infused."

"There's more," said Dac as he closed the report, the gesture more a capitulation than a stop. "But I think that's the part that got my attention. Uh, is that the problem?"

"Oh, no, Mr. Olson," exclaimed Max, hurt. "The problem is in the next paragraph."

"Oh yeah. Right. I knew that." Dac, embarrassed, started flipping back into the report to find his place. "Can you summarize it for me while I'm looking?"

"Yes, Mr. Olson," said Max, the model of patience in spite of Dac's clumsy snub. "The aliens are making their region of space lighter."

"Lighter?" He stopped flipping. He thought he understood what he read but hadn't internalized it that way. "So?"

"So their space continues to expand," replied Max. "Indefinitely. That's the only possible reason to pump mass on this scale, to change the shape of space. The details are a little esoteric; you can find them in the ..."

"Expand!?" Dac stared at the team, Max too. "Then our space ...?"

"Right!" said Max, beaming in satisfaction. "Our space will collapse!"

"Okay. Satisfied?"

CHAPTER 28

EXODUS

"Dead center, Mr. Olson," said Jason Fielding with a concerned edge Dac couldn't help noticing. "Or close enough."

"Speed?"

"At the top end of instrument range. Very fast. That's approaching relativistic velocity, and closing." Jason looked at the readout again to check and then glanced up at Marcy.

Nod. "Confirmed," she replied. "Accelerating slowly. A real screamer."

"Pappa?"

"Confirmed, Mr. Olson," replied Pappa, "but I show a somewhat lower velocity. Keep in mind that the object's vector is at a severe oblique angle to the Thingy cloud's vector, but largely head-on to it as well as to our own vector."

Jason looked back at Marcy who returned her "Sorry, I can't help you" look.

"Accelerating?"

"Yes, Mr. Olson," confirmed Pappa again. "Slightly and slowly, but clearly accelerating."

"Dead center, you say?"

"I didn't say, Mr. Olson. It was Mr. Field ..."

"Okay! Jason?"

"It is still a ways out, Dac. Confidence level is moderate to high." Jason studied his display for a moment, hoping it might change for the good. "It will center punch the Cloud on its present trajectory."

"Intercepts!"

"On your left, Mr. Olson."

Dac swiveled to his left, interested but irritated. His board had cleared itself; the annual performance report tucked away somewhere. Just as well, he thought, I couldn't make sense of it anyway, much less do anything about it or justify my pay. Seven months sitting on your sling twiddling your thumbs and watching those black prisms spin didn't do much for performance ratings when your job is claiming mineral rights and hauling freight. I wonder if I can claim overage credits for discovering the Thingy, or the alien language or ...

"Okay, what have we got here?" Dac asked himself absently as he focused on the board.

Dac's attention locked on Pappa's display, struggling to apprehend the situation. It showed X, Y and Z views of the vicinity, at maximum range. Fine cross hairs identified the point of interest with appropriate vectors. Nested coaxial probability cones radiated from the point, their axes centered on the point's trajectory. The cones, displayed brightly in colored gradations from light blue at the outside to red at the trajectory axis, unambiguously revealed the impending collision. In spite of its colorfulness, the array stood spell-binding and ominous.

Dac jerked viscerally when the array shifted slightly, reflecting updated data.

The Cloud nestled within the inner cones, green and menacing in spite of its spiral galactic shape. The Cloud had evolved into a classic Sb spiral that was too obvious to be coincidental. Its overall spin even duplicated the rigid disc that had mystified astronomers from Hubble on.

"What is that thing? Pappa?"

"Unknown, Mr. Olson."

"Jason?"

"It's a ship. Leveraged, I'd say."

"Leveraged!?" Dac hesitated as he recalled a mental construct of the old Milken drive from his academy days. "Leveraged! What makes you say that?"

"It's a point source of radiation. Too strong to be an asteroid; asteroids don't radiate electromagnetic energy. Albedo too high at scanning frequencies for an asteroid, even ice." Jason was thinking out loud and Dac let him. "Too hot to be space junk. Far too fast to be an asteroid. Too big to be a clipper. Too fast to be a clipper." After a moment, "Nothing goes that fast anymore, Dac. Hasn't for nearly a century."

"Conclusion?"

"It's still a ship." Jason paused to add, "One of ours."

"Anyone else?" No one else on the flight deck had the experience to challenge Jason Fielding. Few even knew what leveraged meant.

"Pappa?"

"A high probable on Mr. Fielding's analysis, Mr. Olson. Searching." Even Pappa respected Jason's experience. Dac noticed Pappa's clipped syntax which hinted urgency.

"Gerry. Contact?"

"I'm assuming it *is* a ship. Nothing yet, Mr. Olson," replied Gerry Ast, duty communications officer. "If it is a ship, they should respond. Even allowing for radical Doppler I should have them. No response, Mr. Olson."

Dac turned back to his board. No real change. The blip, whatever it was, would pass through the Cloud if it didn't make a course adjustment soon. If it *could* make an adjustment. No problem yet, it seemed. Still things didn't look right.

"Confirmed, Mr. Olson," announced Pappa. "It is a ship, Earth origin. I retraced its trajectory and probable levers. I am certain it is an Iowa class personnel transport, registry Winnebago." Pappa paused, and then added, "Complement of 257 crew and 13,784 passengers, plus appropriate baggage and freight. One of the last leveraged ships made, one of only four Iowas, and very old. There's an interesting fact about ..."

"Good Lord!" Could have been anybody. Murmurs.

"What in Hell's Roadmap is it doing out here in the Bubble?" asked Dac, not expecting an answer.

"Probably the same thing we're doing here," answered Jason. "Looking for elbow room."

"Excuse me?"

"The Bubble," replied Jason. "We're here because there isn't anything else here. That's why they call it the Bubble." Rueful pause. "At least there wasn't. Leveraged ships need a lot of empty space to work up that kind of speed, along with a very low probability of collision with space junk over extended time frames. Same as us."

"Yeah, but what are they *doing* out here!" Emphasis on doing.

"They're colonists." Jason flipped a few switches and rubbed a panel to fine tune the image. "Going to save the universe, or something like that."

"Correct, Mr. Fielding," added Pappa. "Their registry indicates they set out from Earth nearly three hundred years ago. And Mr. Fielding is correct about the leveraged drive. An interesting fact ..."

"Well, can we hail them?" Dac was uneasy about the disturbing display indicating a possible collision, and it showed. "Do they know about the cloud?"

"I have no response yet, Mr. Olson," replied Gerry Ast. "Do they use standard frequencies?"

"Yes," said Pappa. "They do not have EPR, of course, but they should be scanning all standard electromagnetics. They should respond."

The display on Dac's board tightened, the probabilities jumping a notch as the blip streaked inexorably toward its destiny. The cones intensified, indicating enhanced danger. The proper motions of the cloud and the ship indicated collision at present velocities in a bit over seven hours, through a point about a third of the distance out from the center of the Cloud.

Dac put his finger on that point.

"Density?"

"Somewhat less than one thousand Shafts per cubic kilometer, Mr. Olson," said Pappa instantly, anticipating Dac's concern. "But that is not the whole problem."

"Then what in Hell's Tenderizer *is* the problem!" barked Dac, giving Pappa pause in spite of his prepared response.

"The ship will intersect the Cloud at 22.57 degrees to the plane of the Cloud's ecliptic." Pappa responded. "Their path through the Cloud will be nearly 13,000 kilometers long, at an average density of approximately 730 Shafts per linear kilometer for the transit. However, some areas in the ship's path are as much as a hundred times more dense. Given the size of the ship, it will collide with at least," pause, "somewhere between 600,000 and 800,000 Shafts in less than a second."

"Good Lord!"

Absolute dead silence on the flight deck. No one could think of anything better to say and so said nothing.

"Prognosis?" said Dac after a moment to fathom the implications.

"Given that scenario, the ship will not survive intact, Mr. Olson."

"Gerry?"

"Nothing."

"Well, dammit, do something!" Dac tore his eyes from the display and eyed his staff fiercely, then with compassion as he read their faces. "Do what you can," he said softly. "We have some time yet. Reports in one hour."

Dac set aside the conflicting reports from the investigation into a drunken fight and knifing two days earlier. Fights were not common, but they were inevitable, no big deal. Knifings? Rare but every bit as understandable as the fight. Nobody was seriously hurt and company policy covered the situation. But the alcohol! Who in Hell's Pub was making alcohol? And why, when safer intoxicants are standard issue? Some lady involved? Lordy! Where were the Societal Accommodators and the Pharmacists? Note to look into that.

Dac rubbed his eyes thoroughly, smoothed his eyebrows and reached for the coffee on the stand beside him. Later, he thought. Two good slugs and he was ready for Pappa's report.

"Pappa. The Winnebago. What's the deal on that?"

"It was built by GM/EU for an ethno-political-religious minority that wanted to start all over again with a perfect civilization on some new planet of their own," replied Pappa. "Commercial traffic still runs into them occasionally out here."

Lots of those over the years, Dac thought, with some understanding. In fact, back in his young rebellious years he had ...

"According to my news media archives, the Winnebago set out a few centuries ago with everyone who could pay their way and take the pledge," resumed Pappa. "Lots of fanfare at first, Pilgrims and all that, but they faded from the records after a few decades and from memory in a century. Only a few intermittent reports have surfaced, mostly automatic navigational bursts and accidental sightings. The few close contacts showed they were apparently under no distress and needed no assistance. They were tracked for about a century and then largely forgotten."

"Centuries!" Dac had to wonder at their adventurous spirit if not their prudence. "How did they make it this far?"

"The Winnebago used the Milken leveraged drive, maybe the last still operational, the technology long surpassed." Pappa paused to switch to a different archive. "The massive amount of fuel needed in the Winnebago's time was a serious impediment to interstellar space travel, forcing flight patterns into extremely long loopy slingshots to save energy. The length of the trajectories required for interstellar travel meant ships had to be extremely fast to be feasible, even to relativistic velocities if reports are to be credited. Hence the Milken Drive, the name an obscure joke, the humor long forgotten. The drive requires a long slow acceleration to incredible speeds, using space's interstitial gravitational gradients, and equally long deceleration."

"What were they looking for? Besides Paradise, I mean," asked Dac. "What was the plan?"

"They hoped to find a place to land when they got there without knowing exactly where they were going. The endeavor made sense to them even though the ultimate goal was extremely distant, at least by their standards and experience. The name of the Winnebago's expedition was ... *is* ... A Leap Of Faith." Dac reflected on that.

"Where were they headed?" asked Dac. "I mean, did they know where their Paradise was?"

"Apparently not, at least not in any detail or certainty," replied Pappa. "They did have good astronomical data showing several Sun-like stars with Earth-like planets in the Woodrell sector. That was good enough for them."

"Woodrell?" Dac had to filter that out before responding. "They expect to find Paradise in Woodrell? That's a badland now. Full of pirates and fugitives. That's the last place to find Paradise unless they planned on doing a lot of proselytizing."

The tragic feature of the Winnebago's expedition was that the sector of space they apparently intended to colonize was long since taken. Shortly after they embarked, ram mass conversion drives solved the fuel problem, allowing far more direct trajectories that took far less time, even at much lower velocities. Then the Alcubierre drive became commercially feasible and the Winnebago had been thoroughly leapfrogged by technology; everybody else got there first.

Dac stopped, gulped the now lukewarm coffee and considered that; centuries in space! What mentality, what social pressures would drive a people to undertake that kind of journey! One thing for certain, he thought in counterpoint; they would be really PO-ed when they got to Paradise only to find burger stands, high rent and politics as usual. Dac smiled compassionately and returned to Pappa's report.

"Shall I continue, Mr. Olson?" asked Pappa, picking up on Dac's distracted gaze at the display construct.

"Sure. Any more data concerning their current situation?"

"The Winnebago is huge by any gauge, Mr. Olson," resumed Pappa. "The ship is really some two dozen personnel carriers, lashed to the central drive unit. Each unit is not much more than a refrigerated warehouse, effectively open to cold space to preserve the passengers' sleep, plus a command and control unit."

Warehouses filled with racks of frozen families, thought Dac, popsicles and momsicles and kidsicles.

"And?" encouraged Dac

"The personnel carrier units are each the size of our own ship, the Jobs. The whole structure is nearly four kilometers in its greatest dimension, including antennas and towed nuclear fuel reserves."

"Four kilometers!" Just think of it! Huge wasn't the word, thought Dac.

Dac found his imagination wanting. He shook his head and reached for the coffee. The cup was cold. Fine, he thought, I drink too much of it anyway. He rolled off the recliner, straightened and dressed for the staff meeting.

"That's it?" reiterated Dac. "No contact. No change in velocity or trajectory. Everybody on the ship is asleep or probably dead already. And it will hit the Cloud as scheduled. That's it?"

"There's one more factor, Mr. Olson," replied Pappa.

"Which is?"

"In just under twenty-seven minutes collision will be inevitable," said Pappa. "At that time the Winnebago's engineering parameters and power resources will be exceeded by the physical requirements of an evasive maneuver."

Dac looked around at the others. He felt strangely detached, considering they had more or less conceded thirteen or fourteen thousand lives. They showed no particular emotion in return, whatever they were thinking. They all knew the story of the Winnebago by now. What it was doing out here. Why it didn't know about the Cloud. Why it didn't respond. But it was all completely out of their ken and control. They could do nothing but watch, the way they might watch the radar image of a remote mid-ocean hurricane on the evening weather report. Interesting maybe, but impersonal.

"Contact, Mr. Olson!" Gerry Ast, very urgent. "I have them!"

Dac took only a second to respond. "PA."

"Sspspspspsssss … ing you. We seem to have a problem. Proximity alarm went off. Don't know what it is. Can you advise? Sssssp … pssssps. … peat. Please identify yourself. We are try …"

"Pappa! Give them evasive course corrections. Now! Give me transmission priority. Now!"

"Done, Mr. Olson."

"You are in immediate danger, Winnebago!" Dac chose his words carefully, enunciating clearly. "Take evasive action now. You have new vectors now. Turn now!"

"Who are you?" replied the Pilgrim's thin voice. "What's going on? Please identify yourself."

"Turn now! God Dammit, Winnebago! We'll talk later. Take evasive action now! We sent to you new vectors. Do it now!" Dac looked up at Jason, pained. How can you make it more clear. Or urgent. "Do you understand, Winnebago?"

"Sssssspspsssps... derstand. Awaiting confirmation. My instruments show nothing ahead. We can't …sspspssps... without guidance council approval. I am energizing the council now. Please ssppsspps..."

"Winnebago!" A little desperation. "Your ship will be destroyed. You are on a collision course with an uncharted physical hazard. Your radar is ineffective. You will be destroyed unless you take immediate evasive action now. Turn now!"

"Ssssps... Thank you for sharing that with us. Ssspss."

"Pappa! Can you download a visual construct of the situation to the Winnebago? Something that will show on their equipment?"

"I think so, Mr. Olson. If they are receiving."

"Don't explain anything you don't have to, Pappa," said Dac, prudently. "Just show them."

"Done, Mr. Olson."

Dac watched his board for any sign of a course adjustment. Nothing.

"Winnebago! Do you have our visual transmission? Do you understand the hazard?"

"Sssp... Understood. What is it? We can't see it. I show nothing. Who are you?" The voice cracked a little. Interference from the Cloud? Fear? Whoever it was, he was entitled to a little fear right now.

"Are you turning?" Christomity! "Have you taken ..."

"They're turning, Mr. Olson." Pappa.

Dac checked his board again just as Pappa updated it. The Winnebago's trajectory had changed. The probability cones shifted, just visibly. The ship's trajectory was not clear of danger, had hardly moved at all. But it was moving, in the right direction. Dac heard a few low encouraging cheers behind him. It was personal now.

"Heaven's Help Line! Pappa! Give them live updates. You're their eyes now."

"Yes, Mr. Olson."

"Winnebago. Status?"

"Ssp ...sted! Full power. I don't know if ... No. Oh, no! ..."

"Pappa?"

"They appear to be oscillating, Mr. Olson." Pause. "The Winnebago is broaching."

"Sspps ...king up. Lost number seven and eight! No response on ..."

Dac stared hard at his board. As he watched the Winnebago's trajectory sprang into three diverging lines, one somewhat more intense than the others. The probability cones still intersected the Cloud, only slightly aside from their original position. They did not move during a long hard watch.

"Pappa?"

"They seem to have lost structural integrity, Mr. Olson. Their ability to compensate is extremely limited. They are trying to turn the command units. The rest of the ship is without control."

"Prognosis."

"The collision is inevitable, Mr. Olson."

Dac rose from his seat, looked again at the board, and turned to leave only to be faced with the flight crew. They were stunned, saddened certainly, but their steady eye contact told Dac he had done what he could. And nothing else could be done.

"I'm afraid," he said slowly after a moment, "we have managed to wake them only to witness their own deaths." Pause to hold each of their eyes for a moment. "They may have time to make their peace as they see fit." Pause. "Let us hope others would be so kind to us."

CHAPTER 29
VARIABLES

"You read this report, Pappa?"

"Yes, Mr. Olson," replied Pappa. "In fact I ..."

"And you concur?"

"I have no problem with the conclusions," confirmed Pappa. "I have been involved with ..."

"That's not what I asked."

"Are you asking if I concur," asked Pappa, "in the sense that I participate fully in the stated conclusions of the report without reservation?"

"Yes."

"Yes. In fact, I ..."

"And you agree that the Shafts are mass pumps."

"Yes, but ..."

"And the aliens are pumping mass out of their space?"

"Yes." Pappa paused, assuming Dac would cut him off again. Finding the air clear he added, "I should add that ..."

"To us, here."

"Yes. Well, not to *us* exactly but ..."

"And that makes their space, uh, lighter?" Dac was fast approaching his limit about things physical.

"Yes, Mr. Olson," said Pappa. "The cosmological constant is a function of ..."

"So the lighter alien space will expand?"

"As far as we know, Mr. Olson," explained Pappa, "all space is expanding now. The aliens ..."

"Okayokay! So their space will expand faster? Or longer? Or farther What?"

"Forever."

"Forever what?"

"The lightening of alien space will allow it to continue expanding without limit."

"There's a limit to the expansion of space?"

"The theoretical limit is related to the escape velocity of the universe," replied Pappa. "If the matter in the universe is going fast enough it will continue to expand. If not, it will eventually collapse. This is all in the report, Mr. Olson."

"And the aliens are pumping out mass to make their part of the universe go faster?" asked Dac, ignoring Pappa's not too subtle jab. "To exceed the escape velocity?"

"No, Mr. Olson," replied Pappa, with a slight little boy sing-song. "Theoretically, we think they are trying to change the effective escape velocity in their favor."

"Ah!"

Dac considered Pappa's statement and managed only to confuse himself more. He had read the team's report several times over and found the turgid prose numbing. They must have had too many commas on hand, he thought, and had to use them up. They sure had a shortage of periods!

He was reluctant to keep asking questions of Max which only revealed his admittedly limited grasp of cosmology, so he was boning up on things with Pappa. In private. Pappa's tutorial mode was patient to a fault, but his emulators often confused Dac's sometimes redundant questioning as a lack of attention and prodded him gently as would a school marm.

"Summarize that for me again, Pappa."

"The shape of space is a function of the quantity and density of the mass in it," began Pappa, one more time. "The shape of space in turn influences the movement of bodies through it. This influence is manifested locally in the gravity well associated with a planet or star.

"Similarly," Pappa continued, "the universe as a whole shapes its own space and influences the movement of the matter in the universe. This matter is moving outward, so to speak. Expanding is a more precise term.

The pertinent question is whether the matter will continue to expand forever without limit, or eventually collapse into the point from which it theoretically emerged.

"The seemingly critical factor is the value of the cosmological constant. The value of the cosmological constant, in spite of its name, is a variable, a function of the quantity and density of the mass in space, as well as time." Pappa paused according to programmed methodology. "The cosmological constant, therefore, is a measure of the shape of space and its influence on the movement of matter in space. The ultimate disposition of the universe depends on the value of the cosmological constant.

"The question of whether the universe will ultimately collapse is as yet unresolved. The aliens are apparently attempting to resolve the question in their space to their advantage by decreasing the quantity and density of mass in their space. The decreased mass will change the cosmological constant, the shape of space, the movement of matter in space and the velocity needed to escape the ultimate collapse of space. As a result," concluded Pappa, "their matter's existing velocity, which participates in the overall expansion of the universe, will be sufficient to ensure escaping collapse."

"Okay, I think I've got it," said Dac. "That's Part A. Part B is our end of the deal. If I understand you, the new mass will make our part of space heavier. Then ..."

"Denser is a better term, Mr. Olson."

"Okay, denser. The new mass will increase the density of our space to the point that it will collapse. Right?"

"That is correct, Mr. Olson. In fact ..."

"And you think they can pull it off?"

"Pull it off?" reflected Pappa, understandably struggling to interpret the expression in terms of shifting mass.

"You really believe the aliens will be able to change the shape of space some day, enough to escape collapse."

"It is neither a matter of belief, Mr. Olson," said Pappa, expressing strength of conviction with volume, "nor of time. It is certain."

"And what makes *you* so certain?"

"Because our space is collapsing now."

✦ ✦ ✦

"It's all there," said Max. "It's in the book."

Spook Central exuded smugness. Max leaned back in his chair, arms folded across his chest, displaying a professionally moderate but clear 'I told you so' smile. The rest of the team, Nraa, Tony, Vera, Sci and the others were no more diplomatic but they were somewhat more restrained. Vera?

"I know, I know," admitted Dac in mock humiliation. "But you guys had a head start on me; while you were hunting aliens, I was wasting my time on life support systems and paychecks."

"Right here in the report," said Max, rubbing it in good-naturedly, "on page 137. Appendix XIII: The Rubin-Ford Effect."

"I'll read it later," said Dac, "when I can give it the full attention it deserves." Cough. "Right now I only have time for a few questions. This collapsing space business, you're sure it's happening right now?"

"That's the Rubin-Ford effect," said Max. "The Great Attractor."

"Why didn't you call it the Great Attractor," said Dac with just a touch of petulance. "Maybe I would have recognized it."

"Well, that's not the scientific term," replied Tony. "And up to now nobody thought there really was an attractor out there, a thing. Most scientists were convinced it was only the confluence of random local movement left over from the Big Bang."

"Whatever it is," pursued Dac, "what is it?"

"It's an inflow of matter," replied Tony, "galaxies, into a region of space centered 750 billion light years away, in the direction of Hydra and Centaurus. We're moving in that direction along with a volume of space some 400 billion light years across. Galaxies on the other side of it are moving towards us, towards the same region. The galaxies in back of us," said Tony with hitch back over his left shoulder, "are moving towards it too. Of course, this all assumes a fairly large Hubble constant."

"Of course," said Dac over his eyeglasses. "And you say there's nothing there?"

"Nothing like a super cluster of galaxies has been previously observed," said Penny Ash, "Nothing obvious. It was assumed to be brown dwarfs or dark matter if anything. We know better now."

Dac turned abruptly to Penny. Bright, young, well over two meters tall and hard. A body-builder by reputation and Dac didn't doubt it. Very smart, also by reputation. Dac didn't doubt that either.

"Tell me, Penny," said Dac directly to her, leaning towards her. "What's your personal opinion? Are we going down the tubes?"

"Yes!" she blurted, panicked by the sudden intense attention of the second VP. She looked at the others on the team who were similarly surprised. "Well, not down the tubes exactly, Mr. Olson. But the theory and the observations agree completely, more so than most astronomical phenomena. That's a sure sign of the correctness of a theory; the observed experimental results match the prediction of the theory.

"So, yes," she concluded. "There's something there and it's pulling us there with a force consistent with the presence of vast quantities of mass. The amount of mass is consistent with the observed replication and growth of the Shafts at the observed rate for a period of time consistent with the age of this part of space. I'd say we're going down the tubes."

"You're convinced?" prodded Dac. "No reservations?"

"Yes, sir. No, sir." Straight face.

Dac studied her for an uncomfortable few moments, then each of the others in turn. Dac wasn't challenging them; he was studying them, trying to see into their personal worlds. Did they really believe in their report or were they simply sticking together like a good team, on a point that would never be proved one way or another in their lifetimes.

Max was a dominating character, and given to excess for his own amusement, particularly when there was little riding on it. Most of the team was relatively inexperienced and perhaps too malleable and too concerned with keeping Max happy. Politics is politics and they would be foolish to play the contrarian, outlandish as was the team's position.

On the other hand, maybe it was wishful thinking, rampant confirmation bias as it were. Maybe they wanted it to be so, wanted it so much it became more real to them. Pumps that change space to undo the Big Bang? Come on!

"Okay, given that our galaxy will fall into this drainage ditch," said Dac, trying to shake off his funkiness, "what do we do about it?"

"Paddle like Hell," said Sci User amid chuckles born more of the break in the tension than Sci's comic talent. "Our galaxy is flowing with the local group of Galaxies at around 14 million kilometers per hour, give or take. That's not even a relativistic speed, less than two tenths of a percent of light speed. This ship could get out, in about a billion years. But it would be impossible to move anything like a planet at that speed, much less a galaxy. Impossible. We're going down the tubes." More chuckles.

"I didn't mean that exactly," said Dac, joining in the merriment to save face. "I guess what I was getting at is, if your theory is correct, now what?"

Blank faces.

"You've identified the problem," said Dac finally. "A problem. The ultimate problem. The *immediate* problem, however, is the Thingys." Are? "Now what's the immediate danger?"

Questioning faces.

"Your team charge, remember? What is the immediate hazard and how do I protect the ship, the people in it, and the rest of civilization as we know it?"

"Why there is no danger, Mr. Olson." Max looked surprised. "Other than the obvious hazard of running into one of them, there is no immediate danger. None whatsoever. It's ..."

"... in the book" pre-empted Dac. "Yeah, I got that."

Dac knew the answer; nothing to worry about. The aliens were important, fabulously important, and they will have a major impact on our civilization, our lives. But right now, no problem.

"Tell me," said Dac thoughtfully. "How long will all of this take, what's the time frame for doomsday?"

"Just guesses at this point, Mr. Olson," answered Max. "Billions of years, at least." General nods. "The precise date will have to wait for more theoretical and observational work."

"Then I take it," continued Dac, "the aliens won't experience any results for billions of years either."

"Assuming both effects proceed at the same rate," said Sci, "and that their time is concurrent with ours. Yes. Their goal is to circumvent the end of time, not the middle."

"Then what's their hurry?" asked Dac. "Why would they or anyone else care about the possibility of the universe collapsing billions of years in the future?"

"First of all," said Max, quite seriously, "they apparently do not see the collapse of the universe as a possibility; they see it as a certainty. All things considered, I think I'd take their word for it.

"In addition," he continued, "a few billion years seems distant to creatures who live a few decades at best and can look back maybe 25,000 years on a clear day. The aliens may have started building Thingys a billion years ago, when we were still learning how to breathe air. To creatures like that, looking a billion years into the future is planning for retirement."

"What makes you think they have a billion year life span?"

"Who knows about their life span," replied Max. "Considering the way they write, it has to be long just to have time to read a book. But regardless of their individual life spans, their civilization's span must be almost eternal. At least they're trying to make it eternal."

Dac caught at the spiritual overtones in the word eternal but could not fault Max' logic.

"But," rebutted Dac. "To make that investment! They had to feel something would change as a result of their efforts, something would be better now or a problem would be alleviated now. The benefit is just too far away! What changes for them now?" Dac wasn't really looking for an answer.

"Mr. Olson?"

Dac and the whole team turned to Vera Scott.

"I think I understand," she began, hesitating under the team's attention. "The aliens are old by any standard, ancient. And they're obviously very intelligent. We can assume they are as civilized as we are, with a culture just as diverse and rich. With treasures they preserve in libraries and museums and universities. Preserved for the future.

"Before they built the Thingys," Vera concluded, "they knew their world, their efforts, their civilization and its treasures would inevitably come to an end. As everyone thinks at one time or another, they may have felt frustration at the pointlessness of it all; why work to build if it will all be destroyed and come to nothing. That would be particularly acute if you lived a very long lifetime and had a culture with a very long history.

"So they set out to do the most monumental thing they could do; prevent the collapse and literally create a future.

"Now they know there will always be a future. Their culture has an objective investment in its preservation; there will be a future to leave it to. And the message ..." She stopped, half cocked.

"?" coaxed Dac with an eyebrow.

"... The message is a gift. A legacy to their future."

CHAPTER 30

WAR AND PEACE

"What did I tell you," exclaimed Dac as he read the summary on his private quarters monitor. "War and Peace! A lot of war!"

"I'll say," said Marcy. "And not a Helluva lot of peace. Us poor warmongering humans sure don't need to be embarrassed!"

"Is everybody getting this?" She added with a slow unbelieving swing of her head. "I mean, can anyone in everywhere read this?"

"Well, yes and no. The original message? ... yes," said Dac thoughtfully. "If they have the wherewithal to translate it. The translations we have so far? No. They're the property of the kind folks who invested in the whole translation project, like a copyright."

"It will all get out eventually anyway, won't it?" observed Marcy.

"Sure. But probably only those parts with no commercial or military value. The original message is available to anyone in the universe who wants it. Pappa broadcast it many times to HO on open channels and it's been intercepted by virtually anyone who is interested. Pappa did not encode or protect it so that critical data wouldn't be lost."

"Aren't they all translating it as we speak?"

"They are probably trying, sure. While anyone can have the message, not everyone can translate it; the computer power required has proven enormous and is ongoingly even enormous-er, probably for many years to come." Dac reflected a bit and added, "And there probably isn't anyone left who isn't already tied up on it with the HO consortium."

As a result, those parts of the message that were not released by the consortium were effectively secure from unauthorized access. It would all be translated and made public eventually, of course; that could not be prevented. But it could be delayed until the consortium locked in any competitive advantage to be had, and that was good enough.

"Suspicions confirmed," mumbled Dac. He was fascinated with the story, like everyone, but held an abiding cynical attitude about it all.

"Right from the start I felt everything about the Thingy is evil, Marcy. The crew and half the human race are completely addicted to the alien soap opera, as told by the aliens themselves."

It had taken two painful months for the translated vocabulary and grammar to reach a critical mass. From there on translation began to snowball, relatively speaking. It was now only a matter of applying massive computer processing time. Some parts, the primers the aliens had so thoughtfully provided, were easy, others were impenetrable. To date, however, just less than one percent of the message had been translated, and very little of that contiguous. Results read like a sorting through a pile of shredded newspaper clippings.

Some parts might never be understood but what had been translated was incredible. Incredible not for its glory or scope or heroics or grandeur or magnificence; it was incredible because people did not want to believe.

"I don't know about you," said Dac as he read the latest release, another war. "But I can't help feeling disappointed. You see all kinds of mayhem on the holos, but you know it's just-make believe escapism. This stuff is real and it's as depraved and sordid a tale as anything I've ever read."

"I know," agreed Marcy. "And the worst part is that it's so human. Change the names and you have the Inquisition or the Holocaust or the Scrub."

"And we're just getting a few highlights," said Dac, shaking his head slowly in an attempt to understand. "I don't think the rest will be any better."

The first of the three major parts of the alien message was indeed a history of the race, and it pulled no punches. Most people expected, or maybe wanted and needed, a glorious revelation of triumph and peace and prosperity and security and wealth. And deep down most people hoped some of it would rub off on the human race, hoped it would hold the cure to everything that was wrong with us. They were disappointed, but still intensely fascinated. And profoundly disturbed. The alien story was indeed a soap opera, and a terribly real one.

"Pappa. This is getting tiresome. Isn't there anything more enlightening in the translation?"

"Enlightening?" asked Pappa. "As in socially uplifting or philosophically profound? Storytelling perhaps."

"Yes! That's it!" responded Dac and Marcy as one. "What do these aliens do for comic relief?"

"I am sorry," replied Pappa apologetically. "There is nothing of that sort so far in Part One but I have an admittedly limited sense of humor. Human humor, that is, and certainly of alien humor. However, even at that I can tell they are quite a staid bunch."

"Okay. Let me look at Part Two."

"Yes, Mr. Olson, but you will find little that could be described as enlightening."

The Part Two, by far the biggest, seemed to be a look to the future. It was a treasury of the alien culture; historical literature perhaps, turgid and opaque social or political analyses, something that might eventually turn into graphics, still stubbornly arcane scientific findings, and even more obtuse technological treatises. But it was all perseveringly and doggedly staid nonetheless. Eventually Part Two would probably be the most human-like and commercially profitable but as yet it was too fractured and incoherent.

The Part Three was highly technical, related mostly to the Shafts themselves. It included an analysis of the problem they saw; the ultimate collapse of the universe, and their solution. However, the alien technology was so advanced and different that translation was moving glacially.

Release of this latter information was highly restricted because of the possible military ramifications and security implications, but what was released largely confirmed what was already deduced about the Shafts.

Relative to the demand, translation proceeded at an agonizingly slow pace. The Part One history unwound, tragic episode by epic episode, and held the race spellbound. Marcy called it the ultimate soap opera.

"God," she muttered. "It's a quagmire. It could be the history of the rise and fall of any depraved human empire."

"Yeah," replied Dac. "And the blanks are the worst."

"Blanks?"

"Sure. The untranslated parts." Dac thought for a moment. "Like the best stories that build suspense and then leave you to fill in the unsaid parts. You always imagine the worst. This is a fill-in-the-blanks do-it-yourself horror story."

"But to be fair," said Marcy, "they are completely objective. They don't seem to make any excuses or apologies for their excesses. And they don't gloat over their victories either. They don't seem to have anything like an ego or a political motive. Just the raw facts." They pondered that silently, comforting each other casually as they read.

"Like a parent teaching honesty to a child."

CHAPTER 31

🙣 🙝

CALL HOME

"Let me get this straight," mumbled Dac, mostly to himself. He studied Jason closely for a few moments to be certain he was serious. Jason was serious.

Dac's eyes moved to the others in the group that had approached him in his supposedly private office: Uni Farber, head of the translation team; Marcy Phillips, the best electronics engineer on the PC and Po Washington, mechanical engineer. Their eyes were steady, no sign of a joke. And they were excited.

"You want to call them on the phone and say 'Hello'? Just like that?"

"Well, yes," said Jason, a little embarrassed at Dac's loose translation of what he thought had been a well-reasoned presentation. "My charge was, uh, 'non-language intrusions'. I think that's how you said it. But the operative word was intrusion, to get their attention. I think Uni has a good idea, as good as any. And if they're halfway human in their social development, it'll get their attention. Marcy and Po think it can be done; most of the equipment already exists. I think it's worth a try."

Dac considered their proposition; just give them a call! Well, why not. After all, if they're listening like we're listening ...

"Okay, okay. Tell me this." Dac didn't want to be a wet blanket and chose his words carefully. "What makes you think anyone's listening on the other end? They may have been sending that signal for a million years; why would they be waiting for an answer now?"

"No good reason," answered Po, first on the draw. "But they *are* sending a message to *someone*. Maybe not to *us* exactly, but to someone. Why wouldn't they be expecting an answer?"

"Well," mused Dac. "They may have set an automatic messaging machine adrift. Like throwing a bottle with a note into the ocean, never expecting an answer that would be impossible in the most probable of circumstances."

"Yes," replied Jason. "We thought about that a lot. But if we accept that premise, this whole contact effort is moot. Are we going for it or not? There are not many choices in between."

"True. You're right. We're going for it, mainly because the hazard is real and it isn't going away. Unless anyone's got a better plan ..."

Dac held up an index finger as a placeholder while he thought. "How about the million years?" continued Dac after moment. "Even aliens that write like they do would get pretty bored after a million years! Maybe they're long gone by now. Kaput!"

"True," replied Uni in turn. "But that time frame is only speculation, very loosely supported by some circumstantial evidence based on debatable theories about controversial observations of the hypothetical Great Attractor!"

Uni hesitated and glanced at the others for support, fearing she may have overstated things a bit. She had, and retrenched.

"Uh, the more likely case is that they are contemporary," she continued. "With possible relativistic slippage. They may have a million year history but it's most likely someone's out there right now."

"How so?"

"Because all of the observed activity is contemporary. Because we have never observed an alien artifact before and have no reason to suppose it is anything other than what it appears to be, a real here and now thing that goes back and forth to some real there and now. Because there is a message to someone, which certainly implies expectation of a response. Because ... Well, just because."

"I see," said Dac, keeping a straight face. "Because." Actually, he did see, and 'because' made sense, which is what bothered him most. He had a momentary vision from some old war footage of a tense young sonar operator anxiously awaiting the pong in response to the ping he had sent into the void, the crew set on hair trigger. There was something else that bothered him.

"Why didn't we think of this before, Jason?" Dac's managerial substrata began to surface. "It seems we put a lot of effort into your 'non-language intrusions,' for nothing. Why didn't you try this first?"

"Your first question," answered Uni with a touch of testy, "was fully addressed in the report our team prepared ..."

"All right, it's in the book!" I'd better read that damned thing sometime, he thought. Mental grumble. Maybe Pappa can translate it into English. "But why now, after all this time?"

"Three reasons, Dac." It was Jason, taking control. "First, we didn't have anything to say. We didn't have anything translated but a few disjointed words and a lot of guesses. Now we think we can put together a coherent response, even if it is just repeating their words back to them."

"Hell's Parrot's, Jason! If all we're doing is playing back a recording, we could have done months ago!"

"No, we couldn't," chimed in Po. Everyone turned to Po more quickly than he could accommodate, causing a mild sensory overload. "Well, we *could* have. But we wouldn't have known what we were saying. We might have done something terrible, or more likely been completely ignored because the playback would have made no sense. Like, how much importance would you attach to an echo?"

"Okay, but ..."

"And second," continued Jason. "We didn't have the capability. We just now put together several technologies to make it possible. And the aliens helped us do it!" Smiles all around.

"Go on. I'm intrigued," said Dac, intrigued indeed.

"The first problem in banging on their door to get a response is to be able to identify a response," said Jason. "We figured the most likely response would be a change in whatever it is they're doing. Since the most obvious and fundamental thing they're doing is vibrating at an ungodly rate, the most likely response would be a variation in the vibrations. That meant we had to be able to reliably measure vibrations in that range. The methodology wasn't a problem, at least in the electromagnetic spectrum. It was the extremely high gravity wave frequencies which we don't usually use. No need. We had to build new equipment to assure the reliable precision we'd need.

"Measuring gravitons at those frequencies was tricky," he continued. "We have gravity wave detectors, of course, but they are relatively crude. We upgraded their sensitivity and operating frequencies mostly by synthetically increasing the effective aperture of our virtual lens. Po did it." Nod to Po who beamed appropriately. "That and enhancing our analytical capabilities. Pappa handled that."

"Old theory and technology, actually," said Po. "But we didn't have anything ready-made on board, mostly because there's been no call for it. I cobbled up a few things and it seems to work."

"That's two," said Dac after assimilating both of them to his satisfaction. "And?"

"And three," said Marcy, displaying three fingers triumphantly, "is the loudspeaker!"

"The what!?" Dac had trouble accommodating the idea of loudspeakers in space. "Loudspea ..."

"Well, figuratively speaking," added Marcy quickly. "The biggest problem with talking to the aliens is, well, talking. We have to transmit what we say to them somehow and the only alien vehicle we know of is vibrating shafts. We could receive but we couldn't send."

"Until now?"

"Until now!" Marcy beamed, at Dac and at the others, but mostly at Dac. God! Could she beam! "And I think we have it! We just disconnect a few of the main propulsion units and ..."

"Disconnect ...!?" Dac lurched autonomically, spilling hot coffee into his lap. A secondary lurch cracked his knee cap against the table leg. It was not executive.

Everyone jumped for napkins, or cover, simultaneously. Marcy moved to help Dac. Uni and Po moved for the door. Jason stood firm, amused.

Things came to a stop suddenly when Dac lifted his bladed right palm in the universal signal to stop.

"Okay." Pained pause. "Okay." Dac held his breath and gritted his teeth until that sweet piercing stomach-numbing electric pain subsided into relief. "Okay. Now what's this about dismantling the ship!"

"Well, not the ship," resumed Marcy. "Just a few propulsion units, maybe three. We won't do anything to the ship. Much."

"I'm listening. How much is much?" Dac held the much in escrow.

"We figure the best way to send a signal is through creation and destruction of mass, same as they do, but we'd need to do it as fast as they do it. The only things that fit those parameters are the mass conversion drives!"

Dac stared.

"The drives! They convert mass into energy to drive the PC. But we don't care about that."

"We don't?" Dac looked at the others who looked back like grandpas waiting for the kids to open a present. "Then why did you bring it up?"

"We don't care about the energy," corrected Marcy. "That's not important. The key is the mass that is destroyed to create the gravitons. Mass is converted in pulses, trillions of pulses per second. The process is so fast that most of the time nothing is happening. Each pulse is converted instantaneously and in effect goes out of existence just like ..."

"Just like the shafts!" finished Dac. Dac's turn to beam, with realization.

"Right! And each pulsed mass destruction emits gravitons!"

"Just like the shafts!" they all said in unison.

Dac thought they were about to break out in song, The Rain In Spain or some such, so he reigned them in.

"But what about modulation?"

"Modulation?" Po. "Oh, the signal. You mean how do we control the pulses to encode the message?"

"Yeah." Dac thought modulate covered the point more succinctly, but let it pass. Almost. "Modulate."

"This is a bit technical."

"Try me."

"All right." Not having a clue as to Dac's technical depth, Po sorted his thoughts so not to insult Dac while still being technically accurate. "Mass feeds to the converters on demand, controlled by the pre-conditioners and injection servos. The mass feeders are basically magnetic drivers that concentrate dense plasma into discrete bottled plugs and force them into the converters on demand. Magnetic waves control the flow of mass plugs. The magnetic waves can be modulated so the flow of plugs can be modulated. So the emission of gravitons can be modulated!" Po surprised himself.

"Okay, I can see that." Dac really did, surprising himself. "Why three?"

"We're going to generate a signal that looks as much like theirs as possible. Two units will generate a constant frequency matching the shaft's 'carrier' wave. We think we need two to generate enough power. The third will add the modulated signal."

Dac checked once more for seriosity. Of course they were serious! Hell's Woofers, he liked it! Talking to aliens in their own language! On their own Goddam smart phones! Hell's Ringtone, he liked it!

But. There's always a But.

"But why dismantle the ship?" he asked. Considering he was responsible for the safety of the ship and crew, it was a fair question.

"We want maximum probability that the shafts will pick up as many gravitons as possible." said Uni.

"So?"

"So we have to get the drives into the center of the cloud of shafts," said Uni incontrovertibly. "You don't want us to take the whole ship into the cloud, do you?"

He most certainly did not! But it did not necessarily follow that he had to let them knock the ship apart to avoid the shafts knocking it apart.

"But ..."

"Besides," added Jason. "If something goes wrong, the drives will be far away from the rest of the ship."

"Okay, but ..."

"And there will still be seventy-one drive units left on the ship. It's not like she'll be crippled or anything," said Marcy.

"Yes. That's true. But ..."

"And," added Po, sensing the kill. "If we blow ourselves up you won't have to put up with us anymore."

The comic relief was just right. But.

"But," said Dac to the round of expectant faces. "What are we going to say?"

"What was that all about? You never said a thing about ..."

"What!" grinned Marcy devilishly. "I couldn't tell you."

"I am the CEO, am I not? I am supposed to know everything on board, am I not?"

"Well, yes, mostly. But ..."

"And contacting the aliens is directly in line with my instructions to your team, is it not?"

"Okay. But ..."

"And you knew all about this and didn't say a thing to me. Right?"

"Right. But you see ..." Giggle.

"And you're telling me you couldn't tell me?"

"Well, I guess I *could* have, but ..."

"And you let me sit there looking like a fool!"

"But you looked so sweet that I ..."

"Sweet!" Sputter. "Sweet! A CEO does *not* look sweet in front of his crew!"

"There you're doing it again." Snicker.

"What! What am I doing!?"

"Looking sweet. You really are a teddy bear, you know." Snuggle. Nuzzle.

"Dammit, Marcy," without much steam. "You could have clued me in a little."

"But I didn't want to spoil their surprise. It was mostly their idea, you know. And they wanted to be sure before they sprang it on you. You know, in case it didn't work."

"In case it didn't work!?" Steam up! "You mean you've already tried it!?"

"Well, sorta." Oops. "Not exactly tried it." Massage. "I mean we didn't send a message or anything." Intent gaze. Snuggle.

"Well just what in Hell's FedEx did you guys send? A test pattern?"

"We didn't *send* anything." Hurt pout. "We just sorta ... tested it. I thought you'd be proud of us. Me." Subtle on-call welling of moisture in the eye.

"Aw, Marcy." Dammit all. "I didn't mean to ..." Sincere eye contact.

"Look. I am proud of you. All of you guys. Really." Gentle stroke of shoulder and neck. "I ... I just got worried about you, you know, if something had gone wrong and you'd gotten hurt." Good tack! Good! "I don't know what I would have done if something had happened." Pain. A little more pain. "And you got hurt and I wasn't there to help." There, right on!

"You mean that?" What's he take me for? "You really worried about me? Wait a minute." Move off a bit. "You didn't know we tested it." You sonov .... "Did you?"

"I mean just now, when you told me. Then I was worried." God!

"You knew!" Genuine PO-edness. "You knew and you didn't tell me you knew!" Feigned anger and disbelief.

"I ..." Think fast. "I didn't want to spoil your surprise." Take that! Smirk.

"You were spying on us!" Justified outrage. No wonder it was so easy to talk him into it!

"Spying!?" How do I get into ... "Look. I'm the CEO, right?" Marcy didn't concede the point. "And I have to know what's going on, whether I want to or not, see. So there are, uh, controls built into the system."

"You were spying!" That's it, twist it.

"I wasn't spying!" Compose yourself. "Pappa told me."

"Pappa told you!? So now it's Pappa's fault, is it?"

"I didn't mean it like that!" Lordy! "It's nobody's *fault*. There isn't any fault. Pappa is programmed to flag any unusual and/or unauthorized energy expenditures. A lot of other things, too. It's part of the fail safe systems and the cross-check systems and the security systems and the accounting systems and who know what all systems. I have to know what's going on and Pappa has to tell me. It was just a routine report." She's accepting that. Okay, Now the Confession. That usually does it.

"So yeah, I knew. Mostly. So I pretended not to know." Snuggle. "You know, like when you find out what's in your Christmas present and you don't want to spoil the other person's fun so you pretend you don't know?" Massage. "See?"

"Well, I guess so." I guess so.

"And you did have fun keeping it a secret, didn't you?" Schmooze a little.

"Well, yes." Now that I think about it.

"And you did have fun springing it on me, didn't you?" Stroke, slowly. There. Stop right ... there.

"Yes." Dammit, he knows every spot!

"Well." Soft deep warm voice. "Where's the problem?" A little pressure here, a kiss there.

"Problem?"

CHAPTER 32

OPENING SHOT

"They're gone?" Dac looked absently at his board for confirmation in spite of knowing it was filled with biomass production figures for his quarterly P/L report to the board of directors. "Who's gone where?"

"Who?" asked Pappa, confused.

"They're gone!" confirmed Pete Bravo independently. Pete punched a few icons on his board and mumbled something violent. "Where in ...? They were ..."

"Mr. Olson," interrupted Marcy Phillips, professionally calm but urgent nonetheless. "Maximum scan shows nothing. They are not within detectable range."

"What's gone, Dammit!" Culpable silence on deck. "Pappa, what's going on?"

"Confirmed, Mr. Olson," replied Pappa with no audible hint of concern. "There is nothing within range of my sensors. The shafts have disappeared."

"Nothing?" Dac could not accommodate the idea.

"Actually," qualified Pappa without hesitation, "the debris from the Winnebago is undisturbed, as are the speakers ... mass converter drives. The Shafts, however, are gone."

"But the shafts *can't* be gone!" Dac looked at his display and back at the crew. "Can they?"

The bank of line monitors to the right of Dac's communication control panel lit up like a terminal's landing lights, each silently blinking its own little need while collectively clamoring for immediate attention. Dac punched PA unnecessarily hard and growled, "I know! They're gone!" Punch!

The communication panel cascaded to dark again. One light persisted until it too finally winked out under Dac's glare.

"Okay. Who knows what's going on? Marcy?"

"The shafts just disappeared, Dac." Nobody noticed the familiar, including Marcy and Dac. "They were here and then they were gone. I've checked the record several times and they simply, uh, didn't come back."

"Again?"

"They come and go a zillion times a second. One time they didn't come back. That's it." Marcy could only shrug palms up. God, could she shrug!

Dac looked from Marcy to Pete to Jason Fielding to Nraa Post and learned nothing.

"Pappa?"

"Confirmed, Mr. Olson."

"Confirmed what! They went away or they didn't come back!?"

"They did not come back, Mr. Olson. If they had moved away at that apparent speed, they would have certainly disturbed the impaled wreckage and destroyed the speakers." Pause in unrealized expectation of another question. "They did not come back," repeated Pappa in the off chance that he had been misunderstood.

"Now what?" asked Dac of the crew, who looked as though they needed a little guidance as to what to do next. "Status reports! In my office in five ..."

KLAXON! KLAXON! KLAXON!

"What KLAXON the KLAXONs goKLAXON on KLAXONow!"

Dac slammed the release and scrambled to his desk, genuine flight in his blood but battle tested fight in his hands. Flip this, punch, punch, flippity snap. Punch!

"Pappa!"

"Incoming, Mr. Olson!" Pappa really did manage an understated exclamation, reserved by some thoughtful programmer only for extreme and imminent danger. The result was electrifying. "The coordinates are on your board, Mr. Olson. Collision in ninety-seven seconds. Shall I take evasive action?"

If anything, Pappa's calm precision was even more unnerving than his relatively unbridled exclamation.

"Do it!" said Dac simply, but very quickly. He didn't stop to consider whether it was possible to avoid collision, assuming Pappa would not have asked if it were not. Nor did he consider what the danger was. Collision was precise enough for the next ninety-seven seconds.

There is no sense of motion in a profit center, even under sudden flat out acceleration. The only clue that the thing moved at all was Dac's control board readouts. Right now they indicated Pappa had pumped everything he had into the seventy-one remaining conversion drives. They were all approaching nominal maximum output.

The attitude display rolled as Pappa turned the ship into a quartering race to gain time to gain acceleration.

"Collision in eighty-two seconds. Request to overload." That riveted Dac's attention.

Pause. "Authorized!"

"Seventy-six seconds."

Pappa thoughtfully added red cross-hair indicators to the display to locate the hazard and the ship in three dimensions, the overlay grids scaled in million-k increments. The ship's velocity passed .002 light speed, accelerating. The hazard gained inexorably.

"What in Hell's Hounds is chasing us!" spat Dac.

"Sixty-two seconds."

"Request to shut down all non-life support systems."

"Authorized!" No pause.

Pappa enhanced the display of the deadly race with trajectories.

"Intersection in fifty-seven seconds at present rate, Mr. Olson. Point oh three seven light speed."

Another enhancement showed the hazard's huge size, density isos outlined its internal structure. The illustration was unmistakable.

"Thingys!" Hushed awed disbelief.

The cloud of shafts, billions of innocent mindless black little shafts of pure metallic hydrogen were shrieking out of Hell's Void like a blast of antipersonnel flechettes. They would shred the fragile ship like they had the Winnebago. The roles were reversed now; the Winnebago had plowed into the cloud inadvertently. But the results would be the same. It was coming directly at them.

No! Not directly! Pappa overlaid the trajectory of the cloud's center of mass to the ship's trajectory. Their paths diverged! The cloud's outer fringes would overtake the ship but the dense center would miss.

Might miss. If the ship continued to accelerate. If the density of the cloud was correct. If the cloud moved at a constant speed. If the drives don't explode. If.

"Request to jettison warehouses."

The warehouses! Almost a year's work. And a year's pay and dividends and my career and ...

"Authorized!"

The Hell with dividends, smiled Dac ruefully. I'll kiss the board's butts if I get mine out of this in one piece. Besides, if they survive maybe we can chase them down later. And if they don't, we probably won't either and the point will be moot.

"Twenty-five seconds."

Pappa adjusted the display, tightening the scale and enhancing the detail of the cloud. New projected trajectories.

"Estimated time of collision: twenty-four seconds," intoned Pappa. "Point oh four seven light speed."

Update: "Twenty-four seconds."

Update: "Twenty-six seconds."

"Oh Lordy, Lordy." Dac wasn't much at praying but he made allowances this time. "Hold on!"

Update: "Thirty-two seconds."

"Yes!"

New trajectories, more divergence as Pappa diverted energy into a gentle turn.

Update: "Forty-nine seconds."

"All RIGHT!!" Commotion and relief and tears and grins and jumps and noise. "We did it!"

"Nice work, Pappa!" said Dac, very sincerely. "Hell's Razor, that was close!"

"I beg your pardon?"

"That was close, Pappa. I thought we had it back there. Nice Work."

"Had it? Of course, you refer to the potential of collision. Did you think we would actually collide, Mr. Olson?"

"Did I think ..." Dac looked at the others, a little embarrassed. "You mean we weren't going to hit the cloud?"

"We would have been struck by the cloud of shafts if we had not taken evasive action," replied Pappa incontrovertibly, "but we did take evasive action. If you monitored your board you could see that ..."

"But the request for overloads. Was that needed?"

"Oh yes, Mr. Olson. As you know, the engines are overbuilt by an order of magnitude. The request is a formality only. The limit is there to prevent, uh, I believe the correct term is hot-dogging."

"And shutting down the non-life systems?"

"Standard procedures in a red alert. Surely you are familiar with regulation number ..."

"Okay!" Dammit. "And jettisoning the warehouses! If we weren't in any danger why did you do that!?"

"Why, Mr. Olson." Genuine puzzlement. "The explanation was on your board. As long as we had to expend so much energy to accelerate, I simply turned the ship towards our original destination and launched the warehouses to proceed unattended. At their present speed they should arrive only a little behind our original ETA and make up somewhat for our seven-month delay." Petulant pause. "I thought you'd be pleased."

"Okay. The question is obvious," opened Dac. "Any answers?" He surveyed the conference room. Jason. Hand. Marcy. Bravo. Mead. Ast and Label. Unit One. Their guesses would be as good as anyone's. Better than most, he hoped. He focused on Marcy, for no good reason.

"What!? Me?"

"Yeah. You." Dac smiled gently to relax things a bit. "They're throwing rocks at us. Got any ideas why?"

"Well, for openers," she opened, eyeing the others uncertainly, "we might try to objectivize things a little. We don't know *they* are doing anything, at least deliberately. And we don't know that they're doing it to *us*, specifically."

"Okay," said Dac. "If not them, who? And if not us, who?" Whom?

"Well, maybe those are the wrong questions," she continued. "Maybe we just happened to be in the way of whatever is happening. Like maybe we just happened to be in the way when the Thingy broke up for some other unrelated reason. Like maybe all of this really has nothing to do with us."

"Do you believe that?" said Mike Hand.

"No," said Marcy. "But it might help to organize our thinking if we forget about the idea that the Cloud was taking a deliberate shot at us. Maybe it was just moving away for its own reasons and we stepped out into the street without looking."

"Okay, fair enough," said Dac. "For openers. Any other ideas?"

"I think Marcy is on to something there," said Mike. "The Cloud didn't come directly at us, exactly. It was a glancing shot at best, and it didn't turn to pursue us."

"Good point, Mike." Ast. "But does that mean they ignored us or does it mean they're not very good shots. After all, what would or could they use for gun sights?"

"Wait a minute," chimed in Jason. "What's all this 'they' business? You're presuming that was deliberate."

"That looked pretty damned deliberate to me!" said Ross Label. "I don't know about you but I felt like a duck on opening day looking down the barrel of a 12 gauge double. That was a load of buckshot if I ever saw one, and if it was, they'll take another shot!"

Silence settled on the room. Ross' intuition was respected. He was not given to hyperbole, usually, but his underlying fear was contagious and the metaphor unnerving.

"Give me a consensus," said Dac to get things moving again. "For openers. That was a deliberate shot at us. Agreed?"

No objections. Not even uncertain diverted eyes.

"All right." Dac paused to formulate the next step. "Given that they took a potshot at us, are we agreed that they will likely take another?"

Nods, tentative, but definitely nods. No comments. The direction of the proceeding was obvious.

"And given they will take another swipe at us, I see two options: stay or go. Any others?" Very brief pause. "If not, then I vote we go." Dac shifted his weight to rise, the matter settled. A few chairs squawked.

"Mr. Olson?" It was Mercedes. "Let me see if this makes sense." All eyes turned to Mercedes, unto discomfort. Dac relaxed by way of permission to speak, but he was visibly impatient. A chair squawked again. "What if the machine, and the aliens on the flip side of the shafts, were just reacting to our assault."

"*Our* assault!?" said Ross. "What did we ever do to them!?"

"Well, for openers," replied Mercedes, "the Winnebago pulverized a few hundred thousand of their shafts when it plowed into the Cloud. From their end that would sure look like an assault. It would sure get their attention! If they were paying attention. And it sounds like we all agree they were. Are."

"So you think they're retaliating?" concluded Ross.

"No. Well, maybe. But I think it's more likely they are just making a more or less automatic response to what is probably a fairly common event."

"Again?"

"Well, look," she continued. "If Thingys and Clouds are all over the place and have been for who knows how long, they are bound to smash into asteroids and stars and planets and all sorts of hard stuff from time to time. The Winnebago was nothing compared to even a small asteroid. So wouldn't it make sense that they anticipated that possibility and built in some sort of automatic reaction?"

"Like?"

"Like stopping, like they did. Then maybe feeling around to see what they're up against. You know, like a blind man poking around with his cane. Or maybe like we do when we bump into a piece of furniture in the dark, reach out and feel what's there. But their senses must be extremely limited, so they're reaching out in the only way they can." Mercedes hesitated to formulate an appropriate analogy. "I'd compare it to one of our deep oil exploration drills. Drills aren't equipped for anything but drilling, so if we hit an obstacle we just bang into it until it gives, or start over and go around it. Or ..."

"Or what?" Dac prompted.

"Or maybe just grind the obstacle into dust, like that Ball."

"Ahh," in general from most.

"Okay, then what?"

"Well, and I'm speculating now," God, she thought, as if that wasn't obvious! "Feeling around would tell them whether to destroy the obstacle or go around it. Or if it was too big, a planet say, they would have to pack up and move their operation somewhere else. Considering the scope of their operation, I'd guess they would try the first two options first. Same as we would do."

"And?"

"And nothing." Mercedes stopped, then reconsidered. "And maybe we can give them another sense to help them make an intelligent decision."

"You mean your scheme to send a message to them?"

"Yes. That strikes me as an obvious thing to do. We bump into them accidentally and they react automatically, so we call and tell them, Hey! Time out. Excuse me! There's someone down here in the hole!"

A few smiles at that. Most had not seen this side of Mercedes and appreciated the break in the somber mood which had now definitely shifted to thoughtful optimism. Most were unsure of the reference to a hole, or had it wrong.

"Wait a minute!" Ross. "You're not seriously considering waiting around like a ... a sitting duck, just asking to get blown out of the water!" Ducks again!

"We've been sitting here for nearly ten months now, trying to establish communications. We should just walk away now?" rebutted Mercedes.

"Yes!" Ross did not feel any urgent call to honor in this sort of foolishness. "Pappa seems to think evading that first salvo was no big deal. I think it was just a bad shot. Ask Pappa what would have happened if the Cloud had been coming directly at us. Or if we had ten seconds less time to react."

"Good questions, Ross," said Dac. He eyed Ross askance as he asked, "Pappa?"

"In either case," replied Pappa, "the outcome would have been the certain destruction of the profit center."

"I rest my case." Ross folded his arms and leaned back in satisfaction. "We can't take another chance like that. Who knows where the next strike will be."

"Excuse me, Mr. Label," said Pappa. "*I* do."

Dac jumped at that, only slightly ahead of the others.

"You know!" Dac sputtered, getting his wits together. "They're going to take another shot at us!?"

"Yes," said Pappa, quite matter-of-factly. "As a matter of fact, they have taken forty-seven, uh, 'shots' so far."

"Forty ...!" Dac was almost over the edge. The rest were not far behind. "When!?"

"Just now, while you have been discussing the matter."

"Wh ... Why didn't you say anything?" Dac was incredulous. "That kind of danger flashing all around us and you did nothing!?"

"There was no danger, Mr. Olson," said Pappa calmly. "And the debate was intriguing; I hated to interrupt."

"Interrupt!! I'll interrupt your ..." Dac couldn't talk. Then he did. "Hell's Circuit Breaker, Pappa! What can you be thinking!?"

"I am thinking that there is no danger, Mr. Olson."

"Explain yourself Pappa!"

Dac searched viciously for something to hit or throw or condemn to Hell's deepest pits. "Damn!" He managed, just barely, a seething equilibrium grabbing the desk in a death grip that startled the Unit One officers. "This had better be good, Pappa, or you'll be making change in the cafeteria! Momma can take over just fine."

"DAMN!" Dac folded his arms to prevent a physical relapse.

"The first stroke was an unavoidable surprise," began Pappa like he was reporting today's hydrocarbon output. "The second and third strokes were far removed from our region of space, an admittedly fortuitous happenstance. However, analysis of the first three strokes indicated a pattern that was confirmed by subsequent strokes. The pattern is quite predictable. In fact, I have already made minor evasive maneuvers to position the profit center out of any immediate danger. We can stay right where we are for at least another few days."

"Unless the pattern changes," rebutted Ross.

"Of course," admitted Pappa. "However, the pattern clearly indicates a sweep. Mercedes Mead was quite right in that regard; they are looking for us. However, the pattern is not redundant; they are not searching regions already swept. We are safe where we are, in the center of the path of the first stroke even if the pattern changes. I expect eventually it will have to but it is likely they will continue to sweep new paths, not old."

"Any more questions?" You done good, Pappa, thought Dac grudgingly but genuinely relieved.

"Yeah," said Mike Hand. "Now what?"

"You tell me." Sly smile. "In my office at oh eight hundred."

"I can't believe you're seriously considering a hair-brained idea like this!" Ross Label was on his feet, trying to control his hands and feet and elbows and butt and talk at the same time. "I don't care what HO says! The aliens aren't shooting at them!"

"Look," Dac interjected, smoothing his hair back in frustration while he worked his way past that hair-brained remark. "HO policy says I can, *should* take any reasonable measures to maximize any commercial opportunities; *"Feasible and safe measures commensurate with the main commercial objectives of the Jobs,"* with some reservations and constraints of course. That means there's money in it somewhere, a *lot* of money." Dac eyed his people meaningfully. "For *everyone.*"

"Keep in mind that the Jobs and her crew are explorers and exploiters first and foremost, with a certain amount of danger implied. Like mining and football. But it's all right with them, considering that they, uh, we are on the verge of losing the Shafts entirely. They leave it to me to call. The thrust of their guidance is basically, don't screw up."

"So yes, Ross. It's a little crazy," concluded Dac. "Maybe a lot crazy. But doable and really great if we do it!"

The others in Dac's office looked at each other, embarrassed for Ross but understanding his frustration, more or less. He was only vocalizing what they all felt, that near-diarrhea loosening of the bowls that indicates you are about to do something really stupid and you can't find a graceful way out.

"You saw what it did to the Winnebago!" finished Ross. "It looked like it was run over by a lawn mower!"

In fact it did. Worse. Dac recalled a scene from his youth, a butcher shop in the back of the grocery where he worked as carry-out. A glove that was on display as a warning; it had dragged a hand into a meat tenderizer, shredded, missing a few fingers at the second joint. Another memory, of pop cans riddled by .22 ammo after an afternoon plinking.

The Winnebago looked like that. Another time, a deer that had been hit on the highway ...

"Look, Ross," said Jason. "I don't like it either; there are a lot of things I don't like about the Shafts and the aliens. But I figure Pappa's right. He's predicted a hundred and thirty-seven strokes accurately so far. It's no more complicated than any docking maneuver, just a little faster. The worst that can happen is it doesn't work and we're right back where we are right now. He fixed Ross calmly, smiling, his voice warm and soothing. But we have to try it once. No sweat, okay? Then we go home."

"We go home, right?" Jason fixed eyes with Dac pointedly.

"Yes. We go home. To port. Okay?"

"Yeah, okay," said Ross reluctantly.

"No, *not* okay!" inserted Ross for the record. "The *worst* that can happen is that Pappa guesses wrong and we end up like the Winnebago!" Grin. "But I'll do it. Like I have a choice. You all think it'll work. Well, okay it'll work; we'll make it work. But for the record it's still crazy. Okay, I'm on board. Once!"

"Once is fair enough. Jason?"

"Fair enough," accepted Jason. "Looks like a go!"

Dac looked long at Ross. Should he relieve him of duty on this, this crazy stunt he calls it? Maybe he's right, maybe it is crazy and he's the only one who sees it. In that case I'll need him more than ever to keep us crazies in line. On the other hand, crazy or not, I need cool heads. Ross almost lost it and that makes me nervous.

Dac looked to the others. Jason was unreadable. He didn't like it but he didn't like anything, and he always came through. Mike was grinning, like he was loosening up for the kickoff. Marcy looked like, yeah, all right, whatever. Does she really understand? I'll check later. Gerry Ast? Busy thinking and calculating and planning and working out the details and too occupied to worry. Bravo? Quiet, maybe apprehensive. He keys off of Ross a little but no problem on this. Mercedes? She's composing the message right now, I'll bet. This is her thing, her one big chance, and she's into it already. Hell's Shredder, it was her idea! Hers and Pappa's!

"That's cool, Ross." Dac nodded, just once, to everyone. "Let's make it happen. Once."

CHAPTER 33

NOMINAL

"Point oh four seven three, Mr. Olson." Pappa's voice was set on neutral, which wasn't very much different from his excited voice. Dac found that fact reassuring; the last thing he needed now was an AI full of wobbly chips.

"Nominal," concurred Mike Hand, co-pilot on this gig.

"Jason?"

"Five by five." Jason looked up from his board long enough to smile at Dac from one corner of his mouth. "She'll hold together, Dac."

Dac noticed the un-protocol familiar address. He didn't realize his anxiety showed and in just a moment knew he needed that comfortable touch from his most trusted friend. He turned back to his board and tried to look busy. Then he realized he was looking at the hydroponic tomato production for last month. He quickly flipped to current flight status and narrow-eyed the deck sideways to see if anyone noticed. Everyone was too preoccupied to pay attention to his board. Except Marcy, who smirked appropriately and went back to work. God! Could she smirk!

And what in Hell's Dictionary did 'five by five' mean anyway!?

"All departments: Project status update: Go/NoGo. "Dac's status panel lit up gogogogo. "It's a go." Dac was gratified to see his crew accepting his personal corporate speak instead of that fakey sorta-military lingo.

"Mercedes? Is your message in auto queue?"

"Ready, Mr. Olson," she replied. She was nervous as Hell's Jell-O but she was ready. "Ready."

"Pappa?"

"Point oh four eight one, Mr. Olson. Holding nicely on spec. That should pull us away slowly. All systems nominal."

Comfortable word, nominal, thought Dac. Point oh four eight one. A significant piece of light speed. A factory the size of a small town out playing chicken with a cloud of killer slivers and we reassure ourselves by calling that nominal! That means it's exactly as dumb as we predicted. Ross was right; this is crazy as Hell's Cockroaches.

Simple but crazy. All we had to do was fire this crate up and point her in the right direction. In the direction Pappa predicted the cloud would be headed when it reappeared for its three hundred and eleventh swipe at us. At precisely the right speed to stay in front of it but pull away slowly as they kept power on to broadcast their message. At precisely the right time to put us immediately in front of the cloud of shafts when it popped into existence to rip another swath through space, hunting us. And stay there long enough to transmit Mercedes' message through seventy-one mass converters, all aimed backwards at the cloud. And hope we say something that makes sense. And hope they are listening. And understand. And care. Ross seemed more and more sane every minute.

Dac had to reinvest himself in the strategy. "Forgive my confusion here but tell me again. Why do we have to be in front of the cloud? Why can't we just track alongside it?"

"We can," replied Jason. "The problem is that the cloud is highly flattened in configuration. If we were to ride above it, for example, we would be broadcasting our message through the thinnest aspect. Some areas are much more sparsely populated than others so we might be wasting much of the effect. Since we don't really know how much effect is enough, we feel broadcasting edge-on will be most effective."

"In addition," interjected Pappa, "the direction of the mass converters would drive the ship away from the cloud, which would degrade the signal, and it would alter the direction of the ship away from our intended direction."

"And that's the most dangerous place to be. Right?"

"Yes," confirmed Pappa. "However, we will be pulling away from the cloud at all times. There should be no problem."

"Except for the problem we created for ourselves," grunted Dac.

"There is one troubling consideration, Mr. Olson. The cloud seems to have consolidated somewhat over the last sixty or so appearances. It is still large but much more sharply defined at the edges. I'm not sure about the ramifications of that fact."

"Okay. That's interesting, Pappa but what does …"

"Bingo!" Jason snapped up at his overhead just as Pappa's alarm signaled the reappearance of the cloud. He flipped something and grinned. "Right on schedule. She's all yours, Mead."

Dac saw that Mercedes was already on it, as far as you can be on top an automated process. Pappa had programmed the communication team's message to broadcast the instant the cloud appeared, at full all-out power. At Maximum danger zone power. Readouts jumped as the converters started speaking Thingy talk; otherwise nothing seemed to happen. All Mercedes could do was watch, check that everything proceeded as expected, and sweat. Then we ride it out, the cloud disappears and we back off about a billion clicks to see what happens.

"Pappa?"

"Nominal, Mr. Olson."

"Jason?"

"What's to see?"

Indeed. If they could see the cloud, and they couldn't, it would appear stationary. Two chunks of matter chasing through space at ungodly speeds, relatively almost at rest. The scans were stationary. Everyone on the deck was stationary. Dac's board displayed the point that was the ship next to the cloud. A cloud that had grown to a gargantuan size but vaporously transparent as smoke. A huge galaxy shaped spiral cloud next to a tiny blip like a bird in the path of a hurricane, the arms shaped like scimitars. What was the significance of that spiral shape; design or the natural development of mindless forces? Many of the crew had theories about that; did the Thingys turn into galaxies somehow, or influence development of their spiral shape?

One of the mysteries of galaxies, Dac mused, had been the disc-style rotation; the outlying spiral arms often spin too fast, like the galaxy was a solid disc rather than a whirlpool. They should fly off into space but something held them together. Conventional theory blamed Dark Matter without conclusively finding any, so far. Could that really be Thingy influence?

If they could have seen it, it would have looked like their backs were against a wall. Dac regretted that analogy immediately.

It had to be that close, to make sure the converters' blast was focused on the denser center of the cloud. To make sure the message would be received. And maybe do as much damage as possible, thought Dac with surprise; what if they missed the message and took their blast as an attack!

"One converter shut down, Mr. Olson," said Pappa. "Three are overloading."

Dac popped back into the moment, setting his ruminations aside for more urgent matters.

Nominal, thought Dac. We figured we'd lose a few converters trying a stunt like this. We didn't need all the converters for heavy acceleration anyway; we were already up to cloud speed. We were using the converters as transmitters, providing minimal acceleration. The synchronized pulsed conversions would generate the modulated gravity wave that carried mankind's first message to the aliens. That was the theory. And we were pouring everything we had into this theory.

We can tolerate twenty percent breakage, Dac assured himself. That's why we chose this particular vector; it was pointed straight at the nearest comfort station. We could lose fifty percent of the converters and easily coast on home. It would take a while to get this tub stopped, but we'd get home. Then our tour of duty was over. That was the deal with HO when they authorized this stunt; lots of R and R. Then what? Heroes or goats?

"Four converters down, Mr. Olson, seven on overload. We are holding station nicely."

"We seem to have a problem, Dac." That was Jason, professionally under control but the edge in his voice betrayed there was a problem.

"A problem?"

"They are accelerating!" Jason. "And fast!"

"The cloud is accelerating, Mr. Olson," juxtaposed Pappa.

"That can't be!" almost shouted Dac. Then more calmly, "I thought the cloud always moved at one constant speed! No fair!"

"It always has," said Pappa irrefutably, "until now."

"Then what's happening?"

"I believe that now," said Pappa, this time incontrovertibly, "they have found us."

"You mean they're attacking!?"

"I said they are accelerating, Mr. Olson," replied Pappa. "Directly at us. I don't know that I would characterize their change in velocity as ..."

"Jason, get us out of here! Do it now!"

"Done!" Jason sounded relieved hitting Stomp earnestly.

"Eleven converters down, Mr. Olson," said Pappa. "Eight on overload. We are approaching maximum allowable loss."

"Jason?"

"I can divert power into a turn or accelerate," said Jason. "Probably not both. Your call."

"Pappa?"

"Confirmed, Mr. Olson."

"Confirmed what!"

"Confirmed your call, Mr. Olson."

"Turn! Now!"

"I'll need all the power I can get, Dac," said Jason after a moment of activity at his board. "Permission to shut down the message transmission?"

"Why?"

"The transmission degrades the efficiency of the converters. Maybe three or four percent, but I don't think I can spare it."

Dac looked up to Mercedes.

"Okay! Permission granted!" said Dac after a long moment, "But *only* if and when you *need* it. Clear it with me first. Pappa, keep track of that!"

"Seventeen converters down, Mr. Olson. Four on ..."

"Intercept, Pappa?"

"We are within the outer edges of the cloud now, Mr. Olson," replied Pappa instantly. "Density is approximately one hundred shafts per cubic kilometer in our vicinity."

"Jason?"

"We're ..."

A shriek of torn steel ripped the ship, followed by a thump and a lurch.

"Impact, Mr. Olson. Starboard arboretum. Air pressure dropping." Pause. "Sealed."

"Full emergency alert!" Dac slipped into battle mode unconsciously. It fit nicely. The crew's reaction was almost instantaneous as they were on standby anyway, and hair-triggered.

"Pappa! You're Jason's eyes. Protect our vitals and get us out of here! Now!"

"Affirmative, Mr. Olson." Pappa did not wear battle gear gracefully. "All teams alerted. Nonessentials power downed." Isn't that 'powered down?

Affirmative? Power downed? Dac didn't have time to correct Pappa's archaic lingo. Probably another programmer's way to get even.

Another remote thump and a shiver through the ship. Those little two-kilo Shafts can give us a good whack, thought Dac.

"Pappa! What happens to a Shaft when it hits us?" A new thought Dac hadn't heretofore considered. He sure hoped somebody had. "Does it stop or keep on going or break up?" Afterthought. "And what's the penetration and damage path?"

"The Shafts are structurally extremely persistent," responded Pappa after a moment to analyze damage reports, "but not completely so. They seem to abrade and ultimately deconstruct. Damage path depends on what is in that path. However, they are doing significant damage everywhere. I am most concerned with life support and gas envelope."

"Damage report! All departments!" Dac flipped reports over to Damage Control, Security, and to Maintenance. He checked his board that everyone was busy as Hell's Blender but it looked like things were under control for now.

"Okay. Your turn, Pappa."

"We have encountered almost three hundred Shafts so far, Mr. Olson. Damage is extensive but limited to non-critical components. I have oriented the ship to place the heaviest and least vital components to windward, as it were. The farm was severely damaged due to its being on the up side towards the impending assault. I suggest all non-emergency personnel move to the downwind side of the ship, on the structures furthest from impact hazard. Details are on your screen, Mr. Olson."

"Do it!" commanded Dac without looking at his screen. Pappa knows best. "But let me make sure I understand the situation." Dac composed himself and his personal analysis of the situation. "We're being chased by the cloud of Shafts and the Cloud is faster, gaining on us. Right?"

"Correct, Mr. Olson."

"And the ship is oriented so the heaviest less important parts will be hit first and most, Right?"

"Correct, Mr. Olson."

"How fast is the Cloud moving?" demanded Dac.

"The Cloud is moving at just over .05c, as are we, Mr. Olson. If you refer to the relative speed, or the impact speed, it is closing at about LEO speed, or fifteen to twenty thousand kilometers per hour."

"That's bad?"

"Yes."

"Prognosis?"

"We can probably stand several thousand impacts at this rate, Mr. Olson, given this relative velocity and Shaft density. Beyond that ..."

"Jason?"

"We'll lose her at this velocity, Dac. They're gaining."

"Pappa?"

"Confirmed, Mr. Olson, if Mr. Fielding is referring to being overtaken by the cloud's core before we reach safety."

"Time out! Let me see if I've got this right," said Dac with a hopeless 'I don't believe this is happening to me' grin. "If we accelerate we have more damage where we aren't protected hitting more Shafts faster trying to get away, and if we don't accelerate we have more damage from the increased number of Shafts overtaking us. Right?"

"Yes." Pappa.

"Yes what! Dammit!"

"Yes, you've got that right," said Pappa. "I believe it is again your call."

"Accelerate, Jason. Give her Hell's Leadfoot!" Having cast one die, Dac turned to his board and cast the other. "Pappa! I don't care if you fry every last one of those converters. I want a total energy dump. Understood? Move it!"

"Confirmed, Mr. Olson," responded Pappa. Then uncharacteristically, "Hang on to your ... I believe the appropriate term is junk!"

"Cancel the message?"

Dac hesitated. "No," he said simply. "Now that we have their attention ..."

CHAPTER 34

LOSING IT

"Status!"

Dac knew the status. It was serious. A couple of gigazillion blades were slashing at his tail, his ship was falling apart around him and he was losing power precipitously as mass converters flamed out like flashbulbs. Or got shredded in the metallic hydrogen maelstrom. The converters were exposed on outriggers, and essentially unarmored. And what in Hell's History are flashbulbs!?

Great, he thought as he checked the update on his board, discouraged. Now the Goddam septic tanks just got ripped out! The ship was being gutted like a fish and all he could do was watch.

"Gimme some good news. Jason?"

"We're holding. We're not gaining. I'm trying to slip sideways out of the way but it'll take a while. We should be clear in twenty hours or so." Pause. "If power holds up."

"Marcy?"

"We've lost most of the primary scanning array," replied Marcy immediately. "All forward antennas are damaged or gone. We've cobbled up an emergency retrench position with cannibalized shuttle systems. Free-standing systems are okay for now; they're all embedded and armored."

"Pappa is operational," continued Marcy with a quick check on an overhead display, "but his speed is degraded with the loss of his DeltaQ bank. Some sensors are not completely reliable. Momma has taken over the ship to free up Pappa's capacity. Non-essentials are all off line." Marcy looked at Dac personally, helpless a little, with 'I'm sorry I let you down' in her voice but competent and composed nonetheless. "Holding, I guess."

"Mercedes!" barked Dac. Hell's Oopsies, he thought. She didn't get us into this. More controlled, "Mercedes?"

"No response, Mr. Olson. As far as I can tell we're still broadcasting. Strong. No response." She didn't look up.

"Mike?" He said, still looking after Mercedes.

"The guts are still in order," he replied, terse and hard. "But we're losing too many drives. About a dozen drives overloaded and successfully shut down; they will come back online in a few hours when they cool down and reset. The others are probably slag. There aren't enough left. I can't apply all of the power I've got available."

"Pappa?"

"No significant recent change in our survival prognosis," said Pappa with a disconcerting hitch. "There is one indeterminable consideration."

"Which is?" Here we go!

"Many of the mass converter units have been disabled due to failure of ancillary systems. However," continued Pappa, "if a mass converter unit were to suffer a direct hit at the point of the magnetic bottle, there is the potential of a catastrophic fusion nuclear detonation. I thought you should know."

"Can I do anything about that now?" Dac was frozen.

"No, Mr. Olson."

Dac looked up to see every crewone looking at him. They understood the situation, and soon everyone on the Jobs would know and understand.

Dac hesitated overlong. "If that happens … will we know?" Talk about your morbid!

"No, Mr. Olson."

No elaboration was necessary nor requested.

"Mr. Olson?"

"Yes! What …" It was Ross. "What *is* it, Ross?"

"I have an idea. I worked it out with Momma and Pappa," said Ross, like he was a bit afraid of its reception and needed heavyweight corroboration. "The Cloud has that galaxy structure, rotating spiral arms and all, but perfectly organized and symmetrical. With relatively unpopulated voids between the arms.

"I think we can head for a void, maybe ride it out of here," continued Ross. "We'll have to turn into the cloud and drift with it for a bit, back and fill up the void, but it might take the pressure off. We may not get out as soon but we might get out in one piece. Or in fewer pieces. We'll miss a dense arm full of Shafts coming up. It's on your board, Jason. What do you think?"

Jason checked the vectors Ross had transferred to his board and grunted at the display of the cloud's structure on his board. Dac looked hard at Ross. Jason nodded, almost imperceptibly; he was all but incapable of admitting that a techie like Ross could have a good idea about piloting a ship. Dac looked at Ross again, caught his eye, and said thanks, eyeball to eyeball. Ross smiled. See?

"Jason?"

"Looks good." Grudgingly but with enough respect that Ross could hear it. "It looks like a good bet."

"Pappa?"

"It is feasible, with reservations," hedged Pappa.

"Reservations?"

"Yes, Mr. Olson," replied Pappa. "The proposal will take more time which in turn may mean more collisions overall. I suggest adding another vector moving sideways to the plane of the Cloud as well. It's on the boards."

"And that will take power, which we are running short of?"

"Of which we are running s ..."

"All Right!" manomanoman. "Pappa this is no time for a ... Can we do it or not!?"

"Yes."

"Okay! Do it, Jason!" commanded Dac ramped up to full authority. "Now is good!" Jason did it instantly, one click ahead of now. Almost ahead of Dac.

Dac's board scans rolled with the maneuver and the ship seemed to creak inaudibly with the strain. Silence reflected the crew's concentration as they willed the craft into the turn vicariously; aside from the display, there was no sense of the motion.

"Pappa?"

"Thirty-two drives down, Mr. Olson. Fifty percent."

"You don't need all available power, Mike?" Dac knew the answer, with so many drives down.

"Yes, sir." Mike looked to Mercedes and the contact team. "No, sir. But ..."

"Pappa, pour everything you can spare into that message, maximum dispersal." What have we got to loose, he thought. He looked directly at Mercedes. "When we're down to twenty good drives, kill the message. Until then I want to be heard all the way to Hell and back. Understood?"

"Yes, Mr. Olson," said Pappa, correctly interpreting the metaphor. We have twenty-seven functioning drives now, Mr. Olson. At the present ..."

The ship lurched downward and skewed violently, with a ripping blackboard screech that terrorized the flight deck. The crew sprang into action, largely ineffectually.

KLAXON! KLAX!sptt.

Dac's snapping hand guillotined the alarm before it really got up to speed. "Think we aren't alarmed enough!?" he thought. You can klax your little chips out when things get *really* serious. Right now tell me something I need to know.

"Structural integrity has been compromised, Mr. Olson," announced Pappa. "Assessing."

I didn't want to know that, Dac grumbled to himself. He slipped back into his seat and stroked the board for information.

"Damage!"

"We lost the starboard burb, Dac," said Jason, unbelieving. "That compound turn just left it behind!" Jason concentrated on his board, afraid to take his eyes away lest something more terrible happened. His jaws were clenched in frustration, his eyes welling in rage. "Something must have been ... So many drives out ... Uneven power applied a torque ... Too much damage ... I couldn't ..."

"Casualties!" required Dac. "Were there ... How many people?"

"One moment, Mr. Olson," replied Momma. "One hundred and thirteen crew and EEs. Some families. Mostly biomass and agribusiness, two warehouses."

"We lost seven drives with the burb, Mr. Olson," said Pappa. "We are down to eighteen functioning drives."

Dac watched as Jason struggled to regain control of the remaining superstructure. One burb, gone! Seven hundred thousand tons of metal and air and food, and one hundred and thirteen people. They would live for a while, hours, while their chunk of life ablated in the cold firestorm of Shafts. Children not knowing what was happening, mothers and fathers who did.

The scan rolled again as Jason eased the lop-sided hulk into some stability, tweaking the remaining drives gently, mumbling into the board as he worked.

"Mr. Olson?"

"Mr. Olson?" Pappa. "The message?"

"Yes," said Dac simply. "Kill it." He couldn't look at Mercedes.

The crew sighed collectively, finally. More than anything else, turning off the message meant they had failed. They had lost. Whatever chance they had to make something of this disaster, it was gone. All that was left was to hang on, to survive.

"Recovery, Mr. Olson?" It was Mike. Dac realized that Mike's ex and his preschool daughter were on the burb. He looked to Mike and to the others. There was no real choice.

"No, Mike," replied Dac firmly but paternally. "If ... when we get out of this, we'll look. Okay?" Mike nodded but didn't, couldn't answer. Others went back to work, mostly glad they didn't have to make that call.

Some watched their boards, fascinated by the breakup of the derelict piece of their ship, the small town they had to leave behind. Others distracted themselves in their work, trying desperately to believe that it still mattered.

Dac was a board watcher. He had friends on that, that what? That scrap heap out there spinning to its doom? It was still a space ship of sorts, he reminded himself. It was doomed but it was still a free-standing ship. As if that were good, he thought ruefully. Each burb was more or less self-contained and capable of limited free flight. If it had power and working drives. And barring an accident. But that burb out there was powerless, already heavily damaged and relentlessly stalked by an accident. What did they have left now? Hours? In their place, facing the inevitable, would I rather forego the hours and be done with it? What else, he wondered, could go wrong?

"Dac?"

It was Jason, under his breath. Dac caught the trace of fear in Jason's voice, a brittle overtone he had never heard before, and looked over to Jason instantly. Hackles up!

"What is it, Jason," said Dac, hushed and tired, the command gone from his voice.

"We're out of balance, Dac, bad. I can't maneuver into the void. The burb and too many flameouts. I'll have to crabass this crate nearly forty degrees to maintain control."

"So? Do it," said Dac. "What's the problem?" he added, sensing, knowing he did not understand the problem.

"We're exposed, Dac. I can't keep the heavy mass as a shield." Jason looked up at the ceiling. "That's an outside wall, Dac. A class III meteor shield, two sheet metal skins, and a few feet of insulation and mechanical stuff. Then space. And that's upwind," he concluded, nodding upward. A distant whang underscored Jason's analysis of the situation.

Dac looked up, imagining cold space glaring in through shredded panels. Clear space. Stars. And little black shafts rifling through the ship, ripping through the flight deck, through people. Life pouring out into space. Dac looked back to Jason, seeing his fear and not even trying to hide his own.

"Options?"

"We have to get squared away," said Jason. "I can't add drives; I can only shut them down. That's not enough to counterbalance. We'll have to jettison the port burb. Soon."

Dac stared hard. "Pappa! Are you monitoring?"

"Yes, Mr. Olson."

"Analysis!"

Pappa took a long time to respond. Performance had degraded significantly, Dac Knew, but he hoped accuracy had not.

"Confirmed, Mr. Olson," replied Pappa finally, visual display only; Pappa was still able to pick up on the private nature of the dialogue. "The flight attitude required for reliable control with the remaining battery of drives and the present mass distribution force exposure of weak aspects of the command module to probably overwhelming intrusion."

"Remedials?"

"Mr. Fielding's recommendation is sound, Mr. Olson."

"Alternatives?"

"None, Mr. Olson," said Pappa distantly, "but I might suggest maneuvering the detached burb to the front of the command module as a shield."

Jason smiled a 'Nice work Pappa' smile at the overhead speaker and began working out the procedure.

"Momma?" It can't hurt to get a second opinion.

"Momma?"

"Momma is not responding, Mr. Olson," said Pappa. "I'm checking for ..."

"Now is a good time, Dac." Jason's urgency was compellingly understated. Dac hit PA.

"We have a problem," he began tentatively. Criminitly, he thought, that'll sure get their attention! "Abandon the port burb now! The port burb will be jettisoned in ..." he glanced at Jason, "fifteen minutes." Jason nodded, with a slight sideways head twist. "Repeat! Emergency Jettison! Abandon port burb! Do it now!" PA off. "Count it down for them, Pappa."

Several of the crew looked up in amazement, not having heard the preliminaries, but they bent to their support tasks immediately upon internalization. Transfer air and water. Upload data banks. Move people, count heads.

"Ten minutes," intoned Pappa's autonomic alter ego.

Disarm atomics. Shut down drives and power plants. Move people, count heads. Verify evacuation compartment by compartment.

"Five minutes."

Count heads. Depressurize. Seal bulkheads. Secure the burb for recovery later.

Later. Right.

"Emergency Jettison protocols complete," announced Jason after several agonizing minutes. "On your mark. Mr. Olson."

"Mark." Quiet but firm. "Cut 'er loose, Jason."

One long moment.

"She's gone, Mr. Olson."

"We're down to eleven drives, Mr. Olson," said Mike Hand. "Stable."

"Shielding burb in place," after several tense minutes. "Let's get out of here."

Stable, thought Dac. We're balancing the port burb on the nose of the command module like a trained circus seal with a ball. Pushing it like a tugboat pushing barges up a river. We're down to, what? fifteen percent power, no backup computer and Pappa's getting twitchy, twenty percent of personnel lost, heavy damage and more certain. Stable. I don't think I can stand much more stability.

"Prognosis?"

"I've cut power to save what drives we have left," said Jason. "If they hold, and the cloud accelerates at a constant rate, and nothing else goes wrong, we're out of here in forty hours. Give or take a tad."

Jason looked up at Dac and Dac nodded. Like they knew what they were doing and had everything under control. Dac recalled an old joke about not needing much time to look at a hot horseshoe. Whatever in Hell's Burlyque a horseshoe was.

I can just see it, he thought. Walking into an HO debrief with a box full of bolts and fenders and spilling it onto the table. "Mission accomplished," I would say. "Got any more little jobs for me?" Right. Jobs. If I'm lucky I'll spend the rest of my career hauling toxic waste. Hell's Dice, if I'm lucky I'll be dead. Like those hundred and thirteen SOBs out there. That's all I'm entitled to.

Dac looked at his board sullenly. The white display board curved around to 80 percent of his peripheral vision, like the inside of an eggshell. Brilliant matte white with colored displays scattered about within reach. Directly in front of him was Pappa's display of the cloud and his ship. Ships, now. The rotation of the cloud's arms sweeping like a scythe away from the command module, toward the lost burb, like the arms of a hurricane embracing an island that can't run away. They would get the worst of it in a few hours.

Overhead, temporarily out of the way, were the final production figures for the fiscal year. To the right of that his to do list, the last entry, "Arrange going home party." Dac swept his hand across the list, erasing the party. How about a 'staying alive' party' he thought in a funk, or a 'don't kill any more of your friends' party! Or a ... What in Hell's Floaters was that!

Dac's attention was drawn to an incidental motion on his board and found nothing. It took a second to realize what he noticed was actually something that disappeared. Another second to realize what wasn't there.

"Oh, no!" Jason with uncharacteristic agitation. "Oh baby! It can't be! Lordylordylordy!" Jason was a blur of activity. "Nononono ...!"

Jason was out of control, a sight so rare it froze Dac in fear. He knew in his heart there was inevitably one more disaster due and payable. This sounded like Hell's Foreclosure, only the particulars in escrow.

The flight deck erupted in turmoil, people shouting commands and running in circles, flipping switches and stroking boards to resurrect dead systems. Status lights blinked furiously as whole panels flashed to life. Dac turned his attention back to his board but it still didn't register.

"Pappa! Hell's A Poppin ...!"

He had to shout to hear himself over the commotion.

"Status!"

"The cloud," pronounced Pappa, slowly above the frantic activity, "has stopped."

CHAPTER 35

STOPPED

"Stopped!?" repeated Dac incredulously. "Stopped?" Pause. "Stopped!?"

"Yes, Mr. Olson," repeated Pappa after a pause, searching for an alternate meaning to Dac's third question. "Stopped," said Pappa finally. "It is now motionless," he added, just in case.

"Then we're safe!" shouted Dac. Then more restrained, "We did it! We're home free!"

"Not quite," said Jason, in more reassuringly better control. "If I don't get this heap turned around ...!"

A dull ping brought a hush on the flight deck. It sounded exactly like the first plump raindrop of a summer thunderstorm, smacking a corrugated steel shed roof. Another, a duller bong by only a little. Then more, closer. An explosion!

"Come on, baby," murmured Jason, throwing his body into the effort of turning the ship. "Hold together now. That's it. Come on." Gentle. Coaxing. Lightly stroking his control interface like a determined but gentle lover.

"Will somebody tell me what's going on?" Dac's daydreaming had left him a notch behind the situation, his anxiety a direct function of his ignorance. Nobody paid him any attention.

"Pappa!"

Pappa responded with a well timed KLAXON!!

"Collision hazard," clarified Pappa. "Immediate and extreme danger."

"Collision? But I thought the cloud stopped!?"

"Quite, Mr. Olson. However, *we* did not stop," replied Pappa, irrefutably succinct as ever in spite of his impaired capacity. "We are now leaving the stationary cloud at relatively slightly more than a fraction of one percent of light speed. The effect will be a secondary collision. Excuse me, Mr. Olson, if there's nothing else, I'm a little pressed at the moment."

"Uh, yes. Of course." Stunned, Dac turned to Jason but hesitated, seeing he too was more than pressed. He gathered himself in a moment and reconsidered. I'm the boss, after all, he thought. Act like it!

"Pappa! Situation!"

"We are in a relatively thin region of the cloud," replied Pappa quickly realigning his priorities, "in a void between dense spiral arms, traveling approximately along its length. We will intersect an arm in less than ninety seconds. Please refer to your board, Mr. Olson."

Dac turned to examine the display. Pappa laid out three XYZ views of the situation, centered on arbitrary axes imposed on the cloud of Shafts. The cloud showed the now familiar spiral galaxy shape. A red dot marked the location of the ship, a blue line its trajectory. The red dot was moving very fast.

The ship was in a trough between arms, just inside the outermost. Its present trajectory was roughly parallel to the arm, cutting a thin chord to one side of the spiral, but it passed through the arm as the arm curved in front of them. The angle of the ship's trajectory to the arm was small, the transit long.

"Problem!"

"We will encounter a large number of Shafts at extremely high relative velocities, Mr. Olson, on the order of ten thousand incidents concentrated in a period of approximately two one-thousandths of a second."

"I still don't see the problem, Pappa," challenged Dac. "At that speed the shafts will just vaporize against the burb up front. We can just plow through."

"Yeah. Except for one thing," grunted Jason. "We're going backwards!"

"Backwards!?"

"You got it!" Jason squirmed throwing body English all over the flight deck as he desperately manipulated machine commands to bring the ship around. "We're about to pitchpole!"

Dac stared at Jason, hard. Pitchpole! An old nautical term; overtaken by a large following wave. The term was ancient, graphic and completely unnerving.

Dac finally realized the nature of the problem. They had outfoxed themselves. In order to avoid more serious damage, and unable to outrun the cloud, they had headed for the relative safety of the void between the density arms. Pushing the port burb ahead of the ship, they had slowly headed into the cloud in a side-slipping maneuver. They allowed cloud to overtake them while they were pointed into Shaft storm with the port burb between them and the cloud. Now that the cloud had stopped, they were breach to the wind as they in turn barreled into the cloud with the burb-shield behind them.

"Pappa! Prognosis?"

"At the present attack angle, the command module will not survive intact."

"Recommendation?"

"I concur with Mr. Fielding's present action, Mr. Olson. May I recall your attention to your board."

Dac turned to Jason. Jason glared at his board. Dac looked up to his display. His ship was approaching the density arm along a trajectory that changed as he watched. Then a second trajectory appeared, almost parallel to the first. They converged at the density arm.

"What is that, Pappa?"

"That, Mr. Olson, is the starboard burb. It is derelict, more or less following us into the cloud. In effect, it is now ahead of us on our way back out, in relation to the stationary cloud. Mr. Fielding is attempting to place us directly behind it, in its wake. We will follow it out."

Wake!? The word paused Dac, with mixed implications. He looked again to Jason who was concentrating intensely on his work, oblivious to Dac and everything else. Brilliant, he thought of Jason. Good fast hard precise reactive thinking under extreme pressure.

And ghoulish, using a coffin full of your doomed friends to run interference.

Dac thought better of that. We're using their ship, not those people; they were doomed the instant the cloud stopped, if not before. Maybe they're already dead. And maybe we're doomed too, but they've unwittingly given us one more chance. Don't we have a right to take it? Dac considered that he was having a little difficulty being completely comfortable with that analysis.

Dac pondered his control board, watching the two points of light converge, plunging inexorably to their mutual fate. After all, he thought, I didn't make the cloud stop. And I didn't make it accelerate when it wasn't supposed to, he added. Yeah but, he replied to himself, you did put us right in front of it. Ross told you it was a hair-brained idea, but it was your call and you put us here. And you put them there, out in front.

"Mr. Olson?" It was Mercedes. Puzzled. "I have something!"

"How's that?"

"I have a response from the cloud!" Heads popped up. All of them, even Jason's.

"A response! What does it say!?"

"I don't know, Mr. Olson." Mercedes' eyes were wide open, her expression helplessly blank. "The translation system is shut down. You know."

"Okay." Pause. Damn!! If he was going out on this he'd sure like to know what they had to say before he went. "Okay."

Dac turned to his panel and watched the two points fast approaching the density arm, now almost one point. The starboard burb would impact the arm in a few seconds, then the command module. He studied the board, trying to see if the ship would be safe behind the burb. Even if it were directly behind, he thought, is that safe? Like there was an alternative.

He looked around the flight deck, looked at his crew, individually and as a team. He looked at people, faces, bodies, tools, actions, expressions, intensity, lights, noises, procedures, systems, rules, machines. But he saw desperation, hope, frustration, anger, fear, resignation. He felt all of that himself, maybe enough for all of them, but not enough to change anything.

"Initial impact in ten seconds, Mr. Olson." Initial impact, the burb followed immediately by the command module, two heartbeats separating them.

"Thank you, Pappa." Even Pappa, a friend he would miss.

"Five seconds." This is it, thought Dac. We make it through and go home, or we don't. Whatever, it'll be fast.

"Initial impact," said Pappa.

Dac braced himself, eyes locked on the board.

"Correction," said Pappa, apparently surprised. "One moment."

"One ...!" Dac almost had a hernia. "Hell's Stopwatch, Pappa! What ..."

"There has been no impact, Mr. Olson."

Dac looked around the deck, surprised that in fact there had been no impact. Equally stunned. The rest of the crew fared no better. Scramble to see what had happened.

"Pappa!"

"The cloud has disappeared, Mr. Olson. It is no longer within range of my sensors."

"Jason?"

"Empty space, Dac."

Damn! Was I imagining things? Dac remembered all too clearly the last time the cloud of shafts had disappeared. They were just reloading.

"Danger?"... "Anyone?"

"We're clear." "Nothing." "No trace, Mr. Olson."

"Hypothesis, Pappa?"

"None, Mr. Olson."

"Projection?"

"None, Mr. Olson."

"Guess!"

"None, Mr. Olson."

That wasn't fair, thought Dac. To conserve capacity, he had long since shut down Pappa's guessers along with most of his emulators.

"Anybody know what's going on?"

Nothing.

"Then let's go get that burb!" Dac looked to Mike. "We're gonna play Hell's Hockey and get the puck out of here!"

CHAPTER 36

LAST TESTAMENT

Dac pulled back from his board, stretched long and hard, rubbed his eyes long and hard, and flopped back into his recliner. He slipped his feet from his slippers and scrunched his toes into the nubby and slightly bristly industrial grade carpet. Dac relished the chance to relax, finally, after nearly a year chasing the Thingy and being chased by its offspring. Sitting here now, trying to reconstruct the events, Dac felt the reality of it fading and he was giving it a good push along.

The rest, the sleep, the regular routine, they all did wonders for his equilibrium and brought him back to a familiar reality. When it came to reality checks, theoretical aliens were no match for personnel relations, repair and maintenance schedules, payroll accounting screwups and coffee.

"Especially coffee," he said aloud, deliberately invoking the favor of the Gods.

He found it hard to think of the next item for his report so he stopped. His final report, he thought as he got up, would have to wait for a fresh pot of coffee.

It would have to wait for the aliens too. Or rather for the aliens' last message, if it was a message. If it was for us. If we could translate it. If it made sense. If it made any difference. Mercedes was on that right now, he thought. Better be.

Aliens. Dac had often wondered what they looked like, how they talk, how big they were … are. Most of the crew imagined the same, one way or another. Right now there is no clue but there might be a picture of them buried in their message somewhere. Like that Voyager space probe we sent

300

out back in the twentieth century with a picture of us naked humans, but it probably wasn't too revealing.

Dac's image of an alien looked a lot like the movie versions, mostly by default. Aside from the penchant for men in rubber suits, Hollywood didn't really have any better idea what they looked like. Hell's Architects! We didn't even have anything like a door or a window on that Thingy. At least that would have been a clue to their scale; they might be giants.

"Pappa?"

"Yes, Mr. Olson?"

The mechanical voice over the speaker was lower pitched and slightly slower than usual. Dac noticed the question mark inflection. Good Old Pappa would have been much more expository, or declarative. Whatever the word is, Pappa sounded a little detached and formal.

"Are you okay, buddy? You sound like you still have a few cracked chips." In fact, Pappa had a *lot* of compromised chips and systems. He had lost a major part of his architecture in the debacle and was only now getting back on his virtual feet.

"Yes. Thank you for your concern, Mr. Olson. I am feeling much better lately since BE engineers began revamping and upgrading me."

Dac was closely following all of the repair work on the Jobs, particularly Pappa. The crew of the Biological Engineering ship was doing miracles putting things back together, with remarkably effective if cobbled patches and bailing wire. Whatever in Hell's Hardware bailing wire was.

But Pappa was getting golden gloves executive treatment; upgrades to the latest and best computer components, almost doubled memory capacity, all new ship-wide sensors and instruments, upgraded AI programming and enhanced human-sensitive fuzzy logic. We pretty much cannibalized that BE ship.

"I understand the upgrades require some temporary but significant intrusions into my personality in order to migrate to my final configuration." Pappa paused thoughtfully, Dac thought, but he couldn't quite identify how he knew that thoughtfulness. "It is a bit technical, Mr. Olson. I hope you understand my being a bit stilted. I should feel better in a few days."

"I understand completely, Pappa." Dac really did understand completely but wanted to let Pappa know he was paying attention. "Just get well ASAP."

"Thank you, Mr. Olson. Will there be anything else?"

"No, Pappa. But you behave yourself and do what you're told."

"Chirp"

"Wait, Pappa! There *is* something. Have you found anything in the translations that tells us anything about what these aliens look like? Anything personal about them? How they talk and sound and smell and walk?"

"I have been asked that question many times, Mr. Olson. My stock answer is they look like men in rubber suits." Pappa paused to see how his attempt at humor worked. Nothing. "But seriously there is nothing of that sort yet. Not a word."

"Thank you. And keep up your spirits." Dac smiled at the small joke, then realized Pappa probably didn't see that. "And I appreciate your fun side. Really."

"Chirp."

Whatever else is in the report, I'll have to wait for Mercedes' translation of that final alien message; it may tell us why we survived to write this report. And maybe why the aliens, or rather their artifacts, are completely gone without a trace. HQ will want to know about that! And it may tell us if our message, the grand missive from the human race to the aliens, was received. And whether it had any impact on the situation, or we just lucked out. I want to know *that* he thought; it was personal.

Dac rose from his chair and meandered across his study to the kitchenette to slosh out his cup. He stepped around the up-ripped hole in the center of the study's floor, a daily reminder of the damage from the hail of shafts that nearly shredded his ship. This particular shaft had angled through his study into the closet, ripped through his set of dress uniforms and went on through to kill journeyman electrician Omaha Tedeo who was working on another repair at the time. He didn't miss the uniforms; they always made him feel like a bit part in an eighteenth century Viennese operetta. But Omaha ...

Repair of this, his personal shafted hole was a long way down the list of priorities, thousands of priorities. Dac had resigned himself to side-stepping it a long time ago and hardly noticed it any more. He would probably miss it when it was gone.

His coffee cup sloshed merrily in the running water. It was once white, with a cheerful bearded gnome in bas relief facing the right-hander, given to him by a managerial mentor at least ten years ago. In fact, he thought fondly, she had mentored him somewhat beyond the official curriculum. His cup was no longer even remotely white. The coloration always reminded him of his grandfather's meerschaum pipe; mellow and striated brown top to bottom with a jolly bearded ogre or something carved into the bowl. Grampa told him once the face was really Santa Claus. I still believe it was.

He looked at his own coffee mug thoughtfully, rubbing his thumb over the patina of coffee past, long since turned to varnish, or some such. Whatever it was, he never washed it any more than grampa would scour out his pipe bowl. Slosh only, in clean water, no soap.

He fumbled with the coffee maker, spooned in a double charge of coffee and filled the water place.

Water? Right. Somebody once calculated that on a two-year junket like this every drop of water passed through a human body more than three hundred times. And that was when everything was working right. Until they get the water purification system back up to full capacity it might be double that, or ten times that. Sometimes Dac was sure he could taste every one of them. He could sure smell them. He winced and spooned in two more dollops of coffee.

He winced again and spooned three dollops back into the can. Rationing, he thought; better make it last. What hydroponic capacity they had left went for essentials only, and all stores were strained on this extended voyage home. When this coffee is gone, that's it until port. Eight months without coffee! Yeow!

He dumped the water in the toilet, per his own conservation directive, to recycle it through another human body. How long would that take, he wondered. Hours? Minutes? He looked grimly at the droplet bellying down from end of the water spigot. How long ago was that in a human body?

Seeing no viable alternative, he reluctantly filled the teapot with what he pretended to be fresh water and set it to boil. On high. Nuke it good, he thought, more in deference to his aesthetic sensibilities than any hygienic requirement. He went back to his desk and to the report. Where was I?

Food production. The farms had taken a terrific beating but were back in production on a limited basis. Details, production figures, repair schedules, etc., etc. They were up and running again but more importantly, Dac thought, people were up and running again, working again, at normal jobs doing everyday tasks. Things were tough for a while there, until the BE ship finally arrived.

Details, damage triage, repairs, costs, etc., etc. The three supply and support ships helped patch the containment shells and replaced as much air and water as they could spare.

Details, figures, etc. Way too many ceteras. The roster showed the BE ships off-loaded nearly 60 percent of the ship's complement, mostly casualties, kids and non-essential EEs, followed by personnel lists, casualties, liability analysis, functional impairment. BE helped rebuild two dozen drives and replaced ten hopelessly terminal drives with their own. When we get up to full power, we'll have about two thirds of the drives we started with. Close enough.

Details, retrieval of the lost burb, costs, time, salvage estimates, etc. More help was due in a few months. So they were safe and eating adequately for now. It was all in the report.

The report. The 'What In Hell's Snafus Happened' report. The 'How Could So Many Things Go So Wrong So Fast' report. The 'How Do I Keep My Job' report. The 'Mostly Baloney' report.

But it had to be done and Dac had to do it. He had to explain to HO why the aliens built the Thingy (who knows), why they broke it up (who knows), why they attacked (who knows), why they stopped (who knows), and everything else (who knew!). Lord knows Dac didn't.

Lots of speculation, but not much hard knowledge. By now the media, true to form, had over-speculated every punkin-headed critique, no matter how outlandish, beyond recognition or any chance of rational recovery. Outlandish! That was certainly an appropriate use of the term, probably for the first time ever. But now he had to give the whole episode one more reprise, as though being closer to getting killed made his guesses more valid than any other. At least he had one final opportunity to put himself in the best historical light. He was genuinely thankful for that!

The Thingy was an enigma at best. Maybe we would have a clear understanding of them someday, when the translation of their history was complete but that would shed no light on what had happened out here, to his ship and to his people. That was for later, not now.

Dac shook his head at the first whiff of fresh coffee. Heaven's Percolator that's good! he thought. Somebody sure knew what they were doing when they invented coffee. He filled his comfortable old cup, slipped his feet back into his comfortable old slippers and moseyed back to his comfortable old recliner.

Maybe he was getting too old and comfortable for this kind of work, he thought. Not that the last year would ever repeat itself soon, and not that he didn't handle it well. This weighed against that, maybe he handled it as well as anyone could. Now that it was over he was glad it was over; he had satisfied his curiosity about aliens.

Aliens. No trace of them, now. The only evidence left from all of this, this close encounter, was the damage. The wrecked Winnebago, his own wrecked ship, and the message, of course, although that wasn't a thing really. Everybody was out looking for them, looking for more Thingys, but no luck so far. And everybody was scanning the skies for more messages, but no luck there either. They'll probably find the aliens again sooner or later, but right now there's no sign of them.

The message. Messages, Dac corrected himself; there were two. The first message had been repeated verbatim thousands of times over, the autobiographical story of the aliens. Everybody knew about it and followed the release of each newly translated sordid segment like they followed the soaps. Something like two percent of the message had been translated so far, loosely, in fragments, bits and pieces. The rest would take years, maybe lifetimes to get everything right.

The second message was sent just once, extremely short relatively, and as yet untranslated. It was their presumed response to the message we broadcast to them while they were chasing us, received just before they stopped chasing us. Why did they go away? he wondered. Do you suppose it was something we said?

No. The message to the aliens was composed by a committee of some 200 politicos who included every contribution by every group that could spell its own acronym. It seemed as though they were all appealing to a higher judge, as though the aliens might somehow shed light and grace on their words and confirm the validity of their particular political or religious or ethnic or socially aware view of the way things ought to be. As though just sending their words was equivalent to the aliens' acceptance and approval of them; like getting a proclamation of left-handed scissor day read into the Congressional Record.

The message was something like: Greetings. We look like this and talk like that, and do things this way and that way, and sing and dance, and pass all these really neat laws to solve all sorts of problems, and these are our religious beliefs and we want you to see the light, and we have all of these neato inventions and machines, and here's how we do business and make money, and we want to talk to you and cut you in on the profits, and blahdy-blah-blah-blah, and please respond, and have a nice day.

He smiled again. Yes, he corrected himself; maybe it *was* something we said.

"Mr. Olson?"

It was Mercedes Mead, her head poking around the frame of the open doorway. Dac could see an entourage behind her, the Translation Team.

"Come on in," said Dac with some enthusiasm and a wave. He found it easy to be enthusiastic lately without a crisis du jour. "It looks like you have the whole crew with you. Any news?"

"We have it! We have a translation!" said Mercedes, straight-faced but with pride and eagerness bubbling over. She literally skipped into Dac's working anti-room, moving to let the others sidle in, and formally presented a sheaf of papers to Dac with an uncharacteristic flourish. "At least a good working first draft."

"All right! Let's take a look at it." Dac took the papers and smiled up at the team. They all looked back at him expectantly. "Should I read it now?" he said, as in 'Can I open the present'?

"I ... we thought you would want to see it as soon as possible, Mr. Olson," replied Mercedes, grinning to the others. "Before the media get hold of it and distort it all out of shape."

"Yes, indeed!" he said, and began to read.

MEMORANDUM

To: Dac Olson, Vice President and CEO
            IPFTA / SBU Jobs

From: Translation Team:
            Mercedes Mead   Uni Farber
            Winnie Logo   William Stewart
            Ad Blanker   Patrick Grey
            James Klein   Pappa & Mamma

Re: Preliminary translation of alien message.

Following is the preliminary translation of the alien response to the message sent by the JOBS, received immediately prior to their disappearance. The translation was produced by the Jobs on board AI computer (Pappa) using the latest HO translation algorithms. This translation must be refined and approved for release, of course, and pertinent uncertainties have been noted. We believe it is, however, fundamentally accurate. The numbers were added for reference only. The preliminary translation is followed by what the team feels is a looser but more 'socialized' translation. The ellipses represent completely unknown elements. [TT] is the Translation Team referred to above.

The alien response:

1. '...' (Apparently their name for us, related to their word for "other than us." Translated hereafter as "you" or "your" as appropriate.) are not identified within (consistent with?) project engineering design parameters (unplanned?) and probably represent an application of '...' (undecipherable proper name?) type variability principals (unexpected), with emphasis, in a chaotic milieu.

   [TT: They initially identify us as a glitch in their grand plan but seem to warm up to us later. We think this means they think we weren't supposed to be here, as in "What are you doing here?"]

2. You are new to '...' (Apparently their name for themselves, i.e., the immediate authors but possibly their whole people or political edifice. Hereafter translated as "us" or "we" as appropriate.) We do not know you. We have no record of you. We do not know where you are. It is not possible to know where, with time dilation element assumed, you are.

   [TT: No further translation necessary. This is an alternate restatement and reinforcement of their first statement. The last sentence may indicate they see this as a pure accident, as in "I shot an arrow into the air". Confirmed by statements below.]

3. You present as (appear to be?) a life order without archival substantiation (lacking official recognition?) and an unlicensed territorial occupation.

   [TT: Did they call us undocumented aliens? They do seem to feel we fall under their jurisdiction.]

4. We can have no awareness of damage to your life but we find receptively plausible (accept?) as fact your unverifiable statement of injury.

   [TT: This is a qualified admission of error. They are taking our word on this, possibly indicating some social awareness or sensitivity, and assumption of honesty on our part.]

5. Our awareness of your presence is limited, with regard to scope rather than depth, by lack of appropriate lifesign-specific feedback through our without attempt to conceal (admittedly?) limited specific feedback (unsophisticated?) effluent conduit.

   [TT: The last phrase might be translated as discharge sluice, drain or sewer. Sounds like a self-effacing excuse; "We didn't think to put life sensors in the exhaust pipe." There may also be a little responsibility shifting here; "What did you expect when you live in a sewer?"]

6. We experience sudden fear of imminent actuality (alarm?) and concern, with moderate disbelief, that you grant concessions in failure of forceful interface (defeat) in formal conflict resolution suspension of legal parameters (combat?). This is structurally and logically conscripted (based?) upon studious reflection of your "..." (apparently own) erroneous assumptions. Your expression of our

dominion and your submission is neither possible nor desirable. Tribute is not relevant.

[TT: There must have been no overt aggression involved on their part.]

7. We accept life's common right (moral?) responsibility (lit: self incrimination) and extend it to the unanticipated negative outcomes of our otherwise '...' (undecipherable) neutral acts. This extension of responsibility is neither expected nor required under our established conflict resolution precedence inventory (law?) or other more broadly discriminating societal requirements (customs or religion?).

[TT: We found it tempting to believe that a lawyer wrote this part in an attempt to take the moral high road, anticipating a lawsuit. As later statements show, this qualified acceptance of responsibility costs them nothing.]

8. We higher than otherwise, with modest brightness, experience uprightness and cessation of concern in respect to your lacking in persistency structure. In consequence, do, with forcefulness, not omit the red (lit: expressed in Hz!) in your deliberations, with reaffirmed strength.

[TT: we haven't a clue.]

9. We express fear of self-inflicted discomfort due to exposure to possible loss of prestige and convolution of '...' (undecipherable) accruing to us for other than with care and foresight (prudent?) choices, causing the unwanted and undesirable consequences that force project reevaluation and remanifestation.

[TT: We think someone was embarrassed about a screwup and heads will roll. This is a remarkably honest admission, but again it costs them nothing. Can they possibly understand human nature well enough to try to garner a little sympathetic understanding?]

10. We express, with intensity, concern that termination of life functions among your living and damage to your assets occurred. We prefer, in absolutes, without qualification, that the life cessation and physical loss had not occurred and experience discomfort, with maximum intensity, which damage did occur.

[TT: Sounds like an apology, indicating a social conscience.]

11. We experience '...' (uncertain, possibly an intensifier?) discomfort as a consequence of our inability to reverse damage to you or reinstate (compensate?) appropriate value for the damage.

    [TT: Seems like genuine frustration and regrets.]

12. We assert and affirm under '...' (long undecipherable phrase) that the effluent conduit be relocated and not reacquire (be replaced? be reconnected?) in our life span or in that of all scions (buds? descendants?), holding your space inaccessible (off limits?) until your collapse and extinguishment.

    [TT: We believe the last word refers to the next sentence.]

13. We experience pain, with tolerable intensity, upon consideration of the possibility of your failure, with moderate emphasis, to understand with maximum precision (lit: employment or implementation?) the impact of our imposition on your space is probably, with moderate uncertainty, not amenable to restructure (irreversible?).

    [TT: They seem to place considerable importance on our knowing what to expect. It also seems that our analysis of the effect on space was correct.]

14. We experience sudden unanticipated realization (surprise?) that you accommodate the encodement of the legacy (the message?), with maximum reverence, and that you are able, with diminutive denoting indulgence towards the student, to compose coherent thought using the code of the legacy, with maximum reverence. The sophisticated technology implied in the existence of your communication is perceived with favor. These qualities are unique in our other than '...' (proper noun, probably their generic name for themselves as a people?) experience.

    [TT: This is a genuine, if left-handed compliment. We think it also implies their awareness of other alien species!]

15. In contrast and counterpoint, your unauthorized acquisition of the inviolate by agreement (copyrighted? privileged?) information transfer objects (content?) of the legacy, with maximum reverence, violates our privacy and that of '...' (undecipherable) for proper objective (for whom it was intended). We assimilate (take?) the reality of your translation of the legacy, with maximum reverence,

in spite of universally accepted prohibitions pertaining to the interception of such inviolate by agreement private communication to be evidence of your lacking, maximum degree or quantity, interindividual congress precept awareness.

[TT: Ouch!]

16. We state and record your communications in the '...' (undecipherable. archive? data bank?) that authorization-restricted personnel may at will reconstruct this encounter, with high degree of ambiguousness, to immediate awareness and examine it in controlled circumstances that preclude intellectual corruption.

[TT: We are not sure what to make of this, probably thought police at work. We were probably insulted again.]

17. We experience discomfort upon consideration of our inability to reconcile the '...' (uncertain; counter revolutionary? contrarian?), with maximum rejection, principles formulated in your initial communication expressing desire for expanded empire building (commercial?) relations with your ultimate communication indicating your desire to terminate what you apparently perceive as formalized domination determination confrontation (lit: combat?).

[TT: We would have trouble reconciling them, too.]

18. Analysis, with utmost attention, of your communications indicates that we have, with emphatic denoting no possibility of error, no common basis for gain-producing, with maximum '...' (possibly value exchange system?) consideration, intercourse. The lack, with emphatic negative, of object (purpose?) to the pursuit of commerce is obvious and elementary (lit: underlying truth?). The possibility of negative consequences, with '...' (long phrase seeming to be a comment on their society?), from continued contact override. Therefore, we will, with intellectual emphatic implying irreversible decision, not intentionally contact you again. Do, with force, not attempt to contact us for the reason, with maximum certitude, that we will not respond.

[TT: That's clear enough; we don't have anything they want. Don't call us, we'll call you. Whatever the reason, they are certainly anxious to end communication.]

[TT: Some of the team felt perhaps there is something they don't want us to know. Another group felt perhaps they are afraid of us! What possible reason could there be for not communicating if, as they state, dominion or tribute or submission is not possible? Surely an exchange of ideas is desirable, or at least neutral. Political or ideological pollution and social upheaval is another possibility, considering their history.]

[TT: Still another possibility is that, like all technological developments, the Thingy could be used as a weapon. That, combined with our demonstrated ability to translate their message, would give them reason for concern. Could we develop our own Thingys and retaliate?]

[TT: However, we all concur that, considering their level of technology and their stated desire to be left alone, we might best leave them alone.]

19. We express, with emphasis, our desire, with reasonable sincerity, with no qualification, that of all possible random occurrences, you experience only those you perceive to be desirable.

[TT: Nice touch that.]

End of translation.

Following is a loose reinterpretation of the translation, with liberties that may not be completely defensible.

1. You were not expected. We don't know why this happened.
2. We don't know anything about you, and because of space/time considerations, we probably could not have known about you.
3. Our official records do not know about you either.
4. There is no way we could know about hurting you, but we'll take your word for it.
5. We know our sewage equipment is not designed to detect life under these conditions. We really didn't see a need for it.
6. We are surprised and disconcerted that you thought you were being attacked and felt a need to capitulate. You are wrong on all counts.

7. We accept responsibility for your injuries even though we don't feel we have to.

8. You share responsibility for your problems. Whatever you did, don't do it again.

9. We're a little embarrassed about all of this and it will cause us problems too, so don't push your point.

10. We're sorry about the damage and deaths. We really wish it hadn't happened and wish we could put things back the way they were.

11. However, we are sorry we cannot put things back the way they were.

12. You can be assured the sewer will be moved away and will not return.

13. We want to be sure you understand that your space is collapsing and the process is probably irreversible.

14. We are surprised and impressed that you can read and write our language. You are unique in that respect.

15. On the other hand, you have been reading our private mail and you should know better.

16. We are not sure about you and these events, but we are saving your messages so the proper authorities can examine them in detail.

17. We can't reconcile your two messages.

18. However, we can see that we don't want to have anything to do with you. Contact with you is not to our advantage and may be dangerous. Don't call us.

19. Good Luck

End of translation.

"Sewer!?" Dac held the report at arm's length, flipped a page or two as though that would change the translation somehow, and repeated. "Sewer?"

"That's our best guess Mr. Olson." replied Ad Blanker. "We cross-checked that as best we could; there aren't many occurrences of that exact word. It's probably correct."

"Sewer," Dac repeated. "What does that mean. Well, I know what that means," Dac corrected, "I mean, have we been slugging it out with a sewer pipe in their garbage dump? That's it?"

"It appears so, Mr. Olson," said Mercedes. "That is consistent with some of our earlier speculation, that the Thingy was just the dumb end of some machine."

"However," added Uni Farber, "that doesn't necessarily mean it's dirty, even by their standards. And it doesn't imply anything, any more than the byproduct from a manufacturing operation is an affront or a challenge. Their 'effluent' is simply temporarily unused stuff; waste from one operation that can be a resource for another."

"The hydrogen?"

"Right."

"It sounds as though they are completely aware of the impact of their, uh, unused stuff on our space," observed Dac. "But there's something that doesn't ring true here."

Dac looked at Mercedes and the others. They were professionally proud of their work, rightfully so, and stood tall. However, Dac noted, they looked conspiratorially to each other as Dac looked at each of them.

"Most of this doesn't seem to have any relation to the message we sent them. The references to, uh," Dac flipped back through several pages, "defeat in combat, dominion and submission, tribute." Dac looked up without raising his head. "Tribute?"

Ad Blanker smirked. Fax Klein glanced to Bill Stewart who smiled back to Mercedes. Mercedes flushed.

"Mercedes," said Dac. "You stand convicted. What's not in the report?"

"It's all there, Mr. Olson," replied Mercedes. Snickers from the others. "All of the translation is in that report."

"Okay. What am I missing?"

"I was going to tell you, Mr. Olson," said Mercedes finally. "But there wasn't time." She looked at the others. "We, I, uh, changed the message we sent to them."

"Changed the message!" repeated Dac. "You mean we didn't send the message the HO composed?"

"Oh, yes! We sent that, over a hundred times, right up to when they started chasing us!" Mercedes smiled at the others.

"I don't know if that's what caused them to chase us, but that's when it started. They were chasing us, and catching us. And I thought we needed to send a short clear message that could not be misunderstood. So we, uh, I surrendered!"

"Surrendered!?" Dac was incredulous. "Surrendered." A flat repetition without rancor.

"What, exactly, did you say?"

Mercedes handed a single piece of paper to Dac. Dac cleared his throat, checked the others uncertainly, and focused on the paper. It had four lines of copy centered on the page, in small compressed machine script. It read:

```
                    STOP ATTACK NOW.
      WE SUBMIT. YOU DOMINATE. WE ARE DEFENSELESS.
      MANY DEAD. ARTIFACTS DESTROYED. SPECIFY TRIBUTE.
                    STOP ATTACK NOW.
```

"You're right," said Dac. "You surrendered." He considered Mercedes' articles of capitulation, and then flipped back to reread the alien response. It made a whole lot more sense in the context of war and peace.

"Apparently," he said finally, "they didn't like the HO message any more than I did."

"We," corrected Uni. "If we had received the message we sent, we might have attacked too."

Dac smiled ruefully at that. There was a reason, he thought, that he preferred life in space, away from the political world. Worlds, he added; they were all alike. He understood Jason's frustrations and bitterness towards everything HO, and apparently the aliens shared his, our, opinion. Dac felt a new respect for the aliens for their astute reading of our words.

"When did all of this occur to you?" asked Dac, back on the subject. "You had to have some time to put this together. If I recall, things were a little dicey."

"You mean when did we write the message?" rephrased Uni. "The idea occurred to us long before we sent the HO message. We felt there was a real chance that we were being attacked, rather than just being swept, and we tried to think of the best ways to stop an attack. Submission is the most universal defense against attack, except when the attackee is food. That didn't seem to apply here, so we prepared the surrender. We figured in either case, they were attacking or they weren't, it would get immediate attention and action."

"Yeah," added Ad Blanker. "If they got the message, and bothered to translate it, and understood it and it made any sense, and they were inclined to do anything about it, and they *could* do anything about it, and do it in any meaningful time frame."

"So you had this strategy all worked out in advance?" asked Dac.

"Right," replied Mercedes. "Well, actually several strategies. With Pappa's help. In fact we had a dozen different messages prepared, to be ready for any turn of events. Like if nothing at all happened, or they answered with another message, or asked for more information, or ..."

"Pappa was in on this!?" Dac stopped, realizing immediately that Pappa had to be in on any translation to or from the aliens; their language was beyond any human ability. So he took another managerial tack. "Why wasn't I informed?"

"You were informed," said Pappa. "It was on ..."

"I know," cut in Dac. "So how did you know they would go away right in the nick of time?"

"We didn't, of course," said Uni. She lost her satisfied smile and replaced it with a little fear and guilt. "In fact, Mr. Olson, we screwed up badly."

"How's that?" Oh boy! Just wait for HO's ...

"Well, we wanted them to stop their attack, or whatever they were doing. And they did. But we apparently said 'stop moving' instead of 'stop attack'. We didn't realize that we would keep right on moving through the stopped cloud." Uni stopped to choose her words. "Sorry about that. We should have had everyone involved and anticipated that happening."

"Chirp." Pappa. "The messages *were* on your board, Mr. Ol ..."

"All right!" Dac held Mercedes fixed while he compiled the story in his own mind. "Let me get this straight. First we got in front of them on one of their sweeps, so we could send the HO message. Then we sent the HO message. Then they used that to determine where we were and accelerated at us, to do whatever it was they were sweeping for. Right?"

"Right."

"Then you sent your message and they stopped, per the terms of your surrender. Right?"

"Right."

"Then just when we were about to hit the arm of the cloud, they disappeared. Right?"

"Wrong," countered Uni. "They sent their answer to our message and then disappeared."

"Okay. Right." Dac thought about that. "Then why did they disappear just when they did? They couldn't have known where we were in the cloud, could they? Or that we were about to blast through it?"

Silence.

"We talked about this" said Mercedes after a moment. "We think it was just plain stupid dumb blind luck. They looked at the messages, just like they say, and decided they didn't want anything to do with us. And pulled out, just like that. I think we can take their last message at face value; they basically said 'oops' and split."

"But we're talking about less than two minutes time altogether," objected Dac. "Would they have time to translate the messages and make their decisions and act in that time?"

"You forget that they didn't have to translate," said Mercedes. "We *did* send it in *their* language, not ours."

"And we don't know what time factor is involved," added Blanker. "They may have taken a century to make their decisions, or their equivalent period of time. Who knows?"

"It did sound like they thought about it at some length," admitted Dac.

"Or maybe it was no decision at all," said Uni. "Any more than we would stop to think twice about throwing an undersized fish back in the pond. They may have simply followed established protocols."

Dac could relate to that. His primary job was to implement and administer established proven policies. Only there were no established and proven policies for aliens and Thingys and shafts and surrenders.

"I only have one last question," he said to the team. "A decision, really. And we need to be together on this."

They looked at Dac, knowing the question.

"Understanding that we were probably exceeding our commission just by engaging in unauthorized negotiations with a foreign state, do we include in my final report that you, uh, we, uh, maybe the whole IPFTA, Inc. surrendered without firing a shot?" Pause.

"And incidentally lost the greatest commercial opportunity in the history of hisserkind! And billions, trillions in profits! Profits that our employers promised to their nice investors when they put together the alien translation consortium. Profits that were pledged to finance the huge expedition that is due to arrive even as we speak!"

"Not to mention a few fantastic scientific discoveries. And probably revolutionary cultural enlightenment. And new forms of entertainment, and mathematics, and medicine and, and ...! Do you think we can include our surrender in the report!?"

Absolute dead silence.

He knew their answer, even without looking at their blanched faces and stunned eyes. He knew his own answer.

"You didn't!"

"I thought I just said I did," said Dac. Mock consternation at this challenge to his veracity.

"I know you did," agreed Marcy. "But you didn't!" she contradicted. Hand over mouth sniggle.

"Look. It's done. I did what I had to do. We all agreed."

"But Pappa! He knows all about it, doesn't he!"

"He did."

"You didn't!" Mild shriek of gleeful surprise.

"I just said ..."

"But they'll find out, won't they?" A little more genuine concern there than Dac expected. With a residual smirk.

"Who'll find out?" he said. "There are only eight of us who know." Pause. "Nine. And we all agreed." Pause "Almost all." Meaningfully.

"Oh, I'll never tell!" Wide-eyed open-faced cross-my-heart honesty. "But I'll deny I ever knew you!" Snurk.

"Thanks!" Make that eight, he thought.

"Don't get me wrong! I think it's great!"

"How's that? I thought you ..."

"I do."

"Then ..."

"I said I'd never tell. I think it's great that you risked your career for this but I didn't say I'd risk *my* career for it."

"That's clear enough. I think."

"Now wait a minute! Fair's fair; I didn't ask you to tell me, you know!"

"Look. Let's forget it. Okay" This is going nowhere. Snuggle. "What say we ..." Snuggle interruptus.

"I don't want to forget it." Sit up straight. Indignant. "What if they find out!?"

"I told you." Gentle reassuring voice. "Nobody ..."

"But who'll believe it?" Sincere, with a little hurt.

"Who'd believe what really happened?" God! She's using that hurt little kid bit again! "Look. We keep our cool." Smile understandingly. "Play to their egos." Back of hand to cheek. Good. "No problem." No problem.

"Well, I don't know." I know you'll *pay* for this, Mr. Chief Executive Officer Olson!

Give in a little, smile. Good.

"That's better." That's better! Now move closer. Slow! Deep urgent voice. "I'm sorry I upset you." Good tack! "How can I make it up to you?" Look innocent now, innocent. Small of the back. there!

"Well, for starters you can ..."

God, can he!

CHAPTER 37

APPENDIX ONE

MEMORANDUM

To: Officers and Directors
                InterPlanet, Inc.

From: Chief Executive Officer Dac Olson
                IPFTA / SBU Jobs

RE: Final alien message translation

Following is the final translation of the alien message conveyed to the human race immediately prior to their disappearance.

This is a refined translation that reflects the essential meaning of the message. The original has been forwarded to the proper authorities. Study of the original transcription may result in slight modifications of this translation, but we believe that it is essentially correct.

This message was received in response to the message we broadcast to the aliens during their final search sweep. It may be profitable to review the sequence of events leading up to this message to put it in context.

We believe the aliens misinterpreted the collision of the Winnebago with the cloud of shafts as a simple and common mechanical encounter, such as with an asteroid. They then proceeded to sweep the area to clear it of other debris.

Since the sweep pattern was precisely systematic, we attempted to position ourselves in front of one of the sweeps in order to broadcast our message to them. The broadcast required considerable power from our mass converters. This outlay of power was perceived by the aliens as another obstacle to be removed and they accelerated in order to destroy it. This acceleration was unexpectedly out of pattern with that of previous sweeps.

In the process, the IPFTA / SBU Jobs was overtaken and sustained considerable damage.

It appears, however, that the aliens finally received our transmission, realized their mistake and broke off contact after sending the following message:

Greetings to humans, with reverence and intensity.

We acquire your message in interest, with intellectual intensifiers. We declare your language skills, evidenced by your translation of the Legacy, with utmost reverence, to be superior, with utmost qualitative comparative, in relation to all known other-than-us species. Your technical knowledge is worthy of praise and commendation.

Your interesting words, with profound depth of feeling, will be preserved for all time in honor and admiration among our philosophers and students as being among the greatest bodies of literature and thought produced by all sentient species.

We regret that physical barriers and engineering considerations prevent further intercourse. It is not possible to sustain communications. The instrument, with reverence and awe, absorbs a large proportion, with maximum intensifier, of our total common energy resources with known and discrete limits, and must be moved for use on much more urgent and '...', with utmost reflexive, projects.

In addition, the mass transferal and concomitant energy consumption coupled with the time/space differential to stress the matrix of space such that '...' is inevitable if the interface is sustained beyond '...' engineering limits. The result would be catastrophic to both of us.

In addition, our laws, with reverence and spirit of utmost strict adherence, do not allow diversion of owned-by-all resources to commercial enterprise for the profit of the artificially selected, with reflexive denoting inward looking, individuals.

We therefore reluctantly withdraw from your vicinity, with timewise implication, according to our without-change schedule, with emphatic rigorous rigidity, in order to prevent complete '...' to both spatial delimitations.

We regret that because of the aforementioned engineering considerations we cannot pursue the interesting, with breathtaking startleness, commercial opportunities you propose.

Our imposition on your space was planned to be temporary and is now at an end. We will, with assurance denoting moral certitude, contact you again during the next phase which begins in the '...' afterward.

Good luck.

(End of alien message.)

Attached is my final report concerning the events not previously documented, primarily the period from the initiation of the message to the aliens to the present. Supporting material is provided in the Appendix.

Attached is a listing (Appendices J through M) of casualties, the damage to the SBU Jobs, repairs completed, a schedule of repairs to be completed and projected costs and related matters.

Also included is a listing (Appendices R through T) of liability suits already filed and those who have registered their intention to file suit.

Also attached is my letter of resignation which I have submitted in order to accept a teaching position in the Zuckerberg sector.

"Okay. Satisfied?"

Printed in the United States
By Bookmasters